Wade

A NOVEL

J. A. CARTER-WINWARD

B₀₁₀NARY PRESS

© 2021 J.A. Carter-Winward. All Rights Reserved

Published by Binary Press Publications, LLC (www.0101press.com)

Paperback I
SBN-13: 978-1-61171-040-3
ISBN-10: 1-61171-040-5

Ebook
ISBN-13: 978-1-61171-041-0
ISBN-10: 1-61171-041-3

For
Bella, Laurie, Lacy and Cherry Rose

Wade

A NOVEL

J. A. CARTER-WINWARD

"It's too amazing being human—
even when it looks like it's going all wrong,
that has to happen
for us to understand what's right."

—Bella Cummins
Bella's Hacienda,
Wells, Nevada

PART I

1

The doctor had suggested it was all in his head because of his wife's death.

It's only eleven in the morning and his day yawns open like the desolate landscape whizzing by him as he drives down I-80 from Elko back to Wells. He thinks of how he'll fill his day. His days as an insurance salesman should have prepared him for retirement, but all it did was teach him to think too much. Sitting across from people who had that look in their eyes that somewhere along the line, they figured out they weren't going to live forever. Their mettle slapped up next to their belief in God and Heaven and then on the other side of it, the pragmatics. Wade saw that the pragmatics usually won out, and what had once been eyes lit up with holy fire and faith were now heavy with uncertainty and fear. Yeah, an insurance man deals in fear; he has to. Fear and pragmatics. And then thinking too damn much.

Early retirement isn't all it's cracked up to be, he decides. Of course he'd looked forward to it when he was younger. Back then, he had the two boys, Ann at home, and visions of campouts, fishing trips and barbeques filling his mind, as if his young sons would never age, never leave the nest to have their own complete lives with him as only a small part of them. He hardly ever sees Milton anymore. Henderson isn't that far away, but his son never makes the trip. How old is Milt now? He'd be thirty-two. He has two daughters and Wade gave up remembering their ages long ago because they are two and four years of age to him forever. His granddaughters are like their mother, his pristine daughter-in-law: they like the finer things in life. Camping with them would be out of the question.

And then there's Cole. Wade feels a twinge, and the emotion runs the gamut from pride to disappointment to guilt all over again when he thinks of his younger son. So many things lost. And now as Wade enters Wells, he thinks of the lost things, including his fingers.

A fifty-minute drive to go see a "specialist." The specialist who told Wade he can't find anything wrong.

Wade had argued with him in his head the whole drive home. He said all of the things a strong man would say, a reasonable man would say, an educated man. Wade hasn't felt strong in eight months. No, eight years.

Right, so because you don't have an answer, I'm makin' it up, that it? Mister Specialist Doctor who went to medical school while I was raisin' two kids and supportin' a family? You little pissant worm. Fuck you, okay? Fuck you.

But Wade had tried to look thoughtful in the doctor's office. He tried to *be* thoughtful. *What would make me deliberately lose movement in three fingers on my right hand?* The thought that comes to him suddenly is that he'd have to start jacking off with his left hand if it got any worse. *Then,* he thinks, *maybe it wouldn't feel like me. It would feel like someone else.*

Wade pulls into his drive and he's surprised to find his front step empty. Usually when he's gone for a time, the step is occupied by his surly neighbor Durward, or as Wade knows him, "Dude." He peers over to Durward's house and the blinds are still closed. He turns off the car and decides to check on him before he goes in to make his lunch.

Wade steps up to Durward's door and raps three short knocks. He looks down and sees the cracks in the foundation of Durward's cinder-block cottage. He knows his foundation looks the same. He wonders if maybe it's time to move somewhere else. Somewhere where no one knows his name and no one knows his story.

The door opens suddenly and abruptly stops as the chain strains between the door jamb and Durward's angry face.

"Oh, it's you." He closes the door, unchains it and opens it wide. Durward is holding a broom. "Thought it was another damned salesman. I'll kill the next one come by."

"Had some sales people come by today, didja?" Wade steps into the musty living room, complete with the smell of bacon and something sour covered by bleach.

"Yesterday. But they been comin' back here like they forget, see. But I don't forget. Sons of bitches," Durward mutters. He places his broom against the wall and Wade realizes that the broom is a weapon for the "sons of bitches."

Durward had lost his wife more than 20 years ago and has been on his own ever since. He takes meticulous care of his yard and house, and informs Wade how his roses are doing every time he sees him. Wade's yard is a tangled mess. He just mows the lawn now, nothing more. The flowers and such had been Ann's domain.

"You want somethin'?" Durward shuffles toward his chair and sits before Wade can answer.

"Naw, I'm all right. I usually see you outside or on my lawn pullin' weeds."

Durward's face breaks into a puckish smirk. "I turned in early, then late last night."

"What are you talkin' about?"

Durward points his finger in back of him. "Millie came by, brought me dinner again."

"Mildred? Next door?"

"Yeah. She made me some home-cooked chicken and rice. With some of the beans from her garden."

The twinkle in Durward's eyes is unmistakable. Wade stares at him and knows his mouth is open. Could eighty-three-year-old men still *do* that?

"So you...you and Millie? I mean...she spent the night?"

"Naw, she left after. Wanted her own bed 'n' all. But this bull still got some horns." Durward's smile broke open to reveal his straight teeth, yellowed with the slight gray tinge of a hard-boiled yolk.

"Jee-sus. I had no idea."

"Oh, she been courtin' me for months anyhow. Bringin' me the meals, comin' to visit. That's what my mother woulda called 'forward' in her day. But I don't mind it one bit. I told her she could call me Dude 'cause it was familiar and all. She liked that."

Wade's thoughts involuntarily turn to Tammy, and he shakes his head to jostle sense into it. "I had no idea that…no offense, Dude, but you're gettin' on and so's Mildred."

"Well, yeah, but that don't go away, see. You're still a man, 'til ya ain't. It's the meals, I tell ya. They think they gotta court your stomach." Durward chuckles, then he points a shaky finger at Wade. "You got yourself a Millie, Wade. You just don't know it."

"What are you talkin'? Tammy? Dude, that wouldn't be right."

"Why not? I see her car over, she's bringin' ya meals."

"It's different with me and Tammy." Wade couldn't believe he's taking romantic advice from the world's leading authority on orneriness. Whenever he'd seen Dude and Mildred together, Dude still carried himself like a cranky old dog and not like a man courting a lady at all. Well, maybe not a cranky dog--gruff. He had been gruff. He can't picture a woman responding to gruff.

"Dang, boy, you slow?"

"Tammy is my sister-in-law, Dude. Wouldn't be right. And anyway—"

"To get technical, she ain't. You ain't married no more. You gotta live your life or it'll shrink up and fall off." Durward's face breaks into a grin.

"She's family. What would I tell my kids? 'Oh hey kids, your Aunt Tammy spends the night now.' Wouldn't be right. And anyhow, I don't see her like that."

"Well, she's a bit of a mouse, but she's a warm body. You take that with a cold whiskey and you got yourself a smile on your face come mornin'."

Wade doesn't want to talk about cold whiskeys and warm bodies, especially Tammy's. Tammy, his sister-in-law for thirty-three years, his helper with Ann when Cole had gone away. Her stringy brown hair and almost chinless face. And anyway, warm bodies are something he can't even remember. He feels a slight irritation growing and he can't pinpoint where it comes from, but it makes him restless in his chair, so he stands up and slaps his thighs.

"I'm gonna get, Dude. Talk to ya later."

"Ask her for a pot pie. That's a good signal. You can do all sortsa innuendo and all."

"Thanks, Dude."

Wade walks out of the screen door and looks over at Mildred's house as he stands on the front stoop. It's all closed up as if it's vacant, like so many houses on 3rd Street lately. He catches a visual in his mind's eye of old Mildred, spread-eagle on Durward's bed, and his eyes clamp shut.

"God damn that horny goat. I'll be seein' that in my head all day long."

He walks toward his yard and a minute stirring, low in his gut, warms his insides as he recognizes the feeling. It brings with it a rush of disappointment and sadness, heavy and dark in his chest. He recognizes his yearning and knows it's still wound up, still clinging to his late wife.

After his Spam and eggs, Wade vows to eat better. Whenever Tammy brings dinner, she always has a fresh green salad or cooked peas. He places his hand on his belly and sinks his fingers into the softness. The mushy midsection has been creeping up on him like time itself, and although he notices now and again, it hadn't fully hit him between the eyes until now.

That horny old goat had gotten him all bothered. His thoughts run into sexual release everywhere he turns—except when they go to old Mildred, then he feels an icy cold shower spray his mind and douse it with "yuck." He tells himself he's healthy and normal to be turned off by an eighty-something-year-old woman. Then he feels red creep up on his neck. The distaste comes from her body, or what he perceives it to be. Bony, sinewy, hanging skin—the body his wife had had the last year before she died.

He used to carry Ann to the tub and she weighed nothing because that's what cancer does: eats away until there's nothing. Ann used to joke with him that she finally found a diet that worked. He sees the red, angry scar on her chest from the mastectomy in his mind, and all of this, old Mildred, Ann, all of it, doesn't stop the yearning in his lower body as he wanders into Ann's bedroom. He stands in the doorway of her sunlit room and looks at the perfectly made bed with the pure white bedspread. The room seems strange now, without the oxygen, the hospital bed. It's just a room now, and he remembers long ago, her plump backside sitting on the edge of the bed folding laundry, looking busy, always so busy.

He walks in and, out of habit, pulls the bed cover down to expose the sheet, then he sits on the bed's edge, and for all of his melancholy thoughts, his pants feel tight around his loins as he feels his dick full and practically pulsing. Trying to make his right hand into a fist, his three errant fingers stay stubbornly stuck in the same position.

He lies back, furtively looking at the window with the lace curtains, certain someone's face will hover in the frame and catch him, but he eases his zipper down anyway and pulls himself free.

Nothing wrong with thinking of your dead wife and touching yourself, he thinks. *This is me, missing her. This is me, wishing she was here.*

But he knows deep down there are too few memories of his wife that way and so he concentrates on the sensation of his two fingers stroking. He keeps his eyes closed and tries to conjure up the images from magazines he'd seen, the Internet, the girl at the *Stop 'n' Go* mart who's too young to think of that way, but she is a real, tangible presence in his mind and so it's her in the bathroom there at the *Stop 'n' Go* and he won't let her image out of his mind.

Sweat forms on his brow and upper lip and he spits into his hand and strokes faster, feeling his immobile fingers inertly touching his dick while his two fingers work it. His breath is ragged and the images keep coming of Mildred and the old goat on her and Tammy with peas and salad and then the girl and his fingers, the doctor who told him nothing's wrong and the receptionist at his work who is too old, too plump, but who has nice lips and so he thinks of her lips, too, as he rubs, re-wets his fingers and rubs some more.

And then he almost hears his wife's voice and opens his eyes for a brief moment to check for her but she isn't there and so he rubs and winces, his face bunched up in concentration but he remembers it all too well now and the scene plays vividly in his mind but he keeps stroking in vigorous jerks.

You don't take your undershirts out of your work shirts and then I wash 'em and they get all dingy. See? Don't you think I got enough to do without separating your shirts for you when I do laundry?

I'm sorry, I'll separate the shirts. I just take them all off at once and forget.

I'll tell you what, you don't appreciate me and all I do, Wade Kendall.

It's ten o'clock at night, Annie—

—and you think I like rinsin' off your dishes? It's everything, you don't care about anything—

Why you pickin' a fight right now? Jesus H. It's always somethin', right?

Because I'm tired of it, I'm tired. Can't you see I'm tired?

Look, come into the bedroom and be tired in there with me.

I'll sleep in here tonight. You know you snore.

Come in for a little while then.

What, so you can sleep like a baby and I get to lie there awake and then wipe myself clean and come here and lie awake all night while you're sleepin'?

Annie...

He says her name out loud and he feels his arm tense and the tendons ache but he rubs and the girl in the bathroom is on the counter with her legs open and she's so young and then he has Mildred in his arms, carrying her to the tub with her petal-thin skin touching him and Tammy's shy smile is in front of his eyes and it's then he stops because his cock stings and his two fingers aren't enough. He's getting soft.

All he can hear is his ragged breath. His face begins to cool, the sweat running down his forehead towards his hair. He looks down and that's a mistake because his belly swells and obscures his visual of the bottom half of his dick.

"*Fuck me.*" He lies there breathing and finally tucks himself back in his pants and shuts his eyes. He decides to go to the *Stop 'n' Go* to buy Vaseline.

The diffused light from the white curtains suddenly makes it too bright, too clear, even for a nap. Out of habit he makes the bed again, wishing he could crawl into it. Anything to put over his eyes to dim the glare of the small room.

The pension forms had taken him an hour to do because he can't type anymore. His three digits, like disobedient children, stubbornly refuse to obey. The pension he'll receive would make sure he was pretty comfortable, as long as he didn't head to Wendover and do a drunken-fool thing like play the machines again. Ann had nearly knocked him clean out of the house after that.

It is approaching the worst time of day. Wade dreads two o'clock because it's after lunch and the prospect of the long stretch of time before dinner depresses him. He measures his days in meals now, in the arrival of the mail, the occasional errand. The routine he'd set up for himself doesn't include anything worthwhile anymore, but when Annie was around, there had been all sorts of routines. Two o'clock had been when he'd gone in and given her limbs a massage, waited with her until the next dose of pain medication was due. He was on guard then, like a tough bouncer, using mental brute force on the pain that had wracked her frame. He tried to be a barrier against the pain taking over her mind by playing silly games with her, like twenty questions. He would make up stories about clients he'd sold policies to and embellish them until he saw the small, weak smile creep up on her face.

That didn't happen, she'd say.

I swear to God, the guy insisted I insure his dog 'cause it was his farm's security system.

Wade smiles and looks at the clock.

Tammy would be there at six tonight. It's Wednesday. Mondays, Wednesdays and Fridays she still brings him dinner, even though Ann is gone. Eight months and she doesn't say why she still comes; he doesn't ask. It's as though both are afraid to break a fragile spell, a delicate illusion that Ann is still there, the human bond that had grown frail and ghostly.

He feels sorry for Tammy, he realizes that now. To him, she had always been Ann's plain and unassuming sister—not even his sister-in-law, because he can't seem to define her in relation to himself. But now it's just Tammy and him and until this morning, before talking to Durward, it wasn't weird. Now it feels weird. He feels an expectation resting on him like a heavy hand on his neck. The thought had never occurred to him to take Tammy out, or hell, even make her dinner himself, which he is fully capable of doing. He knows he should tell her to stop coming, but panic seizes him when he thinks of it; that, and the suspicion that he is her last tie to her sister and she needs him as much as he needs her.

Tammy is nine years younger than Ann, twelve years younger than him, which makes her only forty-four. *That's the prime of life*, he thinks.

At least when he compares how he feels at fifty-six to how he felt at forty-four. Tammy has never been married. She'd been with a guy in the military for a long time, but that relationship was mostly letters and his occasional leave before going active duty again. Wade wonders if she'd slept with the guy. It seems impossible to him, but he knows she had to have. *Right*? The guy wouldn't come all the way to a stink hole like Wells, Nevada to stay with her in her shitty green trailer if he wasn't getting laid. Wade tries to banish these thoughts because he can't picture Tammy that way. When he pictures women, he tries to picture their faces contorted in pleasure, like the pornos he's watched—but not Tammy. And not Ann. He had never seen that look on Ann, and when he thinks of that, he feels like a failure, all over again.

What the hell do you think you're doin'?
I wanted to try something—
Well you're not trying that! That's filthy.
It'll feel good, Annie—
I feel fine, just do your business and be done with it. Come on now.

His nose and upper lip begin to tingle as tears form in his eyes like a slow leak in a spigot. He sniffs but allows the tears to tumble down his cheeks. No one is there to see. If she had only let him make her feel as good as she made him feel, he could have saved her, saved all of it. He's so sure.

He hears the mail truck outside.

It's two-fifteen.

2

The collar on his shirt is tweaked a little and he doesn't know why it matters now. He doesn't know why he changed shirts anyway other than his t-shirt felt too casual, as if it didn't show appreciation for the trouble Tammy takes in bringing him dinner. Not to mention he dabbed some aftershave on his chest and he hasn't worn aftershave in over three years so the smell is in his nose and seems to be seeping from every pore. He can even taste it.

And it isn't because anything has changed for him. He still can't see Tammy the way Durward says he should see her, but he's aware that she's coming now, and that's something he'd taken for granted. He feels ashamed he'd not really thought of it before. The thought occurs to him to take a washcloth to his chest and rub some of the smell out, but then the doorbell buzzes.

He opens the door and Tammy is holding a tray with a covered dish and a smaller dish with cellophane. *Peas.*

"Heya," he says.

Her eyes are down on the food, but they flit up to him briefly and she smiles a small smile without a word as she steps through the door.

He realizes he always feels pressured to speak when she's there because she hardly says a word. He checks his impulse, but it kicks in anyway.

"So what have we got tonight?"

"Uh..." Tammy disappears behind the wall between the kitchen and living room and then he sees her through the little Moroccan window in the wall—the thing Ann fell in love with when they bought the place. After she sets the tray down, she speaks.

"I got homemade mac 'n' cheese and peas."

"Great! Sounds great."

So why is tonight so different? Why is the silence so deafening around them? In his hurry to change and drown himself in aftershave he'd neglected to set the small table. As she reaches for plates he comes to life and moves to the kitchen.

"Sorry, I forgot to set the table."

"I can do it," she says, her eyes looking directly at him.

"I can, too. You did all the work, let me get it. Here." He holds her chair out for her and immediately regrets it as a small blush creeps up her face.

What am I doing?

Before today they had moved past each other like synchronized ghosts, getting their own beer from the fridge, dishing up their own plates, and now he's ruining it with his aftershave and his damn manners. He wants it to be like it was before, but it feels like a tiny shift has taken hold in him and he has to stop himself from dishing her plate up for her. Ann had been gone for eight months. Does this happen after eight months? Suddenly your dead wife seems really gone and other women appear in Technicolor, with shapes and sounds and nuances that had once been invisible? He looks at Tammy's face and sees mascara and a bit of brown, light-brown eye shadow. Had she always worn makeup? Had he just not noticed or is it new? Does she feel a shift, too?

He picks up the salt and feels bad that he shakes it over the macaroni. She never adds enough salt to the mac 'n' cheese and someone at one time told him it's rude to add salt to his food in front of the chef. But he does it anyway. He can hear her chewing. He knows she can hear him because Ann told him his mouth was like an echoing cave and you could hear everything, even the words he doesn't speak.

"So, have a good day?"

She shrugs. "My day off. Had to clean. Place was a mess."

"You should do something fun on a day off, dontcha think?" Good God, is he flirting? Does he even know how? Or is what he just said within the normal realm of conversation with someone you aren't aware of sexually?

Another shrug and then silence.

"Yeah, I went to the doc today. He tells me I can't move my fingers 'cause it's all in my head."

She looks up briefly and shakes her head. "What do they know anyhow. Doctors don't know shit. Look what they did for Annie. Nothin'."

"It'll be eight months on Saturday. Can you believe that?"

He regrets saying it because a shadow crosses her face. "Seems longer somehow."

"Sometimes. Sometimes it seems like yesterday. Depends. Today it seems like yesterday."

"You gonna stay here?"

He looks up at her. "Why wouldn't I?"

"Oh, I dunno. Memories or somethin'. I'd do anything to get outta here. I don't got anywhere to go anyhow."

"Well my family's here. I mean, you're here so I wouldn't go." He begins kicking himself mentally in the head over and over. He clears his throat. "I mean I go see Cole n' all. I can't be too far from him."

"When you goin' to see him next? Saturday?"

"Yeah, that's the day I see him."

"How long's he got?"

"He says he'll be out after he's served a year, but I know he's just tellin' me that. The sentence was five."

"Mm, parole, maybe."

"Yeah."

"How's Milt?"

"Oh, he's fine. I think he's fine. Never hear from him."

"Never liked that wife of his. She don't like us. Too small-town for her uppity self."

He nodded, lifting his beer to his lips. He didn't want to talk about Milt. The feeling of failure thumps in his chest when he thinks of him. Milt, the successful attorney in Henderson, who can't admit he came from Wells. Wade can't admit that he's prouder of the son in prison because of what he'd done for his mother. Milt had visited three times and made it to the funeral, and that's as far as he'd been willing to go.

"You wearin' makeup or somethin'? You look different." Mental kicking resumes.

"I wear it sometimes. Just when I feel like it."

Don't say it looks nice, don't say it looks nice...

"Looks nice."

Tammy says nothing but the small smile tells him she's pleased.

Jesus Christ, I'm going to go over to Durward's tomorrow and kick him 'til he's dead.

When Tammy finally left, Wade let out the internal sigh of relief he'd been storing up all evening. He doesn't know if she'd felt the same tension, the same weirdness, but he hopes it was all him, all in his head and things would go back to normal soon. She would be back Friday and then he'd tell her. He'd tell her she didn't need to feed him anymore, that she could just come around once in a while for small talk. And of course he'd see her at work, at the Flying J where she's a cashier. Yeah, he'd see her when he went in to buy gum and beer. She wouldn't take it personally, he's sure. He just knows she can't keep doing what she's doing. Something is going off the rails, and he's sure it's him.

And he feels like a sort of a jerk that he didn't invite her with him that night to Luther's Bar and Grill, but he never invites her so why does he feel like a jerk?

Luther's had been renovated in 2008 and inside it looks like a log cabin, though it still stinks of beer and fried things and old musty wood beams, but it should since it's been around since before Wade was born. It's where his dad went almost nightly to drink himself into a stupor before his mother came to pour him into the car and then pour him into bed. Wade's father had been a harmless drunk. He was jovial and friendly, slurring his love murmurings to Wade's mother and his kids with his red nose and his lazy smile. Wade had been a drunk once, too, until he realized his drunk was a mean drunk. It was when the boys were small, when he still had the young man ya-yas spouting off around and inside him with nowhere for them to land. But Ann had taken a stand, so he cut back.

Now he drinks beer with half tomato juice to slow him down. It's worked for twenty years, and Wade doesn't like feeling mean.

When he walks in, the music's too loud, as it always is. Gerry sits at the table closest to the bar since the bar is too high for his wheelchair. Junior is at the bar and has Wade's glass already filled halfway with Bud Light.

"Wade, how goes the struggle?"

"Junior, what the hell? Hey, how come you don't go by 'Luther'? Junior just don't seem right."

"You been comin' here all this time, you just now ask 'bout my name? What's wrong with you? Anyhow, Luther's my daddy. Junior's me."

"I don't know. I feel weird tonight and it just popped into me. I looked atcha all gigantic behind the bar and you just don't look like a 'Junior.' You can crush two cars together with your bare-assed hands."

Junior gives a hearty laugh and his belly shakes behind his white t-shirt. "And don't you forget it. Here's your bloody beer, you pussy."

"Gerry, what the hell? How's it hangin'?"

Gerry looks up from his drink and smiles. "Lower than ever, you dumb fuck. What the hell you doin' here?"

"Comin' to see a couple of sad-assed douchebags like you. What else is there to do 'round here?"

Junior slides the bloody beer along the bar and Wade takes it and snags the seat across from Gerry. "Any word from the VA?"

"Yeah," Gerry smiles wickedly, "they still can't find my legs over there in Ee-raq. Guess them towel-heads ate 'em."

"I mean about the pain in your left one, smart ass."

"They says it's some phantom thing, like my nerves still got memory or somethin'. Fucking doctors don't know anything from anything. But my willie still works, so what's there to bitch about?"

"Well thanks for tellin' me that, Gerry, I can go home and have me some fuckin' nightmares now."

Gerry lets out a hearty laugh then a fit of coughing seizes him. "Ah, glad I can give ya somethin' to jerk off to." *Cough, cough, cough.*

Gerry points to Wade. "What's about you? You go get checked out with your hand thing?"

"Huh, doc said the same thing to me. Some phantom thing 'cause of

Annie and all."

Gerry falls silent and his smile moves to a straight line on his face. It's his show of respect. Wade's grateful that some things are sacred and they both know what is sacred between them.

"How you doin', then." Gerry raises his eyebrows and sips at his beer almost daintily.

"Good, I'm doin' good. You know, every day gets better."

"You seein' that lady you met a couple months ago? She was Pete's niece or somethin'?"

"Yeah, and nah, that was only the one-time deal, one date. Between you an' me, and don't tell Pete this, but she was itchin' for a man to take care of her and I just ain't that keen on havin' someone around all the time."

"Didja do her at least?"

"None of your fuckin' business."

"That'd be a 'no,'" Junior pipes in.

Wade casts a squinty gaze over at Junior as Gerry chuckles.

The woman is a waitress at Mama's Cafe, where Wade gets his breakfast. She had been nice enough, but Wade felt her neediness on him like burrs trapped in a mangy dog's fur and he hadn't asked her out since the one date. Every time he goes back into the cafe, he tries to be nice to her, but she sets his plates down rough just the same.

"Well there's always the hen house," Gerry grins.

"Not for me there ain't."

"What?" Junior and Gerry say this almost simultaneously and Wade looks at them.

"I'm not some dipshit who's gonna go out and pay for it. Jesus."

"You never been to Mamacita's? Even when you was married?"

"Never been." Wade looks at the two men, whose mouths are both open.

"How can you be a man in this town and never been to Lil' Mamacita's? I think you're the only man in this goddamned town, Wade Kendall. You should be sainted or knighted or somethin'," Junior laughs.

"Or a queer," Gerry says, laughing in his beer.

"I never needed to pay for it in my life, I ain't gonna start now."

"It's a rite of passage, Wade. You been alone a long time. It ain't bad.

The girls there are real nice." Gerry winks at him. "Hell, I go up there whenever I can and there ain't no complainin', I'll tell you that. There's this one gal there who—"

"Stop. Just shut yer mouth right there, Gerry, so help me. You give me another visual of you and I'll puke in your beer, I swear to God."

"Well, your loss, asshole. Them girls are nice, just sayin'. Some are young, too. But there's this older one there, too, and she's real nice. I'm always askin' for her. I've asked her to marry me at least a dozen times. It's all in fun, but I swear to God, she ever says yes, I'll marry her, whore or no."

"Make her an honest woman, will ya?" Junior says from behind the bar.

"Yep, tell her I can go all night if she'd let me."

"Why don't you tell her that now, you asshole, " Wade says.

"I can't afford to go all night there! Shit, break my bank."

"And there's another good reason not to go. I ain't got much of a bank to break."

"Oh hell, it ain't that much. 'Bout two, three hundred for half an hour. You go to them VIP rooms it's more, though. But they're nice—they got them hot tubs there, right in the room."

"Hot tubs? No kiddin'. Huh."

Wade had seen the "hen house" his whole life; you couldn't live in Wells and not know about the hen house. It was just northeast of the town on a road called *Mamacita Highway*. It had been there, rumor had it, for over 140 years. It's the main attraction for the truckers that move through town on their way from Elko or Wendover, and even farther than that. But Wade had never been inside, never set foot in a place like that. It seems too demeaning, paying for someone to suck your cock or let you fuck her. He figures if a woman wants him like he wants her, then that's the proper way.

Or you just jack off in the shower, he thinks. It's worked for him for over forty-five years.

Wade stares in his beer and sees the bubbles rise and the loneliness envelops him like a pair of giant, supple arms.

There's no Ann. There's no one. What would it hurt if you had to pay? On some level they gotta find you pretty okay, right? It's not like they would be too discriminating up there. So what if they get paid? Maybe attraction exists there, too.

No, he says to himself. *If I'm gonna get off, it ain't gonna be with someone I pay for.*

After distracted small talk and more insults, Wade pays his tab and heads for home. He walks into the night air and he thinks about the warmth he'd felt earlier. He imagines what warmth would feel like if it was for real.

Wade admits to himself the curiosity he's had since he was twelve. *The hen house. The ol' cathouse. The brothel.*

What went on in that salmon-pink, one story double wide-looking house with the darkened windows? As a teen, he and his friends used to drive by it, hoopin' and hollerin' late at night, throwing beer cans in the parking lot, and that's as close and as brave as he'd been in his life.

No one would know. But he can't ever go there because *he* would know and it breaks some sort of vow inside him that tells him he's worth the trouble to get a woman properly, get her right. Of course, the women out there who are looking are looking for men like him for one reason and one reason only: to catch him. He'd felt that the second he'd taken Pete's niece, Cindy, on a date. He paid for their dinner, they'd watched a DVD she'd picked out (*The Notebook*, about the sappiest piece of shit he'd ever seen) and then he took her home. He'd shaken her hand. Now she sets his plates down all rough when he goes to Mama's Cafe. Mama's Cafe is owned by the same woman who owns Lil' Mamacitas. So technically, he'd already given her plenty of money. He's practically been right inside that hen house.

He drives straight home from Luther's to 3rd Street, between Wells Avenue and Starr, where he's lived for thirty-three years and he doesn't even look toward the Great Basin Highway 93 that leads to that dingy overpass that leads to...there.

He doesn't even look. He drives west.

With his truck in the carport he feels settled. He feels ready to face the "empty," all that empty that waits inside the door of his house. Ready or resigned, he's not sure which. He thinks of Tammy again, like he'd been doing all evening. Wondering what kind of company she'd be after eleven p.m., sitting on the couch, watching some rerun of a rosy time in Somewhere, USA, and that's all he can think of now. Somewhere in the USA, someone is coming home to another someone and they won't be alone. And he doesn't kid himself for one minute about why he feels alone.

It didn't start eight months ago when Annie died, it started the first time his blushing bride stopped blushing, stopped pretty much everything he'd looked forward to when he thought marriage meant you got to be with the woman you loved in *that way* any time you wanted. He'd been had a rude awakening. But he never stepped out on her—never. He'd had women make eyes, he'd had opportunities. When he'd started at the insurance company, job training at twenty-two, and those older housewives would meet with him, talk about their husband's death like they'd already buried them…those women, blinking too much, smiling and such, bending over too much. Oh yes, he'd had opportunities. But he kept his promise to Annie to 'have and to hold,' only Annie, she dropped the *hold* and just *had*. She had him. And all he'd wanted was to have her back.

He walks in and the smell of dinner is faint, but it's there, a residual of the evening. Had he brought Tammy along, she might be there with him now, and who knows what could happen after eleven p.m. with a woman like her? But if he is telling himself the truth, it isn't her body parts he wants, but her *body*, in the near, physical sense. Next to him. Looking at his face. Hearing his voice. Responding. Something, anything but the death-silence of the house with the air conditioner bumping and grinding to a halt as the temperature inside the house begins to cool.

Talking to a woman is like an excavation. You have to dig, scrape, brush away the bullshit to see what it is she wants. And even then that can change on a fucking dime. Then the expectations, like another life form, attach to the both of you and soon, there's three of you sitting, talking, not saying anything, saying everything, and never understanding a fucking word of what goes on.

The one thing that makes sense is when the physical distance closes, lips press, eyes shut, hands caress and breathing quickens. That language, that universal language, makes sense but he's a stranger in a foreign land, there. He isn't sure how he could get it up, make it last, make anything happen with a real woman ever again. Even his fucking hand rejects him now. No, the loneliness comes from somewhere deep, somewhere penetrating inside and he can't see any way to make it shrivel and die.

All he wants is a conversation. Someone to listen and to listen to.

"All I want is a goddamned conversation. Nothing wrong with that. Without the bullshit. Just straight talk. Just someone. "

Why not? Why the fuck not?

He grabs his keys and walks out the front door. The truck is still warm as he starts her up and backs out. He heads northeast to Exit 351.

The word had never been used when he thought of himself or his life. *Adventurous.*

But that's how Wade feels as he drives over the deserted overpass that seems to go on and on, like a mouth yawning into the depths of a blackened gullet. This is not a desperate man's climb into the depths of the pathetic; this is an adventure to see a piece of history—a colorful, flavorful part of his past, his *town's* past, and he's ready to break through the barriers that have kept him at bay because it's what a man of adventure would do. Wade decides he is now a man of adventure.

And he only has forty bucks on him. Not that the thought even enters his mind to hire a lady for the evening. That would cross the line from adventuresome to pathetic and he's not pathetic. He's curious. Curiously adventurous.

He can't afford to travel far or much, but he can go alone to camp, fish—hell, drive to Henderson and drop in on that kid of his and remind him where he came from. Win over that wife of his with his charm, his spirit of adventure that has been born this night of all nights in Wells, Nevada on a Wednesday at eleven twenty-three in the p.m.

He turns left onto the unkempt road and the two cathouses glow softly in the black of the night. One is Mona's Ranch. It is a stone's throw from the parking lot of Lil' Mamacita's. He wonders what sort of competitive drama occurs there hourly, daily, weekly, and what the difference is between the two. How do these lonely men choose where to go? One is salmon pink with a modestly blazing neon sign telling its customers it's a "gentleman's club." There are bare bulbs hanging from the awnings lighting the path to the front door. The windows are dark-tinted, but light seeps through, letting him know that life resides inside, squirming, squirting, writhing with adventure.

Mona's Ranch is painted just like a hen house, with a red exterior and white trim. It's a little smaller than Mamacita's. He'd forgotten the size of them, because now as he approaches the two structures, he sees there have been additions--they are not simply wanna-be double wides, but full-on buildings with courtyards, fences, decks.

Two long-haul semi-trucks are parked to the north and he can't tell which lot they're roosting in. Mamacita's has four vehicles in front, Mona's, two. It's as if a final, godly nudge at his shoulder tells him that Mamacita's is indeed the place for him. Hell, he might even meet a couple of guys to chew the fat with and wouldn't that be something?

He pulls his truck into the lot and decides not to worry about whether someone recognizes it. Fuck 'em if they can't handle the new, adventurous Wade, who is there to satisfy his curiosity and embrace all of the goings-on in his little town. His red and white Chevy is a 1978 half-ton in perfect condition, and he's babied her and kept her running for years, recognizable to anyone in town. So fuck 'em.

He sniffs his pits and checks his breath and pulls out a stick of gum. He's a gentleman, he belongs in a gentleman's club and he'll not be a leering lech of a man, there to waste his money on some poor, unwilling woman who has the look of a thousand miles traveled down dark roads. No, he isn't that guy. But then he thinks of Gerry telling him of the young girls there, too and that brings back that feeling of adventure because he is old enough to be their father and he'll be respectful and understanding. He will visit them, never use and abuse them, and he will be their favorite customer, like a beloved uncle, someone to call on them and tell them funny stories of selling insurance to old ranchers and farmers with three-legged watch dogs.

The door to Lil' Mamacita's is black with a bulb overhead to light the porch. Even though the sign says to ring the doorbell, he tries the door anyway, unsurprised that it's locked. He raises his finger and presses the white button, hearing the bell echoing indoors. For one moment he hesitates. But his pounding heart has flooded him with energy and curiosity and his adventure cannot end with him turning-tail and running for the safety of his truck and home.

The door opens with a whoosh, cool air, warm light and a smile on an older woman's face.

"Well, hello, and welcome to Lil' Mamacita's! Come on in." She steps aside and Wade nods his head in greeting, feeling the bravado slip through him like hot taffy and pool at his feet. His feet seem stuck in the taffy mass as he walks, his steps unsure and slow.

The woman places her hand on his back and his whole body flinches involuntarily. He looks at her in apology. She pats him a few times. "Oh, now, we don't bite. Come on in, grab a drink with us. I'm Belle. What's your name, honey?"

"My name's, uh, I'm Wade. Thanks."

"Wade, you from around here?"

"I am, yeah, I've, uh, lived here my whole life, if you want to know the truth. But I'm new here."

"No *kiddin'*." Her eyes are wide and she looks as though he just told her about the discovery of a new night creature, one with magical powers. "How's it you've lived here your whole life, ain't never come to see us, huh?" She smiles and it's warm and inviting and he feels settled the moment her eyes bore into his. This one doesn't miss a thing, this woman with smile lines a mile long and crinkles near her eyes that reveal age, mirth and wisdom, all at once. Her teeth are straight; lines encase her smile. He realizes he's talking to Mama, *the* Mama of the house. Some people would call her a legend, famous at the very least. He's already started his adventure.

"I just never been, that's all. But tonight seemed like a night for talkin'. I mean, seein'..." he trails off as she leads him into a long, narrow room with a bar, and two high tables with chairs. A man in clothes too warm for summer sits at a table with a girl who's smiling, nodding her head. She looks briefly up at Wade, smiles, and then her gaze returns to her companion. She wears a short, hot-pink dress and heels. She's young.

Wade feels caught up in a current and he's not sure how to reach shore. He needs to make his intentions clear, needs to grind his taffy-covered feet in the muck of the bottom of this stream and hold fast. It's then he realizes his mistake. The ATM sitting at the side of the bar awakens him and he stops short.

These women aren't here to entertain him. They aren't here to chat with him and relieve his loneliness, and they aren't a party to his new sense of adventure. These women are here to make a living, and suddenly, as if the current crashes him to the bottom of the pool, he feels a sense of crushing shame fill his chest like a flood of water.

"'Scuse me, Ma'am."

Belle speaks softly to the bartender, another older woman who isn't as quick to smile, and then Belle's eyes light on him again, and she smiles that fifty-dollar smile. "What can we getcha?"

"I—I think I've made a mistake. I'm sorry. I shouldn't be here."

Surely a woman of such wisdom can see inside his mind, see what he's thinking, not make him explain. She sees the confusion, the misunderstanding, as surely as he feels it and will let him go without incident, without embarrassment. Instead, she grips his upper arm tight.

"You hold on, now. Let me get you a drink. I'm lookin' at you and you got a story as to why on tonight of all nights you happened into my place, Wade from Wells. You just sit, 'cause I wanna hear it. Then you can go on out if you like. Deal?"

Her earnest gaze melts him on the spot and he nods. "Could I get a bloody beer? Plain tomato juice and whatever you got on tap."

"Bev, get our friend Wade here a bloody beer. On the house. My treat tonight, Wade. You have a seat, honey, and I'll sit right here and you got my ears."

She pulls out a barstool for him and props herself on the one next to it. Her hand hasn't left his arm.

Suddenly his adventure has turned into a fool's errand—like a giant idea shrunk itself right in front of him into a tiny circle of thought that keeps getting smaller. He'd walked in with half-closed eyes, but now they're pried open, the full light of the situation unfolded, and it is clear as a crystal stream.

Wade looks into those deep blue eyes Belle has fixed on him, and he can't tell her about "adventure." He can't tell her about the new Wade. So foolish, so *not* him. He is not adventurous. He's the guy who steps with slow steps into a lake, feeling the incremental rise of the water from his toes to his feet to his ankles. He waits until he's used to the water before he takes one more step. That's who he is.

He sighs and says it again. "I shouldn't have come in here."

"And why not?"

"I had these ideas…these crazy ideas. I didn't think it through."

"Some of the best ideas aren't thought through all the way, Wade. Sometimes you gotta just jump in."

He laughs to himself. "I never jump in."

"Maybe it's time you do."

"What are we talkin' about here, Belle? Because I didn't come in here tonight to do what most men come in here to do. And that was a fool thing."

"I think you came in here for the *exact* reason these other fellas come in. You didn't want to be alone."

Wade glances up at her and her stare shoots him between the eyes. She has him pegged and he doesn't know if that feels right or not— to be so easily read, so transparent. He shrugs. "No, you're right. I didn't wanna be alone. But this 'aint no social club. It's a business and I shoulda thought that through."

"Listen. You and me talkin'? That's just bein' human. Everybody needs to talk. So tell me what brought you in that door, huh? How 'bout we start there."

Wade looks up at the lights strung along the top of the bar. In front of the lights are bras and panties, stuck up with pins and tacks. He catches a glimpse of himself in the mirror behind the great selection of liquor bottles lining the shelf. He looks old in the light. He looks like the thousand-mile stretch of highway.

He doesn't want to start this way, but he can't help it. It's the most logical place to start.

"My wife passed. Eight months ago."

Her hand squeezes his arm tighter and he doesn't flinch. It feels warm and heavy, like the air outside. "Sorry to hear."

"And…"

And what? He has friends. He has people to talk to—hell, just tonight there was Gerry and Junior and Tammy…almost every day he's talking to Durward. He couldn't tell her why he was there anymore than he could tell himself.

He shakes his head. "And I guess I was tired of the same ol' same ol' every day. Wanted to see somethin' new."

"Well, ain't nothin' wrong with that. You want a tour? I can show you all the rooms, you can meet—"

"No, no I don't wanna waste any more of your time. Thank you for the drink."

He stands and when he stands, she follows. She grabs him and wraps her arms around him and holds on tight. The feel of her against him is like a blanket of comfort after a bad dream. Unsure at first, he finally wraps his arms around her and she stays there until he returns the intensity of her bear hug. She holds him away from her and smiles.

"See, you can't buy that anywhere, Wade. You can't. But you can always come here and get one for free. You understand me? Now, you wanna leave, go ahead. But you understand you always got a home here at Mama's."

His throat is a rusted pipe. "Thank you, ma'am."

He doesn't want to leave anymore, but the warmth of the place is too seductive, too smooth for him to trust. He doesn't finish his beer; he nods once to her and walks out the front door, feeling all at once lighter than the breeze and heavier than the darkened sky.

3

The irony affects him every time.

In order to get to *Wells Conservation Camp*, a minimum security prison, Wade has to drive east through *Independence Valley*. There are signs posted for no hitchhiking because of the prison. *Independence Valley*, the place you go to lose your freedom.

It's Saturday, and Wade is heading southeast to see his son.

Tammy hadn't come over the previous evening. She called him and told him she couldn't come by and he'd assured her he could get dinner on his own, not wanting to have the talk with her over the phone that maybe she shouldn't come by at all with dinner—ever. That was an in-person talk. A way to let her out. Or more importantly, a way to feel her out, see why she keeps coming. Maybe all he needs is that information to get him out of the mind-numbing confusion he's been feeling lately. Maybe all he needs to hear is one word, maybe two, and the answer will appear as clear as the day's sky why she comes. But then he doesn't know how it will clear him at all because any scenario makes doubt roil up inside of him and then he feels a sense of dread.

He pulls his truck into the usual spot, always empty for him, and approaches the gray building with the glass doors.

The inside looks more like a low-budget doctor's office than a prison. He supposes because it's a minimum security place and they want visitors to feel like their loved ones are not so much in prison as being held in a harmless, even benign place. But Wade doesn't fool himself about any of it. His son's in prison and in a very real way, he feels safer knowing that Cole's locked up, safe, rather than "out there."

Cole Kendall had been raised with a larger sense of leniency than his older, successful brother. Wade wishes he'd been stricter about the partying, the late nights. Then again, Milton, his oldest, never seemed interested in the parties, only in escape. Cole had seemed rooted to the spot, to his friends, to his home more than Milt ever had. The boy had never shown ambition except to score the next good time. Wade can't blame himself entirely, but he does just the same.

He goes through the security—a one-man operation— with familiarity as he leaves his keys, wallet and pocket lint in the tray before he enters the visiting area. Then he waits for them to bring Cole in.

This wait, this wait seems never-ending and too short, all at once. He's there just long enough to drink in the gray, industrial carpet and the beige tables, the windows all around and the gray-tinged white-painted brick walls. He wonders if the counseling they offer in there is really helping Cole or just getting him ready to try something new and more dangerous on the outside. His son is ingenious at trying new things.

The door opens and Cole walks in, looking thinner than Wade would like. He's wearing a gray work shirt and Levi's. His smile is crooked, friendly, and Wade's chest fills like a helium balloon when he stands to embrace him.

"Gettin' skinny, boy. They feedin' you?"

"Yeah they are. I just work real hard all week. God-*damn* it was hot out there this week. I get plenty of water but there's no shade on the highway."

"Doin' clean-up?"

"This week. Next week we're headin' into the mountains for trail maintenance or somethin'. Be nice to be in the cooler part. You're looking skinnier than last week, Pop. Are you eatin'?"

"Your aunt Tammy's bringing me food still. And I cook. Course I eat. Been sittin' on my ass like a lazy sonofabitch. This retirement shit's killin' me. But enough about me—"

"How's the hand, Pop?"

Wade holds up his right hand. "Still broke. See this? I'm tryin' to move 'em, they just won't budge."

"You know, that's a brain issue, there, Pop. That's what that is. It ain't mechanical. It's your brain."

"The doc don't know. He talked about an MRI. Maybe there's somethin' to that. Anyways…what they got you doin' besides working the highway and trails? You still seein' that counselor here?"

"Yeah. She's nice. She thinks I got some genetic thing that makes me all *predisposed* for addiction. But I been clean eight months, now, Pop. I feel real good, if you can believe it."

"They tell you anything about parole yet?"

Cole looks at him with a touch of mirth in his eyes. "I don't know, Pop. I'm only in here 'cause I'm not dangerous. I mean, I did what I did and…well they don't take it so lightly, I guess."

"Well it ain't forever. You gotta make a plan for when you get out. You're young still. You got your whole life ahead."

Cole brushes this away. "I don't care about my whole life. Fuck, all I got is right now. You know? And right now I got nothin'. I'm not bein' all dramatic or anything. Just sayin' it."

"You listen to me, Cole. You couldn't ever see past that nose of yours. Time goes by, just like that. Then you're out, then what? You gotta fly right. You gotta make good. You're smart."

"And what am I s'posed to do with a GED and a prison record? Work at Flyin' J my whole life?"

"What, you got bigger plans? Tammy could get you on. You could move up—"

"I don't want some shitty job in town caterin' to truckers and fuckin' locals and pissin' my life away. I wanna travel."

"Jesus, Cole. That takes money to travel, I can't even travel. You're thinkin' like a kid."

Cole reaches over and covers Wade's hand with his own. "Pop, let's not do this again."

"You come live at home with me after, you can take classes on the Internet. You can—"

"What, become a phlebotomist or some shit? Come on."

"No, you—"

"Pop, I can't be in the house. I can't. I'd see Mom everywhere. I see her everywhere now. I wonder…I mean, I don't know if she knows I'm here. She was so sick when I got…"

"Hey, you listen to me. Here's what your mom knows: you were at her bedside *every damn day* while I was at work. You were takin' care of her, readin' to her, bein' there. *That's what she knows.*"

Wade's eyes begin to burn with tears and he sniffs and sits back in his chair.

"Yeah," Cole says. "But what if she knows about this."

"Well," Wade pauses, "I know 'bout this. And you're still my son and I still love you. Wherever she is, she's doin' nothin' but lovin' you, same as me."

Cole stares at a point just past Wade's head, his eyes moving from side to side as if a scene plays only for him and he's caught in it. With red eyes, he meets Wade's gaze.

"I just didn't wanna disappoint her. You neither."

"Look, the way I see it, we all make mistakes. Just this mistake landed you here. Shit, son, your mistake coulda been takin' one too many pills, and then what? This thing here's a blessin', if you want to know the truth of it. That's how I see it. You said so yourself, clean and sober. See what I mean?"

"I guess that's right. It's just that, I don't know what I wanna do when I get out. The pickin's are slim. For a guy like me, anyhow."

"Look, you get a good job, work hard and then you gotta be patient. That's your one thing, Cole. You want everything now when you ain't gone and worked for it, now, see? Patience."

"It ain't like when you were young, Pop, when you could just graduate high school, then find a career. They want you to have college now, and specialties and skills and things."

"And all that takes patience."

"But I mean companies, they invested in you back then, but now it's all on paper."

"Companies still invest. Look it, you're young. You might need to try on a few things before you decide what you're gonna do. Each job brings a different thing. My job I learned all 'bout insurance, but dang, they didn't teach me 'bout people. I learned that all on my own. And when I learned 'bout people, Son, I learned 'bout myself the most. I learned what makes them tick, then I learned what makes me tick. You can't buy that kinda education anywhere, in any college. You see what I mean? Your Mom, now she used'ta tell me I think too much. She'd always complain and say, "Wade, you'd be a lot better off you stop thinking so much 'bout things. She was probably right. But it made me good at my job, see."

"You think 'bout Mom? I mean, is it hard to be in the house an' all?"

Wade wrestles with the shift and with his reaction. He doesn't know what Cole wants. There are a million things that are true: yes, he's lonely. Yes, he misses Annie—or misses the idea of her. But he doesn't miss the illness, the constant worry for her. He doesn't miss watching her fade away and the hopelessness in her eyes. The truth of it for him is that he's glad she's free, and with that, he's glad he's free as well. He decides to take a safe, middle ground.

"Sure I do, I miss her. But I ain't sorry she's in a better place, neither. She's outta pain, an' that's what I think about when I feel blue."

"I hope she don't know I'm here, Pop. I don't want her to know I'm here."

"Cole, I toldja—"

"No, Pop, you don't get it, see. She may be out of pain 'cause she's gone, but if she knows I'm here, where she is right now? You can bet it's causin' her all kinds a grief. An' I don't want that, Pop. I don't want that." Cole's voice cracks as he bows his head. Wade places his hand over his son's. Even now, the boy's more worried about his mom than his own skin. Wade shakes his head. He knows as sure as the day's sun why this boy's that soft spot right in the middle of his whole self.

"She don't care where you are, Son. She just cares you're safe."

Cole looks up and sniffs, smiling a little. "You think so?"

"I'd bet on it."

They sit in silence and Wade wonders if Annie can really see them. He hopes not. Not because of Cole, though. He doesn't want Annie seeing *him*. For some reason, he feels like he would be the bigger disappointment.

Durward is sitting on Wade's front porch with his back straight like a watch dog. He squints as Wade pulls his truck into the carport and cuts the engine. Wade doesn't feel ready to deal with Durward today. The visit with Cole has left his chest heavy with disappointment and pain. The shared memory of Ann's illness, her death, the aching absence of Milt—it all leaves him with a tangle of dark emotions inside him.

Durward has a plastic sack with him and Wade knows what's in it.

"Dude, it's hot today. You're wearing long pants, you're gonna cook."

"Eh. I brought you these. Millie don't like 'em in my house, she says."

"*Playboys* in that sack?"

"Yup."

"Didja think about just havin' them somewhere she don't find 'em, Dude?"

"She finds 'em."

Wade picks up the sack and glances inside at the shiny covers. There's at least 20 magazines inside. "I don't know why you waste all your money on 'em."

"Annie liked the *Good Housekeepin'* ones. Now I give 'em to Millie."

"You ain't gonna win that sweepstakes, Durward, you know that."

He points his bony finger at Wade, "You don't know that, you ignoramus. You don't know nothin' about it. I personally shook Ed McMahon's hand and he knows me. He's lookin' out for me."

"He don't got nothin' to do with it, Dude."

"He's my good, personal friend. Anytime I want ta go to California, he said—"

"Durward, Ed McMahon died, buddy. You know that. Come on now. Come inside, I'll getcha a beer."

"It's eleven in the mornin' boy. I got roses to prune. Brought you them magazines, that's all. Millie an' me we're gonna do some gardening at her place later."

"Dude, why don't you make an honest woman outta her, huh? You're too old to be alone."

Durward scowls deeply, "I ain't alone and I like *bein'* alone."

"Jesus..."

Durward totters away, waving his hand behind his butt as though he's leaving a methane trail in his wake. He calls out, "Marriage is for the young. Fellas like you. You're the one shouldn't be alone."

Wade watches the old man creak back and forth, like he's on uneven stilts. He watches him all the way to his front door.

Wade is relieved to get inside, out of the arid heat. He's had something up his ass all morning, and now ever since his visit with Cole, it's pestering him like a hemorrhoid. He pulls out his phone and dials his oldest son's number.

To his surprise, Milt answers.

"Milt? It's your dad. How's things."

"Dad, good, good, things are great. How…how are you? I haven't talked to you in a while. Sorry about that. I've been really busy."

"Yeah. Well busy is good, I guess. Right? Better than bein' bored outta your skull. I feel like I'm bored outta my skull most days."

"So did you finally end up taking your retirement?"

"Yeah. Yeah I did. Don't know what to do with myself. I was thinkin' of coming to see you, ya know, at some point. Later on. Won't stay there, 'course, no need to put you all out. Just come up, see the kids and whatnot."

"Sure, sure…that would be…yeah. I'll talk to Carol, see what works for us."

Carol is Milt's social manager, wife, drill sergeant, and keeper. She's never spoken more than ten words to Wade, he's sure of it. She's from Henderson, from money. He remembers feeling like a white-trash gatecrasher at their wedding, with his rented tuxedo and Ann, nervous and pucker-faced at his side while Carol's relatives floated among the finery of the country club where they said their vows.

"Well, I can accommodate is what I'm sayin'. I got the time. Like to see the girls before they're all growed up."

"Sure Dad, they'd love to see you, I'm sure."

"Saw your brother today. He's doing good. Real fine. Got him workin' and trainin' for when he gets out."

"That's good, Dad. He's okay?"

"Yeah, yeah. He's good. Got him in the counselin', too, so he's all off the pills. Yeah, it's real good. How're the girls gettin' on? Out for summer I guess."

"Yeah. McKenna's still in dance. She's really doing well. Had a recital last week. Brianna's still taking piano and she's getting really good, Dad. Mom would have loved to hear her play. Mom really liked those old soft tunes, you know, like Deep Purple…she can play that. Well, a beginner's version of that. I told her it was Mom's favorite song, so she learned it on her own."

This warms Wade inside in such a way that he feels his throat close up, eyes moisten. He loves those little girls. They are so polite, so sweet to him. They never judge him. The older one, McKenna, she's shy, reserved, but respectful. Brianna clamors onto his lap when he comes, and he loves it—until her mother tells her to stop treating him like a jungle gym. But he never minded kids treating him like a jungle gym. He just wasn't used to girls, is all. He knows he can't rough- house with them, so he's always careful and gentle, like Annie told him to be.

Wade makes sure he's mastered the cracks forming in his voice before he responds. "Well, I miss those girls, you know. Miss you too, if want to know the truth. I still haven't seen where you work or anythin', you know. You've done real good, Milt. You know I'm proud of you."

There is a long pause on the other end of the line and Wade wonders if they got cut off, or maybe he's been put on "mute," but then Milt clears his throat.

"Thanks, Dad. I appreciate it. Look, I gotta go. I've gotta get McKenna to dance and Carol needs me."

"Well, listen, you can call me any time, you know. I'm just here and, you know, maybe someday I won't be. Is all I mean to say. Life's short. I mean…hell, I don't know. Just give your ol' man a call sometime, is all I'm tryin' to say."

"I will, Dad. I'm sorry. Life gets so busy… you know. I work a lot. I'm sorry. I'll be better about calling."

"All right. 'Bye. You tell those girls their Papa loves 'em. Say 'hi' to Carol for me, too."

"Will do. 'Bye, Dad."

Wade presses "end" and is left with that desolate feeling he always has after talking to Milt. Plans made that are never set, never kept, and always empty.

He pulls out a magazine from the bag and looks at the young woman staring seemingly into his eyes as he reads the captions on the cover.

Mansion Photo Shoot: A Steamy Peek into the Grotto
A Passion for Betty Page
UFC's Softer Side

An Interview with Kanye West.

He doesn't want to read the articles. He wants the pictures because they take him out of the "father" mind and put him into a "man's" mind, which is only a little less painful in the middle of an arid, hot day.

It was not on the daily roster of Things To Do, but Wade finds himself back at the cafe anyway at 1 p.m., ready to order a prime rib sandwich, Mama's specialty. The thought of eating at home alone, especially after the chat with Milt, left him feeling like he'd go bonkers listening to himself chew. Maybe it's because he hadn't seen Tammy the night before and that unsettled him. Made him hungry for company, for people. So Mama's Cafe it is.

He sits in his usual booth, the one nearest the restrooms. A jute coffee bean sack from Ethiopia is next to him, hanging on the wall. He has every letter and color and thread memorized. It's Cindy's station, he knows it is, but he can't get himself to move, not because he *can't,* he just doesn't want her to *think* it's because of her. And if he moved, it would be. Because of her. He finds he's curiously eager to talk to her and he's not sure why. He glances over to where the waitresses congregate, watching for her. So far she's not appeared, but then she does.

He sees her and then sees *her* see *him*. Her eyelids drop incrementally, although no one would notice. But he notices. He seems to notice every tiny thing about her as she grabs a menu and a pitcher of water. It had been two months since that first dull date, and he hadn't called again. He knows the women gossip. Her ego had probably been bruised. He wants to make that right somehow and he's not sure how until the idea strikes him between the eyes. It's so obvious to him, then and there.

He's going to surprise her, he decides, right on the spot.

She saunters over and doesn't meet his gaze. "What can I getcha to drink."

"I'll take an iced tea. How, uh, how you doin'?"

She looks up at him, brows knit. "Fine. You want sweetener?"

He remembers why she didn't do much for him, now. It's a small thing. Her lips are full and nice, she's young, hell, only about 39, but her nose is sort of…pudgy and short, too far away from her upper lip. Reminded him of a horse. He dispels the thoughts because who is he? Some man in his mid-fifties, thinning hair on top (although not much gray), big enough bags under his eyes to carry hay bales, thin lips, jowls. He wasn't a beauty contestant. So who was he to judge her horsey face?

"Yeah, some Sweet n' Low, please. Hey, you got glasses."

"Yeah, can't see what I'm writin.' Must be gettin' old."

"You ain't old, you're young."

"Yeah, not so much."

"Hey listen—"

"I'll be right back with that tea--"

"Hold up a second, I wanted to ask you somethin'."

She puts her hand on her hip and practically glares at him. He wants to shrink back in the seat, say "never mind" and let her get the drink. He's never been good with hostility. But he takes in a deep breath and leans forward, hunkers down for the rejection surely to come.

"Yeah?" she snaps.

"It's been a while, you know...since I seen you and I thought maybe I could take you somewhere tonight. You know, like...out. Again. Or somethin'."

Her hip juts out further. "I don't know..." She looks around at the other tables, then back at the waitress station where another girl watches them intently.

"Not a *date* exactly..." he stammers.

"*Not* a date?"

His radar flashes warning lights. He's in the Land of Womenspeak, the place he's only seen from the perimeter, the place he's never been able to infiltrate despite three younger sisters, a wife and a lifetime of talking to women. He can't see anything in this strange land: no buildings, no town, no life, but he knows it's a real place because they live there in perfumed and powdered glory, talking gibberish to each other all day long.

"Well no, yeah it's like a date. It is—what I mean is, I'd be takin' you out is what I mean. But not anythin' fancy, or anything."

"So you ain't takin' me to the prom?" One half of her full mouth cricks up a notch and he knows he's being teased. The best defense against Womenspeak is to let them have you. And when all else fails, throw them a compliment, even if it makes no damn sense at all.

"I think I'm too old to go to the prom, but you ain't."

She purses her lips like she's thinking. "I don't know."

"I know it's been a while. I just thought maybe we could, you know, just hang out or—"

"I get off at five. Pick me up at six?"

"Yeah, at your house."

"We eatin' or should I eat before?"

"Yeah, we're eatin'. I'll bring a corsage or somethin'."

She laughs, "I thought you said it ain't formal."

"I was kiddin'. It ain't formal. Just…you *deserve* a corsage is all."

Her eyelids drop again, looking at him like he's trying to sell her a stretch of land in a marsh. "*Uh-huh.*"

When everything else fails in the Land of Womenspeak, the best option for a man is to shrug and smile. So he does.

She looks around. The other customers are busy with their plates, drinks, and conversations, but she looks around all the same, as if an audience awaits her reply. "All right. See you then."

Wade nods his head and watches her hips sway a little more as she retreats. He doesn't ask himself what he's doing. He knows. He's making a mistake. A big mistake. He recognizes the stink of his mistakes the second they ease out of him.

Cindy's a nice lady, a nice girl, but she wants something from him he's light years away from being able to give. But maybe they can take it slow. Maybe her horse face will become beautiful to him and maybe she won't mind his slight protruding belly. Maybe two imperfects make a perfect and maybe it's time he just stops reaching for an unnamed, elusive idea of a woman and starts accepting what's in front of him. Maybe the whole mess of men and women is a creation of the modern culture and they had it right back in the day. Like the cavemen. Wade can be a caveman. He provides the meat, the woman provides the hearth. And when all is said and done, the ancients nestled down together near a fire and kept themselves warm with each other's bodies and the promise of another sunrise.

He fooled with the idea of bringing her flowers. But he didn't want to set a precedent. A dangerous precedent, already set two months ago when he asked Cindy out the first time. To be fair, back then he'd been dying of loneliness without Cole around, with Annie gone, and Tammy just the ghost of Annie bringing painful memories and awkward silences to his doorstep. He knew Cindy was divorced, moved to Wells because her uncle lives here, and who knew? She might have been dying herself. So he asked.

Then he did it again and now he pulls up in front of her stone house and parks. He wonders if he'd worn cologne the first time they went out. He's pretty sure he didn't. But he does tonight and wonders what that translates to in Womenspeak.

When she opens the door he's flustered because she's wearing a dress. Simple, cotton, but a dress. He thinks now he should have sprung for flowers, although where he would have gotten them, he has no idea.

"Well, look at you, all ready for prom, " he smiles.

"It's hot out. Dresses are cool."

"Well okay. You ready?"

"Sure. Where are we goin'?"

This is the part he's hoping would be charming, although now it seems pathetic. He thinks of changing his mind, taking her to Luther's, but he sticks to his guns. "My house. I made you dinner."

"Well..." she says, sounding impressed. "Didn't think you were a cook."

"I'm not. But I tried."

The truck ride is silent and he knows he should ask her about her day, but that always sounds like a tin-can question. He wasn't much for small talk, so why pretend? He once heard that comfortable silences are golden. Or is it "silence is golden?" Whatever it is, it feels anything but gold, it feels like cold water from a hose hitting his back and he shifts uncomfortably in his seat, wishing he could think of something witty or ingenious to say. He's mildly panicked because he remembers nothing of their first date. He knows he'll ask her a question he's already asked and so he hopes she's as dead in the memory department as he is.

"I hope you like steak. You like steak?"

"I like steak. You grillin' steaks?"

"Yeah, I got 'em marinatin' in some special stuff, you know, a recipe."

"You made a recipe. Wow, I'm impressed."

He smiles to himself because the "recipe" was a packaged mix he'd mixed with vinegar, water and oil, but she doesn't need to know all that.

He pulls into the carport with a groan. Durward is on the porch looking at them curiously.

"That's my neighbor, Durward. He's over a lot. C'mon."

Wade gets out of the truck and is pleased that she lets herself out. He isn't sure of the rules anymore, how to treat a woman. He'd opened the car door for her and she hadn't gotten mad, but what to do after? He decides modern women are terrifying.

"Dude, what the hell? How you doin'?"

"Came to see if you're busy, but looks like y'are."

"Cindy, Durward."

She stands rooted to the spot and smiles at him. "Hi, nice to meet you."

Durward has a huge grin on his face. "Well, it's nice to meet you, too. Glad to see ol' Wade ain't spending his Saturday evenin' alone again."

Wade smiles a tight smile. "Thanks, Durward. We're goin' in to eat now, so I'll talk to you later."

Durward smiles bigger. "Well now, that's nice. That's real nice. You two have some fun, now y'hear? Paint the town red or somethin' like that."

Durward walks toward Wade and slaps his back hard. "'Bout time, you sonofagun."

Durward shuffles toward his house and Wade looks at Cindy with a grimace. "He's old. Means well, though. We look out for each other."

Durward has bionic hearing.

"I look out for you!" Durward calls back. "Get you laid!"

Wade winces again and Cindy laughs. Almost made it without Durward humiliating him. He doesn't tell Cindy just how he looks out for Durward. The old guy would hate that. He won't even talk about it with Wade. Wade wonders if Millie knows.

Cindy pats his arm, still laughing, and Wade thinks maybe it's a good thing Durward said what he said. Maybe it broke the ice a little, set the mood. Wade has no intention of sleeping with Cindy, but after a few bloody beers, maybe that will change? He tries not to think about the *after* part. The awkward part. The "take-her-home-when-will-you-call-again" part.

Cindy steps into his house almost gingerly. He moves into the kitchen and she follows, then stops at the doorway, leaning one hip on the wall. "I should make one thing clear, Wade, after your friend said what he said…"

"What's that."

A blush creeps up. "I don't know. Maybe this is the wrong time. I guess I wanna know first why you haven't...called?"

He'd been waiting for this question. He was prepared. "I'm sorry 'bout that. I had a lot of stuff to work through. I think last time was too soon."

The widower's excuse. This seems like something a person fluent in Womenspeak would understand.

"Well a *phone call* don't hurt anybody. You didn't even *call*..."

"I'm sorry. I know I should've called. I just didn't feel right for a long time."

"And after two months, you feel right now?"

He pulls the marinating steaks from the refrigerator, then turns them over in the bag. "I don't know. Maybe." He looks for an escape. "I'm going to fire up the grill. Here, you wanna drink? I got beer and, well, you like tomato juice?"

"Ew, no. I'll take a beer, though."

Wade pulls a cold one out of the refrigerator and hands her a glass. Should he pour her beer? He hands it to her, unsure. By the look on her face he's sure he should have poured the beer, but it's too late now. He walks out the front door and goes to the side yard to turn on the gas. He wishes now it was just him and Durward out here, cooking steaks, talking. When he walks back inside, Cindy had poured him a beer and tomato juice.

"To starting again." She lifts her beer glass. They touch glasses and he drinks, gulping it down.

"So what do you want, Wade," she asks. Her eyes probe him and he's immediately on edge. *Want*? This is a tricky Womenspeak question, he can tell. He wants to find the right answer. He knows it isn't "steak and salad." He also knows he can't beg off with an "I don't know what I want." So he lets her scrutinize him while he ponders it. Finally:

"I guess I want someone to talk to. I mean, don't you want that? Isn't that somethin' people want?"

"Well, you can talk to Durward, can't you? Or your friends at the bar. Why you wanna talk to me?"

He hears the profanities in his head echoing.

Goddamn fucking hell I fucking hate talkin' to women. Okay, that's not fair. She's got a right to know. But know what? His intentions? For the rest of the evening or his life? Why is it so goddamn fucking hard?

"Well, uh, you seem nice. Aw, hell, I don't know. Why you wanna talk to me?"

"'Cause I like you. You're funny and sweet. And I can tell you got a big heart."

Wade wants to slap his head. That would have been a fine answer to give her. Leave it to her to take the perfect answer. He clears his throat.

"Well, I uh, I wanna talk to you 'cause you're different. I mean, a different person with a whole 'nother life behind you. And I could listen to you, ya know, 'bout your life. And learn somethin'."

Not bad, not bad...

She smiles. "Oh, I've had a boring life. Ain't been anywhere, done anythin' interesting. Failed marriage, and I work at a diner. What's so big about that?"

"Well tell me about your thoughts, then."

"My thoughts...my thoughts are that you don't do well by your lonesome. You need a woman in your life."

Wade is on instant alert. She continues. "Look, I don't wanna seem forward or anything but you know, I'm pushing forty. I just don't have time for games. That's just where I'm at."

Wade hears her words, but he hears them on some other level that resides with his inner panic button. Games...games...he isn't even sure what constitutes a game. Was asking her out and then not calling a game? If it was, how was he supposed to know he'd played it? What are the rules? Wade's mind flashes as if an H bomb just went off, clearing all reasonable thought from the landscape. Wade exhales and decides that once again, playing it safe is his best bet.

"I'm glad you said...uh, well you told me where you're at. I wish I was so sure."

"Well, let me help you with dinner like a regular person and let's forget all this talk. Let's just *be*, okay?"

"Salad and dressing's in the fridge. I'll go check on the steaks."

He walks outside and feels like a bug's gotten under his skin. Like it needs to be pried out. She's in his house and all he wants is to take her home again because she's in there with a whole shitload of shit: her expectations, her wants and needs, her whole life ahead of her and it's clear she could see him in that life. But he can't even see himself in *his* life, let alone someone else's. He can only see the dusk coming and the comfort of an empty bed with no expectations crowding him right out of it at dawn.

Dinner had been pleasant. Cindy helped him clear dishes and rinse, and now they sit with their drinks on the couch. Both of them face forward. Wade's on his fourth bloody beer, so he's not feeling anything, and he wants to.

"I'm going to get another beer, you want one?"

"Maybe one more." She smiles up at him as he stands. He hadn't thought about the *after*, since he was finally used to having someone there to be with, to *talk* to. Now, dumbass that he is, he's got nothing to say.

"Here ya go." He opens the bottle for her and she grabs it, having abandoned the glass a couple of drinks ago.

"No blood for your beer this time." She raises her eyebrows in a question.

"Well, yeah I think I'd like to *feel* the beer, or what's the point."

"What's the point?" she asks rhetorically.

Uh oh.

"Well, yeah." Wade tips his head back and drinks down half the bottle in one guzzle. A burp escapes and he chooses to ignore it with a small fist to his chest.

"You want to *feel* the beer? What, you wanna be *drunk*?"

"Not drunk. Relaxed."

"Oh, well, I'm relaxed." She scoots closer to him then leans her torso on him, head on his shoulder. Every muscle in him tenses just as he wills himself to unwind. She must be able to feel the steel rods going through his body. He breathes out to try and loosen up, but then it feels like he's trying to loosen, like a spade coming down hard onto dry, cracked dirt.

He looks down on her head. Her head's big. Too big. Her forehead, specifically. He was trying to figure out what it is about her face and he realizes her head's a lot bigger than his. Well, it seems a lot bigger. He thought it was just the nose-lip thing, but it's all sort of weird. She has a weird face. He lets his eyes wander down to her chest. Not ample, but not flat, either. Her thighs are a bit plump, but he likes them curvy, always has. He lifts his left arm to put it around her shoulders. He wishes something played in the background. If he turned on the T.V. now, it would be weird. The noise from his own breathing is deafening as he breathes through his nose. Holy fucking *God* he breathes loud. It whistles. He opens his mouth and now he's mouth-breathing and that's not much better.

She nestles closer, her head rising up, and moves toward him. His chest flutters for a moment as she closes the distance between them and his mouth receives her kiss more passively than he'd intended. But suddenly a hunger roils inside him and he practically drops his beer as he pulls her body to him and concentrates on the feel of her mouth on his. They are moving over each other's mouths, his breathing heavy, hers heavy, her hand wandering over his chest leaving lightning trails of energy in a blackened sky. He is keenly aware of every place their bodies touch: sides of their hips, hands, mouths, tongues, chins, cheeks, his chest. His hand wanders over her breast and she kisses him with new vigor so he takes it to mean she likes that. He squeezes her breast in his hand and tells himself to pace it, not go too fast. Women don't like "too fast."

His dick is straining in his jeans and he feels like singing a Hallelujah Chorus that it still works, still responds, isn't dead or dying from lack of attention. Cindy is making little moaning noises that he finds endearing, and her face looks almost beautiful up close with his hand cupping her cheek and her eyes closed. He thinks of the steps.

The proper steps.

Over the shirt, then over the bra. Under the bra, mouth on neck, slide down to breasts, hand over pants, hand *in* pants then over panties, hand under panties….so close.

But he doesn't know what to do with a dress. It would force him to move his hand under the dress right away, and is it rude to just ignore the panties and try and get to the over-the-bra step? It will be awkward at best. Maybe she'll be bold and just pull the whole thing off. Wait…was she waiting for *him* to do that?

Ah, he'd been neglecting the kissing so he reels himself back and focuses on her mouth again. Suddenly she pulls back, looks at him, then kisses him again. Heart pounding, he wonders if she wanted to tell him something. It would be nice if she would just tell him what to do, what she wants. He opens his eyes and regrets it—he wishes she looked better to him. He wonders if this makes him a pig, making out with a woman he doesn't find attractive. He has an unwanted visual of Tammy's face, with her delicate, mousy features that suddenly seem extremely attractive to him in comparison. His hard-on loses some juice so he tries to stay in the present, feel Cindy's body, the wetness of her mouth. His hand on her breast, how long had it been since he'd cupped a woman's breast? He thinks back and realizes.

It's been over seven years.

He tries to wrap his mind around that. Annie was sick for the better part of three years…and before that…she was always unavailable. She didn't let him touch her. If they kissed and he got too passionate, she'd stop him with a hard hand to his chest. With these memories his dick withers on the vine, he feels it. What is the matter with him? *This* woman isn't saying "no," *this* woman is responding. He moves from her lips and clamps his mouth on her neck, kissing up the side and she presses her body into him. Suddenly her hand reaches down in between his legs and he freezes. There is nothing for her to feel there but soft, limp flesh. He wants to keep kissing her, but when her hand squeezes and then retreats, he is left with limbs like wet rope and a steel bar going through his neck and head.

She eases back from him and smiles weakly. "You okay?"

He looks her in the eyes for a moment. She is not attractive. Not at all.

"Apparently not," he says.

"What's wrong?"

He tells her the truth. "I started thinkin' about my wife. I know I shouldn't have. But there it is."

"You poor man." She wraps her arms around him and he can almost hear the dull thud of a heartbeat in his throat. He's trying to pin-point the emotion. Gently he pushes Cindy away and stares at the wall behind her. The feeling isn't embarrassment, it isn't grief, it isn't sadness. Yes, there it is…the feeling. It wells up in him like an overflowing cup, bubbling and soaking the sides of him, spreading all around, a thick liquid running simultaneously through him and away from him, getting away, running, tripping, falling, soaking the floors and ceilings and carpets with its stink and tackiness. He breathes heavily and his eyes search the floor for meaning but there is no meaning, no reason, no certainty, only the realization that he's got to be alone.

"I need to take you home." He stands and grabs his keys.

"Did I do something *wrong*?" Cindy's voice sounds confident, like she knows it's all him, and that feeds the unrest gurgling in his guts.

"Let's go."

He relishes the silence in the truck this time. There is nothing that can break his silence. She doesn't speak and he can only hear the hum of the truck. When they arrive at her house she sits in silence in the passenger seat for one heartbeat too long. He knows it's nowhere near fair, taking it out on her like this. Impatient, he glances at her, the desire to push her out of the cab overwhelming. Cindy's eyes grow a little wide. She opens the door and lets herself out, slamming the door behind her. He doesn't wait for her to get to her doorstep; he screeches away and doesn't start to breathe normally until he's home.

Seven years. *She hadn't touched him for seven fucking years.* And before that? Before that there was hardly...his whole married life. Desperately wanting, always turned away. Sitting heavily on the couch, his hands grip the sides of his head. His eyes fill with tears then, and his mouth opens in an anguished, silent scream.

Durward is still shaking his head.

"How does that happen? She wasn't too bad lookin'. Hell, boy, *I* coulda gotten it up for her. She had some nice curves."

"I don't fuckin' know, okay? I just couldn't. She's weird lookin'." They sit in Durward's living room and the noise from the air conditioning unit in his window makes it so they have to practically yell.

"She's weird lookin', ya flip her around."

"Jesus, Dude, it's more complicated than that. 'Flip her around.' What's the matter with you."

Durward chuckles. "When we was younger, me and my wife, we done all kinds of things like that."

"Well good for you. Meanwhile she's probably told half the town I've got a fuckin' limp dick."

"She won't tell nothin'. That makes her look bad too, ya know. People will wonder what she's got wrong with her. Naw, she won't say nothin'."

Wade can tell Durward's just trying to make him feel better. He didn't tell him about the anger. He doesn't want to tell him about the anger toward Annie. There's a certain sacredness that comes with the memory of the dead. They get reborn in memory and become different people than they were in life. All of the negatives become a vague part of their humanity, while all of their positives stand out like the sum total of their characters. No, he can't mention the anger. There's also the matter of loyalty. That, and shame.

"If she does, I'm screwed."

"If she does, you got plenty of ways a provin'er wrong, now. One right across town, you ask me."

"What are you talkin'? The cathouse?"

"Well sure."

"Nah. You ever been up there?"

"Cathouse? Sure. When I was younger, sure. After the missus passed, it was somethin' I did. Got expensive though. Then I stopped carin' so much about it. So you gonna go?"

"No…just askin'. My buddy was givin' me hell about never bein' there. Hell if I can't get it up, what's the point?"

Durward leans forward and points at him. "You need to get to a doctor. My brother had himself problems with his manhood and they found the cancer in there. You had your wazoo checked?"

"What the hell are you talkin' about, Durward?"

"You know they stick their digit up yer wazoo and feel around, see if it's got cancer."

"It's a *prostate*. No I ain't gotten it checked in…well I don't know when. Five or so years."

"Does it take you a long time to piss?"

"It takes everyone a long time to piss."

"No it don't. That's a sign. Wade, you go get it checked, I mean it now. You make an appointment tomorrow and go get it done. You get the cancer on that thing you'll never get it up again."

Wade thinks back to his failed jerk-off sessions, last night with Cindy, the fizzling attempts to piss…and his heart jumps a little in his chest. *Shit. What if it's physical?* He'd been so concerned with his three fingers he hadn't stopped to consider the rest of his body.

"All right. I'll call tomorrow and have them check me out, okay? Can we talk about somethin' else now?"

Durward nods his head. "Good. Mine's fine. I can get him up most every time."

"Thanks for that."

"I'm just tellin' ya. Ol' Millie's startin' to act a little weird on me, Wade. I think she's gettin' the bug."

What do you mean 'the bug'?"

"She's been bringing things over, like a robe for after." Durward scowls.

"Nothin' wrong with her bringin' a robe. She's probably modest or somethin'."

"Modest my ass. She wants her stuff here. Look, she left the casserole dish in the drainer there after she washed it out."

"So?"

"*So*? Why don't she take it home with her?"

"Durward, has it occurred to you to *take it to her*? Like a gentleman?"

Durward waves at the air. "I'm a gentleman to her just fine. It's the way things're done. It's the way she's always done 'em, but now she's changin' it all up. Women get the idea, see."

"Well, Durward, what's she getting outta all this? She's doin' the cookin', sounds like she's doin' the cleanin', now you're sayin' she's the one who carries it all back and forth, *and* she's givin' you sex. What's in it for her?"

Durward looks genuinely shocked.

"Well, she gets me around! I help her with the heavy liftin' in her garden, the mulch, I keep her company, and I ain't the only one havin' a good time after hours, boy, let me tell you that. I know how them lady parts work and I work 'em—"

"Shit, don't talk about that to me, you'll make me sick."

"What, you think only super models do it? Shit son, you're 'bout as dumb as they get you don't think every size, shape 'n' age don't rut like pigs. That's what we do, all of us. You been lookin' at too many titty movies you think it's just the beautiful people doin' it."

Wade rolls his eyes, "It's not that, Jesus. It's just you're like…well you're my friend and I don't like thinkin' about it and Millie, she's this nice old lady, and I don't like thinkin' 'bout *her*—"

"She don't look too bad in the buff, Wade. I'm tellin' ya."

"Enough!"

"Fine. Get your wazoo checked. It's why yer pecker don't work, guaranteed."

"I toldja I don't wanna talk about that!"

"Well why don't you get on home then, you don't wanna talk about yer dick or my dick, what the hell's there to talk about!"

They stare at each other with hostility for only a moment before both men break into grins and bust up laughing.

It is ridiculous, all of it. Wade thinks to himself that everything that's happened has been so absurd, it can't possibly be true. But his thoughts are troubled and all he can think about is cancer in his wazoo.

4

Wade thinks of how many doctor visits he's had, just for himself, since he was fifty. If time were to be measured only in doctor visits, rapid aging would occur from birth to age two, and age fifty to death. They are a countdown to mortality and the theme music to his life's soundtrack seems to be Burt Bacharach's greatest hits and The Commodores as they play in soothing melodies over the ever-present speakers hidden in the ceiling.

He wonders if heaven has a waiting room like this one, with plants and pink and blue crisscross wallpaper and gray carpet. A woman in pink scrubs at the front desk handing you forms. Instead of insurance information, heaven would ask for the churches you attended and for how long. If your answer is N/A, you'd be given a different form, like the health form, where you check off your medical history, only it would be a moral history. *Masturbation: Y, N or Don't Know. Circle only one please.*

A young mother comes in with two children and one child is already crying. He keeps saying "no" and the mother murmurs "yes" and "ice cream." Wade considers being helpful to the boy by saying, *hey little guy, it could be worse—the doctor could be shoving his finger up your wazoo.* But he's glad he has enough impulse control and wisdom to keep that from slipping out, no matter how irritating the boy's whining has become.

The door to the back opens with a *whoosh* and it's as though time stops; a moment of chaos intrudes into the calm setting, action has interrupted the passive. He clenches his asshole.

"Wade?"

Wade stands, but not before winking at the little girl, who silently stares with wide eyes at him as her brother continues to wail in an almost automatic noise even he's forgotten about, like a symbolic protestation of what's to come, nothing more.

Wade steps past the nurse, who wears scrubs made to look like denim. They used to be all green. Nurses need variety in their uniformity, now. He thinks that's an ironic commentary on life itself as she asks him to step on the scale. He wills himself not to look at the number; he does anyway. He tells himself his clothes are heavy and he'd eaten a big breakfast.

"How are we today?" she asks, as she probes his ear with a thermometer.

"We're just fine, thanks." He's two people today. One person who is at home, reading the paper, the other, here, ready to be digitally violated.

"Okay, let's get us back to a room, here." She walks ahead of him and he watches her ample ass sway from side to side and thinks that there are fewer morepleasant things in the world than watching a woman's ass sway, no matter how big or small it is. And what else do people look at but the nurse's ass as she walks? The duck watercolors on the walls? The beige doors, secretly closed with God-knows what kind of viral or bacterial-ridden people lurking behind them?

They walk into a chilly room and he looks at the exam table with a shudder. He sits in a chair rather than on the table. She sits at a laptop and begins typing.

"And why are we here today?"

He wanted to tell her that "we" are here to get our assholes probed, but he didn't think she would appreciate the humor. These days you can't say shit like that to women. They sue you.

"I need an exam. Uh, prostate exam."

"Okay and what symptoms are we having?"

He feels an inappropriate urge to laugh, so he turns his head away and coughs. "Uh, some trouble urinating and uh…some trouble with some other things that aren't functioning like they should, or like they used to, uh…in that area."

"So, some sexual dysfunction?"

He wanted to say, *yes 'we' are a little limp,* but he appreciates her use of the word "some," since that sort of lessens the shame. "Yeah, some of that. Not all the way, you know, just some trouble. There."

"How old are you, Wade?"

"I'm fifty-six."

She smiles. "Well, just so you know, these are normal symptoms for men your age, but it's very good you're getting checked. You should have your prostate checked every year, okay? Prostate cancer affects one in six men, but if you catch it early, it's very treatable."

"That's very encouraging, thank you." He speaks to her formally, as if she's his teacher. He laces his fingers together on his lap and lets his eyes wander without moving his head.

"Make sure you head back to the lab for blood work when your exam is done for your PSA test, okay?"

"Okay, thanks."

"Okay, I'll read off a list of your medications, you tell me if there's any changes and then we'll get your blood pressure."

She reads off his allergy medications and his heartburn medications. *Si, correcto.*

The cuff goes around his arm and a pulse meter on his finger. After it deflates, she makes an unhappy noise.

"Everything okay?"

"Your blood pressure is a little high compared to last time."

"Well, I'm a little stressed out."

"Yeah. He'll still want to talk to you about it. Do you have a headache at all?"

"No. Was it that high?"

"Higher than we like. He might want you to get a blood pressure cuff for home and take it for a couple of weeks and see if it goes down. If not, we may need to look at getting you on some blood pressure meds. Okay, go ahead and undress and put on that gown there. Dr. Murphy should be right in."

She pats his arm and stands to leave. After the door closes behind her he feels his face flush and his blood pressure *really* rising. *Is this their schtick? Telling us we're on the brink of death, ensuring they can get us on another medication?*

Wade is immobile for a moment as he looks at the gown on the table and suddenly the music overhead seems very loud.

Yeah you're once,
twice,
three times a lady...
and I love youuuu...

The Commodores sing and he doesn't feel like the music plays his soundtrack anymore. Now, he thinks the better soundtrack would be circus music. His life's got it all—danger, mysteries, and of course, him, the laughable clown.

Wade gets home as the mail truck pulls away. He's got a new blood pressure cuff and medication on top of it. For some reason, this depresses him more than he can stand.

He almost wants to let the junk mail pile up for a few days in protest, but he picks it up all the same. He considers going to Durward's, but he knows the old goat will dig him with slippery asshole jokes the whole time, so he goes inside with his paper haul. A letter slips to the floor among the Chuck-O-Rama fliers and contact lens ads.

He picks it up and sees the letter is to him but he doesn't recognize the sender. He'd worked for an insurance company for thirty-four years and this isn't from them. He opens it.

The check is for eight thousand dollars. He reads the letter.

All the years Annie had worked at the front desk of the Rest Inn Motel, she'd been paying into a small insurance policy. He holds the check in his hand and something stirs inside him. It feels like tenderness but it masquerades as incredulity. She had been worried about him. And her meager paycheck got dinged, probably a dollar-fifty, to provide for him if she passed. The argument comes back to him in vivid color. How he'd asked her to put the money in their checking account when she started working and how she'd told him the money was hers.

So my money is ours and your money is yours?

That's right, she'd said.

He'd argued with her long into the night and the crickets and stars seemed to all be on her side as she told him his job was to support them and if she had money, she could support herself and relieve his burden a little, but it made no sense to him at all. It's not like he's frivolous with money; on the contrary, he is very conservative, always has been. But she wanted that independence, that account of her own to draw from and to this day he doesn't know what she spent it on. She didn't spend it on new clothes or on anything fancy. He wonders if she secretly played the machines. It seems like something she would have done on the sly and not admitted to him.

And now he holds the fruits of her labors in his hand and the crickets and stars all laugh at him.

Tammy wears her usual baggy t-shirt and jeans, but tonight he detects perfume. Wade wonders if it's her old perfume that she's worn for him a million times and he's just noticed, or if it's new. Where does a woman buy perfume in Wells? Could she have driven to Elko or Wendover to buy it? The Internet? Is he insane?

He'd started on the whiskey early. He bought some lemonade to drink with it and he's trying to pace himself as she warms up the chicken and rice in the microwave. She looks at the whiskey bottle, then at him, one eyebrow raised, but she says nothing, which doesn't surprise him at all. He decides his goal tonight is to make her talk to him. Tell him about herself.

"So I've always been curious 'bout that guy you saw a while back. Dennis or somethin'? The military guy. Whatever happened to him?"

She shrugs, her back to him. The microwave hums and she's facing it as if she powers it with her will alone. She looks over her shoulder but doesn't meet his gaze. "He just stopped comin' around. I think he had another girl somewhere. Picked her, I guess."

"So he just stopped coming? Calling? Have you ever asked him?"

"He was too slippery to ask anything to. Nah, he never called. I figure good riddance. He wasn't ever gonna commit to me or nothin.' Don't know why it ever happened."

"Well do you, I dunno, miss him or anything?"

Shrug.

The microwave stops and she opens it to retrieve the steaming glass dish. Grabbing pot holders, she holds it with both hands and sets it on the table. She sits and shrugs again. "Some things. Others, not so much."

"Like what do you miss?"

She clasps her hands together in front of her plate like a prayer. Then she picks up her fork. "Just things."

"Like?"

She finally meets his gaze and her stare is hard. "Like *things*. Like I don't wanna talk about it with *you*."

A crimson flush creeps up her neck and Wade tries to look away but it's something he's never seen or noticed before and it compels him to stare at her. The hand holding her fork comes down hard on the table and her eyes snap to him again. "*What?*"

"I'm just askin' is all. I don't mean to pry into anythin' personal. Shit. Just conversation."

"Well converse about somethin' else. My love life ain't up for discussion."

Her love life. She has a love life. Wade lets that sink in.

"I mean I talk all the time about missin' Annie. I figure you must have somethin' you wanna talk about."

"Well, not him. I miss Annie, too. We can talk about that."

"See, I don't *want* to talk about that."

"Well, I miss her. And for a lot of reasons, too." She looks up at him. "Not just for *that* reason."

"What reason?"

"You know." Her eyes are now glued to her plate.

"I don't know what we're talkin' about here." Wade's head has begun to hurt as he takes another sip of his drink.

Tammy's fork comes down on the table. "I know what you may be thinkin' and it 'aint true, all right?"

"*What* am I thinkin'?" Wade's head is still submerged in Tammy's phantom love life and her agitation confuses him. The food sticks in his throat. He's in Womenspeak now, he can feel it.

"You *know*," she says, her eyes back down at her plate.

"I honestly don't," he says.

She swallows and stares at her plate. Then she looks up, silent. After a moment, she lets out a harsh breath and says, "The money, Wade! You're thinkin' about the money! I'm fine and I don't need any help."

"What? I don't-I don't know what you mean by 'the money.' I don't get you." His mind races for an explanation as he thinks of the check in his wallet.

She lets a huff of breath come out again, then shakes her head. "She never told you."

"Told me what?"

Tammy scoots her chair back and looks around. The red on her neck had crept up to her face and she's flushed. "Annie helped me out, okay? I mean before I got the raise at Flyin' J. And I got more hours, ya know that right? So I don't need no more help. But she helped me for a long time 'cause I was goin' to lose the trailer, get evicted. I thought you knew."

Wade stares at Tammy and his head swims around in little circles with her words. He can't quite pluck them out to look at them. They sink each time he reaches in to grasp one.

Finally, one word sinks in, then another. Annie helped her out. Annie worked for a different reason than he could imagine, and now everything has changed on a dime. A literal dime. "No, I didn't know."

Tammy keeps coming by thinking...what? Thinking her brother-in-law would now pick up where her sister had left off? All this time, he thought it was for the company. For him. Was it habit that she kept coming, or had he missed the gist of it altogether?

"Well, I picked up more hours...and so I'm fine. I thought you knew, so now I feel dumb that I brought it up."

He sits in front of her and she changes before his eyes from something nurturing into something helpless. Something he's got to be responsible for. And the three meals a week—what has that cost her? Did she leave every night wondering why she left empty-handed except for a clean dish? Had he been that big of a fool?

"Why didn't you tell me you needed some help?" He still feels the food caught in his throat and his stomach has closed off, no more space to fill. Yet everything inside feels hollow.

"I don't. I said I don't *want* your help. I toldja I was *fine* now." She's angry, angry that he'd not known. Maybe resentful she had to ask. His own resentment builds dangerously and he pushes away from his plate.

"You know, I—this...you don't need to come around here anymore. I don't want to be eatin' your food knowin' it costs you—you shoulda said somethin'. I woulda helped more. It's just...you don't need to come around no more."

He stands and grabs his drink. Walking out of the kitchen, he moves into the living room and that isn't far enough away from her. He wants to be as far away as possible while that check in his wallet seems to call out a name. And the name isn't his.

When he comes out of the bathroom, Tammy is gone. He takes another shot of whiskey and walks outside. The heat of the evening is oppressive to his lungs, as if the air is shutting him down from the outside in. He peers over at Durward's house and the curtains are open, but nothing stirs inside. He takes long steps and heads straight over there because he blames him for planting the cockeyed notion in his head to begin with that Tammy was coming for him. He'd tell the old goat he was wrong, tell him he might have hit a jackpot with old Millie, but Wade wasn't lucky, not one little bit.

He raps on the door and the doorknob jiggles and he's relieved that Durward is home. The whiskey has loosened his tongue and he feels ready to spill whatever beans come to his dry lips. But when the door opens, he looks down to see the diminutive Mildred smiling up at him. She still dyes her hair penny red, but the gray is at her temples, her roots. She smiles and looks pleased to see him.

"Well, hello there. Come on in. Durward's in the lavatory."

"Mildred, how you doin'?" Wade's voice is crumpled, like his shirt, like his insides. He tries to access the polite veneer he needs but it feels temporarily muted by the whiskey and turmoil in his mind.

"Oh, fine, fine. You want to eat? We've got plenty."

"Just ate, thanks. Maybe I can come back another time."

"Oh, nonsense. Sit down, here. Can I getcha some iced tea?"

"No, I'm fine—"

"Well look who wandered over." Durward emerges from the hallway, still pulling his pants up over his belly. The belly is the only thickness on him. The rest of him is as thin as a starved chicken. Durward sits heavily on the sofa and Millie smiles at him.

"Can I bring you your iced tea, Dude?"

Durward speaks a little louder than necessary. Maybe Millie's hard of hearing? "Yah, yah bring me the tea. You want one?"

"Naw, I'm okay, Mildred, thanks."

She shuffles into the kitchen and Durward smiles evilly. "Lasagna tonight."

Wade whispers but it comes out harsh. "I need to talk to you. You was *so wrong*."

"What was I wrong about? You drunk?"

"No, I ain't drunk but I wanna *get* drunk."

Millie pops in the room, all smiles. "Here y'are. I'll leave you boys to chat while I make the salad." She has an impish twinkle of her own and Wade feels like steam blows from his ears as she turns the corner.

"I found out why she's been bringin' me meals and all that and it ain't for my charmin' personality." Wade glares at Durward.

"What then?"

"The wife was payin' her upkeep. Givin' her money from her paychecks. Practically supportin' her. She kept thinkin' I'd pick up where Annie left off. I told her to get the fuck out."

Durward puts his hand on top of his bald head as if slicking back hair. "Ah jeez, well, didn't see that comin'."

"Yeah well, neither did I. And now…now I got this check, see. From an insurance policy Annie had. And I think her sister's angling for it."

"You ain't gonna give it to her, are ya? That would be fool-crazy. You keep that money and use it. She got a job, right? She ain't a cripple. You don't dare give her a penny of that, Wade. You hear?"

Wade searches the room, looking for somewhere to put his anger because it isn't directed at Durward anymore. It's across town, in a cemetery with a gravestone that says "Beloved Wife."

"If Ann wanted her to have it, she'd a got her a policy, right? That check's for me. Right?"

"Damn straight it's for you."

"But you know, Dude, now it's got me thinkin' about all the other things I don't know. Things Annie did, you know. Without tellin' me."

"Well, you got to find out. You got papers she kept somewhere?"

55

"She's got this file in the closet. Little expandable thing."

"I'd be tearin' that thing apart. God rest her, but your wife, she was keepin' shit from you, and you'd better find out what else she was keepin'."

Wade's anger simmers inside him like heat coming off the pavement. His thoughts are a tangle of confusion because if he's completely honest, he's not that upset Ann had helped Tammy. Tammy had always struggled. Hell, if she had told him, he might have even been okay with her helping Tammy out. So why the anger? Was it for Ann? For Tammy? For himself at what he'd done, how he'd just kicked her out?

"I'm gonna go, Dude. I got things I gotta figure out."

"Well, all right. You go on then. Don't drink too much."

"Yeah, you have yourself a nice evening, now." He calls out, "Bye Millie. See you later."

She comes around the corner and her eyes look pained as she smiles. "You come over any time ya like, Wade, dear. It's nice seein' ya."

When she retreats, Durward raises his eyebrows and whispers, "See? Thinks she owns the place now."

"Cut it out, Dude. You got a good woman there."

Durward mutters, "They all want somethin'. Figurin' out what, that's the thing."

Wade shakes his head and as he turns to leave, he hears Millie humming a tune and catches a glimpse of her in the kitchen, puttering around—just as if she owned the place.

5

Saturday used to be the days he'd looked forward to. For some reason, he still does, even though the day brings with it the bittersweet visits to Cole and then an uneventful stretch of time before he wanders out to Luther's. It's time for dinner and he knows he can't avoid the cafe forever. After a depressing and monotonous visit with Cole, he decides a dinner out would do him some good.

He wracks his brain to try and remember if Cindy works Saturday nights. She's usually there in the day, so he can avoid her, possibly. Not that he's trying to *overtly* avoid her; Wells is a small town. But the scrapes from their date still sting and he wants time to heal them before exposing them to sea water.

He thinks back to his foolish evening the night before. Going through Annie's file like a madman, only to find pay stub after pay stub, thousands of dollars gone into thin air. Or gone into Tammy's pockets. And if he's honest with himself, had Annie told him? He would have probably helped her out himself, too. But when he thinks of Tammy and why she came over, that produces a deeper sting, worse than his date with Cindy.

He walks into the cafe, not seeing her, and goes to his table. He might have gotten lucky and she's gone for the day. As soon as he releases the breath he's holding, she comes around the corner and their eyes meet. He looks back down at the menu, intent on reading every entree description as if it wasn't already imprinted in his head. She appears at the side of the table.

"Somethin' to drink?"

"Iced tea. Please."

He says this without looking up at her. He doesn't want to know what expression she carries on her face. He feels the rush of air as she sets down his water and retreats.

Great, just great. Probably thinks I'm stalking her or worse. I just won't look at her.

She brings his iced tea and slides the sweeteners across the table as she does it. Waiting with her pad of paper, he dares a look up in her general direction but avoids her face, her eyes. What would he see in them? Contempt? Anger? Friendliness? Forgiveness? None of the above?

He tries going over the night in a quick movie reel in his mind but can't find where she had been at fault, only his own anger and general fucked-up-ness that had caused the evening to swirl into dirty toilet water. She *ahems*.

"Yeah, I'll have the prime rib sandwich."

"'Kay." She leaves and he lets out a breath he hadn't realized he held. What is he going to do? Start going to Subway for every meal? This is the only real restaurant in town. He has to make it work. He has to make it right but he has no idea how. However he does it, though, it can't be here. He needs to drop by her house, tell her he's sorry. But he wants to be honest about the *whys* of it. And the *whys* are unclear to him.

One thing is clear and that is he's not attracted to her. But he can't tell her that. A newly divorced woman hearing she isn't attractive to a guy like him? That would shrivel whatever straightness she has in her spine. No, he couldn't do that to her. She's a nice gal; he can't just devastate her with his inability to look beyond her face.

He refuses to use Ann as an excuse. He knows that isn't it. Was it the sex? He remembers that he never called the doctor back. They had left a message for him to call, but it hadn't sounded urgent. Hell, if he had a problem in his wazoo, they'd be more…urgent, right? He dismisses the thought. *I'm fine*, he says to himself.

So what is it? What was it? He remembers that night, spilling rage into tears, spilling tears down his cheeks. He remembers feeling rejected, even though Cindy hadn't been the one to reject him. Had she? No. But that's the only thing he feels, and along with it, anger. His *anger*. It surrounds every emotion that comes up. He tries to remember...

He jumps as the iced tea is placed on his table. Against his own better judgment, he glances up at Cindy. She's standing there with her head down, her feet shuffling. He has to say something.

"Look, I gotta apologize. Again. Seems like it's all I'm good for."

She meets his eyes and smiles a small smile. "Look, I just don't want things to be awkward. You're a good customer and I don't want—"

"Naw, I really am sorry, Cindy. You're a great gal, and I just—"

"You just ain't ready. And that's *okay* you ain't ready. Tells me you were a good husband and a good person. I just think we should be friends, can we do that?"

He breathes out a sigh of relief. "Yeah, we can."

"Good. I'll be back with your dinner in a bit." She smiles again and walks away and Wade feels relief, but on another level, he feels like a royal asshole. What had she said in her Womenspeak tongue that had made him feel like he was two feet tall? She had been understanding, kind. What had he expected? Anger? She's too nice of a lady for that.

He tries to relax, but he feels jumpy, as if he should expect a cold slap. Sipping his iced tea, he glances over to see her approaching with his food. He wants to tell her the truth, but can't figure out what that is.

"Here ya go. One prime rib—"

"I just feel angry so much." He blurts it out and wants to suck it back in his lungs.

She looks at him and nods. "Losin' people we love makes everybody angry, Wade."

"But I ain't angry at her or you or...I don't know."

"Wade, I think you're just fine. You know, maybe you're just one of those guys."

"One of those guys...what?"

"You're just one of those guys who does it once then goes it alone. Like your neighbor friend, there. Nothin' wrong with that. You just don't feel right with anyone else. It's okay to be alone. I ain't one of those, though. I want someone in my life, ya know? Anyway, enjoy your meal, okay? I'll check back."

She walks away and Wade stares at his dinner, the steam rising off of the tender meat. *Like his neighbor friend*? Is that what he's like? His life, spent with a family, has been reduced to *alone*?

His appetite gone, he stares straight ahead and thinks of that word, *alone*. It almost sounds like a moan, a sad cry coming from dry lips in a dark, silent night. The word isn't new to him, of course, but it feels strange bouncing around in his head. *Alone*. Now that he had no one, maybe he finally feels at home with it. It wasn't right feeling alone while another living, breathing body shared his house, his life. Now that Ann's gone, he's maybe right with himself. Right with…things.

Thinking of Tammy, he shakes his head. No, that's wrong. He isn't one of "those guys." He may have never had it before, but something inside tells him he isn't meant to be alone. Maybe no one will ever share his bed or life again, but that doesn't mean he can't share *something* with *somebody*. Strangely, he hadn't felt alone with Tammy. But that's all over now.

He wants to call Cindy over to him again, make her take her pronouncement back, as if she'd laid some curse on his head to be fulfilled with the changing wind outside and the coming of winter. He wants her to take it back, as if she alone had the power to settle it for him, then and there.

But he knows that only he has the power to undo the spell. All it would take is a little adventure and the courage to walk through the door.

Wade drives with measured speed up 6th Avenue until he loses sight of houses, then flips around and takes a right on Humboldt. He zigzags between each street, looking at the houses in the waning light. He's trying to find the adventurous spirit he'd had that first night. All he feels is a heavy lump in his gut. He allows a heaviness to settle in his torso, allows his ass to sink into the hard vinyl of the truck's seat. He makes a note of each street he passes: Baker Street, Castle Street, Lake Avenue, Ruby Avenue…he knows every street and yet he's never paid much attention to the houses. All small and humble, like his. Some unkempt, but most trimmed and maintained, as if all of the pride of each resident rests in the small patches of grass out front and the miniature flowerbeds under the picture windows.

He had always taken pride in his own house, and Ann had kept up the flowerbeds in the yard. He had let his yard go and that wouldn't do anymore. He decides that tomorrow, he would go out and dig in the flowerbed that has been invaded by weeds. Ann would want that. Maybe he'd plant something new there—maybe even some dwarf trees or a couple of shrubs that would turn colors in the fall.

Driving up and down the roads, he finds he's doubled-back and driven several more than once. But that's how it has to be in a town like Wells; every road leads to the same place, and every street feeds into another— unless you plan to leave. Then it's one road, one exit, and you're gone, speeding into the desert, away from the self-containment of a contained life.

In the corner of his mind, nestled among the chaos, he knows the roads he drives are all distractions from the one road he wants to get back to. But he can't make his mind forget the word *alone*, can't reconcile how going to that place will somehow make that word dissolve forever. Driving by the diner would melt his resolve. He circles the block and gets back on Ruby Avenue and follows it around until he gets to 7th Avenue. Over the train tracks and he's on 8th Street, which leads to 10th Street, which leads to Mamacita Ranch Road.

He sees the neon lights glowing in the distance and a tight fist that has been in his belly since he left the diner seems to uncurl in his gut. The memory of the place comes like a rushing stream of comfort and understanding. Yes, there is hesitation. Yes, there is the unknown. The thing that consumes his inner blind spot is the *why*. Why would that place arrest that seemingly eternal condition of *alone*? He doesn't know, and he has no plans further out than the rotation of each tire over gravelly road, inching closer by the second to a place he doesn't understand. Lust doesn't compel him; curiosity no longer compels him. It's something that goes deeper than all of that and like a true blind spot, it remains unseen, unknown, only the faint glimmer of understanding that the spot is indeed there.

The parking lot is crowded tonight and that only makes him pause for a moment. He may see someone he knows, he may not. Would it matter? Does it? No, not tonight. Tonight he is anonymous, even to the people who know his name. He is just a man tonight, just a soul, looking for souls with whom he has no other ties, no other connection but the same floor under their feet.

He rings the doorbell. Him and his soul.

He feels foolish for expecting Belle's face to be the first he sees. Instead it's a woman he doesn't know and he feels that sense of "specialness" he had felt with Belle evaporate. He is just another guy, just another customer to this woman, and he doesn't know why that matters so much.

"Hi, welcome to Lil' Mamacita's. Come on in."

He sticks out his hand, hoping to make a good impression. "Hi, I'm Wade."

"I'm Leslie, the manager. Come sit and let's get you a drink." She places her hand on his back and he doesn't flinch this time. He's monumentally proud of himself.

"I'll just have a beer."

It's the same bartender from the last time he was here. He remembers she didn't smile. He remembers he'd never spoken to her and now he's left alone with her while Leslie scurries into the far hallway on the other side of the bar. Looking around, his scalp sort of shrinks in on itself; he's the only man in the bar despite all of the cars outside. He doesn't allow himself to think where all of the other drivers are. He knows and that's enough.

The bartender brings him a beer and slides a napkin in front of him before she sets it down. Still no smile. Her face is lined like striated rock, like she's excavated through dark, mysterious canyons to get to where she is. Her face isn't unkind, it seems more distracted, like she has a million more canyons to traverse and doesn't have time to stop for water.

"Thanks," he says.

"Sure. You wanna start a tab, honey?"

Her voice. That's where her warmth lies. It's a gravelly, smokers voice, but it's soothing and filled with understanding. She isn't so foreign to him, now.

"Sure, but can I ask—is Belle here tonight?"

"Oh, she ran to the liquor store real fast—we ran outta gin. I forgot to order it last time." Her tone is friendly and she taps the side of her head at her negligence.

"Do you…remember me?"

"Sure, you was here a few weeks ago, wasn't ya? You n' Belle was talking here at the bar. What's your name again?"

"I'm Wade." He reaches over the bar and offers his hand. She takes it and smiles briefly, the lines shifting and changing around her cheeks and eyes.

"Bev, nice to meet ya. They'll be out in a jiff, so hold on."

"Oh—oh, no wait, I just came here to talk to Belle, I didn't—I—"

Bev looks into his eyes and hers are wide, mirroring his, trying to understand. But it's too late. Bustling in the doorway to the hall announces the women as they come pouring out into the room. His breath comes out in one hard and fast *whoosh* as he watches them with dismay. Now leaving would be even more awkward, more of a slap in the face, and he berates himself again for coming here in a time of need.

Leslie is all smiles as she comes and stands near him. "Here they are. Ladies, this is Wade. Introduce yourselves."

He wants to wriggle away, become invisible. All he can think about now is the ATM in the corner, the humiliation awaiting him when he tells them he's wasted their time. He wonders if he can choose no one, thus buying himself more time until Belle comes back. She understands him. It might save him.

There are five women, but three of them are more like girls to him since they look younger than his sons. Most of them sport robes or long sweaters, but it's clear they all wear revealing clothing, maybe even lingerie, underneath. All wear stripper-heeled shoes. He looks at their feet, then forces his eyes up. They might think he's some foot pervert if all he does is look at their shoes.

He hears the lilt and cadence of each of their voices, but beyond the words, "Hi, I'm..." he hears nothing. Not one name sticks in his ears or to his mind. The faces all blur in front of him and he can't focus on any one because all of their features become a collage of glossy lips, eyelashes, soft inner elbows, silken throat hollows, delicate fingers fingering the material of their cover-ups, creamy skin and elegant ankle bones.

They all stand in front of him, smiling and he hardly registers the doorbell as it rings, but he hopes it's a company of truckers ready to pluck each girl out of the line and leave him in peace. Instead, he hears a familiar voice.

"Well here he is." Belle has an arm around a box filled with liquor. He jumps to life and takes it from her as Bev stands behind the bar, one eye on him, the other on the girls. Wade sets the box behind the bar and stands, careful to keep his eyes on the madam.

"Belle, I need to talk to you—I—"

He glances at the lineup and his face is taut with distress. Belle looks at him and he is sure he's made another mistake. When she had said "Come back any time," she'd meant, "Come back when you grow a pair." He sighs.

"I need a minute," he says to her, then glancing at the lineup. He's hoping she'll give him an out.

"Wade, right?" she asks. "Wade, you take all the time you need. Why don't we let him finish his beer, ladies. You come on out in a while. I'll come getcha."

They all smile brilliantly in one synchronized smile, and leave through the door through which they'd entered. He breathes a defeated sigh. "Thank God."

Belle smiles at him. "Here, you enjoy your beer. I've gotta go back to my office and I'll be right out. Then you and me, we're gonna have a conversation."

Belle walks in the opposite direction from the door to another hallway, right past the ATM. Wade's whole self shifts inside as he watches her walk past that machine and disappear into the bowels of the house.

His first beer is three swigs away from being finished when Bev slides another one in front of him. He watches out of the corner of his eye as a man leaves, one of the women behind him with her hand on his back. He wonders how that guy feels at that moment. Relieved? Guilty? Satisfied? Lonely? All of the above? He sets his gaze straight forward and meets his eyes in the reflection of the mirror behind the bar. His ears are pricked for any sound of Belle's return.

After he's halfway through his second beer, she appears. She places her hand on the bar and calls Bev over. "On that next order, be sure and leave off the gin. I got plenty for the next two weeks."

Bev nods her head and continues doing busywork behind the bar. He's not sure if she doesn't talk to him because she doesn't talk to anyone, or if it's just him. Does he have a "leave me the hell alone" sign on his forehead? Probably. Belle scoots a stool out and climbs up.

"How you doin', Wade?"

"I don't know. I guess all right. I ain't got nowhere else to go tonight.

I didn't think it through. Again."

He turns and looks at her eyes and she's got crinkles in the corners as if to smile, but her mouth is a straight line. "I think you came back here because you got some idea in your head about what you want, but you don't recognize you got the idea. You know what I'm sayin'?"

"I don't know. Maybe."

"Look, we can talk, you and me, but I don't think that's why you're here. I think you want more than a barroom conversation. Hell, you could get that anywhere, any bar, am I right?"

"Yeah. Yeah, you're right."

"It's straight forward here, Wade. There ain't no complications. But even though it's straight, it's also real complex, if you think about it. That's probably why you're so fidgety and worried. I think I can help you, but you gotta let me. So you gotta trust me."

Wade takes a long drink of his beer and waits. Bev is watching them out of the corner of her eye and he wonders if Cindy had been all smiles, but on the other side of things, she had squawked long and loud to anyone and everyone that his peter doesn't work. Do they all know about him here? The thought makes him want to turn tail that second and run, never come back.

"I had some kinda realization or somethin' tonight. See, there's where I'm at, and there's where I was…and then there's where I wanna be. And none of them match up. Does that make any kinda sense?"

"Sure. You got some dissonance goin' on. You know what I mean by 'dissonance'?"

He knows what the word means in a vague sort of way, but not enough to really define it for her in words. He shakes his head, then nods. Then his mouth screws up and to the side and they both laugh.

"Shit, I don't know if I oughta say. I guess I know, it means things ain't workin' out, is what it means, in a sense. Hell, I seem to step in a pile of shit no matter which way I turn. You ever feel that way?"

Belle nods, "All the time. But I step in it anyway. Crap on a shoe 'aint the worst of life's problems. And no cursin' allowed in here."

"Huh?"

"No cursin'. You can say anythin' you want in the private rooms, but out here in the bar and parlor, we ask for polite talk."

"I'm sorry, Ma'am."

"You're all right. Anyway, you were sayin'?"

"It's about a woman. Or women, I guess, more than one. Not that I'm any kinda Don Juan…all of the women in my life confuse me. Someone said to me, in a nice sorta way, of course, that I'm just gonna be alone. Part of me thinks that might be okay. Another part is kickin' and screamin' at the thought."

"Well there's alone and then there's *alone*. You know what I'm sayin'?"

"Yeah, I think so. As in lonely."

"Right. I'm alone all the time, Wade, but I ain't ever lonely. You can have both. You can be alone and not be lonely."

"I can see that."

"But I think you're feelin' both. It's why you keep comin' back."

"It's just kinda complicated—"

"Aw c'mon. Why do you think you're the only guy who's lost a wife or someone or had women troubles? Heck, oldest story in the book. Too bad there ain't a Book of Adam. We'd be hearin' all his confusin' stories about how the mind of Eve made him bonkers."

Wade laughs, "Ain't that the truth."

"Look, there ain't no games here. You don't gotta over-think anything. Now, I'm gonna go back there and get someone for you to talk to. Okay? You gotta trust me on this, Wade. All right?"

"All right."

Belle hops off of the stool and strides toward the hallway. His mouth is instantly dry, so he takes another swig of beer. Within seconds, Belle emerges with a petite woman in her forties. She wears a sweater over a short dress. He vaguely recalls her from the lineup, but only because her heels looked a little different than the others. They are clear plastic all over.

"Wade, this is Lana. Lana, this here's Wade and he ain't ever been here before. Why don't you talk to him and get him comfortable?"

He allows himself to assess her and she looks like someone he could ask out on a date. Not beautiful, but friendly, kind-looking. A girl-next-door feel to her. Pretty in her own right and her smile is genuine. When she sits, she places her hand on his thigh and squeezes. His physical reaction is immediate and he doesn't know if he should celebrate that it still works, or worry that it'll take over everything.

"It's nice to meet you, Wade. You nervous?"

"I'm okay. You want a beer or somethin'?"

"Nah, I'm okay. Had a couple already tonight. We're not allowed more than that."

"Oh, okay."

"You hungry? We can order you food from Mama's Cafe and have it delivered."

When she mentions the diner he searches her face for any meaning, anything that tells him she knows who he is. But her eyes are only curious; nothing in them indicates he should worry. His paranoia makes him laugh to himself.

"I'm good."

"So where you from, Wade?"

"Here. All my life. Where you from?"

"Oklahoma. Been here seven years."

"You like it?"

"I love it here. Love working for Belle. Love my customers." With that she leans over toward him to grip his leg again and his eyes drop down to her cleavage. Heat rises to his face. He wants to be so different from the other men who walk in here, but he's exactly like them all. He's just less honest with himself about the *why*. As he sits with her, the why becomes painfully obvious to him.

"I've never been in a place like this. Never done this."

"Well, there's no pressure. How 'bout you let me give you a tour? Don't you wanna know what's behind this bar? I'll bet you're dyin' to know what's behind this bar." She smiles and her face suddenly becomes beautiful to him and he's not sure why. He thinks it's maybe because it's all for him: her smile, her words, her breath, her voice. All for him.

"Yeah, okay. I guess I am curious."

"Come on, let's go." She stands and her hand moves to his back, then she puts her arm through his, as if they are going on a walk down a promenade near the ocean.

They walk past the ATM and she points to it. "Here's that for your convenience."

He is committed in a totally different way now. He knows he'll be back in one of those rooms tonight, with Lana. His body becomes a heartbeat; blood pushes out and reaches every part of him, he can feel it, and when it releases, it's an ebb in the ocean, pulling the shore into itself. He's closing in on himself and expanding, all at once. He can almost hear the waves of blood crashing into his very organs. Especially one organ.

"...and this here's the other V.I.P. suite and it's got a hot tub, too. And a shower. This is fifteen hundred for an hour."

He's heard her say the prices about the other rooms, but they don't gel in his mind until now.

"Wow, that's a lot of...I mean, that's more than I—" he is almost relieved. He can make an escape based on his bank account. His pride is at an all-time low tonight. What's one more blow to the ego for him?

"Well, hold on, now, I got my own room. It's right here. Come on in." She opens the door and it looks like a regular bedroom. There's a dresser, a closet, and of course, a bed with a nightstand. He takes it all in, including the K-Y jelly on the side table and the various negligees hanging in the open closet space.

"You live here all the time, or..."

"No, only a week at a time. Then I take a week off. Sometimes just a weekend if she's expecting a full house. I got another place outside here I live at. Here, you sit on the bed. Right here. Come on, I don't bite."

Now he seems to be made of breath. It comes out of him in long gasps and he takes in volumes of air just to keep from floating away. He sits on the bed where her hand had patted like an obedient child and she smiles at him.

"Now," she says, "we stay in here it's five-hundred. For a whole hour. How does that sound to you?"

He licks dry lips and wants to tell her he doesn't know what to do. Doesn't know how to close the gap between them. His hard-on has retreated and he wonders if he were naked, if he'd look like a Ken doll.

"What if...what about if it's only a half-hour?" His voice sounds so far away, his fingertips tingling with sensation.

"Well that's two-fifty, then." Her hand rests on his leg, as he sits sort of side-saddle to see her. She leans over to him and kisses his cheek, a soft, lingering thing that causes a tightness in his chest that is unbearable.

Then his eyes do something he wills them not to. They fill with tears and he can't stop them. She's so pretty and warm, and would she understand if he told her he had to go, leave this place, because for all of its glitter and satin and softness and allure, it's the realest place he's ever been? Her eyes are the realest things he's ever seen? How could he tell her that he wants to be here more than he wants to be anywhere else in this world, but he can't be here. He can't…can he?

He reaches his hand up and places it on her leg, mirroring her hand on his. His hand is practically on fire, damp with sweat and trembling.

"Just a half-hour, please," he whispers. Her hand comes up and covers his hand and they sit there for what seems like a very long time. His eyes still shed tears, but he doesn't have the energy to feel humiliated by them. She smiles and pats his leg.

She hands him a tissue and he unceremoniously blows his nose. But that's not going to scare her away; nothing will and he tries to remember that.

"Now, you doin' better?" Lana smiles and he nods his head. "Good, so lemme ask you—is there somethin' you see you want me to wear for ya?" She points to her lingerie and stands. "You like black? Pink?"

"What you got on is fine. It's—you're fine."

She removes her long sweater to reveal her short, red dress. As she turns to drape the sweater over the chair he sees her whole back almost down to her ass through criss-cross strings on the dress.

"Okay Wade, so here's how it works. You pay me now and then after, if you liked how things went, you can tip me if you want."

He feels fused to the bed. He'd have to go out to that ATM, just as he knew he would. He wonders if that will break the spell he's under and hopes with all his might that it doesn't.

"Well, okay then, I'll be right back. I hope I can find your room again."

"I can walk you out if you like."

"Nah, I got it."

He leaves her room with hesitancy, not wanting her to disappear, not wanting to give her time to think it through. What if she can't do it with him after all? What if he's just too repugnant for her? What does he want her to do? God in heaven, what does she want *him* to do?

Standing at the ATM, his hand shakes as he slips his card into the willing slot. He can't remember his PIN. He uses it every other day and tonight it escapes him. He raises his finger to the keypad and lets it go on automatic and it does. It performs just as it should and he chooses a cash amount that will tip her well.

There are a couple of men in the bar but he can't look at them. No, this is not where he makes eye contact with anyone. He isn't ashamed of what he's about to do. He's ashamed that he didn't just decide to do it—that it had to be spoon-fed to him by women who understand more than he does, know more than he ever would. In the Land of Womanspeak they had conspired to pull a stranger in from a blustery night and offer him shelter, a warm meal, and a soft bed.

The door to Lana's room is closed and he wonders if that is some signal that he's been denied. He stands there, unsure, and then the door opens to Lana's smiling face.

"You get lost?"

"No, sorry…"

"Come on in." She steps aside and he shuffles in as if hands push him from behind. When the door closes behind him she stands and waits. The money. He holds the bills for all to see in his hand and he's ashamed again.

"Ah, sorry, here's two-sixty, but that 'aint your tip, it's just—"

"I know how ATMs work, honey, it's okay. Now here's what we're gonna do, okay? I'm going to go take this money back to the office, and you stay in here and take off your clothes. There's a sheet you can get under on the bed if you're feelin' shy."

She leaves him there and the word "shy" just doesn't cut it. He hadn't been naked with a woman for so long he tries to assess what he'd seen in the shower that morning and what she'd be seeing tonight. He shudders. He wishes his balls didn't hang so low. He wishes his dick was bigger. Wouldn't that solve all of his immediate problems? If he had a King Kong dick? As a matter of fact, he thinks a huge dick would solve every problem in his world.

He pulls off his shirt and looks in the mirror. He vows to do sit-ups every morning from tomorrow on out. He thinks back to two months ago and curses his past self for not having this foresight. His pants come down and he fumbles with his socks, suddenly aware she could come back while he's undressing, and how un-sexy that would be.

Safely under the sheet, he's panicked by his wet noodle. He curses

Cindy and that doomed night they'd had together because it has clearly fucked with his head. The door opens and he's hoping he'll have time to tell her about himself. He figures talking would relax him and get him in a better head space. She removes her dress in a quick, efficient motion and he takes in her body and gasps under his breath. A definite tingling is going on down below and he tries to ride it. But then she douses him.

"Okay, stand up, Wade, lemme get a look 'atcha."

"You...you wanna...?"

"I need to look." She motions down at his crotch with her head. "Come on, it'll only take a second."

He moves like he's on autopilot while still under the sheet, preserving the illusion of modesty until he stands before her. He's pleased that he's not shriveled completely. She grabs a baby wipe from a container on the dresser and kneels in front of him. The wipe is warm as she wipes his dick and balls down with it. *Cleanliness is next to Godliness?* He wondered who he could ask about this ritual.

"Okay we're good to go. Why don't you lie back on the bed, honey."

The moisture on his dick is cooling him down and shriveling him up so he doesn't know what he's going to do. He opens his mouth to speak, but she climbs on top of him and rubs her small breasts down his torso and he feels the tingling come back. Her breasts are now on his dick and as she moves them over it, he sighs and lets her move. He can't talk to her now. He can't tell her what he wants or how he feels because she now has her face nuzzling him and the thought occurs to him that she might take him in her mouth. Annie had done it once, as in once inside her mouth, then she had gagged.

Lana moves to the side and grabs the K-Y jelly from off the nightstand. Squeezing some in her hand, she encloses his dick in her wet fist, moving it in a slow rhythm.

Soon he's glistening and hard and the fact that he's not a wet noodle after all brings a huge sense of relief. There is nothing wrong with him. Nothing at all. When she reaches behind him, up on the window sill, he springs to life and places both of his hands over her breasts. They are soft and pliant, her belly is soft—again, a girl-next-door, not some untouchable he couldn't see himself with outside of this place. A crackling noise and then he sees the condom. Of course. He hadn't thought about that. She places it on the tip of his head, then uses her mouth to slide it on him.

Lana doesn't gag. She doesn't seem to be disgusted by it, by him. The only barrier is the latex as she swallows him deep in her mouth, the pleasure focused on his dick and pooling into his belly and chest. All warm, all soft, all wet. Everything concentrating on this one part of his body—the rest of him isn't even there, doesn't even have to be there. But he's in the moment and no past or future exists. He wants to tell her how it feels but she has gone to work on him and he thinks it would sour it, sour her actions, and he doesn't want sour; he wants the sweet feeling of warm, soft, wet to be neverending.

Again he wants to talk to her, tell her in color and sound and shape and music the things going on inside him, but before he can utter a sound, she turns her back to him, straddles him and begins to pump up and down on him.

His hands automatically move to her waist but he wants her to stop. He has the one part of him unable to speak wrapped in her warmth and it seems to have taken over, while his mouth and mind try to find words.

What do you like to do?
What's your favorite color?
Mine is green.

The tingling in his spine overtakes him and soon he is thrusting his hips to match her and suddenly, the tingling explodes and the familiar release spreads through his dick and stomach and then he's still. It had taken less than two minutes, he figures. But he feels too tired to contemplate any of that. His mind tells him his seven-year dry spell is over. He finally got laid.

Another part of his mind responds by saying *so what*?

She slides off of him and moves around to kiss his forehead.

"Didja have fun?" she asks, a lazy smile on her face. He finds his voice.

"Sure, yeah. I mean of course." She moves off of the bed and wraps a robe around herself and then he sees his shirt on the chair. He sees the door that he must exit, probably soon. The warmth he had felt just moments before evaporates.

He sees his empty bed at home and the darkness converges on him as it seems to swallow him whole.

PART II

6

Now that he's on two blood pressure medications, Wade doesn't check it like a maniac twice a day. Maybe three times a week, if he's thinking about it. But this morning, he took it and even with meds, it was high. He doesn't know why. The letter from Cole didn't foretell anything bad, really. It's just that he never *gets* letters from Cole and when he got one on Thursday, his mind raced. All it said, in the end, was *I got news.*

Wade pulls his hat down over his ears, the December wind chilly as he walks through the parking lot toward the door of the Conservation Camp. Wells had had an Indian summer, but just like a rabid dog, the weather turned at the end of November into a frothing, mad cold.

The building is warmer than he'd expected inside, and he waits, legs jittery, hands rubbing together, although the room feels almost cozy. He only glances at the two other people in the room—a young woman talking to one of the prisoners. They are bent over the table, speaking feverishly about something good, or something gone terribly wrong. He can't see their faces, he only hears the rise and fall of their voices like a vigorous tide.

What news?

Cole walks in, looking brighter than Wade had seen him in weeks.

"Heya, Pop." He smiles and the couple talking takes a moment from their exchange, as if they need to inhale more oxygen to begin a new torrential rain of words.

"Well, now, don't you look like a cat just ate a mouse."

WADE

Wade can sense when his blood pressure is up by the burning in his ears. They are red-hot, although he knows he should be calm.

"No mice, Pop, just good news."

"Well you coulda told me it was good in your letter."

"I wanted to surprise ya. So, guess what?"

"Yeah? Go on."

"I'm up for parole next week!"

Wade's eyes blink as if in slow motion. He shakes his head, but feels the smile creep up as he watches his son's face transform into that of his ten-year-old self the day he caught a lizard with his bare hands.

"What the hell? You only been in here less than a year—"

"I know! The counselor gave 'em a good word, I guess, and for good behavior 'n' all. And technically it's a first offense for the forgin' thing, so...so yeah, Pop. What do ya think?"

"I think that's some great news, son. There's gonna to be a hearing and all that?"

"Next Thursday. Pop, I could be outta here for Christmas!"

"Well that's fine, Cole. That's really fine news. You want me at the hearin'?"

"Aw jeez, I don't know. No, I don't think so, you know. Case it goes south. I'd rather just be on my own, if that's okay."

"That's fine, just fine. I suspect you're gonna need your room ready—for a while I mean, 'til you get on your feet 'n' all."

Cole looks down at his hands clasped on the table and back up at Wade, an apology on his face. "I could probably use that, if it ain't too much trouble."

"Shit, you know it ain't. Be good to have you. What, uh...what are your plans 'n' all. I mean, when you get out?"

"Well, it's a hearing, so yeah, I mean they could say 'no,' but it looks good, Pop, it looks real, real good."

The elation Wade had initially felt is dragged back down to earth by its collar as he thinks of Cole before he'd gotten arrested. The lying, the drugs, the excuses. Then he thinks of his son's presence at Annie's side in those last few weeks, and he decides *that* is the son he will welcome home. His first Christmas without Annie, and he'll have Cole there to soften the sharp edge of loneliness.

"Well, shit, that's some news then, ain't it? That's some real good news. So you'll be lookin' for a job, then."

Same old conversation, same father, same son. Wade doesn't know how to be any different. He sees the weariness in Cole's eyes the moment it comes out.

"I got money stashed away, Pop, don't you worry. I can take my time, ya know. I don't need to settle for some shitjob if I don't want."

"You got some money, do ya. How'd that happen?"

Cole laughs and gives the room an uncomfortable glance. "Well, you know. Mom, she, uh, set somethin' up for me a while back. You know."

"I don't really know, Cole. I mean…what?"

"It's a…well, see, before Mom died she gave me the information. She set up an account for me a few years back. Been puttin' some of her checks in it for me. You didn't know, I take it."

"No, I didn't know."

"Well, don't look at me like that, all disapprovin'. I didn't *ask* her to."

"It's fine, Cole. It's fine. There's just…there are things your mother did that I didn't know of, that's all."

"Well, it's enough for me to get started anyhow. I won't stay with you long, just enough to get my bearings. Maybe go to Elko or Wendover to set up camp."

"Not stayin' in town?"

"And what? Work at Flyin' J or Subway? Drivin' the same old streets with nothin' goin' on? No, I ain't stayin' in town. I'm thinkin' Wendover."

"Wendover ain't a good place for you, Cole, you—"

"I'm done with that stuff, Pop. Okay? I've changed in here. I ain't gonna fuck up again. You gotta start seein' the new me. I'm in recovery. That means for life, now. I ain't goin' back to that stuff."

"Well the 'new you' sure is actin' like the 'old you' from where I sit. You don't want school, don't want a job, don't—"

"Pop, stop already. I got stuff figured out, all right? I ain't gonna ever be like you, stuck in a shit job for shit wages for my life. No offense. And I ain't Milt. I'm me. Just let me be *me* for once in my whole goddamned life."

"Fine, be you. Whatever that is."

Cole smiles and taps his temple with his forefinger. "I got it all figured out."

And Wade's ears, they burn.

Wade doesn't allow himself to think that Cole's parole will fall through. He's decided in his mind that Cole will be there for Christmas, so he hauls the box housing the six-foot-high flocked tree out of the shed and into the front room. He moves the television to the other wall, separates the two armchairs to make room in the picture window, and opens the box.

The smell is distinct: musty, tinged with a powdery familiar odor that catches him unaware. A movie reel of memories cascades past his mind and he wills himself not to spiral down into the dark. He busies himself with finding the tree stand inside so he can assemble the thing, then mentally revisits the shed for the box of tinsel and ornaments Ann carefully packed every year. Last year he had packed it while Ann sat on the sofa, monitoring the wrapping up of each glass ball. His forearms glisten with the flocking. He hears the shuffling on the front step before the pounding on his door.

The rapping is urgent, and he can't think of who could possibly be out there. He glances out the window and sees Mildred without a coat. She sees him and starts talking, but he can't hear her. Her face is stricken.

He stands, slightly alarmed. He's never seen Millie on his front stoop, not once. He's glad he'd shoveled and salted that afternoon as he opens the door. The chill causes him to brace, as he'd just warmed from his recent trip to the shed.

"Millie, where's your coat!"

"Wade, I need you to come over to Dude's—he's...something's very wrong...he woke up from his nap and he's not right, something's not right, he—"

"Okay, slow down, Millie—slow down. Lemme get my coat. And where's your coat? You're gonna catch yer death."

He regrets saying it as he grabs his parka, feeling like the word "death" is a word he should avoid saying in front of old people at all costs, like the word itself will bring the event closer. He has a sneaking suspicion why she's there and doesn't know quite how to tell her, because there's always the chance Durward is sick.

They hurry down his walk, but the roads are snow-packed. He quickly grabs on to Mildred's arm and navigates them across the snow.

Durward's house is silent when they walk in and Wade's breathing becomes deeper as his heart pounds.

"He's in here..."

Mildred leads the way down the hall and when Wade enters the bedroom, he sees Durward crouched in between the bed and the wall, eyes wild.

"Dude—"

"Shh!" Durward snaps his head and looks at him. His whisper is harsh. "Be quiet, get down. Damn fools, *get down!*"

Wade looks at Mildred, who then looks back at him. "He woke from his nap and this is what he's been sayin'."

Wade takes Millie's arm and gently pulls her down to the floor to the side of the bed.

"Stay here," he says to her. Wade crawls around the bed until he's right in front of his friend, who has his hands up to his ears, cupped as if he's trying to capture sounds in the air.

"Dude, we're all down. Coast is clear."

"Naw, it ain't clear. That's what they want ya ta think. It ain't clear! I heard 'em in the bushes. I heard 'em. They found me—"

Wade moves in closer and puts his hands on Durward's shoulders. "It *is* clear. Remember? It's just me, you, and Millie here and nobody's shootin' nothin'. Those shots you're hearin' were just them dreams you get."

"Naw, my eyes were open and I heard 'em."

"Look at me. No one heard 'em. No one's there."

Durward's eyes search Wade's face, red-rimmed and teary. His mouth moves as if he's saying a silent prayer. Wade begins patting one of his shoulders. "See that? You're home, now."

Voice ragged as ripped cloth, Durward starts stammering. "Belnap n' Greenwood, they're gone, they were over in the reeds, they were—"

"Shh, they're resting now in heaven, Dude. Been there a long time."

"I got blood on me, I got blood…"

"No more blood. Look at your arms. Look at 'em. See that? No blood. Now turn your head 'n' look over there at Millie. Now see? She's all right. We're all right. We done this before, remember, buddy? What do we call them dreams?"

Durward's eyes look back and forth as his eyes clear, his forehead loses the crinkles. "We call 'em 'glue dreams.'"

"That's right buddy. Them glue dreams get stuck on you when you wake up, but it's just a dream. It ain't real, it ain't nothin'. Just yer head playin' tricks. Just that old goddamned head playin' tricks. No war. No guns. Just blue sky and snow and Millie here. Dude? Ya hear me?"

Durward's head nods and then his hands cover his face. Voice muffled, he says his words quietly, only for Wade's ears.

"Why can't I shake them dreams?"

"'Cause they're made of glue, buddy. Awful, sticky, rotten glue. Been a long time since you had 'em. You're gettin' better every day. Been a real long time since the last one."

"I could hear the screamin'."

"I know, buddy. I know. Let's get you up. C'mon."

Wade stands and holds Durward's forearm. He puts another hand underneath the old man's armpit and they rise together. Durward seems to see Millie for the first time.

"Didn't mean ta scare ya. I got these dreams sometimes…"

Millie stands and walks around the bed. Wade moves out of the way so she can wrap her arms around Durward's middle. "Let's go in the other room and watch a nice old movie. I made us chili. We'll look at the snow outside."

They walk out of the room together and Wade is struck by how Durward wraps his arm around her shoulder, how tender yet protective it is. *That Millie*, he thinks, *she's a good one.*

As he walks through the living room to leave, Wade smiles at Millie as she sits on the couch close to Durward, her hand rubbing small circles on his back. Durward sits on the couch, a dull look in his eyes. Wade knows Durward will be all right. A few more minutes will go by and the gunfire in the old man's thoughts will be silent; the fire, the smoke, the mangled bodies that sank into the mires of Korea will sink again into the depths of his mind, and he'll not speak of it again.

The tree looks good with the three brightly wrapped packages underneath. Wade is wearing a new flannel shirt he picked up at Claire's Western Wear, the only real clothing shop in town. Wade bought Cole a couple of shirts, a pair of Wrangler's and some socks and underwear. He hopes they fit his son's leaner frame.

He's leaving at four o'clock to pick him up. Today, Christmas Eve, Cole will be a free man. Wade's heart is racing, but in a good way.

Milt had called earlier and put both girls on the phone. Wade had felt a little sick inside as he spoke to each girl, so grown-up from when he saw or spoke to them last. McKenna spoke to him like she was a tiny adult. She asked him how he was doing and what he did with his days. She told him about her latest dance recital and Wade wished he had been there like he knew her other grandpa had been.

Brianna was more like a child on the phone, a little shyer with him than in person. But Wade got her to laugh when he told her he would send a horse and buggy to fetch her and bring her to Wells to see him. She told him about the new piano pieces she could play, names of songs he'd never heard of, and he *oohed* and *ahhed* appropriately, as if he knew just how difficult the pieces were. Milt got back on the phone and told him that 'Carol sends her love,' and Wade tried to not let anything come out of his mouth to let on that he knew just how much that meant.

The one promising note was when he told Milt that Cole was coming home today. Milt had known he made parole, but not when they were letting him out. He seemed genuinely happy about that and even hinted that he would take a couple of days from work and drive down for a weekend to see the both of them in the next couple of months. Wade wanted to tell him to bring the girls, but he knew it wouldn't happen. If he wanted to see those kids, he'd have to make the effort, and he resolved to do it soon.

Wade opens the cellophane bag containing Mildred's homemade carrot bread and slices off a thick piece. He's got an hour and a half before he can leave to get Cole. Just as he's about ready to take a bite, he hears a knock at the door.

He doesn't bother to see who it is, he just opens it. Tammy stands on the step with an unsure smile on her face.

"Hiya."

"Well…hey. What the hell? How are ya? I mean, it's good to see you. Come on in."

She carries a paper plate with plastic wrap on it, cookies circling the plate like a wreath. She's wearing a blue fluffy parka and jeans. It had been months since she'd been there, and he'd only seen her at the Flying J a handful of times. She had always been cool and distant. Wade swallows back his confusion and smiles at her. He's a little overcome at how much he'd missed her. As if he sported a new set of eyes, she looked smooth and dainty and pretty. He wanted to get that coat off her, he wanted her to stay.

Handing him the plate, she says nothing. He looks for a sticker or a card, but she only offers cookies.

"Thanks for these—hey, I don't know if you heard, but Cole's comin' home today."

Her face is genuinely surprised. "No kiddin'? For the holiday or—"

"No, no they don't do that with jail. I mean, let 'em out for holidays. What I mean to say is, he's comin' home for good. He's paroled."

"Huh. Well, ain't that somethin'?"

"You know, if you don't got any plans tomorrow, I'm makin' dinner for us. I know Cole'll want to see ya."

Her face colors slightly. "That'd be nice. I, uh, got a friend with me tomorrow. If you don't mind one more."

Wade's mind races over the past few months, her absence, the meals she used to bring. The money doesn't matter to him anymore, just the familiarity of her face and the comfort of its contours and expressions. He feels like he knows all of them. But the expression she wears now is unfamiliar and he tries to think of any other reason she's got a friend other than it's a man. And why should that matter to him anyway? She's family. Right? Family.

"Course you can bring a friend. I mean, yeah. I got a small turkey breast and some potatoes, nothin' special or anythin', just you know. Cranberries in a can."

Cranberries in a can?

He wants to figure out a way to ask about her friend. Just big brotherly-in-law concern, he figures. Right? And then of course there's portions and food amounts to figure out...

She smiles. "I can bring somethin'. A vegetable or somethin'."

"Well I got frozen peas and that stuffing mix and some gravy mix. I think we're good."

"I can bring more cookies for dessert."

"Okay, that'd be...real good. Yeah."

He can't be nosy. He lost that right, but in his guts he knows this friend is a man. He decides he's glad for her. She deserves a man. Yes, she's needed one. And Wade is her brother-in-law and that's how she'll introduce him and that's who he'll be. He'll open a beer with this guy and they'll talk sports and politics. They'll laugh and get a little tipsy and talk about his work and how Wade likes retirement. Wade will ignore the feelings that tumble inside of him when he looks at her face and hears her voice. He'll re-dress those feelings into brotherly love and care and he'll do what he can to make them into a family again. He'll make this guy feel welcome and accepted and they'll bond like men do when they don't share a woman they both love.

Cole wears his new plaid shirt as he sets the table.

"So who's Aunt Tammy bringin'?"

"Aren't you a little old to be callin' her 'Aunt Tammy? How 'bout you call her just 'Tammy.'"

Cole looks perplexed. "I always call her Aunt Tammy."

"Well cut it out. Makes her feel old."

Wade winces at the lie and stirs the frozen peas in a small saucepan. Cole is drinking a Coke and Wade feels slightly guilty that he's drinking beer when Cole is trying to steer clear of everything that resembles drugs. But there is no way in hell Wade can meet Tammy's 'friend' without a buzz on. There's a knock at the door and Cole pipes up.

"Got it."

"Oh hey, don't say nothin' 'bout Tammy feelin' old or anythin', okay? I mean, just..."

"I got it Pop, relax."

Wade breaks up a frozen clump of peas and his ears hone in, a glancing dash of hope in his mind that he'll hear two female voices. Instead, he hears a cluster of voices, two familiar, one not.

Wade turns down the heat on the peas and walks into the living room as coats are being shed and taken by Cole. He stops in his tracks at the small crowd.

"I tried callin' you but you didn't answer. I hope one more's okay." Tammy stands in the living room with a small, wiry man in his forties, and standing behind him? Cindy.

Wade internally shakes himself and smiles. "'Course it's okay. Hey there."

Tammy pulls on the small man whose face is bright and weathered, all at once. "This is Stuart. Stu, this is Wade. And you know Cindy, I guess."

"Uh, yeah, hi..." Wade shakes the small man's hand but his eyes flick to Cindy, who seems a little embarrassed.

"Glad to meet ya, Wade. Thanks for makin' room. Just got into town today. Didn't think I was gonna make it 'til tomorrow."

"Well, we got plenty, so come on in."

Cole returns from the spare room without the coats. "I'll set an extra place, Pop."

Stu puts an arm around Tammy and Cindy hovers behind them, looking at Wade, then at Tammy. She clears her throat. "Well, what can I help with?"

"Oh, sorry, nothin'. I got beer and whiskey and Coke and...water, I guess."

Tammy moves out from under Stuart's arm and heads toward the kitchen, leaving Stuart standing there, and it feels like he's squaring off with Wade, like one of them is about to draw.

"Stu, what can I getcha?"

"I think Tammy's gettin' me a beer."

"Cindy, uh...beer?"

"Sure, thanks."

He walks into the kitchen as Tammy pours two beers in glasses. They are alone as Cole starts talking to Cindy and Stuart in the front room.

"So he's your friend?" Wade asks, getting down another glass.

"Well, it was Cindy, we were gonna hang out together today—"

"Didn't know you knew her."

"Well I met her at Flyin' J, she'd come in with her paychecks. Anyway, she told me she knew you from the diner and we started talkin'. Stu just came in, like he said. I was plannin' on him later, but he showed up. I hope that ain't a problem or anythin'…"

"No, no nothin' wrong with it at all. So how long you been seein' her?"

"You mean seein' him?" She looks at him, her brows in a furrow.

"Uh, yeah, him."

"'Bout three months."

The other room is a swarm of voices and Cole and Stu talk excitedly together. Wade hears snippets, but the oven blower is on and he can't hear much of what they're saying. He pours the peas into a glass bowl and places it on the table. Uncovering the gravy, he sees it already has skin on it. He uses the spoon to pick it off and realizes he doesn't have anything to serve gravy in but another bowl. Where did someone go to buy a gravy boat? Does he need a gravy boat? He takes the foil tent off of the turkey and places that on the table. They are short a chair.

Wade wanders into the living room and can finally hear Stu talking.

"And in a country like that, you wouldn't have even gone to jail, that's the thing. It's them drug companies, the insurance companies, an' of course they got the government wrapped around their pinkies like this." He holds up his pinkie finger and grabs it for emphasis.

"Uh, I thought we could dish up in there and come on out here to eat. Bring out some chairs." Wade eyes Cindy who is eying Cole. Cole is eying her back and Wade retreats to grab a chair from the kitchen.

When their plates are filled, he sits in a chair, Cole next to him, and Cindy on a chair next to Cole. Tammy and Stu sit on the couch, plates on their laps.

"Yeah, Pop, Stu was just sayin' how if I lived in Holland, I wouldn't have even gone to jail."

Stu, mouth half-full of turkey, nods his head and speaks. "Yep. You

WADE

need somethin' in Amsterdam, you go and get it in Amsterdam. They got everythin' legal there and that's what the biggest problem is in this country. Everythin' you need's illegal. What d'you do for work, Wade?"

"I was in insurance, but I'm retired."

"See? Insurance. Biggest scam there is."

Wade glances at Tammy, who chews and stares straight ahead.

"Well," Wade said, "we took care of a lot of people—"

"But it ain't nobody's job to take care of people. See, we got a country full of babies here in the U.S. Wanna be taken care of instead of workin' and savin'. I got my own truck, but I'm strangled by government regulations. Cuts my business in half 'cause I don't work for them big companies, so they restrict what I can haul, makin' sure the fat cats get rich."

Cole points his fork at Stu. "It's The Man. He's always watchin'. But people are catchin' on. Like in Colorado, where it's okay to smoke pot now. And I bet they're making money hand over fist there."

"Yep," Stu says through another mouth of food, "they are. Makin' shit illegal's how you create the criminal class. An' I see this young man here an' I think to myself, 'he ain't no criminal! What the hell's he doin' takin' up tax dollars in jail'?"

"Well," Wade says, "we got laws and they ain't just for protectin' people from other people. They protect us from ourselves."

"Oh, come on. You serious? You need protectin', Wade? I got myself a nine-millimeter in my truck. That's gonna protect me, not some stupid law. And I fight for my own rights God gave me. Government don't got any right to give me freedom. Only God gives me freedom. Government and corporations are what take that away."

Wade's gaze and ideas about Stuart are narrowing in and the picture isn't good. He's beginning to dislike this ferret of a man already.

Cole nods his head. "It's like Big Brother, like that story. If people wanna drink themselves to death, let 'em. Or take drugs. We're all adults."

"Exactly," Stu nods vigorously.

Cindy speaks up, "There are some good things that you don't think about though, Stu. Like old people and Social Security. That's all my mom's got comin' to her after a whole life of strugglin'."

"Well, no offense, but I think that's a sham too. People know they got that cushion, so they squander their money and they don't save up to take care of themselves. They rely on government and insurance and even that don't work half the time."

Wade resents this blowhard spewing his anti-government bullshit here, on Christmas of all days, while his son sits there and agrees. Wade wants to remind Cole that if it weren't for the law, he might be dead of a drug overdose, and is that what he thinks should have happened?

"Well," Wade begins, "Cole you forget you was in real trouble last year. If you'd been left to your own, you just might not have made it."

Cole looks at him, a hint of hurt in his eyes. Stu speaks up. "Hell, he'd be fine. When somethin's illegal it's twice as allurin' and we want it more and more. He'd-a been fine if drugs was legal. Drug companies, doctors, hospitals, they're all in on it. Hell, I've gone my whole life, never had health insurance. Won't give the bastards one cent of my money."

Wade's food is getting cold. His stomach is in knots. "So you must got a huge amount of money, then, savin' up for if you get cancer or somethin', huh? 'Cause my wife, she had cancer, and even with insurance I'm still payin' those bills. How you plan on payin' if you get cancer?"

"I won't. I get it, I'll just let it take me. I don't need no doctor puttin' poisons in me just so I can die anyways."

Tammy looks at Stu. "She was in a lot of pain. You think that, but you'd be in a lot of pain."

"Well then shit, gimme morphine and I'll turn it up. I have the right to decide *that*, too."

"You say that, but you don't know." Tammy returns to her plate, a subdued look on her face.

"Sorry 'bout your wife, Wade, I don't mean nothin' by it. Just sayin' is all. We're too dependent."

Wade and Tammy's eyes meet for a moment and he can feel Cole's stillness next to him as a heaviness settles in the air. "Well, Stu, I see what you're sayin' but I can't agree with it all. I mean, you're a truck driver, ain't ya?"

"Yep. Got my own rig."

"So say you hit some icy patch and you jackknife and get real hurt, real bad. Some driver on the road finds you and calls an ambulance. Then you go to the hospital where they save your life. You got no insurance, see, so what happens is folks who got the insurance have to eat the cost of your hospital stay. So you got folks takin' care of you and you don't pay nothin'. Seems like that ain't too self-reliant to me."

"Well that's how the system works, even though it's wrong, Wade." Stu's eyes are hard like that phantom patch of ice and his chewing slows.

"Well, I know how you can fix that, then, Stu." Wade smiles a small smile. "Just have a letter posted your cab there says, 'If I am in an accident, please let me lay here on the side of the road to die, because I ain't got no insurance and I don't want to be a burden on the government or society.' Then I guess you got the right to not have insurance. Then you're walkin' the walk."

Wade and Stu lock eyes for a moment. Stu's sharp features seem to sharpen a little more, as if honed by a hunting knife. Then a slow smile spreads on Stu's mouth and his face breaks into a grin, lines gracing every surface of his skin. "That's a hell of an idea. Good thinkin' Wade. Walk the walk. I like it."

"Can we talk about somethin' besides politics? C'mon Stu, we always have such nice conversations when you don't get all hot-headed over politics." Tammy looks at Stu, and Stu smiles.

"You're right. We talk 'bout all sortsa things. You like football, Wade?"

"Not really." Wade looks down at his plate, wanting an out.

"Cole, let's talk about you," Cindy pipes in, turning her whole body to face Cole. "How you like bein' out and a free man?" Cindy's eyes sparkle at Cole and Wade has a sudden lead-ball feeling in his gut as he sees Cole's eyes give her the once over—twice.

7

Cindy had wriggled her way into staying at Wade's after Tammy and Stu left.

We can take her home later, can't we, Pop?

Wade had stared in mute amazement as his son and Cindy nattered on about all sorts of shit he just doesn't understand, like *energy* and *journeys* and *soul* and shit. Jesus, he wishes he could go back to that prison and ask them what the hell they're selling in there to transform his son into some hippie.

Sitting there in his living room, he felt like the most awkward third wheel ever created, or like a wheel on one of those grocery carts that wiggles and spins out of control so that only the use of brute force will make it move in a straight fucking line. That's how he'd felt, so he left, even though he wanted to stay and make sure nothing happened. Which is ridiculous because they're easily eleven years apart and Cole's a good-looking kid. Wade doesn't calculate in his head how long it had been since the boy'd gotten laid.

He isn't sure what concerns him more, that she'll tell Cole they had gone out, or that she won't.

Wade drove straight to it, like a part of him was grabbing himself by the shoulders and saying, *you've got no choice in this. This is the place you're gonna be.* All of the ambiguity of the previous summer has left him.

He's surprised and relieved that Lil' Mamacita's "open" sign is lit. Who works Christmas night? Girls with no family? That depresses him even more than his own fucked-up situation, and he already thinks that's pretty fucked up.

He sits in his car and looks at the building, snow on the roof, icicles dangling from the edge of it. The last time he'd been in, it hadn't done much for him. He wants to blame the woman, Lana, but he can't. She was nice enough. So what is he doing back here? He hopes that the rules for Christmas Day are different from the rules of every other Saturday night. This night, of all nights, he just wants to belong somewhere.

He rings the buzzer and waits. Frosty breath shoots out of him as he looks around the lot, noting the two cars parked in front. He hadn't bothered to look in back to see if trucks are there. He thinks of the truck Stu drives and how it's probably parked in front of Tammy's trailer and he clenches his eyes shut and rings the buzzer again.

"Welcome to—oh, hey Wade, how ya doin'? Merry Christmas! Come on in." Belle smiles at him, a jingle-bell necklace around her neck. She sports a sweatshirt that has the words "ho, ho, ho" on it. He grins despite himself.

"Merry Christmas to you. Nice shirt."

"Ha, yeah, just a little inside joke. We don't use words like that 'round here. But I couldn't resist."

When she shuts the door she grabs him in a bear hug and he returns it with a robust sincerity, jingle bells jingling all the way down his chest.

"Haven't seen you in a while. Lemme getcha a beer, on the house."

"Oh, I don't need that, I can pay for a damn beer."

"Ah, watch the cursin'."

"Sorry. Anyway, I didn't think you'd be open."

Her eyebrows rise with the widening of her eyes. "Oh, yeah, you'd be surprised at how much we need to be open on holidays like this one." She nods, cementing that fact for him. "Oh yeah, you'd be surprised. It's early still. You watch, we're gonna be hoppin' in an hour or two.

"No kiddin'."

He wants to say he's surprised again, but he'd already said it so he nods, agreeing with her. No one is in the bar except Bev, who has already poured him a half of a beer and is opening a can of tomato juice. Wade points at the glass.

"You remembered."

Bev taps the side of her head, as if all of that knowledge and memory is tucked away and the skill with which she wields it is hers alone. Wade takes a grateful sip of his bloody beer, glad to wash the taste of the day away. Belle had left, but she rejoins him and pats his back.

"We only got five girls right now, but I've got six more comin' in at seven. You wanna wait an hour and some? Oh, here they come."

Shit.

He should have prepped for the drill, because he felt he needed to settle first, but he knows why he's here and there's no point in fooling himself or Belle, ever again.

Three girls walk out, the curtain parting like a pair of red legs, and he doesn't see Lana. For some reason, he's immensely relieved, as if seeing her again would bring back all of the darkness he had left with that night last summer. Plus, he'd feel compelled to choose her again, lest he hurt her feelings. He tries to focus now, tries to see them without looking like he's picking out a melon at the grocery store. He doesn't know how to convey *respectful* in his gaze.

"I'm Dina."

"Hi, I'm Amy."

"I'm Sienna."

Dina is the oldest as far as he can tell. She's got ebony hair and dark caramel skin and his brain tells him he should pick her because of her age. But he tells himself that age doesn't matter anymore—just look at Cole and Cindy, right? Age is a number. Only a number. Looking at the three women, he wonders where their families are.

He smiles and nods at Amy, a petite woman in her thirties with platinum blond hair that goes to her waist. Fake tits, definitely fake tits, and a skinny boy-body that he can't find a curve in. Finally his eyes settle on the last girl, and for the life of him, he can't remember her name. Younger than the other two by at least ten years, she is no more than twenty-three, maybe twenty-five. She's very curvy, what some would call plump, but he doesn't mind that, actually likes that, in fact. It's the opposite of Tammy, opposite of his wife before she died, and this night is about doing the thing he least expects of himself. He clears his throat.

"I, uh, forgot your name…"

"That's Sienna," says Belle, next to his ear.

"Oh, okay, uh, well…"

"Would you like to talk to Sienna, Wade?"

"Yeah, sure, that'd be great."

Sienna's wide almond eyes are a deep brown, her skin like raw honey. She smiles at him and walks toward him, one foot in front of the other, balancing on precariously high heels. Her shiny, straight black hair is parted down the middle.

"Hi, I'm Wade."

She takes his hand, her grip limp, but her skin is impossibly soft. "Hi, nice to meet you."

"That's an interestin' name you got there. I mean, it's a color, ain't it?"

"Yeah, it's a color." She scoots next to him and crosses her bare legs. Her short, black miniskirt rides up to the tops of her thighs and he tries not to stare at her ample cleavage. He can't quite look into her eyes just yet. That niggling part of his brain is at it again with the age thing, mostly because he sees himself as her job, her 'have-to,' her necessary evil, and he doesn't like it. Not one bit.

"So you workin' on Christmas...you got family?"

"Yeah, I've got family in Utah. That's where I'm from. Where're you from?"

"Here. Well, I was born in Elko. Moved here when I got a job workin' insurance. Well, when I got married."

"You still married?"

"No." Wade doesn't want to have that conversation, not again and not with her. He doesn't want death sullying the mood. "And my son's home, sorta ran me outta my house tonight. Long story. Anyway."

She smiles and then does something that leaves him with shock waves throughout his frame. She reaches over and takes his hand. There is nothing sexual about it, it's just warm and comforting and it makes her seem so much wiser than her years.

"So tell me something about yourself that's unique, Wade. Anything."

He opens his mouth, then closes it. How is he unique? Nothing comes to mind. He reaches for his beer with his right hand without thinking, then stops.

"Well, uh, here's somethin' weird, I guess. See these three fingers? I can't move 'em. I can feel 'em, but can't move 'em. Doc says there ain't nothing wrong with anything. Says it's all in my head or somethin'."

She reaches over and wraps her fingers around the three fingers, squeezing them together. He can't help but picture her hand around something else and he wonders if she does it on purpose.

"You can feel that?" she asks.

"Yeah. Just can't move 'em."

"Wow."

"So you next. What's unique 'bout you?"

"Oh, I'll show you. But you have to wait. Don't worry, it's not weird or anything."

"You'll 'show me'?"

"Yeah." Her smile is wide. "I'll show you. Okay, so if you could be anywhere in the world right now, where would you be?"

Her face is open, eyes searching his, and he suddenly feels like she is really with him. She isn't just doing a job, she's asking him—searching him for a piece of him he didn't know was missing. Her eyebrows arch beautifully. His heart is a battering ram against his ribs as he takes in her face.

"I guess I'd be on a beach somewhere, nice and warm and sunny. How 'bout you?"

She tucks her hair behind her ear and looks down, then up at him again, smile deepening. "That sounds really nice. Me too."

He doesn't tell her he made that up. He doesn't tell her that right there, in that room, is exactly where he wants to be.

Wade feels her hand in his, soft and warm and he doesn't want to let go. He also wants to be practical, wants things to go smoothly.

"Can you hang on? I'll be right back."

"Sure, I'll be here."

She releases his hand and it almost tingles from her touch. He makes his way over to the ATM. He feels that sense of adventure return, but maybe it's because his savings account is bulging with money. He suspects that has only a little to do with it. He takes out the bills, enough for a whole hour and a hundred for a tip. When he comes back into the room, Sienna's eyes light up and his cynical mind can't understand how she can fake that so well. It occurs to him that maybe it's for real and he decides to stop second-guessing her motives as he takes the seat next to her again.

"I hit the ATM," he says. He regrets it instantly and looks away.

"Okay. So you told me where you would wanna be, now tell me about your family. You have kids, right?"

"Yeah, two." But he doesn't want to talk about his family; he *knows* about *his* family. What he doesn't know is all about her and that's what he craves.

"What about you? You said you're from Utah. What brings you out here?"

"Well, this job. I live in Utah two weeks out of the month. Two weeks, I live here."

"No kiddin'? It's only 'bout four hours or so from Salt Lake, I guess, right?"

"Actually about three. I live in a small town, north of Salt Lake. Brigham City. So it takes me about three and a half hours to get here. I like the drive. I listen to books."

"You listen to 'em? Like tapes?"

"Well, no, it's audiobooks. It's on my iPod."

"No kiddin'? What kinds of books you like?"

"All kinds. I don't like romance books, though."

"Oh yeah, why not?"

"They're stupid. I like books that mean something, you know? Like, books that go deep into what life is about. Books that talk about humanity."

"Wow. That's…I didn't figure, I mean, shi—shoot. So, you always like those kinda books?"

"Well, not when I was in school—high school, I mean. But when I took college classes I took a lot of English Lit classes. I learned to love books like that."

Wade can't remember the last book he read and he feels ashamed, suddenly, as if this bright, young college student sits here with some back-country rube. He vows to read a book before he comes back. Maybe she could recommend one? Maybe they would read one together, then talk about it?

"So didja finish college or—"

"No, I…I had a son."

"Oh. I see. Well, that's good, I mean, right? How old is he?"

"He'll be four in February. And yes, that's very good. He's the light in my life." Color comes into her cheeks as her eyes become even more alive than before.

Wade turns from her and sips his beer. This new information causes a sense of protectiveness to well up in him. She's a mother. She's doing this for her son. She changes before his eyes. Then he opens his mouth and regrets his words instantly.

"So why do you do *this*? I mean, I guess the money, but—I—never mind. It ain't my business. Sorry." His ears burn with shame and he wants her to take his hand again. Surely Lana was a mother. He didn't ask her why she was a prostitute. What is wrong with him?

"It's okay. You want to see my room?"

"Yeah, sure. I mean…yeah." Suddenly the reality of going with her strikes him and all he can see in her is the young mother with an almond-eyed boy at her side and he wants to turn tail and walk right out the front door. He also wants to help her. Hell, if he could, he'd give her whatever she needed so she could turn-tail too, go back to Utah, to her small town, and be with her son all month, every month, forever.

Her room is smaller than Lana's had been. Or maybe her bed is bigger. He looks at it. It's made, with a pretty peach and pink comforter on it and he imagines her sleeping in it, on her side, curled up with no makeup on, her hair spread out on the pillow. Breathing out sharply, he doesn't know why he's doing this—like his mind is loading torpedoes and shooting them through his body to douse and ruin his desire. She closes the door behind him and before he can get his bearings, she slips her arms around his neck.

"Remember how I said I'd show you what's unique about me?" she asks.

"Yeah."

She places her hands on the sides of his face and kisses him on the lips. Her lips stay there, gently pressing and he opens his mouth a little for her as she deepens the kiss. His body reacts instantly. Torpedoes gone.

She pulls away and smiles a little shyly at him. "No one else kisses."

His breathing has quickened and he clears his throat and reaches in his pocket so she doesn't have to say it. "I—I got enough for a whole hour—I mean, if that's okay, I—"

She puts her finger up to his lips. "I don't charge for time on a clock. I look at it as time *together*. However long that is. Okay? So for one time together, that's two-fifty."

"Okay," he isn't sure he understands, but she's touching him and that's all he wants to understand. He'd taken out six hundred, thinking he would have an hour. He's confused but he figures it will work itself out. Anything she says—he'll do anything she says.

She takes the money from him without looking away from his eyes. "I'll be right back. There's a robe for you on the back of the closet door if you want to get into it."

"Oh, okay. I will."

He had been doing his sit-ups regularly and his paunch has lessened into something he's not ashamed of anymore. But he also knows he isn't some twenty-five-year-old stud and he has hair on his back, front, everywhere and he thinks of how beautiful she is and…

He comes to life, strips off his clothes and gets into the soft dark-blue robe she showed him. His erection has gone down and he's glad, as if seeing his desire would make her think less of him; then he thinks that's nuts and his brain is all confused again. He stands, but then wonders if he should sit on the bed, but that seems like he's taking things for granted, but then she took the money…he can't quiet his thoughts, can't slow them down. He doesn't know why this girl has him so befuddled in his mind that he can't think straight. He almost jumps when the door opens. Sienna walks in and her smile dazzles him so that the light in the room seems even brighter. When she kicks off her heels, she shrinks down so that she comes just to his chin, and he looks down on her face as she pulls off her clothes.

Her naked skin is like the dark, sandy desert; he'd walked through it, driven past it so many times, the burnt sand and sage, dunes smoothed by wind, swelling then tapering then swelling again, so smooth, the color seemingly all the same, but shadows and light contort every surface, making her like a satin cloth wound around an hourglass. He hardly notices as she kneels down with the warm baby wipe and inspects him, wipes him down.

Then she turns on the bedside lamp, placing a red silky scarf on top of it to mute the light. She then flips off the glaring overhead light.

Where Lana had taken charge, Sienna seems to intuit what he wants, reading his mind as if he has a list of things he desires and needs from her. When he moves to the bed, she lies down next to him and kisses him again, and nothing, nothing else matters but her lips and the feel of her silky skin.

When she breaks the kiss, she looks him in the eyes and brings her hand up to his cheek. "You can do anything you want to. This is our time together."

So many things play in his mind, so many visions, words caught in his throat, his mouth, between his teeth. The thought grabs him by the throat and gut and he wants to ask her permission, and she had said 'anything' but he still isn't sure.

"I want...I'd like to...uh..."

"Tell me, it's okay."

He licks his lips, suddenly dry, and looks down between her legs and back up at her. "I want—I want—"

"Yes...I would like that."

He stops stammering and his breathing deepens, becomes heavy, like he can barely take in enough air. Heart pounding, he lays her back on the bed and moves over and above her. He kisses her breasts, tasting the slight musky scent on her nipples. He buries his head in her neck, smelling her, then he moves down her soft belly mound, soft downy hairs on her lower tummy leading below. Moving down, down, he spreads her legs, slides his cheek across her small strip of fragrant hair, then moving down more, smelling, nudging, and then he can't deny himself another second and he drinks her in and it's all he wants, all he can see. He feels like he's been blinded his whole damn life, and suddenly a cloak is lifted from his vision. It's the moment of fulfillment after complete starvation and thirst and want, and he thinks of the desert again, of her desert-sand skin with this oasis she's allowed him to visit. He crawls to it like a ravaged man and he bathes relentlessly in its comfort.

Wade snorts and jumps. He opens bleary eyes and sees unfamiliar walls, the soft light. The warmth of Sienna's hand and forearm jars him awake even more as she begins gently rubbing his chest.

"Oh shit, I fell asleep."

"It's okay. It happens." She whispers to him and he searches his mind for any clue as to how long he'd dozed. His face grows hot as he realizes he might have stayed longer than he'd planned. She moves in closer and drapes her leg across him. He gently moves it off.

"I'm sorry, I should go. I can't believe I just dropped off like that. Shit."

Sienna props herself up on her elbow. "Look, I don't do the time thing, okay? You collapsed. You must have needed the rest. It's okay. I'm not going to...I mean, I don't take advantage. You know? An hour isn't how I think about it. So don't think I was trying to get you to stay or anything."

Wade looks into her face, her brows knit so beautifully together, her mouth turned down at the corners. She seems concerned that he thinks she was up to no good. All he feels is panic that he had taken her time.

"I know, I know you wouldn't—what time is it, anyways?" He sits up, conscious of his belly, his shriveled dick disappearing as he moves from the bed.

"It's eight-thirty."

"Aw, God. You should've woke my sorry ass up."

She stretches out on the bed, arms above her head and a lazy smile on her face.

"But you looked so peaceful," she says as she stretches. Her back arches and he takes in her whole form and feels himself grow with heat again, tingling, his heart pounding. Well, why the fuck not? He moves over to the bed and wants to get on her, right then, but he's still not sure of the rules.

"Can I...can we...I mean, I'll just go back to the ATM again—"

She reaches over to the dresser and pulls out another condom. "You're fine. Come on...come here..."

He gets on top of her again and he kisses her before she slides the condom on.

When they finish, he's wide awake, keenly watching the clock.

"Now I'm really gonna go. Merry Christmas to me, huh?"

"Merry Christmas to me, too. There aren't a lot of guys who do that. What you did at first...I mean, go down on me like that for so long. It was really good."

Wade's face burns. He doesn't know the language for this kind of talk, can't make himself say the words in his head or out loud. He isn't even sure there are words for what they had done— or at least how he feels about what they had done—in his vocabulary. *Miracle*. That's the word that enters his mind: *miracle*. The smell of her is on him; he can still taste her. It feels more intimate than even being inside her. What had possessed him he doesn't know. He pulls on his jeans and she wraps herself in a baby-pink robe.

"I'll be right back," he says.

"You paid for two parties already. And you tipped me. I don't count sleeping as time, remember?"

"I don't know, see, if I was with, say *another person*, ya know...I mean, I been here for almost four hours. That's—that's a hell of a lot more than I gave you."

"Look, let me tell you how I work. See...I like regulars, you know? Guys I get to know, who come see me all the time. If I break their balls about time, well then maybe they don't come to see me as much, you know? Or they try someone else and I lose them. I like to *like* my guys. I like to keep 'em. You see what I mean?"

"But I feel bad."

"Don't feel bad. Feel good. Then come back. Come see me again soon."

"Absolutely. I mean, you can count on that, is what I'm sayin'." Wade is calculating how much he would owe Lana right now. He'd paid Sienna six hundred. He'd owe Lana two thousand. He really wants to go back to the ATM.

"Come on," she steps into her high heels and almost meets him at eye level again. The pink robe accentuates her light caramel skin and dark eyes and he thinks he's never seen anyone so beautiful in his life. "I'll walk you out."

She takes his arm and it's almost painful to leave the little burrow of her room, like they'd been two desert mice nestled in a den by a hot spring under frozen earth. The noise from the bar is louder than he'd ever heard and he's hesitant to walk out and come upon faces he might know. Then it hits him that she is probably going to shower, change, come out in a lineup in front of all of these men. He stops that thought in his head like a gunshot to the gut. He can't let himself think like that, not now.

He sees the ATM and he stops. "Here, I want to—"

"Next time," she says in his ear, smiling. It's endearing, how she's always whispering in his ear. She tugs on his arm and he moves with her. Maybe she needs him to go; he doesn't want to be a bother to her.

He goes over what she'd said to him, about knowing her customers. *She wants to know him.*

He looks at her. "What book you readin'? Or listenin' to?"

"It's one I read in high school. It's kind of heavy but I love it. It's called *The Stranger* by Camus."

"By who?"

"Albert Camus, c-a-m-u-s. He's French. Or he was, I guess."

"I'm gonna check it out then. So we can talk about it."

"You'd do that for me?" Her eyes are wide, a small, dazed smile on her face.

"Sure, I mean, yeah. I want to."

"I would love that!" She grins and loses about ten years from her face. Wrapping her arms around his neck, she squeezes him tight. "No one's ever done that for me."

She looks into his eyes and his chest fills, like a warm, thick liquid saturates it, as he looks at her white teeth, her full lips. He had kissed those lips. Lana hadn't kissed him. He knows he has to say goodbye, now. Not wanting to keep her any longer, he kisses her forehead. "Merry Christmas, Sienna."

She moves in close and whispers in his ear. "Merry Christmas, Wade."

She turns and walks away with only one backward, smiling glance. He continues to watch the hall, even after she's gone.

This is a dream, only a dream. But this is *his* dream and he will dream of her every night and probably every second of his days, and then the noise of the bar overcrowds his head and his dream of dreams and he turns to leave, but not before glancing in the bar.

Several girls talk to men, all ages, all sizes, the bar more crowded than he'd ever seen it. He's glad Belle isn't there, fearing he and Sienna had broken some sort of house rule, doing what they had done. Or maybe he is the one who has broken rules, rules he should have had in place before he'd ever set a sorry foot back in here. He knows in his right mind he's about as special as a grain of sand on the floor of a desert. But Sienna, she had grabbed a handful of him and kept him, and in that way he did feel special. He doesn't care if it's a dream, a fantasy, whatever. If she's that good at giving it to him, then he's going to enjoy it, drink it in and ride it like a wave.

The faces all blur together in the bar as he makes the trek past the wide entrance leading to the front door—all a blur but one. For a brief moment, his eyes settle on one face at a table, talking to the long-haired blond. At first he can't place him, then he does, the implications jolting him. He had been at his house just hours before. The face belongs to Stuart.

Nine o'clock on Christmas night. Wade thinks of calling Milt to talk to the girls, find out what they got for Christmas. He decides to wait, since they might already be in bed. The truck meanders, moving at a slow, unhurried speed down 10th Avenue. Wade turns on Lake Road to head back into town. On a whim he turns up 6th Avenue and sees that Luther's is open. He hears the Hallelujah Chorus in his head as he parks next to Gerry's van. Another truck is in the lot. Wade really doesn't want to go home. He's aware that he's the only ride Cindy has, but Cole would have called him if she had been ready to leave, and there have been no calls on his cell tonight.

The music inside plays some country rock as he walks in. Gerry is in his usual spot at the table by the bar, and Pete, Cindy's uncle, sits at the table with a beer. He smiles wide when Wade walks in.

"Well lookie here, it's ol' Wade, you sonofabitch. How you been?"

Pete stands to greet Wade and they shake hands, Pete pumping his hand like he's shaking dust from a rag.

"Hey, you off the road for the holiday?" Wade looks around for Junior, who is not behind the bar.

"Yeah, between hauls, that's me."

"Gerry, what the hell?" Wade slaps him on the back and Gerry nods, face serious.

"Well, it's Christmas, Wade, so Merry fucking Christmas." Gerry scowls and sips at his beer. Wade knows Gerry can be a moody fucker, so he just lets him be when he's on one.

"Yeah, you too. Where's Junior at?"

"Had to run home for a second, somethin' to do with the wife. We're holdin' down the fort 'til he come back. So you ever ask out that niece of mine?" Pete's eyes glitter through his bushy gray eyebrows, his beard and mustache the same color gray.

"Oh, uh, we uh, sure, yeah. She's a nice gal. Real nice." Gerry watches Wade with a worried look on his face. Wade looks back at him, an innocent expression in his raised eyebrows and wide eyes.

"What?" Wade says.

"Nothin'," Gerry shrugs.

"What's goin' on?" Pete looks between the two of them. "Whatcha not tellin' me?"

Pete is an excitable kind of guy. He's gushy when he's happy, and a downright grizzly when he's upset. Wade always feels like he's walking on brittle ice when he talks to Pete. One wrong comment, one observation about the state of the country, the world or anything, and like a light switch, he flips to *on* and there's no stopping him.

"Naw, it's nothin', Pete. It's just nothin' came of it is all. I mean, she's a friend now, see. She's a real nice gal 'n' all, we just didn't click or somethin.' But she an' me, we're friends."

Pete nods his head and takes a drink, relieving Wade's fear of an outburst. Then Pete wipes his mustache of foam and leans over.

"So what's wrong with her?"

"What? Nothin'. Nothin's wrong, Pete. You know."

"Uh huh, so why's it you're here an' she's at your place then?"

Wade opens his mouth, but nothing comes out.

"Yeah," Pete continued, "I called her thinkin' she'd be all lonesome tonight, and she said she was at your place. So why you ain't there, huh?"

Wade can see the wheels turning in Pete's head and he doesn't know how to stop them. "Well, she came with my sister-in-law."

"I know that. She had dinner there with y'all. But why didja leave them gals at your place alone an' come here?"

Wade doesn't want to tell him Cindy is there alone with his son. His convict son who just got out yesterday. Wade thinks of anything he can say that will be the truth, but at the same time protect Cole.

"You know women, they like to clean up and chatterbox an' well I just needed to get out of there, ya know?"

Pete studies him for a long time. Finally his face breaks out into a grin.

"Damn, they can talk, can't they? Women can natter on 'bout most anythin' and nothin' all at once."

Gerry clears his throat. "A toast to women and their mouths."

"Hey, watch it, brother, that's my niece an' his sister-in-law you're talkin' 'bout."

"I didn't mean nothin' by it, you old fucker. To women, then. Cheers."

The men raise their glasses and Gerry wipes at his eyes. He clears his throat again and turns his head.

"What's wrong, Ger? Hey, c'mon, it's Christmas, buddy. You're with good friends, here." Pete has his hand on Gerry's shoulder. Wade hears a door close in back and is relieved Junior is back so he can get a beer in him. He brings his hand up to his mouth and inhales. A faint whiff of Sienna stirs him and he quickly pulls and scratches at his nose before turning to Gerry.

"What's goin' on, now, huh?" Wade glances up to see Junior enter the bar, coat still on. "Hey Junior, Merry Christmas."

"Well ain't you all a sight. Beer's on the house this round fellas."

"See that," Pete says, practically cooing to Gerry, "we got us some free beers. Life's good."

"Yeah, sorry, yeah, life's good." Gerry gives off a weak smile and Wade sees that far away look in Gerry's eyes he's seen a few hundred times. The look is there on him like the Ghost of Christmas Past, the haunted visions of what was and what might have been.

Junior brings over large mugs of beer, Wade's without tomato juice, but he's not going to complain about that tonight. Junior actually has a mug in his hands as well. His eyes don't hold any mirth either, and Wade wonders what sort of specter has landed in his life this night.

Pete looks up. "So everything all right with the wife? She pissed you're open?"

"Nah, it ain't that. She needed me to go home an' talk to our second oldest, Ben. He done some foolish, stupid thing an' then told his mama about it tonight of all nights."

"What'd he do?" Wade asks.

"Ah, he went out, joined the army."

The whole table groans. Gerry looks up, his eyes still far away. "You tell that boy to come 'round here, see what workin' for the U.S. did for me. You tell him I gotta wait months for my medical care, still, and you tell him I got stories, stories about nights like this, Christmas nights when them bastards hit hardest, knowin' this is a sacred day, an' how thirteen men died right in front of me on Christmas day, you tell him—" his voice had risen in volume until he was almost blaring like a preacher.

"Gerry, Gerry, it's all right, now. Come on." Wade pats his shoulder as Gerry wipes the tears streaming from his eyes down his wrinkled cheeks.

"You just tell him," Gerry says, softer.

Junior holds his beer up. "A toast to Gerry, an' to the men he lost."

"Friends," Gerry says. "They was friends."

"Here, here," Pete clinks and then chugs half the brew down as they all sit in silence.

Wade looks up at Junior, who towers over the table still. "Our kids do stupid shit, Junior."

"Yeah," Junior nods. "Speakin' of, I heard your boy's out. Parole?"

Wade is instantly on guard. "Uh, yeah, yeah, he got out. Clean and sober and doin' great."

Pete looks at Wade, eyes narrowing. "He stayin' with you, Wade?"

Wade nods. "Yeah, just for a bit, 'til he gets on his feet."

"Uh huh. So, he, uh, there now, at yer house?"

"Yeah, yeah, he's uh, there as far as I know. Yeah."

Pete nods, eyes trained on Wade, as if more questions are to come, but he doesn't say another word, and that's the most dangerous thing Pete can do.

Junior kicked them out at 11 p.m., wanting to go home and smooth things over with his wife and son, and it being Christmas and all. Wade's limbs are rubber, limp and elastic like he has no control. He wonders if he'd had too much to drink, or if it was the visit to Mamacita's that has him all loose and relaxed. He finds he's searching for any reason at all to go back to see the girl, as soon as possible. Before he goes back, he decides, he's going to read that book Sienna told him about. He remembers the title, *The Stranger*, because when she'd said it, he thought it could be about him. He doesn't remember the French author. He'll look it up on Google, order a used copy. Maybe read it in one week and go see her on New Year's. Then the thought occurs to him that she might be off. He mentally smacks himself upside the head for not asking her what her schedule is. For all he knows, she'll be back in Utah the next week.

And he has to think about the money. How far would eight thousand dollars go at Mamacita's? He tries to do the math in his head, but it's fuzzy with beer and the need to sleep. He pulls into his carport and all of the lights are off in the house except the tree lights in the front room. He sits with the engine running, still waiting for the heat to kick on in the truck, knowing it takes a good fifteen minutes for it to warm up but wanting one shot of warmth before he hits the freezing night air to go inside.

He finally turns off the truck and makes his way out, feeling like weighted balls of lead have sunk into his limbs.

Walking in, the warmth makes his head feel even heavier. He quietly curses, knowing that the empty room signals Cole has gone to bed—and Cindy? She had to be with him. Unless Tammy came and got her. No, he can feel it. She's there.

"Jesus H.," Wade whispers. Pete gets hold of Cole, who knows what he'll do. The boy had obviously been starving, or Cindy would not be there. But hadn't Wade been starving, too? And he couldn't, not with her. But then he remembers Cole's age, and at twenty-eight, his hormones would still be on a rampage.

Wade walks into the kitchen and tosses his keys in a bowl filled with push pins, paper clips, some stamps and rubber bands. This is where he has been putting his keys for over thirty years. He'd needed a place for his keys since Annie complained he left them all over, then lost them, and so the bowl came out, soon becoming the resting place for all of the other shit that accumulates in a random bowl on a kitchen counter. Doesn't everyone have that bowl? That drawer? The place where unknowns go, the things you can't put into a clear category. Things with no use in the moment, but with the promise of usefulness in the near-to-far future? Just like him, only the opposite. His usefulness is in the past, and now he sits in his house like a used paper clip, once the object holding everything together, now bent out of shape, misplaced, with nowhere else to go.

He hears a door close and wonders if they heard him come in and had closed it for privacy. He jumps when Cindy appears in the living room. She wears one of Cole's new Christmas shirts and her legs are bare. Wade looks away, unsure of what to say to her.

"You were gone so long, Cole invited me to stay."

"You don't got to explain nothin' to me."

"I'm just telling you."

"Yeah, and I got a cell phone if you wanted to go home so much."

She smiles, a small flicker of embarrassment on her face, "Well, I guess I didn't."

"Jesus," Wade shakes his head and places both hands on the counter, leaning into it. "Does he know? 'Bout you an' me?"

"I didn't say anything. But he could hear it. From anyone."

"Well, there's *that* to look forward to then, I guess. Yeah, that'll be a great conversation for us." Wade is angry, the alcohol bringing a sharpness to his words and voice. He remembers what an angry drunk he can be and breathes in deep to calm himself.

"You can't be jealous," she says. Her tone is coy and his anger broils inside.

"An' you can't be serious. First, I said 'no' to you, remember? Second, he's ten years younger than you and you should know better! Third, he's got his life he's gotta get together, an'—"

"Eleven. He's eleven years younger than me, and so what? Age is a number. How old are you? And you asked me out! So don't be a hypocrite! It's okay for you to see someone so young, but not me—"

"That ain't the point!" They are doing that whisper-yell thing people do when the children are asleep in the next room. Wade's voice is getting hoarse with the effort to keep quiet, but his temper has flared to the point that his real voice breaks through.

"Well what the hell *is* your point?"

"This is my house, is my point, and I get a say in what happens here!"

"Oh, so he shouldn't expect to be treated like a grown-up here, that it?"

Wade takes a step closer to her. "You know your uncle Pete was askin' about you tonight? Yeah, he don't seem too thrilled 'bout you bein' here with my son."

"That's because Uncle Pete thinks I'm forever fifteen years old, that's why!"

"Well that ain't my business. That's between you and him. I don't wanna see you come mornin', you understand? So you either let me take you home right now, or you get Cole to take you, but I don't wanna wake up with some stranger in my house."

She crosses her arms and huffs out a breath. "So, you don't want me and you don't want anyone else havin' me."

Something in Wade's head snaps. "Jesus fuckin' Christ, how'd you get that from what I said? Why can't women just talk like *people*! I told you exactly what I don't want. You made that other shit up right outta your stupid female head!"

"You, Wade, are a *misogynist*! No wonder. You hate women, dontcha? Well that much is clear and I'm glad I found out now before anything ever happened between us!"

He is being tortured in the Land of Womenspeak. She turns to leave and he screeches in a whisper as loud as he dares. "Nothin' was *ever going to happen with us! Holy fucking God!*"

But she had returned to Cole's room and Wade seethes with rage, a limp fury inside him with nowhere to go. And now he doesn't know if he's stuck taking that cow home, or if Cole's getting up to do it.

Fuck me! he fumes silently.

He opens the refrigerator and grabs another beer. Why he thinks it will calm him is not clear, but he chugs it half down when suddenly Cindy appears again in the living room, her coat on.

"He won't wake up. We…he drank a lot."

Wade bites his tongue, literally chomps down on it to not say something cruel like, *he'd have had to be outta his mind drunk to take your horse-faced ass to bed.*

He grabs his keys and paper clips fly over the side of the bowl as he snags his coat and stalks out the front door.

8

12/28/14

    I haven't written for two months but nothing seems to have changed. The men come and go and come and go and nothing changes. And then something does and I feel like the one thing that changes changes everything. I'm tired and not making sense. But I get to go home in two days and see Jacob. That's the good part. Last time I was home he called Jessica "Mommy" and I was devastated. Jessica told him not to call her that, to call her Aunt Jessica, but it still stung. My sister takes good care of him, so I shouldn't bitch. Some girls with kids have it a lot worse. I figure I've got one year left at this place. One year and then I'm done and I'll have enough to find a place we can afford, move, start up school again, tuition, and Jacob and I be together all the time. I just need to keep my eyes on the prize and keep doing what I'm doing. I think I'm playing it right, too. I don't think anyone else here is really doing the girlfriend thing. The kissing, the cuddling. The shit. I told Belle what I wanted to do with parties, to charge by party not by time and she was all right with that, but told me I might change my mind later. I wonder if I will, especially since I think about what happened Christmas with that one guy.

    I had Barking John again last week. I can't connect with him at all and now he's getting creepy with his pictures. This time he brought in all of these pics of amputee women from WWII or something, some kind of camp and he watched me look at them and I said "Why did you show me these,

John?" and he didn't answer, he just had this completely blank expression that feels incredibly scary to me. No, it's scary to all of us, I think. The zero-expression-thing. It just makes you feel like something is going to snap. Anyway, he looked at me with that blank look, then he turned me around and did me, barking the whole time of course. I am so glad he doesn't ask for me all the time. He just picked me that day. Everyone knows about him and the stories are disturbing. I think he's done every one of us at least twice. Too bad he doesn't fall for Amy. If I could wish him on anyone, it would be her. She thinks she is so superior to the rest of us. She's a former dancer, and I guess she figures that makes her better? I don't know. I can tell she's looking for some guy to "Pretty Woman" her. She's drawn to the rich ones like honey. Not that we all aren't, but the rich ones are the worst tippers, at least that's what I've seen. Like we should be grateful that they chose us. The simple truckers, they're the ones who tip. I guess the rich guys give all their money to their wives, so there isn't any left when they want pussy.

 I had another guy who came in and he wanted just straight sex but he insisted on calling me "Mona" and I asked him if that was another girl he liked, and he said "No, I just like the name 'Mona.'" He tipped me $200, so hey, call me "Mona." Then there was this other guy on Christmas night and he was kind of shy and sweet, older but he didn't have whiskey dick or anything. He was new to this, I'm, pretty sure, but respectful. He went down on me, like it was his fantasy to go down on me. At first I thought, sure, why not? Then he kept at it and I actually came. I couldn't believe it. I don't know if I liked that—at all. It didn't feel right, to be honest. I was going to tell everyone at the Tea Party when Belle was asking us about our week, but I felt like I shouldn't tell them. It felt weird and like a betrayal of something if I told them. No, a betrayal that I came. Yes, that's it. I shouldn't have come, is what it feels like. And I shouldn't really let him do that again, maybe. Anyway he stayed for like four hours and I only charged him for two parties. I can't be doing that every time, so maybe Belle has a point.

 Anyway, I guess that's what changed, this guy doing that to me and making me come. It made me wary. Wary of him, maybe, or maybe more wary of everyone. It didn't soften me up, it made me sort of angry, if I'm really going to be honest. As if this is supposed to be enjoyable for me and he was going to make sure of it. Yeah, I think I'm angry. But it's my own *fault and I'm not going to let it happen again.*

I'm really tired and my shift is over and my body is tired but my brain won't shut off. Oh, and that guy who went down on me, he was telling me he would read a book with me. I'm reading Camus and I highly doubt a redneck will put that much effort into reading literature, but it was kind of nice he said he wanted to. Like we are starting some kind of real relationship or something. But that's what I do, and if the girlfriend experience for him is us reading the same book, hey, whatever, I'm enlightening some hick in Wells, Nevada. I guess he was all right. At least he wasn't like the asshole drunk after him who stayed limp even after I sucked him for a half an hour. Then I just hand-jobbed him limp until he came. He tipped me $60 and it took all of my willpower to not thank him profusely for the huge tip. I need sleep. More later. I will write more when I don't have this ache inside, thinking about Jacob. Just a year. If I could take a pain pill, I would. I'd see if it stopped the hurt. But sleep will. I'm over and out.

Wade decides to stop by and see Dude before he heads over to Mamacita's. He always tries to be available on New Year's Eve for Durward, so he's going to head over to Mamacita's early, see Sienna, then come back over to Dude's for the evening, when things turn bad. *If* things turn bad. He figures, why spend the whole of New Year's Eve drinking with Durward, and inevitably talking him down, when he can possibly spend a couple of hours with Sienna? Luther's is out because Cole and Cindy are going there and Wade cringes all the way down to his balls when he thinks of them showing up and what Gerry and Junior will say. He doesn't think Pete's in town anymore, or Cindy would lay low. She probably knows how he'd feel about the whole damn thing. Truth be told, Wade had kind of hoped he and Cole could spend some time together. But Cole and Cindy have been attached at the fucking hip since Christmas, much to Wade's irritation.

The next day is January 1st, and Wade feels the chill burning his ears as he crosses the street. It doesn't seem to truly turn cold until January. In November and December, the cold is muffled by fluffy clouds and white snow blankets, and there's the holiday cheer that warms up eyes and smiles and homes. Then January hits, and the cold is just cold, right to the bone, bleak and gray. The day is fast approaching and he doesn't know how it will feel and this bothers him: February 3rd. Ann will have been gone a year. He has a small sense of dread for that day and he's not sure why. Nothing to look forward to, only the month of February, when the snow drifts turn black and gray on the street, making rimy formations like complex, mottled stone, and spring seems an eternity away.

He knocks on Durward's door and Millie opens it. Wade wonders if she even goes home anymore.

"Hello Wade, how ya doin'? Come on in, Dude's just watchin' a show."

"Millie your bread was delicious. I got one piece before Cole scarfed the rest in one day."

"Oh, how is your boy?"

Wade steps in and Dude sits up, a scowl on his face as he shakes his head at the T.V.

"Cole's doin' fine, just fine. Happy New Years, Dude." Wade bounces on his toes a little, trying to warm up.

Durward's voice is a little loud. "Ain't it funny how tomorrow's just like today and it's a whole new thing, ain't it? A whole new thing."

Wade sees the bottle of Jack Daniels next to Dude, half gone, and he looks at Millie. "Startin' a little early, huh?"

Her face brightens in that artificial way, as if her smile is backlit by a neon sign. "Oh, we've been at it since about noon, so there's that…and so can I getcha some coffee? You got any plans for tonight?" He can see the worry on Millie's face as she looks at him with her gray eyes.

"No, no coffee, thanks. Just came to check on him, and, uh, see what's goin' on."

"Nothin's goin' on, I'm just waitin.' I ain't gonna stay up late anyways, right? We're gonna turn in early and forget this stupid holiday and go about our business. Goddamned leeches. Goddamned leeches just want money and more shit for their big houses…"

Durward picks up his glass and the ice clinks as he takes a swig.

Wade looks at Millie. "Maybe some coffee, Millie. Lemme help ya."

"She don't need help, what're you talkin' about? She makes the best god damned coffee I ever had, Millie does. Dontcha Millie?" Durward starts to mumble to himself as Wade follows her into the kitchen. She turns to him, creases covering every part of her face, her mouth a tight-lipped line. She doesn't say anything, but her face seems to say it all. Wade puts a hand on her small shoulder.

"Listen, Millie, tonight's a rough night for him. He drinks himself silly every year since I known him. Them firecrackers goin' off, they get to him. So he hits the bottle. Sometimes he sleeps through, sometimes he don't. But I was plannin' on comin' over later on, before it all started, you know. What I'm sayin' is, I can help is all."

"Well I been tryin' to feed him and he don't want much of anythin' so I worry. I don't know what to do." She brings her fingertips to her mouth and glances toward the front room.

"You just keep feedin' him and get him to drink some water. Try findin' some good T.V. to watch or somethin'. You gotta distract him is all."

"But what if he hears those firecrackers tonight? What do I do?"

"I'll be over before then, all right? I'll be here and we'll do it together."

Her hand reaches up and he notices how much it quakes. She cups his cheek and pats. "You're a good friend to him, Wade. A good neighbor."

Wade nods and pats her bony shoulder again, leaving her in the kitchen to make something enticing for Durward to eat.

"Dude, how's it goin'?" He sits by him on the couch and looks into the old man's watery blue eyes, heavy-lidded with age, skin, and probably drink.

"You see them? They got them knives that cut through anything. I won some of them knives, not those, but other ones and they don't cut worth anythin'. But when Ed brings me that check, I'm gonna get me some of them knives that cut through all of those things they got on the T.V. there. See that? A rubber tire, a can, not just soda pop but a real can…"

"Dude, I've gotta go, but I'll come back. You eat what Millie brings ya, okay? I mean it. You need to eat."

"Yeah, all right. All right then, you take care. An' you tell Ann hello."

Dude stares at the T.V. and Wade wants to scurry out as fast as he can so Dude doesn't realize his blunder. Hearing Ann's name strums a strange chord in him as he realizes he has no one to say 'hello' to anymore. No one to return and report to. No one to pass on well-wishes and "feel-betters" to. It's just him, and people can say those things to his face and then forget about him as soon as he's gone.

He wonders if Sienna forgot about him as soon as he'd gone. He wonders if she's gone. In his gut he thinks she is because no one could be lucky like that all in one week. No, she isn't at Mamacita's, but he gets in his truck and starts it just the same. He can tell Belle to tell Sienna 'hello' for him, and then she'll know she hadn't been forgotten.

The parking lot is so crowded at Mamacita's he almost turns around. Even if Sienna is there, would he have to wait for her? How does it all work? Feeling self-conscious, he parks in the second row and walks a little south to see how many trucks are in the back. Two, and one with just a cab. He rings the doorbell, a frosted-mist breath shooting out of him.

The door opens and he expects to hear the noise of a crowd, but all he hears is music. The manager smiles at him.

"Welcome, c'mon in."

"It's, uh..." her name is on the tip of his tongue "...Nancy?"

"Leslie."

"Right! Right, I'm Wade."

"Wade, how ya doin'? Happy New Years. We're hoppin' already tonight, but you can have a beer while you wait."

Wade walks into the bar and two men are at the two tables. One guy is talking to two girls at once. He's a little older than Wade, dressed in a suit. He looks like he could buy the place. Like he's from a big city. He's with two younger girls Wade doesn't know and he breathes out a sigh of relief. The other girl he'd seen in the lineup the week before...the long blond hair, older...what was her name?

Bev knocks on the bar and Wade's attention snaps to her. Her eyes are bright and friendly, even though her mouth doesn't smile. "Sorry, what can I getcha? You want that bloody beer again?"

"Yeah, heavy on the blood. I gotta drive in a while."

"You ain't stayin' for the New Year? We got balloons an' streamers an' free champagne—"

"Nah, I got somewhere to be by midnight, but I came early—hey, is Sienna workin' tonight?"

"Um, lemme ask—I ain't seen her but I just got here at four. Hold on." Bev disappears down the hall and Wade twists around as the guy at the table with the blond gets up and shakes her hand, then walks out into the hall toward the front door. The blond sees him and smiles.

"Hey, I remember you. How are you?" She slides off of her stool and walks toward him, a long sweater covering her. Her legs are trim, her tits huge, even though she's very petite.

"Doin' fine. How are you?"

"I'm doing okay—it's been a hell of a day. Busy. So you here for the lineup? Because I can save you the trouble." She starts massaging his shoulders, speaking quietly in his ear.

"No, I mean...I was waitin'..."

Shit, he hadn't seen this coming. How does he tell her he's only here for Sienna? Do they take that personally? And what the fuck is her name?

"Well, I can keep you company." She sits down next to him and rubs her hand up his leg. He feels his body respond and for a moment, being in that place, he feels like it's a candy store and he wants to try each flavor of lollipop. "You remember me don't you?" She says this with a little pout on her full lips.

"I remember you, yeah, just...your name, I can't remember—"

"Amy...as in take aim and shoot." Her hand goes all the way up to his crotch and his full cock suddenly becomes a hard cock, and he starts thinking about the money. He has the money. Then he thinks about Sienna and her kid and how his money seems to be tied up in going to her, all to her, and then the blond's hand seems all wrong there, kneading him and grabbing him and so he takes it and moves it back down his leg. The doorbell rings, and he glances to the side as Leslie appears from the hall and walks toward the door. The barkeep still isn't back. Voices converge in the hall then Leslie appears with two Hispanic men in ball caps and parkas. He turns his attention back to the woman next to him.

"So, I'm, uh, readin' this book called *The Stranger*, and it's about this guy who just seems to go with the flow, you know? He just lets shit happen to him and nothing really fazes him all that much and so one day he just kills this Arab guy on a beach, and—"

Amy presses her full, hard breasts into his arm and murmurs in his ear. "I don't read a lot because I like to fuck. I did my reading in school, so now all I want is sex. I can't get enough. Do you ever feel that way? Because I think we can make each other feel good." Her lips are on his ear, her tongue grazing his lobe. He closes his eyes for a minute, and when he opens them, Bev is back.

"Yeah, she ain't here. She left yesterday. She'll be back in a couple weeks. Usually gets here on Thursdays. We're gonna be doin' the lineup soon if you wanna hang on."

"Thanks," Wade awakens from the slight reverie of the blond's words and he looks at her, "but I was comin' to see someone else, sorry."

Amy puts her finger under Wade's chin and turns his head toward her, and he hates it. He absolutely hates that she did it. He'd seen women do it in a million movies, but he'd never had a woman do it to him before… and he hates it.

"Well, she isn't here, but I'm here. And I could really use some company. You're from around here, aren't you?"

"Yeah, I'm what you'd call a local guy, I guess." He tells himself to simmer down and be polite, but he's planning his escape.

Her hand still moves up and down his thigh, uncomfortably high up, he realizes, and he's not sure how to tell her because it seems like he already had. "So tell me your name again, sweetie."

"Wade."

"What do you do for work, Wade?"

"I'm retired, took an early retirement. I got these fingers here and they don't move. No one can figure out why."

She looks down at his fingers and seems to shrink away from them a little, as if they are contaminated.

"Well, what did you used to do then?"

"I sold life insurance. All my life, pretty much."

"So what's retirement like? What do you do all day?"

What does he do? He thinks to himself. He has a routine, and nothing about his routine can be rendered to her because she doesn't care and he feels that. She's fishing for clues but he doesn't know what kind of information she wants. She's in the Land of Womenspeak and he wants to catch the first coach out.

"I read, " he says, finally. "I'm a reader." He thinks of Sienna, driving home to her little boy, listening to the book he's reading, how they will talk about it, how she will tell him the hidden meaning between each line that he knows he just isn't getting. He thinks of her and his body warms, his thoughts warm and all he wants is for two weeks to scream by in blazing speed so he can see her again.

He puts his money on the bar. "I've gotta go, I'm meetin' with friends in a little while. It was nice talking to you…" Oh fuck, what is her name again?

"Amy," her lids half close as she says it. "I'm *Amy*."

"Right. I knew that. See you around, then."

He walks out into the hall and approaches the front door. He had thought that if Sienna wasn't there he would be much more disappointed. He thought it would ruin his night. But for some reason, it doesn't. He's happy she's home on New Year's Eve with her family and her son. He's happy he's reading that book. His chest feels light and nothing, not even the oppressive cold air seems to take him down. He realizes he hasn't felt like that in a long, long time.

It is still early yet, so Wade goes home and decides to extend the closeness he feels to Sienna by reading their book. The book isn't long—which he liked when he got it--and now he is perilously close to finishing. As he reads, he is stunned by what captures him. He'd never had this happen to him before and the fact that it does makes him yearn, deep inside his chest, like a giant bog of feeling rests inside of him and it's sucking in all of his other feelings, even his organs, deep into it. Tears had filled his eyes and one or two escape down his cheeks. He'd never had a book make him cry.

He re-reads the paragraph again, out loud.

"*As if that blind rage had washed me clean, rid me of hope; for the first time, in that night alive with signs and stars, I opened myself up to the gentle indifference of the world. Finding it so much like myself—like a brother, really—I felt that I had been happy, and that I was happy again. For everything to be consummated, for me to feel less alone, I had only to wish that there be a large crowd of spectators the day of my execution and that they greet me with cries of hate.*'" Wade exhales. "Jesus."

Those words—"the gentle indifference of the world"— those words pierce him and he can't explain the surge of emotion inside, only the desperate need to share it. But the world and everyone in it is indifferent, and the only person who isn't…is *her*.

No, he isn't foolish enough, stupid enough to think Sienna spends one moment of her time thinking about him. Of course not. But he knows real, he knows genuine. Something about her is genuine and he can't place his finger on what that is, but he knows that the other two he had met, Lana and—what was her *name*?—they were not, or at least not in the same way.

He glances at the wall clock in the kitchen. Twenty minutes until midnight. He doesn't want to go back out into the cold, but he'd promised Millie. And in a way, it's sort of a tradition. He wonders if Millie being there will make a difference to Durward, or if he'll blank out just the same.

He grabs his gray and orange parka and pulls a hat down around his ears. The chill wind takes his breath away as the snow and ice crunch under his feet.

He raps on Durward's door and Millie opens it, eyes wide.

"How's he doin'?"

"Well, he's sleeping now. I just hope nothin' wakes him."

"Okay, well, I can stick around, wait for the new year, then you can head to bed, too. You look tired."

"Oh, Wade Kendall, don't you know you can't say that to a woman?"

"What'd I say?"

"'You look tired.' That's code for 'you look like hell.'" She laughs. "Lemme getcha a drink."

"Huh. Is that right? I didn't mean—"

"Oh, look, I'm seventy-eight. If I don't look tired and at least a *little* like hell, then somethin's wrong, ain't it? Don't you worry, I was teasin' ya. How 'bout a beer?"

"Beer'd be great." Did Millie just teach him Womenspeak? Was she to be his guide in that strange and treacherous land? She comes shuffling back in and it's then he sees her bony ankles under her full quilted housecoat. Skin mottled, blue veins, her feet in old white slippers—he looks back up at her without her makeup and sees where he is headed. He sees it in her, and the indifferent world comes back to him, the fact that the world won't take pity on any one person, but treats each person equally and without remorse. He understands now why Meursault, the main character in the book, said what he'd said. No matter how we feel about each other, we're in this shit hole together, and so finally, we're not alone. He wants to tell Millie about this insight. But the one he really wants to tell won't be back for two weeks.

"Thanks, Millie. I think it's great you're here 'n' all. I mean with Dude. What I mean is...how are things? I mean..."

She laughs again, the crinkles around her eyes not hiding the gray of them, her teeth the color of the outer skin of an egg yolk, straight and strangely shiny. "Are you askin' me a personal question, dear?"

"Oh no, I just—"

"Look," she places her hand on Wade's knee, and her grip is strong, even though he can see the prominent veins and tendons, the seemingly stick-like frailty, "I know you worry about me, Wade, don't you think I don't know. And the ladies at church, those hens all clucking 'bout me livin' in sin...lemme tell you. I'm livin' *life*, Wade. That's what I'm doin'."

"Well I'm glad for you. And for Dude. He just, you know, should treat you right is all."

"Oh!" She exclaims, slapping his knee again, and Wade can see the flirtatious girl in her gestures and animation on her face. "He's right and decent to me. You remember my late husband, dontcha?"

"Sure, Walt. It's been...how long?"

"Eleven years since he passed. I tell you somethin' 'bout him. He kept to himself, Walt did. Especially around other people, ya see. But at home, he was not a good man, Wade. He didn't let me outta his sight, not for one minute. Nothin' I did was good enough for him."

"I'm sorry to hear that, Millie, I-I didn't know."

"'Course not. You don't talk about your relations with people. Especially relations with your husband. Oh, he kept me right on down in the dirt, Wade. Mean as can be."

Wade looks into her bright eyes and wonders how she had come out of such a thing with the vibrancy he sees before him.

"But," she continued, "I had somethin' he didn't. You know what that was?"

Wade shook his head.

"I had a choice, Wade. *A choice.* See, Walt was the way he was, but me? I got to choose whether or not I'd buy all that garbage he tried to sell to me. I could buy it, or I could throw it out with yesterday's trash. So that's what I did. When he passed, it was like a dark curtain was lifted from my life. I chose to survive, and now, look at me. I'm happy, and I get to be with Dude, and he lets me be who I am. He loves everything I do. I am *blessed*. I want to tell those ladies at church 'bout all this, Wade, but no one could understand, ya see. No one would understand how the sin was my marriage, 'cause I let myself get beat up every day. Not physical, just in my mind, he'd be mean with his words, ya see. And the Lord saved me by givin' me that choice every day."

"Jesus. You really don't know about people, do ya." Wade shook his head. "I knew that you an' him kept to yourselves, but I didn't know… anythin' else. I guess you just don't know."

"When I heard your Annie was sick, I wanted to do so much more to help, Wade. But I was caught, ya see. Under his thumb. Had to be there for him every minute, every day. He was overbearin' and just--"

"You don't need to feel bad about anything, Millie."

"Well, I'm sorry for you anyway, Wade. I hope you find someone like I found Dude."

"Does Dude talk to you about his, uh…well, the things he thinks? Like how he thinks he's friends with Ed McMahon and all that?"

"Yes he does and you know what? That's just fine by me. We all need to feel special in this world, Wade, an' that's how Dude feels special. So I let him have that. Who am I to take that away? And anyway, I find it a little endearing."

Wade smiles. "It is pretty funny."

She sighs. "We all tell ourselves stories, dear. Some are more fantastic than others, but we all tell stories to ourselves. I bet you tell 'em just like I tell 'em just like Dude. His are just strange to us 'cause they ain't ours."

"I guess you're right." Wade thinks of the story he tells himself about Sienna and he doesn't want to know how fantastic it is. And he's pretty sure everyone's story is different, even if they share it. It's something that makes everyone separate, but at the same time, it makes everyone the same. That's probably the other thing Meursault figured out. The story he told is what separated him, but then they all had their separateness in common. But Wade's pretty sure that if he tells the story about him and Sienna to anyone else, they'd look at him like he'd said he was a friend of Ed McMahon.

Both of them freeze as they hear pops outside. Wade looks at his watch: midnight. He stands and Millie follows him into the bedroom. The light from the hallway illuminates Dude's face as he lies on his back, mouth open in a soundless snore. The pops and booms outside get louder and Wade braces for Dude to wake up, look around wildly, call out. But he stays completely peaceful except for his brow furrowing a little, as if he dreams of his fantastical life, and how important a man he is in it.

9

Wade sees it, but he can't believe it.

Cole parks the bike in front of the house and walks with a swagger that he'd had before prison. He hadn't seen hide nor hair of the boy since a brief interlude around New Year's and a week after that, but only in passing as Cole bolted from the house with a packed bag.

He walks in the front door and Wade tries to look curious rather than outright suspicious. Where in the hell did Cole get the money for a motorcycle? And where the hell has he been?

"Hey, Pop, didja see her?"

"If by 'her' you mean the bike, then yeah, I saw it. When did you get it?"

"Couple days ago. Saw it in an ad. Don't worry, I had the guys at Otto's look at it before I bought her. She's sweet, huh?"

"Cole...are you workin' someplace I don't know about?"

He averts his eyes and heads into the kitchen. "No, I been doin' some fixin' up at Cindy's place. Her uncle's a shit landlord if you ask me. Everything was broke over there."

Wade stands and walks to the edge of the kitchen. "You been gone since Christmas—"

"Not since Christmas, that's—"

"Point is, what, you stayin' there now? What the hell, Cole? She's, what, supportin' you while you—"

"Hey, it ain't like that." Cole turns and points his finger at him, a piece of bread squishing in his mouth as he chews. "I'm helpin' her out."

"Pete know you're 'helpin'' her out over there? 'Cause he don't seem too keen on the whole thing, is what I'm sayin'."

"She don't live there free, Dad. She pays rent. She can have whoever she wants over. Pete can go fuck himself, he's got a problem with me."

Wade throws his hands up, "Fine, but can you see past the tip of your dick? Jesus, how many things you gonna fix before she figures out she's carryin' your ass? I asked you to live *here*, so—"

"—so you can dictate to me what I'm gonna do, where I'm gonna work—no, I get what you mean, Dad."

Cole has switched to "Dad" which means he's angry. Funny; the only name Milt has for him is "Dad."

"You tellin' me you don't plan on workin'? 'Cause that's what I'm hearin' from you."

"I got plans." Cole stuffs another piece of bread in his mouth and Wade feels his irritation growing by the second. He shuts his eyes tight, and then opens them and tries to access the part of himself that knows Cole's goodness, his kind heart.

"Well, that sounds real good, then, Cole. I'm happy for ya. You, uh, wanna tell me what your plans are? I mean, bounce 'em off me?"

"You mean clear it with you? 'Cause we both know that's what you mean."

"Naw, it ain't like that. You're a grown man, been through a lot. I trust you got it figured out. I just wanna hear about it."

Cole's face changes to an impish smile, and he's back to his old self, the anger melted away like snow off a warm window. "Okay…ready? *Storage units.*"

Wade keeps his gaze as even as possible while his brain screeches to a halt. "Storage units, ya say?"

"Yep." Cole smiles a broad smile. "Got a buddy in Elko with a franchise. *Consolidated Self-Storage.* Gonna open up storage units here. I don't gotta do nothin' but collect the rent checks, Pop. It's perfect. There ain't no storage here in Wells, and all them truckers who live here an' wanna rent out their places, they can rent a unit and store with me."

"Uh, okay then. Sure. I mean, how do you build 'em, or do they ship 'em in, and what's the cost to you up-front and all?"

Cole waves his hand. "I'm meetin' with him next week and he'll tell me all about that. He's already got customers for me—people here in Wells who have to drive to Elko for their stuff. Now they can move it here to my place."

"But he'll tell you the out-of-pocket cost n' all right? 'Cause that's usually a lot, Cole, I mean, you know."

"I told you, I got some money. And anyhow, I got a partner."

"A partner? Who?"

Cole shrugs. "Cindy. She'll be in charge of rentin' the units, gettin' their keys to 'em and the books an' all that shit I can't do."

A car is on the train tracks in Wade's head. The warning lights are flashing, the train's horn is blaring, the arm stopping traffic comes down...

"You can't possibly think you can go into business with her, Cole! You don't even know her, first off, second—"

"I know her better'n you do and she's got cash saved up, too. Between us, we're gonna be fine."

"Holy shit, I can't—I can't believe you're gonna invest everythin' you got—Cole, look at me. How many people you think need storage in this town? Enough to support you *and* Cindy? Are you nuts?"

Cole shakes his head. "See? I knew you'd do this. I knew it. You just can't stand that I'm different than you, different than Milt. I take risks, Dad! And this time it's gonna work!"

"Like all them other *risks* you took that I had to bail your ass out of, that it? Jesus, how can you be almost thirty and not learned a *damn thing*!"

"That was then, this is now. You live in the past, Dad. That's your whole problem, right there. The present is a gift, that's what Cindy says. A *gift*. An' I'm gonna open it and if you can't support me then fine, but keep your negative shit outta my way."

"'A gift.' Jesus. You're going to invest everything you got based on a sayin' she found on a fucking *coffee mug?*"

"I'm outta here. I'm sorry you can't be more supportive, but I don't need all your negativity. And by the way, I'll be clearin' out my stuff. Cindy wants me to move in."

WADE

Wade had argued with Cole in his head long into the evening. He knew there was no way of saving the boy from himself. His rage is split, but the lion's share is going toward Cindy, as if she should know better given her age. Wade doesn't trust her, it's as simple as that. The town's pickings of women are sparse and Wade factors that in as well. He finally settled down and decided he'd dive into the book again. It took his mind from Cole and Cindy and put it in an energetic line to Sienna, and he liked that place a lot better.

On the second read, Wade felt like he'd picked up so much more. Seeing the book's meaning from the get-go gave him different lenses through which he could observe it, lenses that caught the spaces between the lettering, each punctuation mark, the margins, the way the sentences were put together. He even cried again at the end, but less out of wonder and more out of understanding the beauty of the meaning he'd grasped.

He's glad he re-read it to freshen it up in his mind before he sees Sienna tonight. They said she'd be in, and he's bouncing off of his four walls thinking about it. He finds himself picturing Sienna there, at his house. What would she see?

The painting on the wall by Ann's great-uncle, a man who'd made a meager living at landscapes, and it is an original, done in blues, Ann's favorite color. The worn couch, in peach, blues, tans, with dark brown wood on the arms. A couple of matching blue-velvet arm chairs. The miniature grandfather clock on the wall. The cross-stitch in a frame with the lyrics to "You've Got a Friend" by Carole King, although Ann liked the James Taylor version better. An old stereo complete with turntable. A console TV, and on top of it, a new, smaller flat-screen, a black, modern blot on the rest of the room.

He stops himself with hands to either side of his skull.

She will never be there. She will never set foot in his house because that's not who she is. A part of him wonders if going to see her is the right thing to do at all—if he should walk away from that place and never set foot back. He wonders if his feelings and vow are of the same intensity as a crack addict who swears upon his loved one's grave he will never touch a pipe again, vowing, promising, before buckling and sinking into the craving for one last hit.

He walks into Ann's room, since he'd never had a chance to clear out Cole and Milt's old room and it's housing storage Wade just hasn't gotten to yet. Cole had left the bed unmade and Wade can only guess, the sheets unwashed. He pulls the pristine white bedspread up along with the sheet and wool blanket, fluffing the pillows. He checks his hands for dirt and remembers what Ann had said when she'd moved into the room.

I don't see why you gotta move in here.

I told you why, Wade. And for the love of Pete, get offa the bedspread! You're dirty!

He remembers standing, looking down at the white cover, thinking that of course he was dirty. He had no business sitting on that white, clean spread. Maybe he had no business touching her because his thoughts were always dirty, always lustful, always wanting.

He finishes the bed, deciding that he can wait to wash the sheets. He stares at it, then with the petulance of a child, he sits on the white coverlet. His mind wanders.

And this is his room…

What was Sienna's boy's name? He makes one up.

…Tim's room, right here. Right across the hall from us. See that? Tim's got his own room and you can be with him here all day, an' take him to his first day of school…

The hen house, Sienna, those aren't his problems at all. His own mind, that's the problem. He's letting it carry him away into the most foolish places he could let it go off to.

"One, you're too old," he says. "Two, you ain't rich, and everyone knows that if a girl that age is gonna shack up with a guy my age, he'd be rich. Even though she ain't like that."

He thinks about her eyebrows, how perfectly arched they are. It isn't impossible, is it? For a woman to want to be loved and for that to be enough? He isn't hurting, he has plenty to live on, if he's honest. Hell, he'd even go get another job, work somewhere while she stays home and takes care of the boy. He'd have all this time to be with him, too, all this time to teach him right, help him. With Wade's help, he'd have Cole's heart and

Milt's drive to succeed. Wade would do it right.

He brings his hands up to his head again and squeezes the sides of it. Letting them drop, he looks at his right hand, his three fingers. Stares at them hard. He wills them to move, concentrating. Shaking his hand, he feels the fingers smack against each other. Using his left hand, he takes each immobile finger and moves it, stretches it, smacks it. He pulls his index finger as far back as it will go.

He shakes his head.

They don't work.

No matter what he does, nothing he wants will work.

He felt like five p.m. was a decent time to show, so he stands outside Lil' Mamacita's, trying not to allow a second ring of the doorbell possess him. It had been almost two minutes. Finally, he rings again.

The door opens and a breathless Leslie smiles at him.

"Hi, welcome.! Nice to see you again, come on in." She holds the door open and Wade, book in hand, walks into the warmth of the hallway.

"Is Sienna here?" he blurts, all hopes of being sly, cool, and detached melting to the floor.

"She is. Didja come here to see her tonight, or do you want the lineup?"

"I'd uh, well, if she's available, sure. It's 'cause I read this book 'n' all and I…well—" *shut up, shut up shut up!*

Leslie laughs and pats his arm. "You're fine, I think she's finally ready—lordy, shift change is hell 'round here. Bev'll getcha a drink."

Wade thanks her and sits at the bar, where a bloody beer is already sitting on a napkin. He's nervous, so he feels chatty.

"How you doin' this evenin'?" He looks at Bev as she counts cash in the drawer.

"I'm thankin' the Lord this week's almost over, is what I'm doin'."

"Oh, sorry to hear. Bad week then, huh?"

Bev slams the drawer shut and he jumps in his seat a little at the sudden violence of it. She walks over to him and leans over the bar, arms crossed, staring at him. "My kid got a DUI this week. Had to bail his ass out an' now he ain't got no job cause he was drivin' deliveries, an' I don't know what he's gonna do, but you know what I tell him? I tell him it's his own dang fault, and when he left home, that wasn't no revolvin' door I have, an' so he better figure somethin' out *quick*."

Her lips purse, all twisted up, while her eyes look straight into his, as wide as full moons. Wade is flattered she's taken him into her confidence, like maybe she sees he's not some unfeeling, uncaring prick, but a person. A real, live person.

"My son has them same troubles. It's almost like you worry more 'bout 'em as they get older and you should be worryin' less, but they keep on fuckin'—"

"Watch the cursin'," she holds up her finger. She grabs a jar out from under the bar. It says "Curse Jar" on it and it's filled half-full with dollar bills.

"Oh, right, sorry. I'm real sorry."

"It's all right. This is just a warnin'. After, it's a dollar a word. Now, you was sayin'."

"Uh, right I was sayin' that they keep on screwin' up and you never get a good night's sleep. Like when they was infants, only ten times worse 'cause the fu—uh, screw-ups are bigger."

She shakes her head. "I don't get it." Standing up again, she looks around, as if trying to find a person to land her spectacular scowl on, and finally, she returns it to him, leaning back over. "I'm an old drunk," she says, voice quieter. "You think he'd a learned somethin' from watchin' me his whole dang life. I tell him. I tell him he's a dang fool, walkin' in my footsteps. Drink's poison for me, an' it is for him, but he don't stop."

"You don't drink an' you're the bartender?"

"Yep." She moves away from him.

"Well ain't that...hard to do an' all?"

She walks back to him, "Honey, I get guys in here every night remind me why I don't drink no more. Every night. It's God's grace. He shows me the worst parts of myself every night." She taps the side of her head, something he's noticed she does a lot, and she nods. Wade nods with her. He vows he will never be one of Bev's reminders, ever.

"Well, look who's here." At her voice, Wade turns and his whole body leaps to attention. Sienna walks out in a white mini-dress with colored hearts on it and high heels. He is so happy to see her, he feels his whole face flush. She wraps her arms around him and he hugs her back, feeling the fullness of her breasts against his chest, and quickly, the fullness in his jeans.

She gasps a small gasp of surprise and picks up the book. "You got it! Did you read it?"

"Twice," he says, smiling at her. Suddenly he's aware of his crooked teeth, teeth that are too small, and he is self-conscious as her bright, white smile and full lips radiate. She reads the back cover, as if she'd never read it before. "Yeah, I toldja I would. An' so…I did." All he wants is to be alone with her. He feels Bev's eyes on him, and wonders if she can see right through him to his silly heart.

"And?" Sienna scoots up onto the bar stool next to him. "What did you think?" She does the little whisper-in-his-ear thing and he breaks out in chills.

Her face is so young. He reaches up and grabs hold of the front of his neck, as if in thought, but he's assessing the skin hanging down. He'd lost some weight, had been doing his sit-ups, but he's nowhere near a young man and for some reason, every physical flaw he has is under a glaring, white light in his mind, when usually, he never takes much stock of how he looks at all.

He clears his throat. All of the intellectual answers, the insights, the god damned *epiphanies* he 'd had exit his skull in a rush. "I-I loved it. I mean it, I really loved it. It…well, to tell you the truth, it changed the way I look at things. A lot. An' that's somethin' when you're a guy my age." He smiles, but keeps his lips over his teeth.

Sienna nods her head. "That's the mark of a good book, in my opinion. Something that leaves its mark."

He wants to tell her she had left her mark, and that's the reason, more than anything, why he'd never be the same. But he knows this is foolish talk. He finally remembers. "I, uh, marked some things…" he takes the book from her and flips through the pages, looking for his notes. The second read-through he'd marked it up a lot more, finding similar things that happened in the story, but in different ways. He had been proud of himself that he could see the patterns, the themes of it. He'd felt like he could still learn, and that had pleased him.

"See here, when his girl, Maria, when she asks him if he loves her, an' he just tells her the truth, see, but that ain't what society wants, an' it ain't what *she* wants. No matter how we feel, everyone wants us to act the same. He doesn't love her, so he tells her, an' that's a mistake. Sort of." He knows it doesn't come out right, so he struggles to say it another way, but Sienna takes his hand.

"Right. I mean, that's really the gist of the whole book right there. You know, the individual versus society and expectation. He's just himself and society can't handle that."

"Wow, you're a lot smarter about it than me, I guess."

"Well, you know, I took a class and we read this. So I get a lot of it because the teacher pointed out a lot of the themes. So it's not like I'm some expert." She shrugs and then her smile brightens. Wade doesn't want her to see the look in his eyes, which he's sure conveys every foolish thought he'd had about her in the last two weeks.

"Yeah," Wade says, "if school was interestin' to me, well had it been back then, I would've liked to learn how to read better, I guess. See, what I liked best was that even though he's royally fu—uh, screwed at the end, you know, he still finds hope in the 'indifferent world.' I mean, he finally doesn't feel alone."

Sienna smiles, looking into his eyes. "You really read it. I can't believe it."

Wade's face burns and he picks up his beer and drinks. "I was wonderin' if we could…I mean, be, you know…alone."

Sienna smiles. "Come on back."

Her room smells of her perfume, as if she'd spritzed it on more than just her neck. He suddenly hates the fullness in his pants, worries she'll see it and think him an animal, a dirty animal who only sees her as one thing, when he sees her as so much more.

It had been a vicious cycle, when Ann was alive. The more she wouldn't do it, the more he'd wanted her, the more she hated him for wanting her, the more they didn't do it…she had called him names, like "dirty old goat," and "animal," and "beast." She would sometimes say them in fun. Other times, she'd say them with an almost matter-of-fact concern, as if something was keenly wrong with him, like he needed to get checked by a professional. It had always left him feeling like a leering pervert. It turned his desire into a cold, damp rag.

Sienna smiles and turns around after she closes the door. She looks at him expectantly.

Wade jumps to life. "Oh, sorry, this is, this is...here..." he pulls out his wallet and pulls out six hundred dollar bills. He had done the math at home and realized that the eight thousand dollars in his savings would not last long at this rate. The thought had panicked him, so he vowed to not be greedy, to only go for one time. But this is a special occasion, isn't it? His second time back to see her? The book?

"You want to pay for two already?" She gives him a *you-should-know-better* look.

"Yeah, if that's okay."

"Okay, well only give me five, then. The tip comes after, remember? Always after." He hands her the five hundred and she smiles and gives him a peck on the cheek. "Be right back. There's your robe."

She leaves and he undresses quickly, her words in his head. *Your robe.* Not *the* robe, not *a* robe: *your robe.* Like it's his and his only. He decides to believe that's exactly what she'd meant.

He wants to open every drawer she has and look through each item, know the story behind every one, but he knows how inappropriate that would be. He doesn't want to invade her privacy. He just wants to know every single thing about her.

He sits on the bed, but he can't shake the word from his head, no matter how hard he tries: *animal.* Even though his erection has gone down: *animal.* Even though he wants more from her than sex. *Animal.* His breath quickens as he clenches his eyes shut and tries to superimpose her face onto the voice, Sienna's sweet face, but it can't quiet the voice, the voice of a thousand refusals, a thousand scowls and shaking heads, a thousand cold nights in a cold bed and eyes unwilling to meet his for fear something meaningful would pass, that he would get the wrong idea, and then it would surface: *animal.* Keeping her mouth firmly shut when he kissed her, lest he get excited. *Animal.*

The door opens and Sienna walks in, almost in a bashful way, and she closes the door behind her. "Now for the fun part, right?" She gestures over to the dresser.

"Oh, we gotta do that every time, huh?"

"Yeah," she says, apologetically, wincing a little.

"I came back here once to see you, but you'd gone back home, so I left. Ain't been...well I ain't been back since."

"Oh, I believe you, but some guys, they go between this house and Mona's and they travel, you know. We just have to be careful." She kneels in front of him and wipes him down. "See? All done."

The mandatory exam of his dick and balls leaves him feeling even further away than he already feels. Even looking at her suddenly feels like a violation, like he'd opened every drawer, rifled through her intimate things.

She still has the shy demeanor, but she slips off the straps of her dress and peels it down to her waist. He steps closer to her and places his hands over her breasts. As if a battery cable is attached to his nuts, he jumps a little and moves his hands away. He hadn't even noticed it before: he still wears his wedding ring. Jesus, how could he still wear it?

"What's wrong?" She moves back over to him and wraps her arms around his neck. Leaning into him, she kisses him and he lets her tongue enter his mouth, even though his mouth feels like an arid, old hut: no life, no moisture, only filth and debris. When she reaches down to feel him, he is limp and shriveled, which causes him to back away from her kiss.

"I'm sorry," he says. The heat from earlier fills his face, only for completely opposite reasons. Along with this heat comes an awful, aching, gut-punch feeling that he can't shake. She smiles and puts her hand on his face.

"It's okay. Let's lie down, okay? Let's just do that."

She removes the rest of her dress and flicks off her shoes. Wade remains motionless, so she slips the already-untied robe off of his shoulders and pulls him by the hand to the bed.

"There, see? All better." He lies on his back and she is under his shoulder, her leg across his hip and lower stomach. "Wade, what's the best book you've ever read?"

He stares at the ceiling, a strange detachment from his own body making him feel as though he floats up from the bed.

"I, uh, well I read a book to my wife when she was sick an' it was pretty good." His voice sounds like someone else's, too. He wants to tell her that her book, *their* book is the best book, but nothing authentic can travel past his lips. "It was this book about some guy murderin' people in this big hotel or somethin', an' the hotel was abandoned, see, so these people were like urban explorers, an' there was this gang of guys…never mind. It was suspenseful is all."

As he speaks, her hand caresses his chest, his stomach, and every so often, she checks his dick for life. But there is no life.

"Sounds scary," she says. "The book."

He closes his eyes, closes them tight, and takes a leap that goes against every instinct he has. "I came here to be with you. And I didn't want you thinkin' I only wanted one thing from you, 'cause I don't. An' it fucked me up. I mean *screwed* me up."

"You can curse in here, it's okay." She turns on her stomach and looks at him; he feels her eyes on him but all he can do is look at the ceiling. "Okay, so I'm going to ask you a question, and I want you to be totally honest with me. No matter what it is, I'll be okay with it, as long as it's the truth. Okay, Wade?"

He tears his gaze from the ceiling and looks into her brown eyes. "Yeah, I can do that, I guess."

"I will do anything you want. But I need to know. What is it you want from me? I can get your mind off of what's stressing you out in a lot of ways, trust me. We can just lie here and talk. You could tell me a story. I could tell you a story. All you have to do is tell me what you want from me." She kisses his chest and lays her head down on it.

Wade bites his lip. He feels tears forming in his eyes and the heat returns to his face because men don't cry in the arms of beautiful young women, and especially beautiful *naked* young women, yet the tears spill out, down his cheekbones to his temples and into his ears.

He can't even answer her question. How could he?

What do you want from me?

How could he tell her he wants everything?

1/14/~~14~~ 15

January is half over and I'm still getting used to the fact that it's a new year. I've been here 5 months next week. Sometimes it feels like I've been here a week, and other times like I've been here forever and a day. I've got to admit the money is good, and it might be worth just staying until I'm really cushioned. But it's not worth it, I know, because I'm afraid I'll get burned out. There are some days when I feel like I'm already there. I've got to focus on getting out of debt and getting back on track. I miss school. Three semesters away. I've got to focus. I called today and Jacob sounded better but tired. I hated leaving him—he was sick with a bad cold. I know Jess is doing her best, but he needs his mom. That's why I can't stay here long term. And I can't let it eat me up, like Jessica said. I've just been back here 2 days and I already wish it was over and I was driving back home.

So I'm writing this to record what happens here, with me, with customers, with the other workers, even, so I can do what I want to do. So here goes.

Today was the Tea Party, which is Belle's term for our house meeting. Belle asked us about our "whys" as in why we are doing what we're doing. Everyone said "money" all at once, big surprise, but then Belle said she wanted to hear from each one of us. Amy started, and she said she wanted freedom and to feel powerful and Belle really liked that. I only write about it because I don't see Amy as all that powerful. She seems like she's always working an angle and I have a hard time trusting her. I don't think I'm alone, either. Lana seemed like she was the most up front when she said it was really about giving her family the type of life she wants for them. Her husband earns pretty good money and so she doesn't have to do this. But because she does, they have a cabin, a boat, a motor home, and she said it actually helps her and her husband's sex life, so good for her, I guess. That's not a typical guy if he can handle her being a sex worker and still be married. When Belle got to Tamarind, she wouldn't say anything. She seemed angry, and that's how she always seems to me. Angry at Belle, angry at us, angry at the customers. I think she hates that they pick her because she's Asian. I don't know, it's just something I feel. There are guys out there who have this Asian thing and you can always tell because they come just for her, they ask for her specifically. Some guys will outright ask if there are any Asian girls here. I guess if a guy asked if there were any

Latina girls here, I wouldn't feel especially bad about that. Even though I'm only half, it doesn't matter. Tamarind, though, she seems angry about all of it. It's not bad enough they come here for pussy, but they make it even more impersonal by wanting her for her just being Asian. And then I worry about what I just said, right there. I read back over some of my entries and I get worried about my attitude. Like I may end up hating the very population I want to help.

Back to the Tea Party. When Belle got to me I told them the truth, said it out loud. I said that I had been going to school to become a social worker, but working here has made me want to go into sex surrogacy. Belle seemed impressed but Dina and Lana kind of rolled their eyes. I can see why they did. If you're here as long as they have been here, it might seem naïve and like a pipe dream. It might also sound like sucking up to Belle, who thinks we are all "sex therapists." The thing is, I figured it out and it would be less training, more specialized, and I would have a lot more control over my clients—not the clients themselves, but who I took on as clients. I would be working with couples, mostly. I'd be helping people like I wanted to with social work, only in a more specialized way.

I told them about San Francisco and the Sex Institute and my goals. A couple of girls wanted to know what surrogacy was all about and before I could answer, Amy piped in and told them it was a kind of therapy, and she said she was trying to do that here, working here. It got under my skin, I'll admit, because sex work and surrogacy are apples and oranges. I told Amy it was different and she got condescending with me and I just let her talk but I was irritated that she was trying to throw glitter on a pile of shit, basically. Or the other way around—trying to throw shit on glitter. Either way, she was making it sound like I was making some excuse for doing sex work to make myself seem better than everyone else. Honestly, at first it was the money. But I think I've found a niche that could be profitable and I could do it for a lot longer than sex work, and I'd be in the mental health field. I don't know why I'm defending myself here in my own journal. Amy just got to me. I didn't want to cause drama, so I just let it go, but I was pretty irritated.

Belle stepped in and she sort of agreed with Amy, which I knew she would, but said that there was a difference and that you could be a sex surrogate anywhere, but not a sex worker and have it be legal. Anyway, I kind of wish I had kept it all to myself, but I wanted them to know I had a plan. I guess in a way I still feel like I don't belong here. But if I'm going to be honest here, I guess I'd say that every one of us feels like we're the exception and we are different than the next girl.

But I know inside I'm different because I do take the time with the customers, and I can tell which ones are really broken. Sure, some men are just men. But others are really broken. And once I get a degree and get certified, they would be the target group I'd be helping.

It's been a strangely ordinary week except for a couple of customers. That guy Wade, he came back, speaking of broken. He was my first customer when I got back and I think he was waiting for me. He was as good as his word and he actually read 'The Stranger.' He was very thoughtful about it and the book affected him deeply and that made me really happy, actually. Wade seems like a real blue collar type, but he's got to be more than that because he really did seem to like the book. He seemed to get what it was about and we talked about it a little. My guess is he's formed a little crush on me and wants to impress me. I've had it happen before, but not real sure how to discourage an attachment that will be awkward if/when it gets out of hand. I told him I was listening to a new book and he said he'd read that one, too. So I don't know. We'll see.

Anyway, the experience with him was very different from the first time. He didn't go down on me and we didn't have sex. He became very emotional and started crying and so I just comforted him and let him talk. He was asking me questions, probing, and I get that he wants me to know he's not like other customers (no one wants to be like everyone else, it seems) but I need to be careful because, realistically, I don't know this guy and I have no idea how obsessive he could get.

But he was really broken up, and I know his wife died, but the emotion didn't seem to stem from grief of losing her, if that makes sense. But the grief was about her. It just feels like something else besides mourning. He didn't talk about missing her or wishing she was still around. But it was definitely about her. I just let him talk and he gave me $500, but idiot that I am, I made him take $200 back. Frankly, it was more emotionally draining than just straight sex, so maybe I should have taken the money. But technically we didn't do anything, and I didn't want him suddenly realizing that and coming back to say I took advantage of his emotional state. He finally agreed to take it back and said that when he isn't all torn up he would come back and we could have fun like the first time. I have to admit, I hope he doesn't come back. I don't have it in me tonight to deal with his emotional baggage, and I definitely don't want him going down on me because that is exhausting, too. It takes energy and I just don't have it, or maybe I just don't want to expend it.

The next night after Wade I had a really strange guy come in, only I didn't know he was strange until after. I'm not sure what to make of this and I want to research it and see if it's some kind of...thing. This guy, he said his name was 'Sam,' came in and he was chatty and ordinary and we had one party and it was all normal and fine. After the sex, before he tipped me, he pulled out this cup with a lid and he told me he'd double my tip if I would pee in the cup for him so he could take it home and drink it.

Even as I write this, I feel a little like gagging. I remember wondering why he had to tell me, why he couldn't just ask me for the pee and then take it without telling me what he would do with it. Or, maybe it's better I know so my imagination doesn't go crazy. To be totally honest, I'm glad he didn't explain more than what he did, though, now that I think about it. I'm just glad. So I did it and brought him the cup. The cup wasn't see-through, so small blessing. So he took it and gave me a $200 tip. Probably the easiest $200 I've ever made, but definitely the most disturbing.

Time for my shift. Time to tell myself how different I am, time for them to tell me how different they are. All of us, just play-acting like we're not whores and johns.

10

He'd been wrestling with himself all day long.

After last night, he has zero confidence he can walk into Sienna's room and ever get it up again. Ann had been right all along. All he wants is sex, and the proof is in that cathouse, in Sienna's room. He went there for sex. It's all he wanted. But he hadn't done it. Couldn't. Where does that leave him?

He told her he'd come back. The thought occurred to him to go there and do what they had done last night (minus the blubbering): talk, nothing more. Wouldn't that make him *better* than an animal? Prove to himself, prove to her, that he was decent? He won't think about proving anything to Annie. It's too late for that, had been too late for that after their first year of marriage.

The book Sienna's reading is on its way. He ordered a used copy online and he'd actually heard of this author. He remembers reading *Of Mice and Men* in high school. But it's a different one by this guy, and from what he'd read online, he thinks it will be a good book for him. The title alone makes him think it's perfect for him: *The Winter of Our Discontent*. Maybe he should spend his time reading it, go back to see her when he's done so they can talk about it. Talk about the book rather than make her listen to his cracked voice talking about long-ago events that should be laid to rest.

He thinks about what she had told him, remembers that he drank it in, craved her voice and words. It was as if the sound of her voice and the feel of her body alone provided the comfort he needed, but what she'd said brought him to life, gave him this intangible rope to hang onto for dear life. *A rope of hope for a dope,* he thinks. But did any other man ask her about her life but him? He thinks probably not. He's already proved he's not an animal, hasn't he? So why shouldn't he go back tonight and make love to her?

And so the wrestling match begins again.

If he's honest with himself, it's the money. Would she talk to him at a bar if it wasn't for the money? She probably wouldn't glance his way if they were just two people sitting at a bar. And that's the hard, cold truth of it. That's the thing that makes the discussion in his head go around and 'round in circles. When someone goes to a shrink, they aren't paying for friendship, even though all they do is talk. They pay for a *service*. Sienna's service is sex. And he'd paid for it, something he'd swore to himself he would never do. He'd thought he was above all that. He finds himself wishing he could talk to Belle. If anyone could help him sort the shit-scramble in his brain, it would be her. His heart skips a beat at the possible solution: go to the brothel, but only to talk to Belle. Be friendly to Sienna, but don't go with her to her room. Leave her guessing.

Guessing what? That he's insane? Jesus, what is wrong with him. Sienna won't care if he goes with her, she'll be in her room with someone else, and that thought is what finally propels him into the shower, into a clean pair of jeans and a button-up shirt, cologne dabbed on his chest; that thought—that if it isn't him, it will be someone else, someone worse than him, someone who doesn't care for her, care about what she thinks and feels, and doesn't she deserve to have at least one man in her life who cares?

He does a final once-over on himself in the mirror, and just as he's satisfied that he's completely mediocre, he hears a knock at the front door. He immediately thinks it's Cole. The boy is making a show of independence by knocking on the door instead of walking in. *I don't live here anymore, Pop, so I can't just walk in.*

Stupid little shit, Wade thinks as he turns from the mirror. The irritation has infused him before he even steps foot into the hallway. He opens the front door and can't keep the shock off of his face.

"Uh, hey, what the hell? How are you doin'?" His eyes widen and the chilly mid-January air smacks his face.

Tammy stands outside with a tray of food steaming under plastic wrap. Corn, peas and carrots, some sort of chicken in white gravy, and two baked potatoes wrapped in foil.

"I hope you didn't eat yet." She watches him with all kinds of questions in her gaze, but he can't make out one of them because he has too many questions of his own. He steps back to let her in. He hadn't seen her since Christmas.

She walks past him into the kitchen and he takes a minute too long to close the front door, his head adjusting to her presence, wondering if he'd forgotten a call from her. But he hadn't. She was just there again, as if no time had passed and nothing had occurred.

"Tried a new chicken recipe. Hope you like it. It's got cream cheese an' cream of mushroom soup. Looks pretty good." She busies herself with setting the table as Wade stares at her in confusion.

"I, uh, didn't know you were comin' by or I would have, uh…I mean…"

"Well you know, even though it's been a while, every Friday night, Monday an' Wednesday, I think to myself 'hm, what should I make us for dinner,' ya know? So I just figured I'd make it an' come on by."

Wade hasn't heard her this chatty…well, pretty much ever. He had always equated her with a small, gray mouse. But now she's as lively as a puppy. Is she nervous? Is something wrong?

She'd curled her hair, like she'd had it in curlers, and the curls bounce with her movements. He thinks they looks good on her, the curls. He wonders about Stuart, if he's on the road now. That thought causes heat to rush to his face as he remembers seeing him at Mamacita's. Suddenly his heart pumps too hard inside, his breath quickens. He doesn't know why the sudden clenching in his chest and body overtakes him. Taking a breath in, his chest is constricted and painful.

"All right," she says, "you wanna beer?"

"Uh…" He places a hand on the back of his neck and her face changes.

"Hey, your ears'r bright red, you okay? Oh, shit, you expectin' someone?" He had never seen her face so animated before, as if she'd had a depth charge to her personality since last summer. She is suddenly chatty and friendly—and concerned for him. His head starts to pound with pain in his temples, and the room feels like a mirage, shimmering in the heat. Making his way over to a chair, he sits down, heavy and unmoored.

"Nah, I ain't...expectin'...I just got dizzy is all. I don't know what."

"You don't look so good, Wade. Maybe you should go lie down an' I'll save the food—"

"Will you, uh, go into my room and under the bed there's a cuff, blood pressure. Can you bring me that?"

The more he thinks about it, the worse he feels. His fingertips tingle and he starts to sweat. She comes into the kitchen with the cuff and plugs it into the wall, placing it next to him on the table. Like an expert nurse, she lays out his arm and wraps the cuff in place. He'd seen her take Ann's blood pressure a hundred times with a machine like this.

The cuff hugs his arm ferociously and he can almost feel the blood pumping through his head. The machine beeps, but he doesn't look at the numbers. His vision is blurry.

"Ho-ly shit. Wade, you need to come lie down, right now. Come on. *Right now.*" She barks her command and he's vaguely aware that he'd never heard her bark before. He'd never heard her raise her voice. The alarm that passes through him is eclipsed by this woman, this seemingly new woman, before him.

She leads him into his room and he reclines on the bed, but she rolls him to his left side. "You stay like that. I want you to breathe, you understand? Just breathe an' I'll be right back."

He stares at the wall, then down at the floor where clothes are heaped for the wash pile. His heart continues to pound and he can't figure out what has possessed him, but if he thinks about Sienna, the pounding gets worse. If he thinks about Tammy, the pounding gets worse. Women are going to kill him.

His eyes close, even though he hears her come back into the room. He feels a cool cloth on his forehead. Tammy mumbles under her breath as she adjusts the blood pressure cuff around his arm again. It squeezes and clicks, but he's much calmer now.

The cuff deflates and with it, Tammy lets out a loud sigh. "Whew. That's better. Man, I ain't never seen blood pressure that high."

"What was—no, don't tell me." He keeps his eyes closed.

"You got medication for blood pressure?"

"Yeah, I take 'em every day."

"Huh. Well then, what you had was probably one of them anxiety attacks. They can feel just like a heart attack, they say."

He opens one eye and looks at her. "How d'you know 'bout all this medical stuff?"

Suddenly, she is shy Tammy again. She shrugs. "Been takin' classes couple nights a week. Medical assisting. I figure, with Annie an' all, I got a good idea 'bout the worst of things. And workin' at Flyin' J ain't exactly job security."

"No kiddin'? Where at? Classes, I mean."

"Great Basin in Elko."

Wade knows about the college because he'd all but begged Cole to take classes there. He had no idea Tammy had any other ambitions besides… whatever it is she does. He tries to sit up but she takes a firm hand and pushes him back down.

"You still ain't in a great range. You coulda had a stroke, Wade, you know that? I'd call your doc first thing Monday and get a higher dose of that blood pressure medication or somethin' if I was you. Or maybe somethin' for anxiety."

His eyelids feel heavy, as if he'd just run a series of sprints down a hot highway. An *anxiety attack*? Was that what that was? And if so, is there *any other way* he could humiliate himself in front of a woman this week?

"I'll go put dinner up. We'll re-heat it when you're doin' better." She stands from the bed and practically stalks from the room. Something is different about her and he can't place it, but the difference changes everything about her for him. Everything.

Tammy would only leave when his blood pressure was within normal range—and he'd eaten all of his chicken and veggies. Wade is tired, but it's only eight o'clock and after Tammy leaves, his head is muddled with thoughts he'd never had before.

Tammy had been dressed nice. Usually she wore jeans and a shapeless sweatshirt, or an old baggy t-shirt. Tonight she had on those tights women wear, the ones you can't see through, and some sort of long, clingy tank top that reached her mid-thigh, with a blouse—an actual blouse, not a sweatshirt. Her makeup was subtle, as was her perfume. Maybe she dressed like that for school? Maybe she dresses like that for Stuart?

His head is swimming with her. The way she spoke to him, took charge. Her whole face changed; she had been smiling, animated, and she no longer had that shapeless, mousy body, in his mind. She is petite but curvy, a little heavy in the butt, whereas Ann had carried a lot of weight in her belly. Tammy didn't have much extra on her. He remembers the slope of her thighs, even while he had been having his "episode." His face burns up again and he resists taking his blood pressure for the hundredth time. He knows it's a bit high, but not for any other reason than he's got an itch. He doesn't allow himself to think about where he wants to get it scratched; he just goes on autopilot, grabs his keys, and walks out the front door.

Friday night late at Lil' Mamacitas. The parking lot is full, really full. But there is no way he can walk away. He won't allow himself to think about Tammy and Sienna as separate. They are one woman to him at this moment. Flashes of Tammy's thighs, her face when she smiled, Sienna's body, all her curves and folds, so opposite of everything he knows about Tammy—but they are one tonight.

He rings the doorbell and waits. Leslie opens the door and her eyes rest on him with the familiar expression of a friend.

"Heya, nice to see ya again. Come on in."

"Busy tonight." She doesn't turn. "Busy tonight," he yells again toward her back. She half turns, nodding.

Bev and another woman are behind the bar, a woman he's never met. He looks into the room and all he sees is the crowd, at least ten guys in the room, and women with bare legs, bare arms, red lips, laughing, flipping their hair, talking. He looks into each corner for Sienna, but she's nowhere in the main bar.

The other bartender leans over to him. "What can I getcha?"

"Oh, a bloody beer, please, just half an' half—" but she's already gone, squatting down in front of the glass mini-fridge to get a can of tomato juice. He tries to catch Bev's eye, but she's filling a pitcher of beer, seemingly in deep concentration. Wade pulls out his wallet, when suddenly he feels a slap on his shoulder. He turns, startled.

"Well, lookie, here. How you doin', brother Wade?" Stuart stands with his hand outstretched, waiting for Wade to take it. Wade stares at him, the image of Tammy floating through his mind: the "before" Tammy with her mousy appearance, the "after" Tammy he'd seen tonight. He doesn't want to think of Tammy in conjunction with the cathouse or with Stuart, but here he stands, eyes sparkling, almost a dare in his smile.

Wade reaches and shakes. He can't smile, can't nod in commiseration. He'd never understand the men who come into a place like that together. It felt like something vaguely queer to him, getting off on knowing your buddy's getting off, just like you. Even when Wade had gone to the tittie bars when he was younger, he had done it alone. Arousal and lust are personal, private. Not something to be shared with another man. He feels his single-minded purpose shriveling under Stuart's gaze.

"I thought I seen you few weeks back, 'round Christmas. Was that you? You was walkin' out with that dark, curvy hottie—Sienna or somethin', right?"

Wade had never wanted to punch someone in the face more than he does right now. Cave his face in for taking her name in vain. His face floods with heat.

"No, I don't think that was her name. Anyway, surprised to see you here." Wade jumps when the bartender yells in his ear.

"*Four-fifty,*" she calls into his ear.

Wade gives her seven dollars and takes a drink, trying to cool himself down, not allowing his mind to wonder how Stu knows Sienna's name.

Stu leans in, talking loud still, but it's more intimate. "Nevada's the last free place in America, you know that? Now all they need to do is get their goddamn hands outta drugs and this'd be the ultimate destination for everyone in this country."

Wade forms a straight line with his mouth, not wanting to argue politics with Stuart, but arguing with him in his mind just the same. He thinks about the "nice" things he and Tammy talk about. They must be really nice things, because Wade can't for the life of him see what Tammy could see in a prick like him.

"See, look here," Stu continues, "a man has needs so they come here. You come here, I come here…in every other state, we'd be breakin' the law or sneakin' around. If a man wants to gamble his life away, it's his choice here, an' that's what freedom is all about. We don't need no babysitters, is what I think."

Wade can't figure out how to disengage, and his head still swims with the fact that Stuart knows who Sienna is. He wants to grab him by his leathery neck and ask him if he's fucked her. He's had to have been with Tammy, and all these thoughts confuse him and enrage him with nowhere to release them.

"So, uh, Tammy know you come 'round here? Wade stares down into his beer, looking at the way the bubbles form in the red juice. He glances up at Stuart, who smiles and holds up his hands.

"Hey, Tammy's a good woman. But I don't believe in that kinda thing... restrictions. Monogamy, another government rule we all buy into. History tells us monogamy is somethin' new. It ain't for everyone, Wade. And hey, no reason when you got a place like this--"

"Okay, but does she know, is what I'm askin'." Wade feels his ears getting hot but he breathes, trying to stay calm. He can almost feel the bruising on his knuckles if he punches Stuart in the face.

"Look, I know you're her family 'n' all, just lookin' out for her. But Tammy, she's a big girl. We don't have any kind of exclusive thing goin' on. She don't ask an' I don't tell. Look, I ain't no dirt bag. She and I, well, it's a physical thing. But there's no need to stir up a hornet's nest, if you get me. I mean, you're here, I'm here..."

"I woulda never come here when I was with someone back in the day. One woman at a time is enough for me." Wade regrets saying it, worried Stuart's mind will follow to a conclusion that he sees Sienna and no one else.

"Yeah, I see what you're sayin'," Stuart nods. "I do. I'd just appreciate some discretion. You know. Man to man."

"Yeah."

"So, you, uh, here for someone special? Or you gonna look at the lineup?"

"No, I ain't here for anythin'. Just a drink. Talk to you later."

Wade moves off of the stool and strides to the hall as he hears a faint "Take it easy there, Wade," from Stuart. He wants to stay there, make sure Stu doesn't go with Sienna, and he knows it will drive him insane if he thinks Stuart would go to Sienna out of some kind of spite. Although the man was clearly worried Wade would tell Tammy. He wonders now if he should have used that, told him his secret's safe as long as he kept the hell away from Sienna. He curses himself for playing dumb. He should have admitted it, told Stuart to stay away from her. You know, "man to man." Yes, he feels like if Stuart knows about Sienna, he will make it a point to get to her. He's a snake, that Stuart. Wade can feel it.

He stands alone outside of the building and a new tug of war begins. The two women in his life, and there's nothing he can do to protect them from a snake. The rage inside of him threatens to barrel out through his fist into anything he can find. He decides to go to Luther's. If anyone can talk him down, it's Junior.

Luther's is even busier than the hen house. Wade looks around in dismay. No tables, the bar full. He scoots past a pair of close-knit couples making their way out the front door and stands on his toes to look in back. Sure enough, he sees Gerry's wheelchair, his back to the bar. Wade walks around tables, says a few *s'cuse me's* to women who drunkenly fall into him while playing pool, and approaches Gerry's chair, parked at the very back booth.

Gerry sits alone, facing into the empty booth and away from the clamoring crowd, his eyes staring straight at the wall in front of him. Wade gets within hearing range and calls out to him.

"Gerry, hey, what the hell?"

Gerry's head seems to turn in slow motion. His eyes are bleary slits and his mouth is slack.

"Heya, there," he slurs his words and Wade takes a seat at the booth and looks into Gerry's deeply lined face. Gerry can't seem to focus on anything. Junior's wife approaches the table. Wade can't ever remember her name. Ah, her name tag: *Wanda*.

She sets a napkin down in front of Wade with a glass of water and yells over the din. "What can I getcha?"

"How about some coffee here, for Gerry?" Wade motions to him with his head, eyebrows raised. She looks down at him and, understanding, hurries away before taking Wade's order, which is just fine with him since he's not thirsty at all.

"So Ger, you been here a while, huh?"

"I been here. I been here, yeah. I been…Pete was here for a bit. I don't think he's…you better watch out for him. Yeah, I been here since 'bout, I dunno, I had me some lunch…"

"You said Pete was here? What do you mean I gotta watch out? What's he sayin'?" Wade is on instant alert and catches sight of Wanda coming back with a mug of coffee and a pitcher of water.

"Here y'are, Gerry. There's some sugar there on the table, now. You drink up. Oh, can I get you somethin'? Sorry, hon."

"Uh, how 'bout a plate of fries here for us, and I'll just have whatever you got on tap."

Food, coffee, and water, that's what Gerry needs. And he needs to tell Wade about that fucking hothead, Pete.

"So Gerry, what did Pete say, buddy? Can you tell me?"

"Oh, he's all bent. Yeah, called yer boy a 'dirty convict' and somethin' else about his niece…somethin'. Hey, didn't you take her out, the niece?"

"Yeah, you know that already, Ger. So, what else did he say? You remember?"

"Nah, he was just bellowin' and bein' an asshole, you know how he got…he gets…izzis coffee? I thought I ordered a shot a—"

"Gerry, you had enough, now, all right? You gotta drink that coffee now. You're gonna be one sick son of a bitch if you don't sober up."

Wanda approaches with the plate of fries and some ketchup. "Here ya go, hon."

Suddenly Wade looks up and Pete is there, towering over them. He's got some weasely little scruffy guy with him looking hostile and bored all at once. Pete just stares at Wade, nodding his head, a small smile on his face, which Wade isn't fooled at all into thinking is friendly. He's not sure how to play it: does he greet Pete and ask him to sit down, offer to buy him a drink? They can commiserate on how stupid his son and Pete's niece are being, how wrong they are for each other, but what can you do, right? They're young, they're stupid. He could do all of that, but Pete's eyes hold more than a glittery cold; they hold accusations and spite and they are darts heading for the dartboard that is Wade's blank expression. And the words "dirty convict" echo in his mind as he sees Cole in a giant mixture of the young man in the visitor's room at the prison, the young boy with the missing front teeth, the easy-going kid who always had a smile for everyone, the devoted child who sat by his dying mother— the son. *His* son.

Pete walks around Gerry's wheelchair so he's standing next to Wade, only a foot away.

"Wade," Pete says too loud.

"Pete." Wade scoots back in the booth, sitting straight, and looks up at him. Pete's mouth twists a little and his eyes dart up to the ceiling, as if he's searching for the perfect words to say.

Pete places his hand on the back of the booth, and another on the table in front of Wade so he can bend at the waist and get close, too close, to Wade's ear.

"You tell that dirty fucking criminal son of yours to get the fuck outta my house. You got that?"

Wade stares down at Pete's mottled hand, and he finds he's nodding, too. His mind is berserk with thoughts, but only one feeling spreads throughout his chest and that feeling causes him to scoot out of the booth in a flash and practically knock Pete backwards on his ass. He wants to return the insult by calling Cindy something, anything, but he realizes that's not the way to go, not if he's going to have the high road. He's glad that part of his reptilian brain can think that clearly.

"My son ain't a dirty criminal. He made a mistake and paid for it! Now you'd best get the fuck outta my face and learn to mind your own business, old man. Them two are adults an' they—"

Wade watches as Pete, as if in slow motion, winds his arm up for a punch. But Wade seems to move in slow motion, too, and he doesn't move in time to dodge it entirely. It clips him on the side of his head, up high, where it probably hurt Pete's hand more than Wade's skull. Wade uses both hands to push Pete's chest with all of his might so that he stumbles backwards and nearly falls. The table with the four people drinking catch him and scream in startled unison. Pete recovers quickly and lurches for Wade, aiming low to catch him around the waist, but Wade thinks fast and brings his knee up, catching Pete square in the chin. This time, Pete falls back and lands on his ass on the floor, looking bewildered.

WADE

Wade is ready to offer him a hand up, tell him that they can talk rationally, stop this craziness, but before he can say anything, an explosion of pain lights up his face as Pete's companion lands a blow to his face, catching the side of his nose and most of his cheek. Wade falls back and feels the room tilt.

He can hear screaming and sees Junior's large form grab the small, ratty man by the back of the collar while yelling at Pete on the floor, but Wade can't hear what he's screaming for all of the clamor in the bar. Wade's back is up against the side of the booth, his eyesight fuzzy, and tastes he the blood in his mouth, feels it tickling as it runs from his nose. He looks down just in time to see Gerry puke all over the fries and table.

⁓◯

The ice on his face feels good, and the bourbon feels even better as Millie bustles around the kitchen to fix Wade a snack. Durward is still shaking his head.

"I'll tell you, that sonuvabitch, I'll tell you what a hypocrite he is. That old bastard, way back when, he did time himself, and I remember it."

Wade's face throbs and he can feel the tender skin under his eye swelling as he sits. After Junior had broken up the fight, he kicked Pete and his rat of a friend out. Witnesses told Junior Pete had started it, so he'd let Wade stay, but it was clear he was on Junior's shitlist, too, even if his name isn't at the top. Wade had immediately called Cole. Told him to clear the hell out of Cindy's before Pete got the bright idea of coming there to finish the beating on the boy himself. Wade could only calm down when he saw Cole's bike in front of his house and the light on. But he doesn't want to go home. Not yet.

"Wait, what? Pete's an ex-con?"

"Damn straight. Went ta prison for assault, beatin' some guy within an inch, got hauled off. Damn hypocrite. That son of yours is a good kid, Wade. A good kid. I'll never forget how he done with Annie."

A faint smell of something unpleasant travels across the kitchen, but then it makes sense as Millie places an egg salad sandwich in front of him. "Dude, you want a sandwich, too?"

"Ah, no thanks, I'm still full from that dinner you fed me. You sit here an' tell Wade 'bout that old Pete."

Millie seems suddenly shy as the light is shined on her. "Oh, I don't remember much. Knew his mother at the church, she seemed very quiet and shy. Like a scared mouse from that brute of a husband she had. Pete probably learned it from him. You keep that ice on, now."

"I am, I will." The ice is melting and trickling down his wrist and arm. He wishes Millie wasn't there in a way because he really needs to spout off about Stuart, Tammy, Sienna, all of it. But he can't do it and admit it to Millie. Wade doesn't think any woman outside that hen house would want to *hear* about the hen house. He remembers driving by it with Ann one night when the other road was closed for construction, how she'd held her hand up to her eye to block the sight of it. The memory strikes him in the center of the forehead like a pointed finger. Wade looks down and his chest warms a little as Dude places his hand over Millie's on the table as they sit staring at his swelling face. Warmth, then a sudden bitterness and anger he can't place.

"So when you two gonna make it official, huh?" Wade smiles, points his half-empty glass toward Durward. He speaks from that bitter place and doesn't know why he feels the words come as aggressive strikes. "I mean, look at you, all playin' house over here."

He instantly regrets it as Millie's face falls and she turns away. Dude leans back in his chair and scowls. "Since when's that any-a your damn business, there?"

Millie stands and begins cleaning the kitchen. Wade's Bourbon had muddled his head, but the look on Millie's face sobered him up right that second.

"It ain't my business, sorry. I just…I just don't wanna talk about Pete no more. Cole's at home, safe, that's all that matters."

"Uh, Wade," Millie's face looks stricken. "What does Pete drive? 'Cause there's a car out front at your place… ."

Wade jumps up, adrenaline rushing through him as he rounds the corner of the kitchen and looks through the big window in the living room. His energy rush drains from him, but he's filled with a different sort of stuff when he sees the car.

WADE

"That ain't Pete's car," he says, scowling. "It's his niece's."
Now he really doesn't want to go home.

⁓

Cindy is crying into Cole's shoulder when Wade walks in. She doesn't look up when he closes the door. Cole's face is a dangerous mixture of anger and panic. Wade walks over to the blue chair across from the couch and perches on the edge. He left the ice pack at Dude's and now that he's inside the warmth of the house, his face starts to burn and tingle. He knows his right eye swells with every pump of his heart.

Cole's nose is flared and he shakes his head, as if someone has just asked him a question he's steadily denying. Cindy's mewling sobs take up the limited space in the room. The room seems smaller than it ever had and her sobs grate on his nerves like fork tines on cheap dinnerware.

"Cole, you all right? No problems over there?"

Cole's eyes widen, "*I'm* all right, jeez. Look at her. Does *she* look all right to you?"

Wade reaches down deep to scrape any dregs of sympathy for her, but the crying had begun to inch its way into his left ear and gnaw in it. Then the thought occurs to him that her uncle might have physically hurt her, and that brings him to a sense of rightness.

"Pete didn't hurt you did he? 'Cause if he did, we're gonna—"

"No, he didn't hurt me," she said in a high-pitched, muffled voice. "He just—he just—"

She can't continue and her sobs get louder, which drains all of Wade's reserves of patience. Doesn't anyone here notice his busted-up face from defending these two lunatics? Wade stands.

"I gotta get some ice."

"Pop, he kicked her out. Told her she can't live there no more. She has 'til Monday to get her things out for good."

"Well, that ain't so bad, I mean, you just find another place—"

"Her rent was four hundred a month. You can't find a house that cheap anywhere. Ain't no apartments, only shit-trailers and they're seven hundred and up for a measly one bedroom—I looked, Pop. We got nowhere to go but here."

"Here?" Wade stops and turns. "Here? You can't stay here, I mean... right? You can't..." his words trail off as Cole wraps his arm tighter around Cindy.

"We got nowhere else to go. It would just be until we find a place after we get our storage units up an' runnin'."

"You're talkin' months. Cole! This place ain't big enough for three grown—"

"We'd stay outta your way, and it would only be awhile. Cindy, she works all the time, an' we'll pay you rent. We'll pay you what we was payin' Pete, right, baby?"

Cindy finally raises her face and Wade fights the urge to grimace at what he sees. Her glasses are fogged, her nose a deep red, her big horse-lips even more swollen than usual. What his good-looking son sees in this woman confuses every part of his brain.

"I'll pay you four-hundred for the one room, bathroom, and use of the kitchen. When I'm not working, I'll cook. And I'll buy food." Her voice is thick with tears, but she seems clear enough in her speech that he guesses she's been practicing it a while. She looks at him, eyes pleading.

Wade feels like an utter asshole, standing there, judging her horse-face, her wobbly desperation spilling from her eyes. He berates himself as he thinks of what four hundred extra dollars a month means for him in terms of Sienna. He can't get his own dick off of his mind for one second. He turns and grabs ice from the freezer. Cracking the cubes free, he pulls a dishtowel out of a drawer and plops the ice on it. He takes his time putting the icetray back. When he gets the pack on his face, the pressure makes it throb, but feel better at the same time.

Wade walks in and stands, breathing through his mouth, since his nose is plugged up with blood and other fluids. The couple stare at him expectantly. There is no way around it. He turns her out, he turns Cole out. And is that such a bad thing? On the other hand, when Cole is around, he feels a sense of wholeness, a sense of purpose. Maybe, with Cindy's help, he can turn Cole around. Cindy would surely side with Wade on the practical side of things, wouldn't she? She's a grown woman, looking for security, and Wade knows security; he sold it for twenty-five years. Not just insurances plans, but the idea, the promise of security, to thousands of folks all over the region and beyond. Maybe she could be his ally in giving his son the reality check he's needed his entire adult life.

Wade makes a face of someone deeply troubled, but he's actually a little giddy inside, thinking of Cole home, Cole listening to him, respecting him. And Cindy, she'd grow to respect him too, see how right in the head he is about such things.

"Well," Wade begins. He pauses for effect and rubs his chin.

"Only for temporary, Pop. Promise. We won't be a bother."

Cindy's eyes are leaking, but she trains her gaze on him and he's reminded of one of those animals that are so ugly, they're actually sort of endearing, and that's how he decides he should view her.

Wade sniffs and begins. "We're all adults, here, ain't we?"

Cole and Cindy nod their heads, holding their breath.

"Four hundred a month, we split groceries, and I think we take turns cookin'. I mean, the nights Cindy's here, it wouldn't be too bad if she got a meal cooked for her once in a while, right?"

She smiles and nods her head in a small movement, gratitude in her expression as Cole cracks a huge grin and stands to hug him.

"You're the best, Pop. An' you just wait—I learned how to cook pretty good these last few months. I got an omelet that'll knock your socks off."

Wade smacks Cole's back as Cole hugs him, keeping his good eye away from Cindy's gaze. He doesn't want to see anything in them. Anything at all. The simple gratitude from earlier had been good enough. Mostly, he doesn't want her to see anything in his eyes. She's from the Land of Womenspeak, and he has a feeling that his crafty scheme would be something a woman would spot from a mile away. She'd be able to read right past his generosity and see what he's really up to.

"So, Pop," Cole begins as he breaks from him, "you and your truck busy tomorrow? 'Cause we gotta move, an' there's a couple of other things—"

"Well, you see I ain't got a lot of space here for storage, I mean, her furniture—"

"Oh, the house is furnished, it's all Uncle Pete's. I just have clothes and personal items, some kitchen things and…well…Cole?"

"Yeah," Cole looks at him. "Well, there's Otis and Whitney."

Wade's mind blanks. "You got kids?"

They both laugh, "No, no, no..." Cole and Cindy look at each other, laughing, as if that was an insane notion all around. As if Wade had gone overboard, and they would never impose on him like that.

"Well, who's Otis and whatever—"

"My pug and my cat."

Wade looks at Cole, his hand holding the ice-filled towel dropping to his side. "The what?"

"They're great, Pop. Otis is house trained, you just gotta take him out during the day, and I swear, he's like clockwork, Pop, so easy, and they're great, the cat's real nice, doesn't claw or nothin', an' she just does her own thing, keeps to herself mostly, and Otis, well he's like my best buddy now..."

Wade's face is filled with blood and the whole side of it throbs anew. He knows he should kill the deal right now. To say he is not an animal person would be an understatement beyond words. He thinks again about Cole, his plans, his future, and a sudden fear grips him. Maybe it's the damn book he read and the new way he's started to look at life, but he realizes that Cole's only shot in life is *him*. And he isn't getting any younger. Cole has to be okay before Wade takes that final trip into the emptiness, the void, and he knows he can't accept or be at peace with that trip if Cole isn't ready. He sighs with a determined grimace.

"Does it bark?" He glares at Cindy.

"No," she shakes her head. Then she smiles. "He snorts, though." Cole and Cindy share an affectionate chuckle.

Perfect.

11

He feels like the poster boy for self-control.

Wade had waited until Sunday night to go back to Mamacita's. He doesn't acknowledge the fact that Stuart had ruined it for him the previous night, and all day he'd helped Cindy and Cole move and get settled in their room, right across the hall from him. He'd cleaned out Cole and Milt's old room and now Ann's pristine bedroom has trash bags, boxes, and bins littering it, once at home in. Cole and Milt's room, now in Ann's. Milt and Cole's room is bigger, so it made sense. He focuses on patting his own back at his magnanimous gesture, but he doesn't think about the reasons behind it. No, he focuses on his monumental restraint. He also avoids thinking about the last time he had been with Sienna, how he'd blubbered like a baby while she caressed and cooed to him. How he'd spent three hundred dollars to cuddle.

Leslie had let him in, but no one is at the bar. He sits and looks around, listening to country music piped in through tinny speakers on the wall. Finally, he hears someone walking down the hall with purposeful strides. He looks up and his eyes meet the penetrating stare of Belle.

"Well, now, ain't you a sight for sore eyes. How are ya, Wade? And where the hell'd you get that shiner?" She comes around and clasps her arms tightly around him. He releases himself into her embrace.

"I'm good, I'm doin' real good. This, it ain't nothin'. Some drunk guy took a cheap shot is all. How 'bout you?"

"Better 'n some, worse 'n others," she smiles. "Hey, let's get you a drink. You want a bloody beer?"

"Just a plain old beer'd be nice. Thanks."

"So you want the lineup, I guess—"

"No, I already know who I wanna see, if it's all the same to you."

"'Course, no problem. Who can I call for ya?"

"Uh, Sienna, if you wouldn't mind." Wade feels a deep blush creep up his neck and face. He sees himself as if he's looking through her eyes, wondering what she thinks of him. *This old goat? And that young thing?* No, no, he won't allow himself to think that way. Not tonight.

But there's no hint of reproach in Belle's face as she smiles and slides his beer toward him. "I'll be right back. You hold tight."

He watches her leave and he's glad he's all alone in there. That's the secret. Come at dinnertime or just before. Then he avoids people like Stuart and all of the other men he secretly judges for being there, while holding himself above and apart from them. He knows why he's there, and why they're there. And it's *different*.

Footsteps down the hall and his stomach flutters while he catches his breath. Sienna walks behind Belle and her smile is bright when she sees him.

"Well, hey, handsome. Oh my God, what happened?" She hugs him, and he notices the difference in her hug and Belle's. Belle's embrace was like a solid spike in the dirt, a fortification. Sienna's is a flower opening to the sun and spring rains.

"It's nothin', honest."

"You wanna come on back?"

Shit, the ATM.

"You go on, I'll be right behind ya." Wade nods and waits for her to round the corner before he slips his card into the machine. He pockets the money in the front of his jeans and walks through the hall, the silence only punctured by the fading music.

He knocks on her door and she opens with a sweep of her hand. "Welcome back."

"Well, yeah, I-I'm sorry 'bout that, the last time, you know—"

"Hey, today's a new day. We don't have to worry about anything but right now. I'm glad you came back."

"Me too." He stands there, grinning stupidly before realizing what's expected. "Oh, right, here, and I'll get in the robe an' all."

"You know the routine now, you're an old hat at this." She takes the money in this smooth movement of her hand, while caressing him with the other. "See you soon."

He pulls his shirt up and over his head, and throws it on the chair. He's already got some heft to his erection, but he's not all the way hard. This pleases him, anyway. He feels he has a lot to make up for, after her seeing him bawling like she had. He feels alive and hungry and wants to devour her, and so he pulls off his boxers and gets the robe on. He feels powerful, like a king.

She comes back in and her brow furrows again. "Your eye looks terrible. Did you get in a fight?"

"Nah, some guy sucker-punched me is all. Ain't nothing to worry about."

"Well, I'm glad you're here." She finishes her inspection and he waits for her to drop her robe to the floor and approach him. She kisses him and it's got a force to it, but at the same time it manages to be soft, like a pillowy embrace with pillowy lips. He moves her to the bed and they sit and she uses her hand to lay him back on the sheet. He wants to grab her, take her, but he has no idea how to realize that vision. What sort of change would he have to make to suddenly be the one on top, taking charge?

She reaches over to the nightstand and unwraps the rubber, but he realizes he's not hard enough for it to slide on. He refuses to let this panic him. She leans down to kiss him while she straddles him, all the while working her hand on him until she slides the rubber on. Once he's hard, it's easy for him to let go, want her, see her and no one else.

He wants to be on top, but he doesn't tell her because she guides him inside her and starts moving on him, her hips moving in some sort of infinity-shaped undulation that causes him to sigh and close his eyes. But he forces them open because he wants to memorize every inch of her, every square inch of her face and body as she straddles him, and just that thought puts him over the edge.

"Aw, shit!"

All he can hear is his own gasps, his panting. He hadn't even made sure she enjoyed herself. She rolls off of him and curls next to his side as his chest rises and falls with labored breath.

"I'm glad you're feeling better," she says.

"Better now," he says, curling his arm so she's even closer.

"So, how's your weekend been?" she asks.

"God damn. My weekend. Huh. Long story."

"Bev said she saw you last night? Who'd you pick? C'mon, you can tell me, I don't get jealous."

It seems like ages ago, last night. The brothel, Luther's, Dude's, Cole and Cindy. But it had just been last night. So much for restraint.

"No, nothin' like that. I didn't pick no one. I was here, but I got side-tracked."

"Oh yeah? By what?"

Then it starts, right as he lies there basking in a glow that fades with each thought, each passing question. He had left Stuart there last night, and Stuart had known about Sienna. The thought shrivels his insides into a dark, glowing coal and he sits up, hands on either sides of his head, elbows on his knees.

"Uh oh, what did I say? Wade?" Sienna sits up, hand on his back.

"Nothin'. It's nothin'." He tries to come up with what to say to her, the not-knowing eating away at his insides. He turns to her. "So, were you busy last night?"

Her eyes change, as if a shield gets thrown up in front of them. Then just as quickly, they disarm and she looks away, shrugging. "Steady, you know. Saturday nights are busy. But I wanna hear about your weekend."

"Look, I just gotta ask you—I mean, it don't matter, it's just that there's this guy and he's—"

"Uh," she places a finger on his lips. "I don't talk about other customers. I don't do it to you, and I don't do it to them." She reaches down and fondles him. "Maybe we can wake him up again?"

Wade knows that's a cold shot in hell as he thinks about Stuart, in this very room, her touching the puny little pecker he surely has in those tight Wrangler jeans he wears.

"I think he's done for the night," Wade says, looking down. "Sorry it wasn't so good for you. I mean, I know I went fast 'n' all."

"Never a problem."

Wade swings his legs to the side of the bed and for the first time, he feels exposed, naked in a way he'd feel in a bad dream, like walking into church with no clothes. He feels so exposed he doesn't even know how to move to get his clothes.

Only when Sienna slides off the bed does he jump to life and grab his underwear. He sees the money peeking out of his front pocket and decides to tip her only after he's covered himself completely.

He can hear the dog's bark from the carport. *Yeah, he doesn't bark.*

It isn't really a bark. It's more like the hacking cough of someone dying, mixed with a growl. Walking in, he sees Cindy and Cole standing in the living room. Cindy is petting the dog, shushing him, while Cole smiles as though he's trying to smooth the whole thing over with an overdose of charm.

"Heya, Pop. This is Otis. He's only barkin' 'cause he don't know you yet. Why don't you come over and say 'hi' to him or somethin' so he don't feel scared."

"It'll get used to me. It's fine."

"Wade, he's a dog, he needs to sniff you, make sure you're okay."

"I gotta have some seal of approval from some shitting furball in my own damn house? No, I'm fine right here. If it comes at me, I'll kick its head. It'll learn."

"Pop!"

"Wade!"

They say this simultaneously, as if he'd seriously punt the animal across the room. He only meant a nudge to scare him. Wade shrugs. "What?"

"C'mon, Otis, lookie, this is Grandpa Wade, see? He's nice." Cindy approaches Wade with the wriggling thing, snorting and growling.

"I ain't its grandpa, and keep it away. It smells from here. Just let it down, it'll smell me fine."

Cindy and Cole are silent as Wade tries to focus on what to eat for dinner. He had left the brothel as the after-dinner crowd came in, no sign of Stu, but his heart pounded just the same. Sienna wouldn't tell him. Just like she didn't tell others about him. *He was just like them.* The dog sniffs his leg.

Wade looks down at the bug-eyed thing, face looking like someone pushed its nozzle into its skull to make its eyes bulge, nose spread across its whole mug like a melted marshmallow. "Okay, dog, here I am."

"Well, talk to him, Wade. You know, like he was a baby or somethin'," Cindy says, moving closer.

"I don't talk to animals, that's the definition of 'crazy' in my book."

"Aw, he likes you, Pop."

"Great," Wade says, unenthusiastically. All he wants is to be alone with his thoughts. But maybe that's a dangerous thing. Maybe it wouldn't be good to sit there, winding the conversation he'd had with Sienna around his head and throat like a constricting snake. A snake named Stuart.

The dog jumps on his leg, his entire lower half wagging and Wade scowls, looking down.

"Yeah, okay. Get offa my leg. He been fixed?"

"Yeah, your leg is safe," she says flatly.

Wade moves into the kitchen and sees the animals' food and water dishes. Great, now he's sharing his eating place with them. This day is getting better and better. Wade washes his hands, as though he'd touched the thing and they were coated with 'dog.' The dog is still on him like glue so he looks down at him.

"Shoo, go on. I ain't got no food, go on."

"You just talked to the dog, Wade. Just so you know."

Wade frowns and looks at Cindy. "Well, I didn't say I wasn't crazy. I mean, look at this stupid situation. I must be crazy."

Cole calls the dog and he snorts some more and heads toward Cole, away from Wade's side.

"Oh hey, Pop, here's Whitney, the kitty. See her?"

Wade looks down at the cat that had stopped in the kitchen doorway as if to pose. The cat stays perfectly still while the damn dog smells her ass and sniffs her all over, as if he doesn't live with her every damn day. The cat regards Wade coolly as Wade regards the cat, and then without much fanfare, she slinks away, her pitch-black fur catching light from the overhead kitchen lights.

Wade dries his hands and motions to the cat. "That's more like it. So where's the cat gonna, uh…she go outside, too?"

"Litter box is in our room—we'll clean it out twice a day," Cole says, holding up the scout's honor sign. Wade scowls again.

"We'll clean it every time she goes, how 'bout that?" Cindy says.

Wade knows deep down he's busting their chops. But why shouldn't he? They are inconveniencing the hell out of him. So why shouldn't he make them suffer a little? But he's the one who's suffering. When he thinks about Sienna, something odd and unnerving settles in his gut, and if he were alone, he'd have to think about that. He isn't sure where he can go now other than his room for privacy.

"So, Pop, you go out to eat tonight or somethin'? We didn't see you at the diner."

"I was out, just out. I don't need no twenty questions every time I come home, do I?" Wade snaps at him, instantly sorry for how hot his answer had been. But he didn't want tabs kept on him. He didn't need an inquisition.

"Jeez, no, sorry. I just wondered if you ate yet. We have some leftovers in the fridge if you want 'em."

Wade points to the dog, lying at Cole's feet. "Them things sleep in your room, not all over the damn house."

He opens the fridge and pulls out a foam take-out box. Suddenly he's not hungry at all, so he puts it back. He wishes the book he'd ordered was there so he could read it. He resigns himself to reading in his bed from now on. The damn animals have the run of the place, it seems. He is aware that Cole and Cindy watch him, not wanting to pry, but clearly seeing something is wrong. Why can't they just take their critters and leave him alone?

Wade doesn't know what to do. Suddenly going to his room alone seems like a bad idea. He walks over while four pairs of eyes stare at him, and he sits on the couch. Suddenly, the cat is there, on his lap, sticking her talons into his thighs.

"What in *the* hell?" Wade holds his arms out at his sides. "Ouch! Get this thing offa me, goddamnit!"

"Sorry," Cindy rushes over and picks up the cat. "In case you're wonderin', that means she likes you."

"Jesus, she likes me so she sticks her claws into me?"

"It's a cat thing, Pop. You get used to it."

"I don't wanna get used to it. Look, I wanna be able to sit on my couch without the damn animals maulin' me. Is that too much to ask?"

Cindy's face looks stricken. "We'll keep them in our room when you're home," she says, voice slightly shaking. Wade feels like a giant asshole. He knows these things are her pets, and she's attached to them, but do they have to be everywhere?

"It's just...aw, shit." Wade looks out the window and sees Millie, hurrying across the road, no coat, arms wrapped around her tiny frame.

"What is it, Pop?" Cole asks, looking in the same direction. Cindy is calling the dog into the back room and Wade stands up to get his coat.

"I gotta go. Now."

"Can I help?" Cole asks.

Wade remembers why he wanted Cole around just then. He looks at his earnest son's face and smiles a small smile. "Maybe. Come on."

"Millie!" Wade says. "You can't keep comin' out without your coat!"

"Oh, Wade, it's bad tonight. He's real, real bad. I don't know what to do!"

"Where is he?" Wade demands, walking toward the house with Cole in tow.

"No, no you can't go in there! He's holed himself up in the bathroom and he's got his gun!"

Wade and Cole whirl around and gape at her.

"He's got a gun in there?" Cole says, shaking his head.

"I don't know if it's loaded or not, Wade, oh, I don't know. He just pointed that thing at me and told me to close the door, so I did! I don't wanna call the police, Wade, they'll just take him in and put him somewhere...oh, I don't know what we should do!" Millie bursts into tears and Cole steps over to her and takes his jacket off, wrapping it around her shoulders.

"C'mon, Mrs. Blake, maybe we should take you home, then my dad 'n' me, we'll talk him down."

Cole had only seen Durward in the throes of his "condition" once, when he'd been taking care of his mother. Durward had come outside in his bathrobe, hollering and diving into his bushes. Cole had gone out and instinctively knew how to talk to the old man, helping him get back into his house and calmed down. Wade knew Cole had that sense about him—that nurturing sense about people. That was Cole's gift, and why people took to him so readily. So different from his oldest son, who seemed to put people off the moment he said "hello."

"Oh, I don't wanna leave him. He needs me there for when he come out." Millie is sniffing and shivering.

"Whatever we do, let's get inside," Wade says, hurrying toward Durward's house. When they're all inside, Wade closes the door gently. No loud noises. Wade decides to use Durward's full name, since "Dude" was the nickname his army buddies had given him.

He motions for Millie to sit on the couch. She still shivers, gripping Cole's coat closed at her neck. Cole and Wade move from the living room to the hallway, in front of the closed bathroom door. No light came from underneath it.

"Durward," Wade says as calmly as he can. "Durward Hanson, this is your friend, Wade. Wade Kendall, from 'cross the street. You had one of them bad dreams again, buddy. Remember what we call them dreams? Hey, my son, Cole is here, my boy. You ain't seen him in a while. Why don't you come on out, and you and me and Cole and Millie, we'll all have a beer and sit on the couch an' talk. How 'bout that?"

Silence from the bathroom. Wade's heart is pounding. He stands in the hall, next to the door, Cole near him. Cole walks in front of Wade and goes to the other side of the door.

"Mr. Hanson, sir? It's me, Cole, remember me? How 'bout you come on out, and we can all sit 'n' talk? You're home, Mr. Hanson. Everything's all right."

Wade hears no movement. He reassures himself that he'd have heard a gunshot, even from his house, had Dude fired at all tonight. The gun probably isn't loaded. His chest feels heavy and suddenly he's worried he'd have another incident like when Tammy was over. His worry makes his head pound with the sound of his heartbeat. He tries to steady his breath, but it comes out choppy. He feels a little dizzy. Wade feels his back sliding to the left, near the bathroom door frame, as if he would pass out, right there.

Despite his efforts to calm himself, Wade is panting now. Through his breath, he manages to speak. "Durward, you got us, uh, you got us pretty worried out here, now, you just need to, uh, let us know you're okay in there. It, uh…was just a bad dream… ." Wade feels his legs slowly start to collapse under him. He hears Millie's voice, but it seems tiny and far away. Movement out of the corner of his eye as she hurries toward him. He doesn't have the strength to tell her to stay back.

"Wade, what's wrong?" Millie has him by his coat collar, pulling him back up. Cole is next to her, calling for his dad to look at him; panic fills their voices. Wade is aware they are both bustling around him, and all he can think of is the wooden bathroom door and how they're in front of it and then, without warning, there's a crack, a huge boom that causes his whole body to convulse in on itself. His ears scream with the noise, and the wooden door splinters out into the hallway. Millie screams as Cole bellows, a roar of pain coming from him, and Wade tries to gain a clear visual of his son.

Then it all fades to black.

Wade stares at the glaring overhead lights as his heart pounds heavily in his chest. The pills the nurse had given him had calmed a part of him, like a roll of bubble wrap around his feelings and thoughts, but his mind still thrashes around like a fish, half-caught on a line. The blood on Millie's face had been so red, as if everything else had turned to black and white. Her screams had been in color, too, only what color, Wade doesn't know. He can't remember anything else.

He'd awakened in the ambulance, the sirens blaring but somehow muted as he lay there with the paramedics checking his blood pressure. The oxygen mask kept him from talking, asking them, and every time he tried to move, they told him to "settle down." He had felt their hands on him.

His mouth feels like it's been dipped in tar, slow-moving, his tongue exploring the inside of his mouth as if it were a new place altogether. He tries to sit up, but he's so sleepy. When the door opens, he expects to see the nurse, or a doctor maybe, but instead he sees Tammy, Cindy behind her. Cindy's mascara has formed black half-moons under her eyes. Tammy's stare is penetrating.

"Tammy, what—what's goin' on? Is Millie all right? Where's Cole—"

"Shh, calm down. Millie's fine. But Cole…he's still in surgery."

The force of her words push him back into his pillow and his pulse rate jumps with the insistent *beep beep* sound as a pulse monitor hugs his finger.

Cole.

"Oh, my God," he whispers through cracks in his throat. The tears spring to his eyes and melt down his cheeks. He needs to ask her how bad it is, but he can't speak. Tammy moves near the bed and places an icy hand on his forearm.

"He's lost a lot of blood, but they told me they think he's gonna be okay."

"Where is he? I need to talk to the doctor, I need—"

"Wade," Tammy says, firm but soft, "you need to calm down. He's bein' tended to."

"Where was he hit?" His heart pounds; the fear seems far away and yet it coats him, all at once.

"His upper chest, the right side. They said it nicked an artery or blood vessel and he was bleedin' a lot, inside too. But Wade, he's strong, and they're gonna take real good care of him, all right?" Tammy is her new, authoritative self, and he looks at her. The comfort of her being there, the familiarity, it settles him as surely as the drugs that snaked through the clear tube, taped securely into his arm.

She continues. "We was worried about you, too. Thought you had a heart attack or somethin'."

"I don't know what the hell happened to me."

"The doctor thinks you had another one of them panic attacks and blacked out. Cindy heard the shot from across the street. Called the police and paramedics. Jesus…if she hadn't…" the implication hangs in the air, bringing a wave of nausea to Wade's entire body.

"Durward, is he--" Wade says, trying to stop the room from tilting in his vision.

"They got him in a psych eval situation. Millie told 'em about his spells. He didn't know what he was doin'. When he came to and realized what he done, he started bawlin' like a baby. He wasn't doin' too good, poor old guy." Tammy's gaze locks on Wade's, testing where he's at. Is he angry?

"Poor bastard." Wade says, answering the unspoken question. He pictures Durward, eyes wild, haunted by a war he had never really returned from, could not forget when his eyes closed and his mind took over the shadowy dreamland of sleep. "But they said Cole's gonna be okay? Right? That's what they toldja? When can I see him?"

Tammy hesitates. "They said things look hopeful. Look, now that you're a little better, the doctor'll wanna talk to you. So lemme go tell the nurse, okay? Just hold tight." With a last squeeze of his arm, Tammy leaves the room.

Wade looks over at Cindy, her lips moving and wiggling as she tries to maintain control. When she meets his gaze, she loses it and her face crumples as she covers it with her hands.

"I shoulda never let him come near that house. I shoulda told him to stay put," she sobs, shoulders shaking.

"It ain't your fault, Cindy. Not at all. If anything, it's mine. What was I thinkin'?" Wade's voice is thick with tears. "I never thought the old bastard'd have a gun."

She takes the two steps to the bed and collapses on him, crying in full-blown grief. Wade's tears dry as he awkwardly pats her back. He wants to lift her away from him, confused by all of the emotion he feels, but thankfully she moves away on her own.

She grabs a handful off tissue and sniffs, wiping her eyes and nose. "I'm goin' up to the surgery waiting room again."

"Well, wait, lemme come with you. I mean, nothin' wrong with me, right? I just gotta get this thing outta me, get my clothes on—"

"I think they gotta clear you or somethin', Wade. I'll tell the nurse to come in here and I'll see you up there. Oh, and you should know—I called Tammy after 911. She knew just what to do before the paramedics got there. If it weren't for her, Cole'd be gone. That's what the one paramedic guy said."

Wade watches her leave and a slight wave of dizziness and nausea hits him again. He doesn't know what's in that bag of liquid, but he had to get up and get to Cole. He stands, holding onto the bed rail, the metal pole attached to his IV moving on its casters slightly, and sees his clothes in a white plastic bag on the floor. When he catches his reflection in the mirror by the bed, he moves in closer and sees flecks of dried blood on his cheek and forehead. A stronger wave pummels his stomach and he makes it to the sink just in time.

After what seemed like hours, Wade was discharged with a higher dose of his blood pressure pills, and a prescription for anti-anxieties. One to take at night before bed, every night, and one that he can dissolve under his tongue as needed, up to four times a day. Wade's attending doctor knew nothing about Cole, but sent him up to the surgical center. They had given Wade a few anti-anxiety pills to take with him, but he was still reeling from the medication they had given him when he came in: something to lower his blood pressure, and an anti-anxiety, straight into his veins. His vision is not quite back to normal as he feels another wave of sick on the elevator.

Wade checks in at the desk and finds the waiting room where Tammy and Cindy sit. Cindy stares blankly at the television. He stops and watches them as he hears Bill O'Reilly on *Fox News* blaming atheists for the fall of Rome and saying how the U.S. is headed for the same fate.

When he approaches, Cindy looks up with a start and wipes at her nose with a wad of crumpled tissue. Tammy had been reading a textbook. She puts it to the side, a crease of worry between her brow.

"They haven't come out yet." Cindy moves her purse from the chair next to her, but Wade sits across from them, his back to the T.V.

"It's after midnight, Cindy. You sure you don't wanna head on back and we'll call you?" Wade knows her answer, but part of him wants to be alone, alone with Tammy. With his family.

"I can't leave until I know he's okay," Cindy says, wiping at her eyes again. Tammy's eyes are pinched, and a gray cast surrounds them.

"I'm her ride," Tammy says, "and I'm stayin' put."

"I-I wanna thank you. Both of you, because if it wasn't for you...I mean, I should have been the one to—"

"None of that. We can't play the 'should have' game here, Wade. What happened happened. You got nothin' to be ashamed about." Cindy stares at him, her nose bright red.

Hearing the word out loud causes his ears to burn. *Ashamed.* That's how he feels. His son gets shot and he has a fainting spell. Yes, he feels ashamed. His built-in animosity for Cindy transforms into a soft sort of gratitude. He goes over those moments in Durward's hallway and he knows he would have taken that bullet if he had thought Cole was in danger.

"I been readin' and panic attacks are a medical condition. There ain't no way you coulda controlled it," Tammy says.

"I don't get what they are, even. I ain't never panicked about anything in my whole life." Wade hears the flicker of anger touching his voice, heating it up.

Tammy leans over. "They're a physiological response, not a mental one. Your body just takes over, is what."

"Well, my body's becomin' more an' more useless every goddamn day then." He thinks about his date with Cindy, then, an unwanted image, and his ears burn.

"Well, the doctors can help you with 'em," Tammy says, looking into his eyes.

"You know," Wade says, "you used to say doctors don't know shit. Now you seem to think they can fix anything." He knows his response is unfair, but along with his self-loathing, the new Tammy feels unsettling. No longer needy, no longer mousy in his mind. And maybe that means he's no longer worthy of her, which is the most unsettling thought of all.

Tammy smiles a small smile. "I said that 'cause they couldn't save Annie. Truth is, doctors can only do so much, that's the bare bones of it. But what they *can* do is a lot compared to a hundred years ago. Hell, fifty years ago. *Ten* years ago. I'm learnin' all about this stuff an' it's somethin'. Truth is, I been considerin' goin' to nursing school."

Wade is forced once again to see Tammy, adjust his inner eyes and look at her in a whole new way, and if he cares for her, shouldn't her new ambition be something he's happy about?

A door sighs open out in the hall, and the three of them are on instant alert, watching the doorway. When the doctor in green scrubs enters the room, he looks around. Eyes on Cindy and Tammy, he then glances at Wade.

"Are you Mr. Kendall?"

"Yeah, yes sir."

"I'm Doctor Ward," he reaches over and Wade stands to face him and shake his hand. "We've stopped the bleeding, but he's still in serious condition at this point. The slightly better news is, he's no longer in 'critical condition.' Small comfort, but it's much more promising."

Wade has a sensation flutter down and through his torso. "What- what's that mean? I mean, what all happened?"

The doctor comes around to stand in front of the three of them. "The bullet entered through here," he uses his whole hand, like he was doing karate chop, "and it nicked a blood vessel and barely grazed the carotid artery. His clavicle bone literally saved him. Had it not hit his clavicle, he'd have bled out in minutes."

"Oh, Jesus," Wade puts his hand up on his forehead to wipe the perspiration that seemed to saturate his skin the moment the doctor spoke those last four words.

"We didn't need to remove the slug, it passed through his trapezius and out the back, but part of his clavicle was shattered. We got as much of the bone out as we could, but he's going to need to stay and get more stable before we go back in to repair it. The most crucial thing is to make sure no other bone fragments are migrating. If they are, it's important that we get him back in surgery as soon as possible, because bone fragments migrating around is...well, it's not good."

"You couldn't find them all?" Tammy asks.

"Our main concern was to stop the bleeding and get him as stable as possible. We did the best we could. He'll go in tomorrow morning for an MRI to visually ascertain whether or not we need to go in to remove more bone fragments. If we do, we'll need to act on it quickly, despite the risk of more internal bleeding. This is the critical stage here, folks. He's still out and we've got him in the intensive care unit for the night. We'll monitor him closely."

Wade's mouth is bone dry. "Well, what if...what if the MRI don't show any bone fragments left, then what?"

"Then that's good news. Then we get him stable and we can perform reconstructive surgery."

"What does that mean, I mean, how do you do that?" Wade's mind is grasping the scope of everything that's happening. He thinks of his son's life, he thinks of the recovery, he thinks of the bill, since Cole has no insurance. Wade's automatic thought goes to what he'd done for a living most of his life.

"Well, there's several ways. Since much of the bone is still intact, we can use a plate and pins to repair it. Depending on how much of it is actually missing, we might need to fuse the bone with screws, but that would shorten the bone and could cause shoulder, back, even neck pathology at a later time. But we're way ahead of ourselves here. For now, we need to watch him tonight, see what the MRI says, and go from there."

Wade stands, "Thanks doc, I mean it. Thanks for everything you did for him. Can I…I mean, am I allowed to see him?"

"I'll talk to the nurse. Actually, if you just want to come with me, I'll escort you in. He'll be asleep, and that's what we want right now. But I'll take you back for a few minutes."

Wade stands on wobbly legs and looks down at Tammy. She reaches up and grasps his hand for a moment. The touch gives him what needs to take the next wobbly steps, one in front of the other, trailing after the doctor into the hall.

The morning is chilly. The furnace hasn't kicked on yet. Wade's eyes feel like they're sealed shut, yet he's awake and knows from the pounding in his heart he's up for the day. After seeing Cole, with his tubes and his monitors and his slack mouth, Wade had broken down. The doctor told him he needed to get home, if only to rest for the big day ahead. So, Tammy had driven all of them home. The vision of Durward's dark house had reached down inside him and filled him with a sickness he could barely stand.

His nose detects coffee. He looks at the clock. Six twenty-three in the morning, and Cindy is already up. He wonders if she has work. He's still wearing his t-shirt and boxers, and when he sees the dark brown spatters on the shoulder, he pulls it off and throws it in the corner. He barely remembers the drive home the previous night. He doesn't remember crawling into bed. It must have been after 2 a.m.

He puts on his jeans and another t-shirt, then a sweatshirt because of the chill. When he comes out, the dog runs towards him, butt waggling and strange growl-whines coming from him. He considers punting it, but its eyes are so earnest as it looks up into his. Like Cole's eyes when he really believes something. He can't believe he's tolerating a dog because of Cole. The dog is Cole's "little buddy." Tears form and then, like a spigot, turn off as Cindy walks into the living room with a steaming cup of coffee. The only clothing she's wearing is Cole's shirt, and presumably underwear.

Wade walks into the kitchen and thankfully Cindy had made a full pot.

"When did you want to leave for the hospital today?" she asks him as he pours a mug. He tries to remember she saved Cole's life, but her clothing, or lack thereof, irritates him. Why does she think it's okay to walk around in her underwear around him? What does that mean in the Land of Womenspeak? Does he say something about it, or is that playing right into what she wants? Does he ignore it, all the while feeling like it's a violation, as his entire being aches for his son? Why does she have to be here?

"I guess as soon as I shower, and as soon as you're ready."

Wade doesn't look at her. He decides to sit in the kitchen at the small table rather than join her on the couch.

"Well, I'm showered, all I gotta do is get dressed," she says.

"Well, why don't you *do* that then." Wade hears the edge in his voice, so Cindy surely did, too.

"I was just waitin' for my jeans to dry," she says, no sound of defensiveness in her voice. He suddenly notices the sound of the dryer in the laundry room. Wade reaches up to his land-line phone and dials. He wants to cut off her presence before anything else comes out. He waits.

Milt's voice is clear, as if he'd been up for hours already. "Hello? Dad?"

"Milt, I gotta talk to you."

"What's up? Everything okay?"

"Milt, your brother's in the hospital. He got shot—it was an accident, but it's serious."

"Oh no. Jesus Christ, what happened?"

Milt's voice trembles with emotion and this is a comfort to Wade and he doesn't know why.

"Can you come down? He's at Northeastern Regional. He may be goin' into surgery today again. I can explain it all when you get here."

"Can you at least tell me the circumstances?"

"My neighbor, Durward, you know. Mr. Hanson. He thought Cole was somebody else. Shot him in the upper right chest. Hit some vital things like part of his artery, I can't remember all the doc said. But it would sure be good if you could come down."

"Let me call work and move my schedule around. I should be there early this afternoon. I-I don't know what to say. I'm in shock. What happened to Mr. Hanson?"

"They got him doin' psychological testin' or somethin'…he wasn't right in the head when he did it."

"I'm sorry, Dad. I'm going to let you go so I can call work and get on the road as soon as I can."

"All right. Thanks, Milt."

Wade hangs up the phone and remembers what happens to families when it's life and death. He remembers that all of the extra stuff, the stuff on the fringes evaporates, and all that's left is your family and what you mean to each other. He tells himself Cole is going to be fine. He tells himself that when Milt gets there, by sheer force of both of their wills, his youngest son would be just fine.

Cole woke up just in time for Milt's arrival.

Cole's brows were knit and although he tried for an easy smile, it came off pained and weak. When the brothers saw each other, there was an almost tender energy between them, like when they were very small, when Milt held his baby brother and spoke to him in unsure, soft tones to reassure him that his world was safe as long as his big brother was around. Wade watched and emotion sort of swelled inside him, filling him up, and he didn't know if it was pleasure or pain—or both.

"So they just fused it together, then?" Milt asks, voice low. He looks at Wade, since Cole seems a little fuzzy on the details.

"Yeah, no bone fragments, they didn't even have to add a plate, just a metal rod. It's shortened by some amount, like point 4 millimeters or somethin' silly like that, so it won't affect his throwin' arm, right, Cole?"

"Damn straight, it won't." Cole's words are slightly slurred. He breathes out hard and turns his face away.

"Cole, you look like you're in pain. Let's get the nurse in here—"

"Pop, I'm okay. I got pain meds."

"What do they have you on, Cole?" Milt asks.

Cole looks at them both, a small smile on his lips. "Well, they got me on as much Ibuprofen as I can stand."

"What?" Wade steps forward. "They got to have somethin' better'n—"

"Pop, Pop…" Cole moves his head once as if to shake it, then winces. "I told 'em that's all I can do. I take my past serious. I can't be takin' anythin' stronger, now."

Wade looks to Milt, and Milt has a look of understanding in his eyes. "Cole, I think that's very admirable. But listen, you'll heal faster if you're not in pain. You have a legitimate reason for taking them now—"

"Yeah, but this is how a lotta addicts relapse, Milt. It's too easy to do it. You gotta know how bad I want that Demerol. But I can't."

Wade looks down at Cole and shakes his head. "You are a determined sonuvagun, Cole, I'll give ya that."

"I think it's a mistake, Cole, but you do what you think you need to do." Milt steps away from the bed so Wade can move in close. He doesn't say anything, he just watches Cole's tortured face. He takes the chair next to the bed and glances at his two boys, his sons, both so different from one another, so different from him. Cindy'd had the good sense to leave them alone once she met Milt, and he was grateful for that, as if Milt would see right through his secret, know that he'd dated her, had her breast in his hand once, and judge him for it. What if Cole did some fool thing and married her? Cindy? His daughter-in-law? Well, at least he'd have *one* that doesn't hate him. Yet.

The nurse comes in and goes to work, checking Cole's vitals. Cole's cheeks are pale, his lips dry.

"You need to try and drink some water now, Mr. Kendall, all right?"

she says, voice lilting in a way that tells Wade she knows Cole is in pain, but she has to stay professional.

"Yeah," Cole says, "all right." She gives him a sip from a straw and he winces at the effort.

After she leaves, the water seems to refresh Cole just a little.

"I gotta have physical therapy and such, when I get out. Doc says I could be outta here by the first of next week, all starts healin' good."

"If all goes well; let's not rush." Wade places his hand on Cole's arm.

"Well, damn, it better all go well, 'cause I got to worry 'bout how much this is costin' me," Cole says, a different flicker of pain on his face.

Wade and Milt speak up at once. Wade stops.

"We'll help you, Cole, it's no big thing. Don't you worry about that." Milt nods his head, then looks at Wade. "Right, Dad?"

"Right, we got it figured out." Wade thinks of his dwindling savings account and the panic that thought provokes in him unsettles him. He'd called it his "Sienna account." Then he feels a wave of self-loathing; a selfish fool.

When Tammy arrives, the nurse tells them only two at a time, so Wade takes his leave. He wonders where the cafeteria is as he walks down the hall, when suddenly he sees a slight form walking surprisingly fast toward him. Her face is pinched, her hair flat on one side. Millie looks about ten years older.

"Millie! Millie, I'm sorry I ain't come up to see Durward yet, we been—"

"Oh, he's doin' fine, now, they got him on medicine for his condition, and he's just so awful concerned about your boy—"

"Cole's just fine, Millie. You tell Durward we know it wasn't his fault or nothin'. You tell him to just get better so we can all be home again."

"I-I hope they let him come home!" Millie begins to weep and Wade looks around in a panic, trying to find somewhere besides the bustling hall to talk.

"Here, let's go over here." He moves her to a side hall and she dabs at her nose with a tissue. "Now, what do you mean they might not let him go home?"

"His son, he lives in Oregon, and he thinks Dude should go live in *a home* up there. Oh, can you imagine Dude in a place like that? They're awful! Oh, if you could just talk to him…"

"Me? Talk to who? What do I say? I mean—"

"Wade, you tell him you'll watch out for him. The police took all his guns, now, so he's safe. An' they said the medicine will help his PTSD, so he should be just fine goin' back home, so you tell him, tell that son of his that he'll be fine!"

Millie's face is pure distress. Wade puts a comforting hand on her shoulder. "I swear, I'll do my best. I don't want the old bastard gone any more'n you do, s'cuse my French."

"He's on the fourth floor. You go see him with me. C'mon, Wade. It's time."

Wade steps off the elevator and can't help but get the willies knowing he's in a psychiatric ward. Something about that seems so wrong. Durward isn't mental, he's just scared because of the war.

The doors sigh open and Wade follows Millie to a room near the nurse's station. Durward sits at a table with a man a little younger than Wade. Durward is bringing a spoonful of green Jell-O to his mouth, the spoon shaking violently. When Wade steps in the room, Durward's face registers shock for a moment. Wade can only imagine the hell the old guy is going through.

"Dude, you old son of a gun, how you doin'?" Wade walks over and as Durward stands, still in shock, Wade gives him a big hug. "We was worried 'bout you, you old dog."

Durward's voice is strained. "How-how's your boy? How—"

"Cole is just fine. He is gonna be *a-okay*. We've all been worried 'bout you, Dude. How you doin'?" Before Durward can answer, the younger man stands from the table.

"How are you, Mr. Kendall? I don't know if you remember me. I'm Jack, Durward's son."

Wade shakes the man's hand, his likeness to Durward uncanny. "Nice to see you again. Yeah, I guess you flew the coop before we moved in, but

I seen you over there a few times. They takin' good care-a him?"

"They are. He's been doing very well, haven't you, Dad?"

Durward seems nervous, his eyes glassy. "Yah, they, uh, they take good care. I'm done with this, maybe I should rest. Wade…I'm…I don't—" tears fill Durward's eyes and his son reaches over and covers his hand on the table.

Wade squats down on the balls of his feet. "You listen to me, you old goat. Nobody blames you for nothin', you hear me? We all love ya, Dude. Cole's in his room bright-eyed and doin' just fine. He can't wait to give you a big hug himself when he can. We'll be barbequin' by summer, you watch."

"Well," Jack says, "he, uh, might come stay with me for a while. I live up in Eugene, and we've got a spare room for him—"

"I just wanna go home, damn it. I just wanna go home." Durward's voice cracks piteously and Wade looks at Jack. The man seems genuinely concerned about his dad.

"Millie, why don't you help Dude get into bed. Jack, can we talk outside for a second?"

"Wade?" Dude looks at him, the whites of his eyes showing.

"Yeah, Dude?"

"Can ya check my roses? Make sure they're doin' all right?"

"It's winter, them beauties are sleepin', Dude. Remember?"

"Oh, a-course. 'Course it is. Thanks, Wade."

Wade walks out of the room and Jack follows. Wade gets out of hearing range and stares at the floor tiles before meeting Jack's eyes. "I can see you wanna take care of your dad. He's—well, he's my best friend, if you want to know the truth—"

"He says the same of you, he kept saying that. He was really broken up about your son. But the police took the guns—have they spoken to you yet?"

"Not yet, but I'll tell you what, me 'n' Cole will be the first to tell 'em it wasn't his fault at all. An' now he's on some medications, I bet he's gonna be just fine."

"Millie told me how good you are with him. I had no idea—about the episodes. He never had them, or at least I never knew about them when I was young. Oh, I remember Mom telling me that Dad suffered from nightmares, but that's about it."

"Look, Jack, you know what's best. But I give you my word, I'll take care of your dad like he was my own, he goes back home. An' Millie, she practically lives there—I mean…not lives there, I-I… just stepped in it, sorry."

Jack laughs and he sees Durward, thirty years ago. "Hey, I'm a big boy, I can handle it. I think it's great, him and Millie."

"So-so you'll think about it? Because they have a good thing, and I check on him every damn day, that is, when he ain't checkin' on me."

Jack lets out a long sigh. It seems to Wade he is a little relieved when he speaks. "I'll give you my number in Oregon. Will you call me, every now and again? Maybe check in once a week? I mean, I call him, but he doesn't tell me anything. Except how great his roses are blooming."

"I'll call you once a week, let you know. I'll make sure he's got his medications. I'll get him to doctor's visits. Hell, I'm retired, I got all the time in the world. I think if he knows he's goin' home, back to the way it was, he'd be a lot better for it."

"You know," Jack nods, "I think you're right. And you've really set my mind at ease, so thank you, Wade."

Wade holds out his hand and they shake. Wade feels at home again, knowing he has someone to look after, take care of. Just like with Annie, only different. Durward's going to get better. He knows everything will be all right. He peeks in and sees Millie sitting on the edge of the bed with Durward. They both have their heads bowed, as if in prayer.

Jack smacks Wade on the shoulder lightly, "I'll go tell him the good news. I'll go tell him he's going home."

Part III

12

The book waited for him, between the screen and regular door. He didn't realize he had done express mail.

Unlike most nights, he suddenly doesn't feel so alone.

Cindy is at the hospital, and Milt is still there, too, but he'll be off soon, now that Cole is out of the woods. Dude won't be home for another week. As long as Cole continues to improve, he'll be coming home about the same time as Dude. Wade goes over the dinner he and Milt had in his mind.

It had been filled with news of the girls, which Wade had eaten up because he missed them so damn much. It was causing an ache in his chest to hear how they were growing up, growing up without their Grandpa Wade. He asked Milt if he could come visit, pinned him down. Milt had been surprisingly earnest about wanting Wade to come. Wade even caught Milt slipping into the "redneck" vernacular he'd used before college, law school. This pleased him, although he wasn't sure why at the time; now it feels like Milt had returned, in small part, back home.

"I sat down with the billing office, Dad, and they're working out a payment plan for Cole. I told them to send the bills to your place, then you forward them on to me. You pay what you can and I'll cover the rest. I want Cole to have every chance there is to start up his business. I don't want him to have to give up his money."

"What money? I keep hearin' about all this money Cole's got, but I don't know where he got it."

"Mom left him about $22,000 when she died, Dad."

"Oh." Wade had stopped and stared at a fuzzy point just behind Milt's head. He'd shook himself and shrugged. "Well, then. I had no idea."

"She didn't leave you...?"

"Well, I got a small insurance payment, that was 'bout it. I also got my pension, social security, an' so I'm doin' just fine."

"Good, because the thing is...if...well, if Carol knew I was paying for Cole's medical bills...I mean especially on my own, she'd knock me a new one. She thinks...well, it doesn't matter what she thinks. Cole's my brother, and I want to help him. But anything you can do to help would be—"

"Hey, I'm his dad, I'm your dad, matter of fact. I can take care of it. I live pretty simple. I mean, I ain't rich, but I'm doin' just fine."

And all the while as they spoke, Wade felt his "Sienna Fund" slipping from him, oozing out of the bank like sand sliding away from shore with a receding wave in the ocean. This made him feel like he'd let his priorities got all screwed up, like he was a terrible father. He hated the twist in his gut that came with the thought.

It had been a pleasant enough dinner, but Wade is glad he's finally home and alone. Standing on the porch, he opens the package in his hand and there it is, *The Winter of Our Discontent* by John Steinbeck. He hopes curling up in bed tonight will afford him the time to at least start reading it. He's itching to see Sienna, but the events of the past week have made her feel far away, removed from him.

Walking into the house he's hit by the smell: animal. Animal *shit*.

The dog is circling a pile of shit in the middle of the living room. Of course they had been gone since seven a.m. He curses Cindy under his breath.

The dog actually looks like it's apologizing. It looks terrified. Wade scowls for only a moment. He realizes it isn't the stupid thing's fault. It's Cindy's.

"Come on...what-the-fuck-ever your name is. Come on, let's go outside, come on." He opens the front door wide and the dog *yips* and runs outside, promptly sniffing the lawn for a place to go.

"Otis!" Wade calls out, suddenly remembering the dog's name. The dog freezes and stares at him. "That's your name. Sorry, go to it. Go do your thing. Go on, I ain't callin' you. Just go take a dump somewhere or piss or somethin'."

Wade gets paper towels and cleans up the living room floor, and all he has is Windex and furniture polish, so he Windexes the shit out of the carpet and scrubs. He tops it off with a mound of Lysol spray over the area. Hopefully Cindy take the hint when she gets back and feel like a pile of shit herself. He doesn't know why he's so hostile to her. But ever since she came on the scene, everything seems to have gone wrong. At least this is what he tells himself.

He thinks again of Millie's talk about stories, how everyone tells themselves a story about who they are and what their lives are like. In his story Cindy's the villain, and so is Pete. In his story he's a hero, but he isn't sure what his heroic acts are. He realizes that everyone is the hero of their own stories, and if that's the case, everyone sees their deeds as something special. So how can he be a hero if he passed out the moment his son got in harm's way? What story can the hero tell himself that keeps him heroic? And if he's honest with himself, he knows that Milt will be paying the bulk of Cole's bills, because Milt deserves to. Wade tastes the resentment inside him like a bitter root. His oldest son married a wife who hates his family, he's estranged from them and keeps his daughters away; he never visited or helped with Ann: Milt is paying his penance, and Wade feels as justified by that as by anything else he tells himself in his story.

He peels off his clothes, crawls into bed and tries to think of all of the ways he is a hero, and all of the ways he plans to be one, maybe to Dude, maybe to Sienna, maybe even to Tammy. He'll swoop down from the sky to save their souls, even at the cost of his own. But that thought is distant and far away as he drifts into sleep.

Durward had come home before Cole. Wade saw Millie carrying an overnight bag over to his house the day his son left him there. Wade wonders if she'll ever set foot in her own house again. He wonders if Durward would want her to.

The sun is out, but it's a winter sun, not quite spring, so the light reflects off of the snow, and its light in the sky is gray as if filtered through a dingy glass. Wade hates the black sludge of the street's edges, the way the snow is nothing but a crust over the lawn. He doesn't bother with a jacket. He just trudges down the driveway, cold air huffing in clouds out of his mouth as he crosses the street to see his friend.

Millie lets him in, all smiles, and Wade sees Durward sitting on the couch, looking as though he's visiting rather than living there.

"Dude, what the hell? How you doin'?"

"Oh, ya know, I'll be fine. These medicines they have me take give a dry mouth, see. And I got to drive to..." he uses his arm and a floppy hand to indicate behind him, "ya know, so I can talk to someone, once a week, ya know. I don't much like talkin' to him, but he's a nice enough fella, he just asks too many damn questions 'bout things shouldn't be talked about."

"That's how they help you get better, Dude." Millie places her bony hand on his shoulder. Then she looks at Wade. "The man, Albert is his name, he said that memories like the war are like water in a bottle that's over full. Soon the water just come bubbling out, is what he said."

"Sounds like a smart guy, Dude. I think it'll be okay."

"I don't know. Seems like he's nosy."

Wade and Millie exchange looks. She smiles a little nervously and Wade chuckles. He'd never been to a therapist himself, but he can imagine how Durward feels. "Well, they're thinkin' Cole will be ready by Monday to come on home. He's got PT—that's physical therapy—in Elko twice a week. Maybe we can work it out so's I can take both of you at once."

Durward's eyes flash a little. "How's he holdin' up. I mean, everything goin' to be all right with him?"

"He's going to be just fine, Dude. Look, think about it like someone accidentally slipped on ice in your drive or somethin'. It's like that. Nothin' you coulda done—"

"Put salt down."

"Well say it snowed more and you didn't have the time 'cause—"

"Always time to salt. 'Specially when people're comin.'"

"Jeez, okay, say that he accidentally ran into one of your walls and broke his nose—"

"Well what would he do a fool thing like that for?" Durward's forehead looks like one of those wrinkled dogs and Wade's about ready to give up on the whole analogy thing when Millie pipes up.

"Dude, what Wade's tryin' to tell you is it's like you were sick with the flu. Someone brings you soup, then they get sick. Nothin' you can do about it except bring 'em chicken soup like they brought you soup."

Durward thinks about that for a moment, then he smiles. "Yeah, he was dumb enough to bring me soup, well, I guess...well, no, that ain't right, 'cause he was just tryin' to help me. "

Wade puts a hand out, "Dude, what we're sayin' is no one blames you. Not me, not Cole...no one. And I bet Cole would love to have you visit. Hell, he's already up an' about at the hospital. They're just keepin' him over the weekend to make sure no infections or any complications from surgery happen and things. You see? So it's all fine. He's already drivin' them crazy with all his talk and whatnot."

"Well good, good," Dude smiles, but a crease of worry still rests between his brows. "And you're doin' all right? They said you had some sorta blackout when he got shot, and they was worried 'bout you."

"I'm just fine. See, I got my own head troubles, Dude. I got anxiety or some shit. Makes me black out. And hell, I ain't ever even been in a war, you tough son of a gun, so don't be sayin' nothin'."

Dude brightens at this. "So they got you on some pills too, do they?"

"Yeah. So we're even."

"Wade, you'll stay for dinner? I haven't had time to shop, but I'm making something for us, probably meatloaf with mashed potatoes."

"Oh, I would...I-thanks Millie, but I got somewhere I'm headin' out to tonight, so, thanks anyways."

"You goin' back to see Cole?"

Wade decides that agreeing with their assumption would do. Better than stammering through a lie that he'd have to conjure on the spot.

"Yeah, yeah, that's right."

"Well, you give him our best," Millie says.

Wade is champing at the bit to get the hell out and get to Sienna. He worries because it's Thursday, and what if she's gone?

"Will do. I'd better run, so you two have a good evenin' and I'll see you soon."

Wade lets himself out into the brisk air. The sun's light has started to drop, casting shadows on snow and houses, the tired street vacant and silent. He needs to shower and clean up, then he's heading down where he can be with her.

He thinks of Millie, sitting by Durward's side, and the stark contrast of what he's about to do hits him full in the center. Durward's got something real, something he can touch and hold, any time he wants. Millie cares about him. The comparison leaves him with a cold feeling in his chest. He'd sworn to himself at one point in his life that he'd never go there, to one of those brothels. When did he lose that conviction? Why had he had it in the first place?

Because he'd wanted something real. His whole life, all he'd wanted was something real. Annie was real. But does real mean trading in what you need? Was sex a need? Wade isn't so sure. It seems to him like Durward and Millie have so much more than sex. And what they have, that's a need. A real need. The prickling thoughts continue to dog him as he strips for his shower, an unsettling heaviness weighing in his chest.

During his shower he wondered if he shouldn't be going to Elko to see Cole rather than to the hen house. Part of him also wondered if Sienna is even there, and that makes a difference. He tells himself he's a good father, and a fleeting montage of proof plays in his mind as he attempts to reassure himself. When nothing stands out, he heads toward Elko to see Cole.

Ten minutes out of town he finds a place to turn around and head back. Cindy is at the hospital; it will be awkward. And he needs to see Sienna, if only to say goodbye before she leaves. He feels like he has important things to tell her. And there's the book he's started. The Steinbeck book has been touching him in a personal way that he's not sure he understands. It almost makes him squirm a little.

Heading back toward town, he doesn't take the usual exit. He goes past Wells to take the last exit. It's the quickest way to Mamacita Highway. The light is amber from the sun sinking low in the west, but he makes out a car along the highway, just past the exit going west. The person walking alongside it has long, dark hair, blowing in the frigid breeze that had come up, the precursor to a storm on its way in. He knows Sienna's on his mind and that's why it looks like her, but he drives the extra few hundred feet past the exit to see if he can help anyway. His heart leaps up in his throat when he sees that it is her.

She ends her call when he parks in back of her and steps out of the truck.

"You got car trouble?" he calls as he walks toward her.

She doesn't greet him with the same warmth as at the cathouse. She almost seems suspicious.

"Yeah, and no one can come get me for at least a half hour, so I was just going to walk—"

"Hey, I got a tow rope. Why don't we tow it over to Otto's and see if he can work on it. Might be closed, but at least you won't be on the side of the road."

She looks at him and a smile forms on her face. She has no makeup on, and the effect stuns him a little. She looks like she could still be in her teens. "I don't know if I should…I mean, Belle has rules."

"What rules? That you can't accept help from an ugly old guy?" He smiles and she laughs, bowing her body forward, causing her hair to dance around in the wind like a flared skirt

"No, it's just…"

"C'mon, call 'em and tell 'em a stranger gave you a ride back into town. I'll pull around and get the tow rope on. All right?"

"All right." Her teeth are chattering.

"What's it doin', anyway?"

"As I started going it just petered out, like I ran out of gas, but I've got plenty of gas."

"Smokin' or anything?"

"No, no smoke."

"Hm, okay, you know how to get towed, dontcha?"

"Uh, yeah! After all the shit cars I've had in my life, I sure do know how to get towed."

He smiles, but his heart is pumping so hard he can barely keep from panting. *This is just me, helping a stranger on the road. This ain't nothin' else.* She gets in her car and he pulls in front of her and hops out, grabbing the tow rope from behind his front seat. He glances up at her behind the wheel of her car as he secures the rope to her bumper.

They ride into town slowly, and the sky is casting gorgeous pastel hues as they pull into Otto's Car Repair and Body Shop. Wade pulls her car parallel to the fence so it's out of the way. When he gets out of the car, she steps out with her bag.

"I can wait here for a ride."

"That's silly. I mean, where do you want to go?"

"Home, actually," she laughs. "It's been a long week. I miss my son."

Wade looks at her face, and the youth in it is lost when he looks her in the eyes. There is no youthfulness there, only a weary blanket covering a tired gaze.

"Listen, I'll call Otto in the mornin' and tell him it's your car and tell him he needs to get on it first thing, okay? I can have him call your cell when he knows what's wrong with it."

"Thank you. Thank you, Wade. You've been very sweet."

"So you wanna go eat? We can—"

"There's no way I can go to dinner with you…I mean no way."

"Well can I at least give you a ride back to Mamacita's? I know you're off work an' all, so I won't stay or nothin', I'll just drop you off. No one need know it was me, okay?"

She looks down for a moment then nods her head. "Okay."

Having her in his truck is so surreal he can barely concentrate on the road. He holds off his imaginings, knows his head will be wild with them when he gets home, anyway. Hell, even if she had said yes to dinner, he wouldn't have been able to eat a thing.

They pull into the gravel parking lot and his spirits drop as she grabs her duffel bag from the seat. "Well, thanks again. Oh, here's my cell number…you got a pen?"

"Uh, check the glove box. I don't know if I do…"

"Oh, here's one in my purse. Can I just use this napkin?"

"Sure."

"Okay, so I should just expect his call in the morning?"

"Yep, I'll have him call first thing, at least to tell you what's wrong with it. From there, you know. You'll have to see."

"Thanks again, you saved my ass tonight." She leans over and kisses his cheek, a chaste kiss that nonetheless stirs him.

He watches her walk to the door, and when she looks back, he realizes she won't want anyone to see who brought her.

When he gets home, he calls Otto.

"Otto, it's Wade. Yeah. There's a gray Ford Focus parked out front of your place. Can you check it first thing? I don't know, sounds like somethin' with the fuel line, maybe the pump. But if you would just get on it first thing then call me when you're done. Just fix it and call me when you're done. Well if it's over a grand, yeah, call me. Otherwise, just fix it."

He looks at the napkin with her handwriting, oddly feminine and girlish. Every letter seems rounded and like a flowering vine. It's only six o'clock, but he's going to get in bed, read the book until he can sleep. Then, as he drifts, he'll think of her in his truck, think of her riding next to him as if it wasn't anything at all.

Wade automatically stands when the bearded man comes out of his office and says, "Durward?"

Durward stands and Wade suddenly feels like he's being scrutinized through to his spine. "Hi, I'm Wade."

Albert, the therapist, who looks like a hippie out of his time, takes two steps toward him. "Hi, I'm Albert."

"Wade. Oh, I said that. Sorry."

"Ah, Wade, Durward tells me your son's doing okay. How are *you* doing?"

"Me? I'm fine. I'm great. I got nothin' to say on anything except that Dude here is our good friend and we want to see him, you know, feelin' better."

Albert smiles a patient smile, "I'm glad Dude has friends and neighbors like you to support him. It makes all the difference in the world."

"Great, that's good," Wade nods. "Well, my son's in PT so I'll be back in about an hour to get him."

"Great, great, nice to meet you, Wade."

Wade makes his way from the professional offices to the other side of the hospital where Cole is getting worked on. He has his book and it's breaking his heart. He should have known with a title that had the word "discontent" in it, that it would be a sad, tense read. He doesn't know why the plight of old Ethan Allen Hawley has him so emotional. Ethan's a good man. And he's getting sucked into things he can't seem to control, all because of his innermost desires. And those things threaten his very soul. Wade is almost done with the book, and he's afraid the ending will make him cry, like the last one had. Sienna comes back in two days. He'd have to talk to her about her books. Maybe she could read a goddamned comedy for once.

Tammy had brought dinner last night and thankfully, Cindy hadn't been there to yap and yip and speak Womenspeak while he sat there like a fool. That had happened the week before and he couldn't get out of there fast enough. The new Tammy had a friend. The new Tammy yapped and yipped.

He also knew Tammy would be at the hospital today. She had something, some training she was doing there, and so he told her to come by and say 'hi' if she was in the area. He keeps re-reading pages because everyone who walks by seems like they would be Tammy, until finally, just as he gets into the book, it is.

"Well there you are." Tammy sits down heavily next to Wade with her butt close to the edge of the chair and her legs spread out.

"Oh, hey, I was just readin'. Sad book." He hoped she would see he is improving his life, just as she is improving hers.

"What is it? Huh, never read it."

"It's about this guy in New England back in the early sixties, and how he's just a store clerk, but he has a chance to be a big shot, see, 'cause he came from a good family, but his chance to be a big shot means he has to do some things that ain't...right."

"Huh."

"Yeah."

Is the old Tammy back? Is he relieved?

"Well," she says, "I just spent two hours learnin' how to find a vein and poke a needle into it. See?" She shows him her arm.

"You had to do it on your own arm?"

"No, we all had to get poked. The instructor, nurse, whatever, she did me. But see? No bruisin' and it stopped bleedin' pretty quick and that's what you want."

"So medical assistant, huh?"

"I'm still thinkin' about nursing school. I think I'd be good at it. You know."

"Well sure you would. I mean, you're so calm and you're confident and people like you, and—" he stops and stares down at his book. He should have stopped at "calm."

She's looking at him, so he meets her gaze and her eyes are questioning. "You think I'd be a good nurse?"

"Hell, yeah. I mean, sure. You'd be a great nurse."

"I appreciate that. I do, I mean it." Her eyes start to leak a little and Wade moves to touch her, but thinks better of it.

"Oh, hey, what's wrong? What's the matter?"

"It's just...I dunno. Nothin'."

"No, what?"

She sniffs. "Stu seems to think I should just stop and be an assistant because nursin' is too hard and the pay an' hours ain't great startin' out and he said I'd be a part of this evil system of insurance companies, an'—"

"You know what?" Wade's face burns with anger. "You know what? You can tell that son of a bitch that just because he's goin' nowhere with no future an' he's a lazy big-mouth, he don't need be pissin' all over your dreams, you know? You tell him that." He hadn't expected to have it come out so angrily, but he could feel his ears burning with rage.

"I don't know. Maybe he's right, maybe I'm too old—"

"You ain't too old for nothin'. I'd support you one-hundred percent, if I was...I mean, I do support, I mean, if I was him, I mean—"

She gets a small smile on her lips. "Stu and I, we ain't like...serious or nothin' anyways. It's not like he can tell me what to do. I know 'bout him."

"What do you mean 'you know 'bout him'? What d'you know?"

"He's just a blowhard. And I know I ain't the only one, if you know what I mean."

"Oh, well...then why you wastin' time with him?" Wade starts to mentally kick himself again, a thing he finds himself doing with Tammy a lot lately. It seems that now that she's opening up to him, he's doing the same and it is the opposite of playing it cool, and he really wants to play it cool.

"He's someone to be with you know. Somebody, you know, to watch T.V. with, an' talk to and have dinner sometimes, an'...you know."

Wade's head is screaming that he is all of those things, he could be all of those things, do all of those things. But maybe he is just her brother-in-law after all and that thought spirals him down into a dark place.

"Yeah, I guess he is. It just seems like you're settlin' an' you shouldn't be, that's all."

She glances at him, a side long glance that makes him want to turn away, but he doesn't. Then she drops the bomb. "I mean…I seen his car at the cathouse. It ain't like I don't know. He don't talk about it, but I know."

Wade seals his lips shut, not wanting to hear what she has to say, but she says it anyway.

"I mean a man who goes to them places? He ain't ever gonna settle down or be right for one woman. Or he's a cheat."

"Well, I'm sure it takes all kinds."

She looks at him then, a hard, long look, and he finds he squirms in his seat under her gaze. "Why do you think men go there, Wade?"

"I don't know. How would I know? I mean, shit, maybe just 'cause they're lonely."

"Yeah," she says, still staring at him. "Yeah, an' so maybe they're settlin' too. Maybe they got somethin' right in front of them an' they just don't see it."

Wade stares straight ahead, afraid to move, afraid to breathe. His heart pounds in his chest and he can't look at her. If she's seen Stu's car there, has she seen his truck? It's not like he's ever bothered to hide it. Her eyes are burning the side of his face. Suddenly Cole walks around the corner. Wade can see the pain on his face, like a shroud. He tries to cover it with his smile, but it never quite reaches his eyes anymore.

"Hey, Aunt Tammy. What's up?"

Wade parks his truck out back with the semies, knowing that Tammy could easily find it if she was looking. Married to her sister for thirty-three years and he's a man who can't commit? A cheat? He argues with Tammy in his mind while he walks to the front of Lil' Mamacita's and rings the bell. When he asks for Sienna, Leslie tells him she's unavailable. Would he like to see the lineup?

He sits at the bar and an unrest settles inside him, like a wind whipping dirt devils up before a storm. He'd brought the book, and goes through all of his underlined passages. One sticks out in his mind and he turns to the page and re-reads: *Does anyone even know the outer fringe of another? What are you like in there?*

What is Sienna like in there? What is she like with another man? Telling him what he needs to hear, wants to hear, just like him. He isn't special, never will be special, and to think it is to be a damn fool. He's a man who'd had principles: he would never go to the cathouse. But he wasn't getting laid, he wasn't getting affection, so he drops into the mud with everybody else, just like Ethan Hawley, and is he any happier? Is he better off?

He sees a portly man in his thirties rounding the corner and he can't help but see who's behind him. Seeing her long dark hair, his stomach drops and flutters all at once. He instantly berates himself for being so gullible. She sees him and he can't decipher the look on her face. It's not unfriendly, but there's a stern quality to it, as if he's in trouble. She holds up a finger for him to wait, then retreats into the hall.

The car. She's going to give him hell because he paid for her car to get fixed. It was only $430.00, but she might not like that he did it. Like she's indebted to him now, somehow. He finishes his beer in one gulp and a few minutes later, she comes around the corner and beckons him to her. Usually she comes to him at the bar and greets him. He starts to panic. What if she tells him he can't come to see her anymore?

When he reaches her, she wraps her arms around him and hugs him tightly to her, and he responds, relieved she isn't telling him to scram. Without a word, she takes him back to her room.

The both start speaking at once. They say "sorry" at the same time, then laugh.

"You go," Wade says.

"Okay, Wade…I…thank you so much. For my car. I felt bad I didn't have your number to call and thank you two weeks ago. But thank you. You didn't have to—I mean, you shouldn't have done it, really. We're not supposed to accept favors from clients, but, like, I didn't tell Belle or anything. So, anyway, just…thanks."

"Hey, no big deal. Okay? Forget about it. I was gonna tell you I finished the book." He holds it up for her to see. Her face breaks out into that girlish grin that makes her look nineteen.

"And? Did you like it?"

"Yeah, I mean it was a little sad, you know? I mean, he got everything he wanted an' then he wants to off himself because he feels like a failure, I mean, right?"

"Well, in a way, yeah. I mean, he does things that are not exactly morally wrong, and to anyone looking in, they can't exactly be called 'wrong,' you know? But when Ethan's son does what he does, it's like a foil for what Ethan has done, in a way."

"A foil? Like 'curses, foiled again'?" Wade laughs. She pulls his hand to sit on the bed with her.

"We read that in class, too, so it's not like I'm super smart or anything, but his son, Ethan's son? Yeah, he's like his mirror, reflecting back to him how he's betrayed himself."

"Now, see? That's just awful, because Ethan, he didn't really do anything so wrong, did he? I mean, he really gave that guy money to get better, an' the guy didn't get better, but—"

"Wade, thank you."

"Huh? For what?"

She looks down at the carpet. He notices it's this industrial hard stuff, dark gray with flecks of color through it. Like a cheap dentist's office. "For the car. For reading the books. It makes me feel…like I'm not so alone. I mean, it's just really nice."

He wants to ask her if any of her other clients read her books, but he knows better. He is special. He lets himself feel special, too. He leans over and when she kisses him, her kiss has a passion to it that stuns him a little. They roll back onto the bed and she hasn't inspected him, he hasn't paid her, it's just them, kissing, pulling at each other's clothes, him smelling her hair, fondling her breasts, which have fallen free of her robe. His cynical mind wonders if this is his payment for the car. Giving him this moment. But his optimistic self tells that other self to shut the fuck up because this is real, right here; you can't fake this. Can you?

She pulls away from him and smiles. "Well, I guess we should play by the rules now."

Wade is jarred back into his mind, and the cynic and optimist blend together into reality. He pulls out his wallet and pays her.

"Be right back."

After she leaves, he wonders what to do. His instinct is to stay dressed and talk to her for an hour, find out who she is "in there." The other part of him is greedy, whispers that he has paid for it, for that release, that closeness, and he should take advantage and then talk. He quickly undresses and waits for her. But he knows nothing is happening *down there*. His dick had been hard while they had writhed on the bed, but he can feel it now. Nothing is happening and nothing is going to happen tonight. His penance, finally, for sliding into the mud.

The blood is all in his face and chest and nowhere near his dick. She inspects him, wipes him down and disrobes and there is nothing he can do but let her take him into her mouth while he tries to enjoy it and clear his head. It occurs to him that she hasn't put a condom on him yet, and the sensation of her mouth should be getting him hard, but it isn't. After a few minutes of no response, she asks him if they should move to the bed and he nods, mute and shriveling, inside and out. Something inside him wants to call out, yell at the top of his lungs, some sort of anger broiling up that he can't place. It's not for her, but it surrounds her, like a black and blue halo, tender to the touch and aching.

"What's the matter, baby?" she asks.

"Uh, nothin'…and could you not call me that? I don't like that word. It doesn't feel…dignified." *Dignified*? He doesn't know why his chest is on fire.

"I'm sorry," she retreats a little, he can feel it, not just in her body, but in *her*. He doesn't want her to retreat.

"No, I'm sorry, it ain't no big deal. I mean, I'm just…I don't know what's wrong with me tonight. Maybe I should just get the hell outta your hair."

"No! Wade, look we can talk. See? We can just talk, like that one time."

Wade had hoped 'that one time' had been erased from her memory because he'd tried to erase it himself.

"Well, we talked all about me, so now it's your turn. Let's talk about you." The prickly feelings have started to bleed onto Sienna, and he wants to say something, do something, that will shatter her calm. She has seen him—all sides, and it's only fair he gets to see her.

"Okay, what do you want to know about me?" She's still distant, but she brings her hand up and touches his arm, moving her palm up and down from his shoulder to his hand, where she takes each finger and gently rubs it in her fist.

"Why do you do this? I mean, besides the crazy good money. I guess I just wonder why someone so smart couldn't find a job somewhere else, doin' somethin' else. Not that there's anything wrong with this, but you know what I mean."

She rolls off of him a little and onto her belly. He looks down the length of her, her ass rising up from the curve of her lower back and he feels a tingle but he's more curious than excited now.

"I usually tell other people who ask me that the same thing: I do it because I like it. But that's only part of it."

"What's the other part?"

She buries her face for a moment and then looks at him. "Can I trust you? I mean, I don't tell people this. Not that I'm ashamed of it," she says quickly, "it's just private."

"'Course you can trust me. I'd never do anything to hurt you. You gotta know that by now."

She smiles at him and rolls back into the comfort of his arm around her. He kisses her forehead, an oddly intimate gesture that arouses him.

"I want to go back to school to get my degree in social work. Then I want to train as a sex therapist and surrogate. There. You know the truth."

Wade thinks for a moment and then has to ask. "A sex surrogate? What, like a person who has sex with people who don't have partners who can, or—"

"No, I help people—well, I *want* to help people who have sexual problems, dysfunction or trauma. I want to help heal people from their sexual wounds. Do you know how many people are walking around, all the time, with sexual wounds, Wade? God, so many."

Wade is silent. Is that what he is? Sexually wounded? Is that why she's drawn to him?

"So do you think I'm wounded?"

"Truth? I think, in a way, yeah, you are. Maybe you got shamed your whole marriage for wanting sex, maybe you got rejected—"

"But that's just how women are, I mean were, back then. Wives did that, right? It's the oldest story in the book. The ol' headache routine. An' my wife, she was sick—"

"Nothing against your wife, Wade—I'm sorry. I didn't mean to blame. It's just what I see. I've had other men—"

"You know, maybe the problem is *men*. Did you ever think of that? I mean, maybe men are just too horny and women are nature's way of sayin' 'no, grow the fuck up and do somethin' else,' you know?"

"I don't believe that. Women are given sex drives, too, and some of them love sex."

"Yeah and maybe they're weird, too." He doesn't know why he's arguing with her, but it feels good to challenge her idea of sex and he doesn't know why. "Maybe sex just ain't that big of a deal."

"So…if I was your wife and I wanted sex every night, or every other night, you'd think something was *wrong* with me?"

Her words jar him and he can't speak. *If I was your wife.* His throat is thick with emotion, and he has a hard time speaking.

"If you was my wife, I'd give you anything you wanted."

She looks hard at him "But you'd think I was weird. You'd think I should be telling you 'no,' is that it? But because I'm a sex worker, I won't say 'no,' right?"

"I don't mean that—I—maybe you're right. Maybe I am fucked all up about sex and things. Maybe I'd need you to therapize me." He smiles at her, hoping to break the tension.

"I thought out of everyone, you would understand. I mean, there are disabled people out there who will never have a partner, so they get a sexual surrogate to experience sex for the first time. Do you think that just because they are disabled, their sex drive is gone?"

He thinks of Gerry in his wheelchair and all desire leaves his body. Had she been with Gerry?

"I don't know, I guess not, huh?"

"No. As a matter of fact, I've had a client in a wheelchair before. He'll probably never get married or have a lover, so he sees me, so I feel like I'm already doing sex therapy and doing some good in the world."

"I didn't mean to make you mad. I'm sorry. I think you're a good person, Sienna. I do, I mean…I couldn't do what you do—"

"Of course not, because men are wired differently than women, and maybe this is my own prejudice, but I think most men are too selfish to ever be sex surrogates, frankly."

Wade holds very still and looks down again at the curves of her body. He feels a shift in the air and it isn't a good shift, nor is it retractable. As if a corner has been turned. Now he sees her, now he knows her, and she's shut him out from the person she was.

"I admit it, I'm too selfish an' I couldn't be one. You're right. I should probably go."

She sighs heavily and moves away from him to look at him. "I didn't mean to be so harsh. We can start over."

He'd fed his anger with the argument, and now it recedes like a summer storm, leaving a suffocating heat behind. He had been angry at her for all of her hidden parts, and now that he's caught a glimpse of them, he can't be angry anymore, but a vision of her in his life has been shattered.

He looks into her eyes and he makes a face that tells her the truth before his voice does: "No, we can't."

13

March 12, 2015

I haven't been writing because I've been really busy. And I have to admit it. Sometimes when I'm here, I just want to be on autopilot and not think about home, Jacob, the future. I feel like I just need to survive the moment. It's not like that's a bad thing, it's just what's happening. I've got three more days until I can go home. The last two weeks have been weird. A lot of shifts. My car broke down and Wade drove up and found me. He towed me, then he paid for my car to get fixed which is completely against the rules. I don't know why he did it other than he probably still has some sort of crush on me. I wasn't sure what I should do about that. I felt shitty for charging him the next time he came in, but he's got to know that's how it works. So he came in and he was limp and he had an edge to him, like he was all prickly. I probably shouldn't have told him about my plans, but I did and we sort of butted heads. He went on the offensive and started dissing men, as if men were all freaks because of their sex drives. What am I supposed to say to that? I also got this weird feeling like he felt some kind of ownership or something. That could have been my imagination. All I know is we disagreed on some stuff and now it feels like this barrier I had with him—the one I have with all of my clients, is gone. I don't know if it's because of the car thing or because I told him I wanted to be a sex surrogate. I've never told anyone except the other girls here, and definitely not a client. He said that sex wasn't that big of a deal, but I think he was talking to himself but aimed it at me. I honestly don't know if he'll ever come back, at least not to see me, which kind of sucks because he is a good enough customer and tips well and he seems safe enough. He didn't ask me what I was reading this time and so maybe that was just his way of getting close to me at first. Every client has their deal I guess. Belle warned me that the girlfriend thing I wanted to do could get muddled, and now I see what she means. I don't know if I could do it any other way, though, and I think that scares me a little. The girlfriend illusion is just as much for me as it is for them.

I did feel safe with Wade. So I guess I learned my lesson. Speaking of safe, I had this guy come in and what he wanted was even weirder than the pee guy. He came in Sunday night. He was a doctor, an anathesieologist (sp?) and when we got to my room, he had a hospital gown for me to wear. He put on a mask. He told me to count back from ten very slowly and then pretend I was completely out. Then he just fondled me over and under the hospital gown. He didn't get on me, didn't even really touch me down under, just my breasts and between my legs, not inserting anything. Then as he did that, he made himself come on the hospital gown on my stomach. And that was it. If I follow this scenario to its conclusion, I'd say this guy is a walking time-bomb. If this is what he does for a living, I can't see him not acting on this fantasy at some point. I wonder if he went into medicine because of this fantasy, or if it developed over time while he was in medicine? I don't know but I should definitely find out what hospital he's at and never go there.

I guess I could look at it in a better light. He's aware enough of the fantasy that he lives it out here rather than in reality. I think thinking about it in a more generous way is good for me. If I'm going to be a therapist, I can't be judging people like that. I guess I have things of my own to work out. But I'm sure school will prep me for that.

I keep coming back to Wade because it was so disconcerting. When I told him about the sex surrogate stuff, it was almost like I needed his approval. Why would I need his approval? And when he didn't give it, it was really—I don't know, it felt really uncomfortable. And maybe it's good he doesn't come back to me because he's limp, for one, but also seems really invested in a personal connection with me. Like he already fantasizes that we've got some 'special' thing going on. I said "If I was your wife, would you think something was wrong with me if I wanted sex a lot" and he got all freaked out and flustered, as if me being his wife was even on the table for me. Maybe I need to get some advice from Belle on this one. In a way it made me sad about him. In another, I got angry and felt like slapping him and saying, *"are you insane?"* I mean, I realize he's new to this, but what a total cliché to fall for the sex worker. And I think when I told him about the sex surrogate stuff, it's like he realized I would never be *"his"* on any level, even in his fantasy, and then this I remember: he told me nothing would ever be the same. Things could be the same for me, so I don't know why they have changed for him unless he really did have the fantasy that I could fall for him. Why can't they accept that the brothel and everything in it is the fantasy? That. Not anything else. It's like he was in such a hurry to make the fantasy a reality, he ended up finding the reality then losing the fantasy forever. Didn't he see that coming? Didn't I? I wish I could call him. I know that sounds dumb, but I wish I could. I would talk to him and tell him to come back. Shit. I don't know what's wrong with me and why I'm freaking out so much about this. He just got under my skin, that's all. I just need to exfoliate. Scrub him away.

I kind of hope that doctor comes back though. Good money for drifting into a nap and maybe I can get him to open up about it. It would be interesting to see what makes him tick.

Wade has nothing to read, so he reads *The Stranger* again because he knows it will give him perspective, and it does. Other than shooing the animals off of his couch and lap constantly, it's pretty quiet. Cindy is working a lot, and Cole is out trying to make the dream of storage units a reality. Wade drops in on Durward every day but he's never there without Millie. Wade told Millie she should just move in, but she chided him and said she liked her house being there just fine. Maybe Millie's the one who needs a break from Dude?

A loud rapping at the door startles him and he thinks Millie's out there, but the rapping is very loud, too loud for Millie and when he sees who's out there, he freezes. Pete's on his porch and Wade doesn't need another bloodied nose. He steps up to the door.

"Your niece ain't here," he yells.

"C'mon Wade, open up. I'm sorry 'bout what I done. I gotta talk to you right now—it's important."

Wade opens the door cautiously and when he sees the emotion on Pete's face, he doesn't know whether to block a blow or ask him in.

"What is it, Pete?"

"Wade, you'd better come on down to Luther's. Just come on down. I'll meet you th—"

"I ain't goin' anywhere 'til you tell me what's up."

"Junior asked me to come fetch you, all right?" Pete turns and walks down and away from the porch and Wade is left staring at his retreating back. He's driving his regular truck so he must be in town for a few days. He's still pissed about what Pete had done, inflicting that smelly vermin on him, his obnoxious niece, and of course, having to watch her and Cole cling to each other like a shirt caught in a cactus tangle. But he said Junior sent for him, so he gets his shoes and a jacket and drives to Luther's. It's only three p.m., the off hour, so what's so urgent?

When he walks in, there are three or four men there, including LeMar, who works at the sheriff's department.

Wade walks in and nobody speaks to him, but they all look at him as he approaches.

"Junior, what's goin' on?"

It's then he sees Pete sitting at a table with a beer and he's got tears running down his face.

"Junior?" Wade asks.

Junior walks around the table and puts his hand on Wade's shoulder. His eyes are misty as well. "Wade, they found Gerry this mornin'. He shot himself. Gerry's dead."

Wade hears himself ask why, but he doesn't really expect an answer. The indifferent world won't miss one more war vet, will it? The indifferent world won't miss one more guy in a wheelchair. And suddenly, Wade is enraged at the indifferent world and decides that everything matters—everyone matters. At least to him. He hadn't realized that his face had crumpled and he sat heavily in a chair and wept while Pete reached across the table and held tight to his arm.

He rings the buzzer and Belle answers. He hadn't expected Belle, but he thinks she must have known he needed her, or needed someone.

"Wade...you look like you been hit by a truck, buddy. Come on in. What can I getcha? Anything?"

"Nah. I just came to see Sienna for just a second, really. No big thing."

"Anything wrong I should know about? You got on with her okay last time?"

"Yeah, oh, yeah. I mean, that's fine. I wanted to ask her 'bout a book, that's all. I know she leaves today."

Belle steers him toward a stool and sits him down. Then she gives him one of her bear hugs.

"You look like you needed one of them. What's cookin' in that noodle? I got some free time, you wanna talk?"

Wade doesn't trust he can say it without emotion, but he says it anyway, his eyes dry and his voice like an arid plain.

"My good friend, he, uh, he went an' shot himself yesterday. No note or nothin'...no reason, no explanation. I mean, I knew he had shit...you know? 'Cause of the war an' he'd gone had his legs blown off, so I know—"

"Oh Jesus. Gerry? Are you talkin' 'bout Gerry? I didn't hear."

"Yeah. I mean, we hung out over at Junior's place, you know. It's not like I had him over to my house or I went to his or nothin'. But maybe I should have if'n I'd known."

"Damn." Belle puts a straight arm on the bar and stares at it. Her eyes have a red rim of emotion and she shakes her head slowly. "We all knew Ger was a troubled soul. Lonely, too. But you never know about people. You can't predict and you can't tell yourself you messed up so they're gone. Everyone gets lonely, but not everyone does what he did."

"I guess that's the truth."

"You want a bloody beer?"

"I could use one, yeah."

Belle moves behind the bar and bustles. There is a heaviness there, now, and Wade wishes he hadn't brought it.

"I just wanna go back in time and tell that son of a bitch how much he means to us, an' how he's left this huge—" Wade stops as the emotion chokes his words from his throat.

"You want me to go get Sienna for you?"

"Yeah, please. Yeah."

"Okay, you just wait right here."

Wade stares at his reflection in the mirror as the afternoon sun streams through the darkened windows. The cathouse seems friendlier in the day, like a regular bar, no money, no pressure, no heartache.

Sienna appears without Belle. Her eyes are red. "Wade…Belle told me about Gerry. I'm so sorry."

It registers with him that she knew Gerry, but it doesn't seem to matter now. In fact, he's glad she knew him. If she did anything for Gerry like she'd done for him, he's glad.

She stands a couple of feet away from him and the heaviness is back. Their last encounter comes screaming back into his mind and he has nothing to say to her that doesn't sound canned or forced.

She tucks her hair behind her ear and smiles a small smile. "Belle said you wanted to talk to me?"

"I know you're leavin' today, but I had to talk to you because last time, I left it…well, it didn't feel right is all. And I forgot to ask you about what book you're readin'."

"I'm glad you said that. I didn't want to leave things that way either. I like having you come here to see me. So I hope we can, you know, start fresh."

Through his grief, his insides warm and expand and he can't help but feel the emotion for her swell, unchecked, inside him. The warning lights go off, but he closes his inner eyes.

"I know I acted stupid 'bout what you said. I was wrong. An' I think I am broken and you were right about a lot of what you said. An' I wanna fix that. I want you to help me fix that."

"We can try and fix it together, how's that?"

"That sounds like a good plan, there, I guess. Yeah. Oh—and the book. I mean, I've gotten real addicted to readin' them books you give me. I wanna know what you're readin' now, is what I mean."

"Well I've read one since I got here, but I have one I'll be listening to on the way home today. Just starting it. Which one do you want to read?"

"You pick."

"Well I could loan you my copy of the one I read while I was here—that way you'll have read it too and we could talk about it—"

"I like gettin' my own copy. I like writin' shit, er, stuff down in the margins and stuff like that so it ain't no big thing to get a copy of my own."

"Okay, it's by Ernest Hemingway—you've heard of him?"

"Yeah. Ain't he the guy who shot himself?"

"Yeah. I'm sorry, we don't—"

"No, it's just weird is all. What's the title?"

"*The Sun Also Rises.*"

"Should I ask what it's about?"

"Do you need to?"

"No, I'll read it anyway, I guess."

"Good. Look, if I did anything to, you know...I'm sorry I got a little hot-headed the last time. I just want things to get back to normal."

"It was me who got hot-headed, an' we are getting' back to normal. I guess I just didn't understand."

"Well, I should have been more careful."

"Careful about what?"

"Wade, you know what I do. I need to keep a certain distance. I know you understand that."

"I understand, I do." His mind is arguing with her. She doesn't need to be distant from him, that's what he wants to tell her, but he knows he can't.

"Just so we understand where things are, you know?"

"Where things are. Yeah, I get that. I'm just sayin' you can talk to me is all. I won't get all bent if you talk to me 'bout your plans is all."

"I appreciate that. So, see you in a couple of weeks or so?"

"All right. *The Sun Also Rises.* I'll order it today."

"And I am real sorry about Gerry, Wade. He was a sweet man."

"Yeah, me too. It leaves you with this feelin'...like time isn't in a straight line anymore. Like it's a bunch of loops, and if you could just jump on one of the loops and go back, you could change things, you could...it all seems so real, bein' able to help him before...do you know what I mean?"

"I understand exactly what you mean."

Wade uses his good hand to pick up his beer. Something doesn't feel right, but before he can place the glass back onto the bar, it slips through his fingers and crashes to the floor.

He grips the steering wheel and he doesn't know why he hadn't noticed before. His grip. It isn't an iron grip anymore, but he feels like he's exerting all of his might—and his fingers won't hold. He tries again, with futility, to move his three left fingers. Nothing. He breathes in deeply and starts becoming aware of himself, his whole body. It's when he gets to his toes that he feels his heartbeat knock wildly against his ribs. He really can't feel the toes on his left foot anymore. He *feels* them, but it's as if they are asleep.

Going to a doctor seems pointless now. They said nothing is wrong. So if Annie caused the three fingers to stop working, is Sienna causing the rest of him to shut down? He huffs in disgust. *Yeah, Sienna's ruining my right hand, Tammy is ruining my foot and Cindy, she caused my anxiety.* Well, he concedes that some of that last part might be true. Cole is home now and Cindy's car is there so he really feels like he has nowhere to go just to be alone and think. *Gerry.* Jesus fucking Christ, why hadn't he called him? Why hadn't he gone to Luther's instead? Why the fuck did he do it? The muscles in Wade's jaw start to tense as he thinks of walking into Junior's place with no Gerry to trade insults with and talk to about things. He thinks of the last time he saw him. How fucked up he was. Why didn't anyone do anything? Why didn't he?

Of course, what could he have done? he asks himself. Gerry spoke of his time in the military in two veins: total comedy or total horror—and the horror stories came in sharp bursts, with lightning speed, a sharpness that made everyone around want to stay silent, and then they were done, gone, buried into the past like so many of the friends Gerry'd lost. And now, lost like Gerry. How many casualties of war were there really, if the government counted the bodies left behind to die on American soil? The helplessness and rage reside along with the grief and it feels like an angry boil in his chest. Guilt twists inside of him. He decides to go see Durward.

When Millie answers the door, she looks a little haggard and Wade wonders if Durward had gone to the bad place again. But Durward is just taking a nap.

"Want me to get him?"

"Nah, I don't wanna ruin his nap or anything, I just feel like I got no place, you know? With Cole there and his…whatever she is, I guess…"

"Well, come sit on the sofa here, I'll getcha a beer."

"You doin' okay, Millie? You look—" he almost said "tired," but he remembered what she'd told him about that. "You look like you're stressed out 'bout somethin'. Dude been okay?"

When she comes back in, her face is brighter. "Oh, he's been fine, just fine. Doin' real good and I think that therapist is helpin' him. His son calls more now, an' that's been good for him. Yeah, we're doin' all right. But you…you look like someone just shot your dog. You okay, dear?"

Wade takes a swallow from the cold beer and stares down at the carpet. "You know ol' Gerry? Gerry Farnsworth?"

"I don't think I do…"

"War vet in a wheelchair, no legs—"

"Oh, I've seen him, yes, that's right."

"He died, and, uh…well, he was my friend. I'm kind of…I don't know how to feel if you want to know the truth. I mean, I feel sad an' I miss him. But there's also other feelin's too, because he killed himself, so I feel angry, too. But 'course I felt angry when Annie died, so I guess that's part of it."

"Oh, Wade, dear, I'm so sorry 'bout your friend. What a shame, that. And goin' in that way. They just don't think about who they leave behind, do they? They're in too much pain. That's what the pastor said to me anyway, when my son died back in seventy-four."

Wade vaguely remembers Millie had lost her son to suicide. He hadn't been too involved with her then, or with her family. "Well that was real nice of that pastor, then. Usually church folk think it's a sin."

"Well, he told us it was up to God to judge the person, not us, and that we had to practice understanding and compassion and so that's what I did and it saved me. Maybe it can save you, too. Oh, I think I hear Dude,

I'll go see."

She stands and moves a little slower than she used to and Wade looks at her shuffling down the hall and suddenly everything seems so fragile: Cole, Milt, his granddaughters, Millie, Dude...and mostly? Him.

He sees Dude pass to the bathroom. The door had been replaced, but the drywall had only a spackled patch on it.

"He'll be right out. Wade, if you'll excuse me, I gotta go home for a while, water my plants and such. I'll let you two boys chatter without me lurkin' around."

"You're not cuttin' out 'cause of me, are ya? 'Cause I can go—"

"Oh no, I was just waitin' for him to wake so I could go. Didn't want him wakin' up all alone. He still gets shook up, bein' alone."

Well then why doesn't he marry you and you move in, the damned fool? Wade wants to say. "All right, thanks Millie. For the talk anyway."

Durward comes out and walks down the hall with sleep still on his face like a heavy wool blanket. He nods at Wade, "I'll get me one-a those, hold tight."

Wade hears the refrigerator open and close, the beer can open with a whisper and pop. Dude walks into the room and sits heavily on the couch. He opens the beer and takes a hearty swig. "That Millie, she's a good one, ain't she?"

"So why the hell don't you get her in here for good, Dude? I don't get it."

Durward looks at him for a long time, and then, after taking a thoughtful chug of his beer, he looks down. "I tried. Turned me down."

"What? Are you kiddin' me?"

"And that was before they put me on these stupid pills that killed my pecker. Now my pecker don't work, she only sleeps here once in a while, but we can't do nothin'. How's that for trussed and fucked, eh?"

Wade puts his hand on the back of his neck, really not wanting to talk about Dude's pecker.

"Sorry 'bout that, Dude. Shit, I didn't know."

"Well, them glue dreams have mostly stopped, an' Millie says I'm better to be around, so she says it's worth it. I'm not sure I agree, but what the hell do I do 'bout it? Nothin.' I dunno. Feels like someone took the spit-shine offa my new car. Nothin' looks right anymore, but they say

I'm doin' better. They say it, so it must be. That make any sense to you?"

"No it don't. I know what you mean, and it don't make any sense at all."

"And that, my friend, is when you got it all figured out. Right there. Just when life is turned upside down, that's when you realize how the whole world works. Upside down."

Wade isn't sure what he means, but on some level, he knows he's exactly right.

⁓

He has his arm around her while her dark hair tickles the side of his ribs. After he and Sienna had talked when he'd last been in, he went on the Thursday she returned and had been in to see her at least five times, but it's the same story. He comes in, his dick goes limp, and so they talk and cuddle. When he's not with her, he jerks off in the shower. What the fuck is wrong with him? After Gerry's memorial, where only seven people showed up, he hadn't touched his dick. Death does a number on your dick, he decides. That, or he just can't be with a woman without developing a wet noodle. His chest burns with the shame of it, but the comfort of her, the way she handles him, it takes out the sting. Mostly. And after the past couple of weeks, he feels closer to her than almost anyone in his life.

"So you really didn't like the book?" she makes slow, even circles with her hand on his chest.

"Not really. I liked the way the guy wrote, though. His style, I mean. But the main guy couldn't even be with the woman he loved, not that she woulda stayed with just him, I mean goin' off with every guy she—"

Wade stops. What more is there to say? It's almost too ironic to be ironic.

She props herself up on her arm. "It has nothing to do with sex, really. He was impotent because of a war injury, and I think Hemingway was trying to say that there's more to being a man than a hard...well, you know what I mean. That's what I think anyway. He was so honorable, the character. See what I mean? I mean, she was ravenous for sex but if you look at the time it was written, women were sort of awakening to their sexuality. So she was a perfect character that way. It just seems like it was a love story with the sex taken out."

"I know, I know, but can't you read a book about a guy without a limp dick though? Next time?"

"But you see, they had authentic love, like our friendship is authentic."

He looks down at her. Her brown eyes are so wide they're like a child's, in wonder, seeing the dusk settle on a desert for the first time, not knowing how bitter cold the night will be. He believes she believes it, and for now, that's good enough for him.

"I ain't like him. I can, I just can't now. Maybe it's got something to do with my hands." He hopes it isn't true. But he erases the truth from his mind. "Maybe I'm just fallin' apart."

"I didn't read the book because of you or anything. I didn't see how it could come across."

"I shouldn't have taken it personal, that's all."

"Did you ever have trouble...you know, before? With your wife?"

"Huh, I would've needed to *sleep* with her to know that." When it comes out of his mouth, he's ashamed.

"I think that's part of the problem. Don't you think that's a reason? Maybe?"

"I had no trouble before...I mean with you. That first time...and then the second time..."

"It was the third time...but that's okay. And back then, you were starving. I think now that things are settled...listen, I have an idea. Let's role play. I learned this in one of my classes about communication with someone difficult, so here, I'm you, and you are your wife. I'm going to ask you to make love with me and you be her, tell me what she said."

He pulls his arm out from under her. "Naw, I can't do that. That'd be too...I can't do that."

"Wade, do you want to be with me sexually? Because we can figure this out together if you trust me."

"It seems unnatural to play-act like I'm a...like I'm her with her bein' gone is all."

"It's just an exercise. Trust me."

Ann is gone, so what does it really matter? Maybe somewhere locked inside of him is the key to her mind. Maybe Sienna can unlock it. Maybe he should just have some balls?

He makes a derisive sound, "Okay, I guess we can. But be prepared to be shot down, is all I'm sayin'."

"What was her name?"

Something inside him screams to get out of there, get the *fuck* out of there before he's humiliated, but he clenches his fists as best he can and says, softly, "Ann."

"Ann, let's make love tonight. I want to be with you and feel you under me because I love you."

"See, I could never *say* that to her because she'd—"

"Oh, oh, you're her, I'm you. Come on. Answer me, Ann."

He grits his teeth together and remembers her face. She looked so tired all the time. Did he not help her with the boys enough? Help around the house enough? "I'm too tired, please just go to bed," he says stiffly. Should he make his voice higher? He feels like an idiot.

"Let me give you a massage then, rub your back and feet. Maybe then you'll feel better—"

"You rub too hard and anyway I know what you're up to and it ain't gonna work so stop lookin' at me like I'm a *goddamned piece of meat!*"

Wade stops and his breath is heavy. *Oh my God...*he shuts his eyes tight and waits for the choking feeling in his throat to pass.

He expects Sienna to give up, now. He wants her to, needs her to. Let him go to his bed, alone, with some dignity, let him jack off under the covers and fall into sleep like he used to, and pretend, as Ann makes his coffee in the morning, that he is loved. It's his fault, who he is, always wanting, like a rutting animal...he feels Sienna's hand touch his face and when he opens his eyes, his vision is blurry with tears.

"I'm looking at you as the woman I love, not as meat. You are the woman I love and this is how I want to show you I love you. And then we can talk about other ways I can show you I love you." She kisses him and he takes a sharp breath in, which makes the kiss seem wild and uncertain and Sienna pushes her tongue into his mouth and he knows they are play-acting now, but what would Ann do? He wants to keep kissing her, he can feel the blood pumping to his far regions, he can almost feel his fingers, he pulls her close to him, but he promised her he would be Annie and so he is. He pushes her away.

"Stop it this instant, Wade Kendall, and get your filthy mind outta the gutter for once. You wanna love me, clean your own damn dishes off!" The anger rolls off of him like a thundercloud over a mountain. He knows his face is red. His chin quivers, his mouth contorts to keep from losing it all and all he wants to do is run.

Sienna is inches from his face, her eyes searching his as his tears stream. He needs to blow his nose, but her hands are on his face and her eyes...

They float into his and suddenly hers brim with tears and her hands touch his face and her head shakes. She sniffs and whispers to him, "Oh, Wade...

He needs to stop the tears, but they fall down his cheeks and now his nose runs unchecked and he can't escape her eyes looking into his.

"Oh, Wade..."

She wraps her arms around him and holds him to her tightly and he silently apologizes to his dead wife for depicting her so well to a stranger who never even knew her name.

14

Sienna leaves today and he feels heavy in his whole body. He mentally counts. He went in to see her seven times in the last fourteen days.

She did give him a book to read, she promised him there was no impotence in it (he hated that she'd used that word). The book is by a guy named Ballard, and it's called *The Kindness of Women*. Sounded promising. He'd ordered it last night and now he has to wait for it and pretend that his world isn't in shambles because she's gone, Gerry is gone, because Cole and Cindy are still in his house, because the damn cat box smells all the time and because in the back of his mind is this niggling, clawing worry as he becomes more and more hyper-aware of his physical body and its failings.

He does have one thing he looks forward to, though, and that's Tammy. She's been coming over every Monday, Wednesday and Friday again and that has been a bright spot for him. On those nights, he's waited to see Sienna until after Tammy leaves. It occurs to him that maybe he's limp with Sienna because he's so stuck in a whirlwind of confusion and such with Tammy. Then he goes around in circles again because she is Ann's sister and his sister-in-law, and they are family. And he also concedes that she mostly seems to come to talk to Cindy, now, when she's there. He looks at the clock and is shocked. It's 9:50 a.m. and he's still in bed. What the hell? He hears the front door close and footsteps traveling heavily down the hall. Then a soft knock at his door.

"Pop? You awake?"

"Yeah, c'mon in."

Cole opens the door, his face shining. "Well, guess what? You're lookin' at a businessman now. I met with the owner of Consolidated this mornin' and signed the papers. They deliver the sheds next week!"

"Oh, well...that's great, but...don't you need a place to put 'em?"

"Already figured that out. Cindy's uncle? Pete? Yeah, he sold her a patch of land just northeast of the Baptist Church there, over off Pacific? Yeah, in there."

"*Pete* sold her that? I thought they was on the outs 'cause of...well, you and everythin'."

"Well they had a sit down, and money talks. He knew that land wasn't gonna move, so he sold it to her for a song and she told him maybe, when things start rollin', she could buy his house, the one he'd been rentin' to her."

Wade sits up and swings his legs around to the side of the bed. "Does this mean she's movin' back into the place then? You're movin' out?"

"Well...not yet, exactly. See Pete rented the place out with a lease, so we gotta hang here a while longer..."

"How long is the lease?"

"Well...it's a year, but Pete said he might be able to change it to six months—"

"A year?"

"Well, Pop, we're startin' a business! We need to save every penny—"

"She's savin' every penny! You're not doin' anything! You're not even workin', Cole. And you got medical bills—"

"Well, now hold on, I mean, you and Milt, you said I shouldn't worry 'bout those, so...now I should worry about 'em?" Cole has the look on his face he'd get as a teen, the stubborn "I deserve it" look in his eyes, and it rubs Wade the wrong way every time.

"How much did you pay for this storage thing, Cole? What did you have to pay to get that franchise? 'Cause until that's paid off, you ain't gonna earn a cent. That's how it works. And if Cindy took out credit to buy that land, which I'm guessin' she did, then you got that to pay back!"

"You know what? I told Milt 'bout it. I did. An' he looked over the contract and said it was airtight an' it was a good thing for me to do. So what the hell is your problem? You tell me to make somethin' of myself, so I did! I am! An' now it ain't good enough because I didn't go to school to earn it, like Milt did, that it? Because I don't rely on someone else to give me a paycheck, like you, that it?"

"Ownin' a business is more complicated that you think, Cole. You don't got any idea 'cause you never took any business classes, you never—"

"I don't need a friggin' degree to own a business, Dad! Oh, and by the way, Milt checked, and a lot of my medical bills are gonna be paid for by Mr. Hanson's homeowner's insurance, so you know what? You're off the hook! An' if you want us outta here so bad, why didn't you say so? We'll go *camp out* for six months, how's that?"

The dog is barking in Cole's room and its incessant noise coupled with Cole's ignorance is too much.

"Yeah, an' what are you gonna do when this stupid thing goes under, like almost everything here does? She loses all her money, you lose all your money and she walks out the damn door and leaves you high and dry? Huh? Then what?"

Cole's voice goes quieter, "She ain't gonna leave me. She's in love with me. You're the one going to end up alone and with no one, so stop layin' that on me! You're the one! You know why Milt don't come around? It's 'cause you don't change, Dad! You expect everyone to listen to you, but you don't listen! I been clean for over a year now and I am stayin' clean. Can't you give me that? Can't you for once, be proud of me?" Cole's face turns red and tears brim in his eyes, and just like that, like always, Wade is overcome with guilt. Cole is trying. Why can't he give him credit? Ever?

"I'm sorry. You're right." The comment about Milt stings him as if he'd been slapped in the face. He tries to see himself through his son's eyes, but all he sees is a blur. A blur and a failure. "You're takin' a risk, an' you've done everything right. And you have been clean. I'm the one who was afraid an' I let that cloud me. I am proud. Cole? I am."

Cole sniffs back the tears and stares hard at his father. "We'll find somewhere else to go."

"No, no...don't do that, now, c'mon. You caught me as I was wakin' up, and the damn dog's barkin' and...no, just—"

"Well maybe, if you wasn't over at the whore house all night you'd be doin' something with yourself instead of sleepin' in late and gettin' laid!"

Wade is speechless. He feels a strange mix of anger and shame, and doesn't know how to respond or what to say. Should he deny it? Does everyone know? Should he care?"

"You got it all wrong, Cole, an' you'd better watch yourself because I'm still your father an' I deserve respect in my house, of all places."

"Right, your house. Well I got news for you. Mom had her name on this house an' she told me that when she died, she wanted you to put my name on it so I can have it when you…go. That's what she told me. So according to mom's wishes, it's partly *my* house, too."

"It doesn't exactly work that way, Cole, but you know this is your house, always has been, an'—"

"Well thanks for makin' me feel so fuckin' welcome!" He turns around and slams Wade's bedroom door after him. After the front door slams shut, the sickness in his gut is compounded by Cindy's voice, coming from the other room.

"Cole? You there? How'd it go?"

And the barking continues.

He should have called first, he knows that. Tammy probably isn't even home. Then he hears her footsteps and he finds he's trying to uncrumple himself, as if he's been folded in half over and over and the wrinkles are all set in him.

"Oh, hey. What's up?" She stands at the door frowning.

"Sorry to drop in all unannounced and all, I just wanted to talk is all." Wade's feet shuffle and his heart pounds as if he's picking her up for a date.

"Sure. Place is a mess. But you can come in."

The only mess he sees are dishes in the sink. The table is covered with school books and papers and she has an old desktop PC set up, the motor in it whirring like it's on its last legs.

"You want somethin' to drink?" He almost says yes, but he's afraid. If it's a can of beer, he could maybe handle it. A bottle, and he'd have to use both hands to hold it.

"Nah, I'm good."

"C'mon, I got your favorite." She pulls the can out of the refrigerator and he feels relief for a moment. He can still hold a can with his right hand's two working fingers.

"Okay, sure." He uses his left hand to pop the top and takes a grateful swig. It's getting warmer and warmer outside as it blooms into full spring, and he'd dressed too warmly for the day. Mostly because Cindy and Cole's clothes had taken over the laundry room.

"I've got a final I'm studyin' for so sorry for the mess."

"That computer looks like it's gonna keel over an' die here soon. Don't you got a laptop?"

"I wish. They're kinda pricey, so I thought I'd wait a bit, see if I can find a deal."

Wade feels expansive suddenly, and he looks at her and shrugs. "I can front ya, or outright getcha one. They ain't so bad. I been shoppin' for a new one just 'cause mine's a bit small if you want to know the truth, an' I want a bigger screen. Hell, maybe you can even have mine when I find one."

"I can buy one on my own, you know, Wade. I mean, I don't need no charity or nothin' from you."

"It ain't charity, jeez. It's family. An' you bring me dinner three times a week...can't I do somethin' nice for you to help you with your...deal you got goin'?"

"You don't need to, but thanks. I got the money, like I said, I'm just waitin'."

"You've been goin' to school and not workin' as much, so how could you have the money, huh? Come on. Let me help." Wade knows from her visits to the house she's only been working half-time at the Flying J, so how is she surviving when she worked before and Annie had to help her?

"Jeez, you're nosy, ain't ya? I *said* I'm *fine*..."

The new, chatty Tammy still surprises him on occasion. He wonders how else she'll change once she starts working in Elko. Suddenly it occurs to him she might just move there if she gets a job, and that leaves a hollow sickness inside him. Then it occurs to him: Stuart. He must be helping her. Maybe he even lives here at her trailer when he's not on the road. The sickness deepens.

"Hey, I just noticed your appliances match the green on your trailer on the outside."

"Well, you been here, what, once? Twice?"

"I been here more than that, c'mon. What, you want me to come over more?" He feels a blush as he looks down the trailer's length and sees her unmade bed at the far end. He feels uncomfortably warm all of a sudden.

"I'm just sayin' you haven't been here a lot is all. So, why you here now, anyways? You haven't said."

He rests the beer can on his leg because the outside is wet now, and he can't keep a grip. He changes to his left hand, but the whole hand is weak. Then he thinks about his toes and then he swallows heavily because now he's chilly when he'd just been warm.

"It's about Cole. I don't know what to make of it all. I mean, I know Cindy's your friend an' all and I don't mean to step on any toes or nothin', but...do you think them goin' into business together like this is a good idea? I mean...do ya?"

"You don't like Cindy." She watches him and takes a sip of her own beer and he's suddenly on the defensive.

"She's fine, I like her fine, it's just—"

"No, you don't like her, it's plain as day. Whenever she talks, you make that face."

"What face?"

Tammy chuckles, "That same face you made when I brought cooked spinach to dinner and saw how bad you hated it. You notice I don't bring cooked spinach anymore?"

Wade had just thought it luck that she didn't bring it. He hates cooked spinach. He makes a *face*?

"I didn't know I made a face."

"Yeah, I think after this long, I know you pretty well, Wade, and you got that face. You make it with Stu. I saw it last Christmas."

"Well, I—it...I don't even hardly know that guy, so you don't know about my face."

She's laughing now, smiling and he sees how pretty she can be when she's laughing and the warmth comes back, but there's also an ache as he thinks of her with Stuart. "I think you just *think* you know my face."

"Right. Speakin' of, he's in town today an' he'll be comin' by any second to use my shower, just a warnin'."

"He...showers here?"

"Yeah, sometimes."

"Well I should go, then."

"Boy, you really don't like him, do ya?"

"No, I don't, if you wanna know the truth of it. I really don't. I think he's an opinionated jackass an' you could do a lot better is all." After it tumbles from his mouth, he searches her face, wondering if he knows it as well as she knows his. He doesn't.

"Well, he's got his moments, don't he? But don't all men have 'em? Anyways, I ain't gonna be seein' much of him 'cause he's got a new job come Sunday an' he'll be gone for at least a month, maybe more."

Wade wants to say "good," but he knows it would come out petty, so he shrugs.

Just then, a knock at the door. Wade stands and the beer slips right out of his hand onto the floor and it foams out and he's all apologies. "Aw, shit, I'll get it, sorry—"

"It's fine, just pick it up an' lemme get the door."

Sure enough, Stuart walks in and Wade meets his gaze with what he is sure is "the face."

"Hiya."

"Wade, buddy, how ya doin'? Haven't seen ya around lately." Is he talking about the cathouse? He wants to throttle him as he looks into his face.

"Yeah, well, keepin' busy."

"Gotta run, gotta shower. Thanks, hon." He kisses Tammy on the cheek and walks past the kitchen, closing the curtain behind him.

Tammy goes to the drawer and gets a towel to sop up the spilled beer on the blue shag carpet. She's on her hands and knees, scrubbing, and Wade flexes his hand, looking at it as if it's betrayed him on its own.

"That was your good hand, wasn't it?" Tammy says, looking up.

"What? Oh, the can just got slick, that's all."

She stands with the beer-soaked towel in her hand. "Uh-huh. Lemme see it."

"What?"

"Lemme see your hand. That one." She points to his left hand.

"Why? It's fine—"

"Give it here, Wade, I mean it."

He sighs, defeated and raises his hand. She squeezes each finger.

"You feel that?"

"I feel all of them."

"Even the ones you can't move?"

"Yeah."

"Squeeze my hand."

"I don't need to—"

"Wade, so help me. Do what I tell ya."

He sighs again and squeezes her hand with all of his might. It feels like he's crushing her hand with the force of it. She frowns. "Wade, you gotta go back in. You know that."

"I'm just gettin' old is all. Just wait 'til you get—"

"Wade. You got to go back in and see a different doctor. You know this could be serious."

"And what if it is? Then what? I mean, you said so yourself, doctors don't know shit—"

"But *you* need to know. Any other symptoms?"

Wade shrugs, not wanting to tell her, but knowing he will.

"Wade? C'mon."

"Fine. I don't feel my toes so good."

Tammy sighs. She tosses the towel into the sink and sits in the chair opposite him again. "I'll go in with you, if you want. I'll go in and talk to 'em."

"I can go in on my own, I don't need a...nurse or nothin'."

"Fine. But you make that appointment."

Now that she knows, it's real for him. Deep down he's known for a long time, but now it seems real. And Stuart is alive and virile and healthy, showering in her shower and maybe she's waiting for him to leave so they can—

He shakes his head. "Sorry I came and fucked up your carpet n' all. I just needed someone to talk to."

"You gotta let go of Cole and let him be a man. He's gonna make mistakes, but he'll be fine. An' he's got me to help, too."

"How can you help? No offense, but—"

"Boy, what you don't know," she shakes her head.

"What? What don't I know, huh? I let you in on my secret, what's yours then, huh? It's only fair."

She looks at him for a long time. "Wade, I didn't tell you this before because I didn't think I should. But Annie...Annie left Cole money from investments she made years ago—"

"Yeah, Milt told me. She left him a chunk of money and put money away for him, I know—"

"Wade, she left me money, too."

"Oh. I mean...okay. I thought she was just helpin' you out while she was workin' an'—"

"Yeah, I know you did. And you thought you'd have to help me too, an' so you kicked me out, thinkin' I was comin' for a handout. I wasn't. Annie left me enough money to pay off this trailer. It's all mine, now. And I got plenty more."

Plenty more?

Wade looks at her and shakes his head. "How? She didn't make all that much, I mean—"

"Wade, she left me over twenty thousand dollars. She'd saved up, started clear back when the boys were young, invested...and she left Cole 'bout the same. I didn't tell you because she told me you could take care of yourself, but she worried 'bout me 'n' Cole. I already had that money 'bout a month after she passed. You didn't owe me nothin'. But I felt guilty just the same. It shoulda gone to you. I'm sorry. The way I can help is I can promise I'll make sure Cole is always okay. I don't know what else to say."

Wade sits silently in his chair. Annie had, what? Forty thousand dollars and she divvied it up between her sister and her son, leaving him a measly eight thousand dollars? What could he have done with forty thousand dollars? He laughs to himself. He knows exactly what he would have done. He'd have helped Cole and Tammy with it. Ann just didn't trust him enough to do it without her.

The worst part of all is that Tammy had not kept coming for money. She'd come for him, and he blew it and Stuart is singing in the shower as he hears the water crank turn off and the stupid asshole's voice singing *Sweet Home Alabama* from the next room.

"I'm gonna go." He stands and wipes his hand on his jeans.

"Wade..."

"I...I'll talk to you later."

"I'm sorry."

He looks at her. "Don't be. That money was Ann's an' she did right by you an' by Cole. I just wish she woulda known that I woulda done right by you, too."

He walks out, hearing Stuart sing, knowing the stupid song would stay in his head all fucking day.

※

It has been two weeks since his marathon seven visits to Sienna, and he knows he can't do it anymore. Not only is half the money Ann left him gone, but Sienna is gone for him in a way. She will never be his, fully his, even if she up and left it all for him this second. A sex surrogate. Jesus. "How was work today, honey?" "Oh, you know, the whole ins and outs of being a sex surrogate." He shakes his head. Does it make a difference for him that she will never be anyone's? In a way. In a way, it takes the sting out. But nonetheless, all of that aside, he is still drawn to her like a moth to a bug zapper on a July evening. She returns today and he's got to see her.

He sits at the bar in Mamacita's nursing a beer he doesn't want, wondering if he cuts back on the alcohol, he'll be able to get it up. And he tries to think of something intelligent to say about the book they read.

They read. *Together*.

The story was just that—a story. The other books he remembers being aware of the writing—the author's particular style. Steinbeck he didn't notice so much. This guy, Ballard, he was a lot like Steinbeck. All story, interesting, human characters that made Wade feel like he was inside of their heads. But this new book hit him in a lot of places, like the Hemingway book had—different places, but places nonetheless: things he didn't see coming, like the wife dying. But hey, the main guy could get it up, and Wade appreciated that. And he had a lot of sex...a lot. He appreciated that, too.

He knows he's Sienna's first customer of the evening because it's 4:10 in the afternoon and her shift started ten minutes ago. When she comes down the hall, he searches her face and finds the recognition he seeks. That, and the pleasure.

"Here he is." She smiles. He stands up and tries to get his mind in the place it goes when he's about to jack off at home. But it won't go there. It gets arrested by her and all he can do is surrender to whatever his body will do.

He follows her down the hall and into her room. *Just once*, he thinks, *don't inspect my dick*. He knows it's her job, but doesn't she believe him by now? That she's the only one?

"So do we have to do the whole wipe-down thing again? I told you you're the only one—anywhere. I mean, can't you just trust me?" The unspoken thing lies between them: he won't be able to get it up anyway, so why bother?

"I believe you. Let me take this down to the office and I'll see you when I get back." 'This' is the money. He takes in a deep breath, trying not to think about his bank account.

She seems distracted today. He reminds himself to ask her if everything's okay with her boy, back home. He decides to be optimistic and take off his shorts. The sheets feel cool on his skin and he sees the K-Y on the table and decides to lube things up. Maybe if he tries to get things going, things will actually get going. She walks in as he's stroking himself and he fights to not cover himself up.

"Ooh, feeling frisky, are we?" She pulls her dress off in one movement and crawls up onto the bed. He uses his left hand and strokes, and he can almost feel something...

She reaches for him and begins rubbing and he loses it—everything stops. He sighs and lies back, staring at the ceiling. She keeps working him—something she had given up on the last few times he'd been in. He tries to put out what feels like flames of shame in his chest.

"It's okay...it's-it's okay. I was just hoping...it's okay. Hey, are you okay? I mean, everything's good?"

She smiles and releases his limp flesh and he's relieved. It's one thing he likes about her. Loves about her. She doesn't ask him if it's her, or what's wrong, she just goes with the flow and that makes his shame wither and he can breathe again without pain.

"Sure, you know. Things are okay."

He pulls her to him. "How's your boy?"

Her eyes flash a little and she looks away. "He's good."

"That wasn't so convincing. C'mon, you can talk to me. Tell me. What's wrong?"

"I just miss him, that's all." Tears come up in her eyes. "Oh, great, now look at me. I just did my makeup."

"I'm sorry. I didn't mean to make you upset. You just…I don't know. You do a lot to help me, if you want to know the truth. So I thought I could help you."

"Well," she says, sniffing back her tears, "let's focus on you tonight. How are you doing?"

"I read that book. I liked that book a lot."

"J.G. Ballard is a great writer, isn't he? You remember that movie, *Empire of the Sun*? Yeah, he wrote the book."

"I don't think I ever saw it, but I remember it—a little boy with an airplane or somethin'."

"Yeah, that's the one! Yeah, he's really good."

Wade looks down at her naked body and emotion wells up in him, a frustration he can't seem to erase, and he's suddenly overcome by it. "Sienna, what the fuck is wrong with me? Huh? I mean, look at you! You're so beautiful and I can't…I mean I can, but then I get here an' nothin' and I feel like I'm just wastin' your time 'cause I can't seem to do nothin' about any of it!"

He's flexing his hands now, feeling how weak they are, feeling the strange sensation in his left hand as he squeezes with all of his might and he can barely make a snug fist.

"Wade, Wade…it's all right. It happens and we'll figure it out, right? I mean, first, have you seen a doctor? I mean…"

"Oh my God…you're right. I didn't even think. That drug…that Viagra, that would help me, wouldn't it?"

"It might. I mean, I wasn't thinking that, I was thinking about you… about you being healthy."

He looks at her and again he is overwhelmed, but it isn't simply her physical beauty, but feelings he hasn't felt in so long…feelings he feels for Tammy, but Tammy is out of reach, forbidden in a way he can't overcome or explain, so it isn't as real. But this—this isn't real, he reminds himself. So why does it feel like the realest thing in his life?

He takes her and pulls her close and kisses her and the languor in their kiss, mouths moving with each other, creates the whisper of life—a stirring, and hope swells within him, so he keeps kissing her and soon her hand finds him. He focuses on their mouths, tongues, and he doesn't soften at her touch, he is at last hard enough to enter her and so she reaches for the condom and he buries his face in her neck and only allows the hope… pushes expectation away.

She climbs on top of him and instead of moving slowly, instead of sitting up and letting him see her, she lies down and pumps him, hard, fast, and he wants to tell her to stop, slow down, hold up, but she moves like a wind-up toy and suddenly he is there and when he comes he shudders and makes a small noise and knows she didn't come, didn't enjoy. As a matter of fact, it was as if he were on an assembly line and she was tightening the bolts of his parts before moving to the next set of bolts. The pain is back in his chest, but for different reasons.

"Well, I guess it still works," he says, hoping the breezy comment covers the heaviness beneath his ribcage, not wanting it to seep into his tone.

"See? I told you. You're just fine. You just needed to clear out some of your past."

"No, it was you. You did it. I just wish it didn't…you know, go so fast."

"I'm sorry, Wade. I know. It's just I have…other customers. You know? I need…I'm sorry, but I need to make money here, and you're so generous, and I do love being with you, it's just—"

"No…no I get it."

And he does get it. She's there to make money, not to cuddle, talk all night with just him. He is such a fool. What did he think? She would just give it all up for him? An impotent old fuck who's running out of his discretionary fund to come and see her? How many men have fallen in love with a prostitute? And that's what she is, whether he likes it or not, whether she likes to be called a "sex worker" or whatever, no one would see her as anything but a prostitute. Except him. To him she was a woman—in a way, his woman—and he knows how insane and stupid he's been.

"I think…I think I should go an' maybe not come back for a while. I think I had some wrong ideas in my head that I need…that need straightenin' out. Thank you, you know, for tonight. I mean it. But I'll leave you to your business."

"Wade, I'm sorry…I have to do this. I wouldn't be here if I didn't have to be. I don't mean that…I mean, not with you, sorry, that came out all wrong."

"Trust me, I think it came out just right. Here." He hands her the twenty- dollar bills. "You gotta make a livin'. But so do I, somehow."

"Wait, don't go yet. Let me walk you out, please—"

"Nah, I know my way. I'll see you again sometime soon. Well, sometime, anyway. Have a good one."

Wade finishes fastening his shirt buttons and walks out as fast as he can. How many ways can a man lie to himself? How many times can he find comfort in the act of love, then have that comfort ripped away as soon as the bodies untangle and separate?

How is it possible to feel so connected, then feel so utterly and completely alone?

Wade walks to the front door, hoping no one sees him, hoping her next customer isn't there, waiting in the wings like a trapdoor spider. Or is she the one in the trap, waiting for her prey?

He recognizes the feeling right away. It's the same feeling he had when Ann would "let him" get on top of her. Get it over with, get it done, get out. Is that his fate? *Maybe it's time for a fresh start*, he thinks. Maybe he ought to just let Cole and Cindy have the house, and he can go rent an apartment in Elko or Wendover, or hell, even move somewhere else, like Colorado or Utah. Wherever his meager finances would allow him to live in a bit of comfort.

Ah, but there's Durward to consider, and watching over Cole is still something he feels he has to do. And Tammy. What about Tammy? Hell, he knows she'll be fine without him. It's him being without her that scares him the most.

He knows going to Luther's and getting drunk is a supremely bad idea, but he heads there anyway with only the idea of relief on his mind.

He walks in and not seeing Gerry is still a shock to him. He even does a sweep of the back of the place, just to make sure he doesn't spot his wheelchair. He looks at the usual table in front and his eyes meet Pete's. Pete nods at him and pulls out the chair next to his.

Well, why the hell not?

"Wade."

"Pete. What the hell."

"Well, ya know. Place ain't the same no more."

"Yeah. I know it ain't."

"Listen, 'bout that night—"

"Look, water under the bridge. Let's just forget it."

"Well I will, but I wanna say that I was wrong 'bout your boy. I was wrong to say them things. Looks like he 'n' my niece are really tryin'. I'm helpin' 'em out, ya know. I figure, they trust each other, they must be doin' somethin' right."

"Yeah, I heard 'bout the land you sold 'em. That was real good of you. I just hope this little…whatever it is, is some good business idea. 'Cause seems like Wells is the place everything comes to die."

Pete startles Wade with a hearty laugh, "Well ain't you just a bag-a sunshine? Jesus, have a little optimism, will ya? Plenty of people here need storage. Hell, I'll be one of their first customers."

"Well, a lot of people just pass through here, an' the town ain't that big, so I can't see how them storage units are gonna be full any time soon is what I'm sayin'. I just hope they thought it through."

"Yeah, well." Pete sips at his beer and nods, saying nothing more. Wade turns around just as Junior comes out of the back room.

"Hey, Wade, what can I getcha?"

"Gimme a shot of JB. Gimme two, maybe."

Junior only raises his eyebrows as he turns and grabs a shot glass. Pete makes a noise like he's thinking something through, then leans over to Wade. "Haven't seen you drink serious for a long time, buddy. What's the occasion?"

"The occasion? Nothin'. That's the occasion. There's nothin'. I got nothin'. That's the fuckin' occasion."

"Whoa. Well shit, son, you sound like you're depressed or somethin'. I know I ain't Gerry or nothin', but I'm still your friend, I hope. What's gotcha buggered?"

"I don't wanna talk, really. I just need a couple-a drinks in me is all." Junior approaches with a double shot and places a hand on Wade's shoulder.

"You okay?"

"Yeah. Yeah. Just needed a place to go. Come to, I mean."

Junior nods and walks away and Pete leans in again. "I guess it's me that put you in the situation you're in and I apologize for that. Must be tough havin' the kids at your place. Wish I'd a waited to rent out the house. I am sorry 'bout that."

"Yeah, well, it ain't really that so much. You know I just got done readin' this book 'bout this guy who was in a war camp during World War II, ya know? An' he grows up and gets married, has kids, and then the wife dies. Then he has this string of women, see, and they all give him somethin' to live for in their own way, an' it just sort of hit me, you know, that I ain't got nothin' to live for, really. I mean, don't get me wrong, I ain't gonna do anything stupid or…I just wonder what it's all about is all."

"Well, that's your problem right there, Wade. Don't read any more goddamned books for starters. They make you think too much an' that's your problem. You think too much. Just let it be, right? Like that Beatles song, just let it be. I don't remember anyone ever promisin' me that life was gonna be one big party. Do you? Life don't owe you nothin'. It's just life, ya know? You got to take it as it comes, quit livin' in the past. Or the future, for that matter. Yep, all's we got is the here an' now." Pete punctuates his speech with a belch and nods his head, as if Wade is supposed to agree.

"Yeah, I guess. So what, I just go home an' watch reality T.V. an' drink 'til I pass out an' that's it? If that's all there is to it, then no wonder Gerry did what he did. That's some bleak shit right there, you ask me. All my life I had somethin' to live for, someone to live for. Now there ain't nothin'."

"You callin' those boys of yours 'nothin'? 'Cause as I recall, you got grandkids, you got those boys. An' they don't tell you, but they need their daddy, even if they don't say so. And grandkids need their granddaddies, too. Hell, you're retired, when was the last time you went and seen them kids?"

Wade stares straight ahead. The burn from the shot has warmed his belly and throat and his head is a little fuzzy, but also, things seem a lot simpler. He hasn't gone to see those girls. Or Milt. And what's his excuse? His daughter-in-law doesn't like him. Well fuck her. She can deal with him for a few days if she has to. Let her hold her nose if she wants, but there's no reason he can't go see those two little girls. Suddenly, Wade's vision is tunneled on Milt, making things right with him somehow.

If only he knew what was wrong.

The ride to Henderson had been a little longer than he'd expected. Probably because he's travelling there. He knows the ride home will feel like a breeze. Wade finishes his call to Cole just as he pulls into the massive driveway. Wade approaches Milt's giant front door and rings the bell. The door opens to bright blue eyes.

"Well, well. You gotta hug for Papa?" Wade squats down on the porch of the massive house and the little blonde-haired girl smiles shyly for only a moment before running into his arms. "Oh, I've missed you, you little monkey. Look at how huge you are!"

"I've grown up to *seven*." Brianna poses and turns in a circle for Wade.

"You *have*. Didja get the present I sent ya for your birthday?"

"Yes, and I got a Barbie Dream House from Grandpa and Grandma Hendricks so it was good because then my Barbie had a house to live in. Well my *new* one did. I have lots of Barbies. "

"Well, then, that's good." Wade vows he'll remember to get gift ideas for this year's birthday on this visit. Wade had called Milt in a panic at the last moment last year as the day of her birthday drew near. Annie had always done it. What to get a seven-year-old girl? Well, apparently, a Barbie.

"Where's your dad?"

"He's in the back cleaning the pool but he said when you got here he'd stop to visit with you. And Mommy's at the spa but she's coming later to make you dinner."

"Well, good. And where's your sister?"

"Kenna's at dance 'til three, but Mommy picks her up. Can you put me on your shoulders?"

Wade laughs, his chest expanding with each smile from the child's face. "I hope so. C'mon, let's see if I can."

Wade hoists her up and walks where she tells him to get to the kitchen, where the sliding glass doors lead to the backyard. Milt sees them and starts toward them.

"Grandpa Hendricks can't do it because of his sick...attic."

"His what?"

"He's got sick-attics."

They step onto the back porch just as Milt approaches, wiping his hands. Milt laughs, "Sciatica, sweetheart. Grandpa has a bad sciatica. It's a nerve in the back, remember? Hey, Dad, how was your drive?"

"Well, long and pretty empty. Stopped in Ely to get some lunch. This is a great yard you got. I can't believe I haven't been here to see this new house a-yours til now."

"Papa come swimming with me!" Brianna bounces on Wade's shoulders and he winces.

"Oof, careful there, your Papa's gettin' old."

"Listen, Bree bug, why don't you let Daddy and Papa talk, and you go get your suit on. Don't forget your sunblock."

"You have to *help* me with the *sunblock*, Daddy."

"I know. Bring it down with you."

Milt lifts her off of Wade's shoulders and she scampers into the house singing.

"My God, she's gettin' big. Still a little girl, though. Still a kid. I bet McKenna's gettin' too old for horseplay."

"Oh, Kenna's in a whole other world, Dad, you have no idea. She's growing up too fast. I mean, she's only ten, but...it's the dance. I don't like it much, but Carol...well, she's insistent on pushing her to excel at it. Of course she pushes Bree at piano, so. Yeah."

Wade wanted to say something about Carol, but bit his tongue. His son had said enough. "Well, expectin' your kids to do a good job is a good thing, I think."

Milt's eyes flash for a second. "Well, some kids make it on their own steam, too."

"Well, you sure did, didn't ya? I mean, I was never one for pushin'."

"No, you weren't. I think that was good for me, but...well, not so good for Cole. But that's neither here nor there. How's Cole doing, anyway?

Still at the house?"

Wade tries to wrap his head around the implications of what Milt said, but he just answers the question. "Cole's doin' fine. Yeah, he's still at my place, startin' up that business an' all. I don't know 'bout that."

"I told him the contract was sound, but I mean, who's going to store things in Wells?"

"That's what I told him."

"You know, Dad, he really looks up to you. I mean, if you pushed him a little—"

"Hold on, now. I push him all the time. It don't work out so good, Milt."

"You? You never pushed him to do anything. All he did was party and you just let him—"

Wade's defenses jump to attention. "You know, when these girls grow up, you can talk to me about pushin'. 'Cause right now, they'll do what you say, just like Cole did. Then he turned fourteen and there was nothin' I could say."

"You could have said 'no' on occasion." Milt's stare is hard.

"I said 'no' all the time. He just went behind our backs an' did what he pleased! You wait, Milt. Don't be lecturin' me on parenting when you got no idea."

"I'm just saying he probably wouldn't be living in your house still, doing this foolish business venture with that woman if you took a stand. That's all."

"So it's all my fault, huh? You turned out great, an' that's all on you. Cole struggles, an' that's all on me. Pretty damn convenient, ya ask me."

"I wasn't saying—"

"No, you can't have it both ways. Either I did somethin' right or I did somethin' wrong. I raised you the same, but I had two completely different kids."

Wade feels the sting of the accusations as if he'd walked into a hornet's nest. He feels his blood pressure pounding in his ears.

Milt sighs and looks away. "It's hot, and I didn't offer you a drink. Can I get you a cold beer? I hope dark beer's okay."

"Whatever you got." Wade stares at the water, its shimmering surface making him thirsty, even though it's an unnatural color of aqua blue. He feels like diving in, sinking to the bottom and trying to find his way back up to the surface with only the light to guide him. Maybe a cold shock to his system will wash away the guilt, the accusations Milt had hurled at him. Maybe Milt is right. Wade thinks about all of the times he's tried to steer Cole, and how all of his efforts seem to get sucked into a black hole. No light to bring him to the surface of the memories. Only regret.

"Papa! You don't have your swimming suit on." Brianna frowns as she skips toward him in her pink and yellow suit.

"It's in my suitcase. I'll go get it."

"Yay!"

He looks in her blue eyes and sees it: the wildness that had been in young Cole's eyes. He smiles. *You just wait, Milton Kendall. This one's gonna give you a run for your money.*

She scampers to the pool's edge. "I'm supposed to have sunblock on," she says, eyes twinkling. With that, she takes a step off and splashes into the aqua blue water.

Carol is much warmer to Wade than she had ever been. Which is to say he could almost call her friendly. McKenna had grown and was still shy with him, but she seemed genuinely glad to see him when they got home. Over dinner, she grew chatty and spoke to Wade of her dance and her friends. She does indeed seem older than ten, and with girls, Wade imagines, that has its own worry. Wade eats the meal, which feels like it came from a restaurant, but not a place like Mama's Café: more like a place whose name he can't pronounce. The girls' chatter and antics entertained him throughout the meal and he paid little attention to Carol and Milt.

"I really appreciate you havin' me for dinner, Carol. It was, well, it was the best meal I had in a long time, if you want to know the truth."

McKenna snickers, "We didn't *have* you for dinner, Papa, or you'd be gone."

"Huh?" Wade smiles quizzically and looks at her.

"Kenna, don't correct your grandfather." Carol raises her eyebrows as she clears the dishes.

"What'd I say?"

Milt gives McKenna a cross stare, but it's twinged with a smile. "She means it sounded like we *had you* for dinner instead of having you *over* for dinner."

Wade chuckles, "Well, then, thanks for not *havin'* me for dinner, and for havin' me *over* instead. Plus, I'd taste terrible. Like a spoiled ol' chicken."

"Ew!" McKenna laughs.

Brianna jumps behind him and wraps her hands around his neck. "Piggyback ride, Papa!"

"Why must you insist on treating him like a jungle gym, Bree? Let Papa go. We're going to watch Kenna's dance video." Carol walks over and pries her little arms from around Wade's neck.

"I don't mind. That's what Papas are for," Wade says, smiling. What he doesn't admit is he probably couldn't lift her at this point. The afternoon of swimming, throwing her in the water, and being in the sun had drained him.

"Well, you look tired," Carol says, smiling at him. He tries to detect anything disdainful in her voice, but he can't. She seems to be actually concerned.

"Well, I got some stuff goin' on. It's tough gettin' old."

"You're not that old, Wade. How old are you? Fifty-five, six?"

"I'll be fifty-seven in September. An' they got me on blood pressure pills now."

"Well," Carol says, "my parents are in their late sixties and they both have their issues. It's only natural you'd be on something by now. How's your hand?"

Wade is surprised she's even talking to him, surprised she knows about the hand. Normally she moves around him like a sullen ghost.

"Oh, still the same. Three dead fingers. No one knows why."

"What do you mean 'dead'?" McKenna asks, wrinkling her nose.

"Well, see, here they are, an' they look all right, but when I try an' move 'em, I can't, see? I'm tryin' real hard to move 'em. They won't budge."

"Do they hurt?" Brianna has her wiry arms around his neck again.

"Well, only if I mash 'em. I still got feelin' in 'em, just can't move 'em."

"Girls, into the family room. Kenna, find the Spring Recital DVD.

That has great shots of you," Milt says.

"I wanna play Papa a song!" Brianna jumps and runs to her father, who scoops her up.

"You go get your jammies on, you can play him a goodnight song after we watch Kenna."

"Is Papa having a sleepover?"

Wade jumps to attention. "No, sweetie, I'm stayin' at a hotel. But I'll see you tomorrow, promise."

"Next visit, Wade, you really should stay here. We have the spare room, now. It's really just for you. Well, for Milt's family. My family's all here, so." Carol shoots an unfriendly glance at Milt, who's giving her a look that Wade can't decipher. Anger? Apprehension? And Carol is talking about a 'next visit'?

They settle in the family room and Wade watches as his granddaughter dances in a part-ballet, part-modern dance with moody music and strangely exotic costumes for children. McKenna seems to hover mid-air with her leaps and has a natural grace some of the other dancers lack.

Milt points to the television. "Here she forgets her cue, but she rallies and you can hardly tell."

"Then why do you bring it *up*, Milt?" Carol scowls at him.

"I'm just saying. you know, in case he saw it. We try and learn from our mistakes, don't we, Kenna?" Milt looks at his daughter, who seems embarrassed as she watches the giant T.V. Wade notices Carol rolling her eyes. Had he been wrong all along about Carol? What is the tension he feels with his son and daughter-in-law?

When the DVD is concluded, everyone claps and Milt tells Brianna she can play a song for them before bed. "Maybe you can play *Deep Purple*. I told Papa you are very good at that one and you play it because of Grannie."

"I want to play another one."

"Play *Deep Purple*, Breebug. Papa will like it."

"I'll like anything she plays. I'm an easy ol' guy to please, ya know," Wade says, wanting to dissipate the tension.

Milt turns to him. "Well, sometimes you don't give kids choices, and other times you do, Dad." Wade closes his lips into a line and shrugs. Clearly he should not have interfered. Carol shakes her head.

"Let's let Bree play what she's comfortable playing, Milt, for heaven's sake."

"You know…fine. Whatever. I'm going to grab a drink. Dad, you want a drink?" He stalks from the room before Wade can answer.

"No thanks, I gotta drive," he calls out.

As Bree searches through a stack of music, Wade looks at Carol.

"Sorry. I didn't mean—"

"It's not you, Wade. It's never been you." She smiles weakly at him and suddenly, everything he'd thought about his son, his wife and his family changes, just like that.

"I'm gonna play this!" Bree exclaims.

Carol glances at Wade, then back at her daughter. "You know Daddy doesn't like *Für Elise*, Bree."

"I bet Papa will." Brianna smiles her devilish smile and Carol chuckles and shakes her head.

"She's got her own mind," Carol says, looking at Wade.

"They all do," Wade says. Carol nods and Brianna doesn't wait for her father to return as she starts playing her concert for Wade and her mother and sister. Milt doesn't return into the room until the song is done and the clapping subsides. Milt stands in the doorway with a large glass of amber liquid.

Wade notices Milt's ears. They are bright red.

15

The weekend with Milt and his family had been exhausting but exhilarating. He felt like a new lens had been placed over his vision, and he found Carol to be less drill sergeant and more peacekeeper. He doesn't know how Milt had become so rigid. He tries to see the part he must have surely played, but he only sees Milt as the son who resents him for things not done, and things he can't amend.

Wade waited to go see her and feels he had shown great restraint. He hadn't seen Sienna for a month, since the last time when she'd told him she had other customers to attend to, and so he'd scuttled outta there with his tail between his old legs. He was hoping the wait would jump-start his dick this time. No such luck.

"It's fine. We talked about you going to see a doctor last time. Did you?"

Wade looks into the pools of Sienna's eyes and shakes his head. "I didn't go. I hate doctors." What he doesn't tell her is that if he goes to the doctor, he'll have to tell him about his left hand and his feet, too. And he isn't so afraid they won't find anything this time. He's afraid they will. "Plus, I went outta town to see my son and grandkids couple weekends back."

"How many grandkids do you have?"

"Just the two. Two little girls. Well, they ain't so little anymore. Seven and ten. But damn I love them girls. I wish I didn't live so far away. But then, seems like my son's glad I do. You know, I always thought it was his wife who don't like me. Seems like it's him."

"Fathers and sons have complicated relationships, it seems to me," Sienna says, kissing his shoulder.

"Yeah, seems like. What about mothers and sons?"

"Well, my little guy thinks I'm perfect still. He's only four. I guess we'll see what he thinks of me later."

"Well my sons both thought my wife walked on water. Never had a problem with her. It was always me. Still always me. One resents me an' one won't listen to me."

"Wade, I wanted to ask you something."

"What's that?" He sits up a little and puts the pillows under his head.

"Have you thought about trying another girl here? Just to see...I mean...just to—"

"You know it ain't you. No...I mean, I don't want every girl here knowin' I can't...I mean...no. I haven't thought about doin' that. You don't...you know...tell 'em 'bout your clients or anything, do ya?"

"No, never." Sienna shakes her head. "But you know, just to liven things up. I mean, there's Sunny and Brinnley and Lana—"

"I went to Lana. Before I met you. It wasn't...like with you. She was nice enough, don't get me wrong. She was just not...*personal*, if you know what I mean."

"But see that's what I mean. You and I...we're so personal...if we made it more about just...you know, *fucking*, maybe you'd have better luck."

Wade's chest feels like it's sinking into his back, like he can hardly breathe. Is she asking him to go to someone else to get rid of him? "But you said you could maybe help me."

"Well...I'm not really trained at doing that yet, so I don't know how to help. I *want* to help, so this is why I thought—"

"If you want me to try someone else, I will."

"It's not about what I want, it's about you."

Wade's thinking is mottled with hurt, and he can't meet her gaze. He gets up and starts to dress.

"Wade, where are you going? I didn't mean to say I didn't want you here. I love talking about the books we read and—"

He clears his throat. "Yeah, I'm reading that Ballard book again, I liked it so much. Seems like all them women really helped him through all his rough patches and maybe you're right. I should think about that for a while, I mean, right?"

"I just know that men respond to 'new.' I'm not so new to you anymore, Wade. That's all." She gets up and slips her robe and high heels on. "Come on, I'm going to walk you out. No more slipping away on me. I'm going to walk you out properly."

They leave her room together and he feels a sense of disgust as he thinks of the amount of money he pays her, just to cuddle and talk. Hell, a therapist is only $75 an hour probably. Here he's paying three hundred a visit. Even if he went to someone else, that money is draining like a desert puddle.

When they get to the area where the hallway to the front door meets the bar, he finds himself staring right at Stuart. Stuart smiles and his eyes roam freely over Sienna. It's clear he'd been drinking by the glazed expression on his face. Wade's chest caves in even more.

"Wade, nice seein' ya again. You wanna introduce me to your friend?"

Wade's entire body is a tense steel cage. He feels trembling in his limbs as he stares at the man with his smarmy grin and alcohol-infused eyes. Sienna's arm is still through his, but she tugs a little, as if to wake him from a daze.

"This here's Stuart." He turns and looks at Sienna, his eyes communicating only what his feelings are. No words, no sounds, only a warning. That, and a plea for understanding. Wade glances at Stuart's glassy eyes, eyes that hold mirth, as if he knows what he is doing to Wade at this moment.

"Yeah, I'm Stuart and I sure do like the way you look." Wade's breathing is heavy, and Sienna moves in front of Wade a little.

"Thanks. If you don't mind, I'm saying goodbye to Wade now, so can you please give us some room?"

"Well, I'll wait for ya right over there, all righty?" Stuart says. He reaches out to touch her arm and Wade reacts without thinking and slaps his hand away.

"Wade…" Sienna holds onto him. "You'd better go."

"Whoa, now, Wade. What was that?" Stuart slurs. "I got every right to pick who I want."

"And I've got every right to pick who *I* want," Sienna says, heat in her voice. "Find someone else."

"Huh, I wonder if your manager knows how unfriendly you are," Stuart's eyes glitter as he speaks, staring at Wade instead of Sienna.

"My manager respects my choices. So go ahead and try. Don't think I don't see what's going on." She steps closer to Stuart. "We don't do drama here, buddy, so shove off."

Stuart finally looks at her and shakes his head. "You ain't my type anyways. Now his sister-in-law, she's my type."

Wade feels every muscle in his body begin to tremble with rage. He can't even make his legs move, which is good, because all he wants to do it tear Stuart's heart from his chest.

Sienna moves in front of Wade and places her hand on the sides of his face. When his eyes meet hers, she says, "Walk away. You start something in here, it's a one-strike deal. They won't let you back. Please. Just walk away."

"Anyone but him." He speaks low, staring into her eyes.

"I know that."

Wade walks on unsteady feet toward the door. He looks back toward Sienna and Stuart is standing a few feet from her. He smirks as Wade opens the door and walks out into the breathy-wind night.

May 16, 2015

I don't know how I'm going to survive the next few months. This job, it wears on me more than I ever thought it would. It weighs on me in ways I thought it couldn't. I wonder now if being a sex surrogate will do this to me, too, even though they are completely different. Maybe I'm not cut out for it. But then I think it's not the sex, it's the emotional drain, and I know every counselor and mental health worker has to learn to deal with that, and I will. I need to stay positive.

A lot of the men I see would not seek out a sex surrogate at all, unless they were pushed into it, frankly. One particular guy came in and it was probably the worst experience I've ever had. He had zero in the way of emotion. Totally flat affect. He didn't want to talk, connect, nothing. He just paid, turned me around and bent me over. I half expected his hands were going to suddenly grab me around the neck, it was that scary. When I mentioned it at the Tea Party, everyone said the same thing: they'd rather have anything, including anger, than that blank NOTHING. I don't think I have ever felt so used. I guess that's the right word. Like I wasn't even human, I was a knot in a tree. I felt like a "whore" in every sense and I honestly felt like crying when he left, not so much out of relief, but the way he'd made me feel.

 The most entertaining client was a guy who said his name was "Bruce," but I highly doubt that was his name, and here's why: he brought in an old cassette player and when we got in the room he put in a cassette tape that played the theme song to the old T.V. show The Incredible Hulk. He started ripping his clothes off (his buttons were snaps, so no damage!) and making the Hulk face, and then he wanted ME to make the Hulk face when he fucked me and my face got so tired holding that angry scowl and trying not to laugh. He tipped pretty well, though and acted like it was totally normal to fuck to The Incredible Hulk theme song. I guess I'm just glad he didn't ask for my pee.

 I don't know what to do about Wade. He's been to see me at least a dozen times, and we've only fucked three times. When I told him he should try another girl, he got all bent out of shape. Then some guy came in and he and Wade were in this pissing contest, me being Wade's object to piss on, I guess. Definitely a territorial thing going on and I just can't deal with that. Wade has become way too possessive. I want to tell him he needs a therapist, but that's not exactly something you say to someone: "you need therapy." I don't know how to help him. I don't even know if I can. I wish he would just go see someone else. He's becoming like human Velcro, and I can't afford to be stuck to anyone here, not anyone. But then when I think of him not being here, it hurts. Part of me is angry about that and another part of me feels like, I don't know, like I am doing something right.

 It's wearing me down, wearing me thin. I am wearing out at twenty-six. My insides are worn thin and one day, my outside might just match it. I don't know how sex surrogacy will be different, and that is what worries me most of all. But then I remember I'm made of strong things, like Jess said. *I'm meant to help people. I just wish I could help myself right now.*

Over at Durward's Millie shuffles in to bring him a beer. He almost wanted to get it himself, Millie looks so beat. Her eyes have lost a certain shine and he wonders if Durward is too draining on her.

He thinks about Sienna, Stuart, Tammy. Talk about a catch-22. But what is he even thinking? Tammy knows Stuart goes to the cathouse… and she doesn't seem to care. Wade wants that son of a bitch to suffer. But what could he say? *Stuart wants to sleep with the sex worker I happen to be in love with, Tammy. What do you think about that?* Jesus. And Wade knows he's in love with Sienna, but in a way that's removed from real life. The idea of her open arms, always willing to try with him, always willing to talk…for three hundred dollars. He shakes his head. Dreams of a fool man. Dreams of a lost man. And he is lost, he knows it. He can feel it when he closes his eyes at night and drifts off to sleep. Sienna makes him feel grounded in a way, and he knows he's headed for a brick wall. He just doesn't know how he will peel himself off of the stones.

He jumps when Millie hands him his beer. "You look like you've got some serious thoughts going on in that head-a yours, Wade."

"Just thinkin'. 'Bout life and things."

Durward sips his beer loudly. "Millie, why don't you let me 'n' Wade talk a little man-talk for a while? Wouldja mind?" Wade had never heard Dude be so…deferential before. Usually it's "get on outta here." He must really have it bad for her. Millie walks over and kisses the top of Durward's bald head.

"'Course. I got plenty to do 'round my place. Indeed I do. The place needs a good dustin' and such."

"You all right, Millie? I know I ain't supposed to say you look tired, but ya do."

"Oh Wade, I just need to get my face on. I'll be all right now. You boys have a nice talk. 'Bye."

After she leaves, Wade can't help but smile. "You two give me hope, you know that?"

"Well, I don't know what I'd do without that woman. I toldja she don't wanna move in here. She still don't. I don't take it personal. I think she likes livin' in sin." Durward has a twinkle in his eye. "And I'll tell you somethin' I ain't tellin' my therapist. I stopped them pills and Millie an' me are like rabbits again."

"Oh, jeez. Are you sure that's a good idea, Dude? You know the pills stop them dreams—"

"That ain't really true, they said they could help 'cause of anxiety 'n' all, but I'll tell ya what really helps my anxiety…"

"No—no, you don't have to. I don't wanna hear."

"Look here, I wanted to talk to ya. I been hearin' little birds talkin' 'bout you. You been goin' to that hen house, ain't ya?"

"Jesus, ain't anything private 'n' personal in this town?"

"You found one you like, that it? You think you're gonna take her outta there an' make an honest woman of her, right?"

"I don't wanna talk about this with you, Dude. Or anyone. Who told you anything anyhow?"

"Millie got wind from one of the ladies at church who got wind of it from her neighbor, Velma Peterson, whose husband talked to—"

"Okay, okay, I get it."

"Point is, son, that ain't where you're gonna find it."

"Find what?"

"What you're lookin' for."

"And how do you know what I'm lookin' for? Could be I'm just horny. All right? An' there ain't a woman in Wells my age who's available. What else am I supposed to do?"

"You wait. Timing. It's everything. And you're wrong about there bein' no ladies, there all kinds of ladies at church: single, widowed, whatever, you just need to get out more—"

"I ain't goin' to church to troll for women, Dude."

"What about that sister-in-law-a yours. She's still comin' 'round and she look like she's steppin' up in the world, with that new car she got and her fancy new clothes. Oh, I noticed. I can't believe you ain't noticin'."

"She's got a male…friend. An' we've already been over this. Why are you bustin' my chops?"

"Well, 'cause you ain't happy, son, that's about what I can tell. You don't seem happy is all."

"I ain't happy for a lot of reasons, Dude, an' one is that my other hand's actin' up. That, and my toes on this foot. Somethin' ain't right. And my...I can't..." He waves his hand in his groin area. "I can't most times."

"Shit, son, that's no good. No good at all. You gotta go in to see someone. It ain't no phantom thing, this is real."

"I know but I don't want them tellin' me it's all in my head again, when I know it's real. But I also...I don't wanna know. Seems like if I know, then it really is real."

Durward shakes his head. "You ain't makin' one ounce of sense, Wade."

Wade stands and walks to the picture window. He looks over at Millie's house. He doesn't have a good woman through sickness and health like Durward does, and it's likely he never will since "sickness" has crept up on him like a serpent in the grass. He's about to tell Durward that maybe it's time he gets out of Wells, but then he focuses.

"Dude...does Millie usually keep her side door open like that? Oh shit!"

"What?"

As Wade bursts out of Durward's front door in a panic, running toward Millie's house, he sees the bottoms of Millie's shoes at the corner of her open kitchen door.

―∽―

The smell of flowers has been choking Wade in the little Baptist chapel, and now they all stand around the gravesite as the preacher intones his words. Durward had been inconsolable for days. Now he stands in his best suit, a dark rust polyester job, with a light green shirt and a striped tie, his bottom lip still quivering as Millie's three grown children stand next to the preacher.

"And we commend this dear woman into your hands, oh Lord, ashes to ashes, dust to dust..."

Durward brings a hankie up to his eyes and presses. Wade stands with Cole and Cindy on the other side of him, his hands clasped in front of him, his own tears dried and a sick thud inside his gut. On the other side of Durward, his son, Jack, has his arm around his father. Jack had made the decision yesterday to take Dude back to Oregon. In his grief, Durward agreed.

Wade understands "the indifferent world" in a whole new way now. When Gerry had died, the world really did seem indifferent, but not in a comforting way. Now, indifferent feels hostile and terrifying to him. This world will rip everything you care about right out of your hands. And it is indifferent to it. He thinks of the book he'd finished for the second time, *The Kindness of Women* by that J.G. Ballard, and how the character's wife had been ripped from him, and how he searched to find her in everything he did thereafter. He searched the women in his life, but never found one to take her place. He searched using drugs, using anything to bring a sense of "solid" to his world, but the gaping wound never closed. It just crusted over with a sense of longing.

Durward's soft weeping makes him glance over toward him. He doesn't remember Dude crying at his first wife's funeral.

Wade has this crazy thought to take Dude to the cathouse. Surely the kindness of those women would soothe his pain. Then Wade realizes that not everyone is in pain the same way. Different kindnesses for different pains. Wade has had brief glimpses of comfort in that place, but nothing has gone all the way to soothing his pain—and the pain isn't what he'd thought it had been at all. He thought he had been lonely. But that isn't it. As he thinks of Millie and Dude and Dude's giddy reports of their newfound, late-in-life romance, he mourns.

He sees Durward's tears and can almost feel the loss as if it was his own. Wade hadn't cried like that for Ann. And now he mourns other things, and the gaping wound will never close. He thinks to himself that there is no comfort to be had in anything or anyone. What had been broken in him will remain broken, no matter how many kindnesses he buys.

The crowd mumbles, "Amen."

Durward looks like a withered old man now. He isn't even able to stand up straight. Wade puts his hand on his shoulder.

"Anything you need, Dude, you know where to find me. You need any help packin'?"

Dude says nothing. Jack clears his throat. "We're not taking much. He's staying with me for a while, then going to a senior community. We're mostly having everything hauled away to Goodwill."

Finally, Durward speaks, voice thick with tears, "And that's what it come down to, Wade. A man's life. What he can carry in a bag. What he leaves behind is…well…nothin'. When you got no one to love, there's nothin'. I got my boys, an' my grandkids and a couple-a great grandkids I haven't met yet, so that's where I'm goin'. Love my family an' be there with them. But other than Millie, Wade, you're my best…" Durward stops there and dabs at his eyes, his lips trembling.

"I know, Dude. An' you're mine. I'm gonna miss the hell outta you, if you wanna know the truth."

"Wade, you should take some vacation time for yourself and come up and see him. See us. We'd love to have you." Jack holds out his hand and Wade shakes it.

"Thanks. It's a great offer an' I just might take you up on it."

"I feel like I got so much to say, and it's all bottled up inside here," Durward points to his chest. "Mostly, she was the best thing ever happen to me, an' if you can find that, Wade, well, it ain't too late, son. It ain't too late." Tears course down his cheeks and Wade embraces him, patting him firmly on the back.

"We'll see you before you leave, Dude. When you headin' out?"

"Goodwill comes tomorrow," Jack answers. "I'm cleaning up the place for the Realtor. I hope you get some good neighbors, Wade. They'll never be as good as this guy, though, right?" Jack pats his father's shoulder.

"No," Wade says. "They never will."

"I hope they cherish them roses," Durward says, voice cracking. "It's how Millie an' me…she came out to admire my roses." He bows his head and Jack gives him a side hug, designed to keep him upright as much as comfort him.

Jack pulls Durward away, his arm around him, and steers him toward Millie's three children, two women and a man standing at the grave facing it, as a long line of people, folks mostly from Millie's church, pay their respects. Wade wonders if her kids even knew about Dude, or had ever met him in person. He hopes so. He hopes those kids know how happy

Durward made their mother, and how their mother had shown Dude the ultimate kindness by loving him back, finding a love, finally, that gave her joy and peace.

16

He'd spent all day at the hospital in Elko getting tests, and now he's eager to get to Sienna. He has no illusions. He won't be making love to her tonight. There are a lot of things he won't be doing. Ever.

Belle is behind the bar and she gives Wade a shot of whiskey.

"I know you didn't order it, but you could use it, couldn't ya?"

"You always seem to know, dontcha. You got, like…I dunno, a gift."

"My gift is *people*, Wade. It's why I do so good here and it's what I try an' teach my girls."

"You know, I may not be comin' back here after tonight," Wade says, looking at her.

"Yeah, I know. I recognize the look. Sometimes we're a band aid, and sometimes we're a cure, Wade. For you, a band aid, I think. And it helped for a spell, didn't it? I mean, you did have some good things happen here, didn'tcha?"

Wade bows his head. "I did. An' you were one of 'em. You…helped me…I guess I can't really say how, other than you helped me see myself. I guess that's a good thing."

Belle leans over the bar and smiles. "When you're as good a man as you are, Wade, it's a very good thing." She picks up his hand and kisses it firmly, with force. Setting his hand back down, she pats it. "We'll miss ya, an' you're always welcome back."

Wade turns and sees Sienna approach, and she's got a weary smile on her face. His smile is weary, too, so he's content that they can be weary together.

When they get to her room, he doesn't even bother to get undressed. After he pays her, he just takes off his shoes and lies on the bed, waiting for her.

"You look tired," she says as she walks in.

"Don't you know that's another way of tellin' someone they look like shit?" Wade thinks of Millie and an unexpected wave of emotion blooms, causing his nose to tingle.

"Wade, what is it?" She doesn't strip either, she just climbs over him and lays her face on his chest, her leg over his middle.

"Lost three friends in two months. Two died, and one, my neighbor, he moved away. I feel like the...like a solitary man."

"But you got me," she pulls back, smiling.

He huffs out a small breath, not quite a laugh, not quite a sigh. "But I don't. Even if I was young and handsome and had money an' could offer you everything, you know it ain't like that. I know it ain't like that. Shit, I've been tellin' myself stories for months, an' now it's time to keep the stories in the books, where they belong."

"You know, I read a quote once that Camus—you know, the author of *The Stranger?* He said something like 'stories are the lies we tell to get to the truth,' or something like that."

"Huh, I guess that's right. So what truths did I get to with you? Other than I can't get it up no more."

"C'mon, don't do that."

"Sorry. I'm bein' serious, though. What true things did I get bein' here with you?"

"Come on. You know I'm not all fake with you. Hell, I even told you what I wanted to do when I grow up," she laughs.

"Yes you did. I didn't ever think sex would be such a thing. But it's funny. I think 'bout my late wife, an' all I remember are the times she was sick. I don't hardly remember when we was happy, or when she was healthy. None of that. I remember when she stopped sharin' my bed. It sticks out like a big, swollen thumb."

"I'm sorry, Wade."

"Don't be. It happened and that was just the way of it. And then you, you shared your bed with me every time I came in, and it was a good thing for me. Even if it wasn't all the way real."

"Wade, that's not fair. You know what I do here...sure the lines get blurry—"

"Oh, for me, for us, the lines get blurry. For you? I think they're pretty clear. I don't mean nothin' bad by that, you know. But I mean, do I really know you? Do I? I think deep down, I do. But it don't make no difference because I'm old, I'm broke, an' I think I'm sick."

"You're sick?"

"We're seein' 'bout that."

"Well, you do know me. I've opened up to you more than anyone...I feel close to you. I think—I really think we're friends. That's real."

Wade looks at her and smiles a small smile. "Yeah. You're right. A good friend. Can't fake that. An' I guess in a way I was a good education. Didn't do much screwin' around, but you sure got in my head, didn'tcha?"

"I want to help," she says. She rolls off of him and lies on her back, like he does, staring at the ceiling. "I wanted to help."

"You did help, you did. You gave me everythin' I needed and wanted an' I'll always...you know, appreciate that."

"I don't feel like I did anything. I do care about you, you know."

"I know. I have to ask, just to make sure I got my feet under me. What's your name?" He stands and turns to her, "Your real name?"

She looks down again, smiling a small smile, "Wow, you...you really aren't coming back, are you?"

"'Sienna.' Such a perfect name for ya. You know, no one names their kid the perfect name. Except my parents, 'course. 'Wade'...movin' slow into deep waters, careful, cautious, no risk. Scared to move too fast, or go too deep. That's me, right there. No swimmin', no divin', no splashin', just...wadin'."

"That isn't true. You can be anyone you want to be—"

"No, that's you. I am who I am, where I am. So tell me, what's your real name?"

"Heather. Heather Lopez."

Wade nods his head, his nose burning along with his insides. Everything is melting under the sun. Everything is weary and unsure. He knews it was going to be over today, but now that she knows it, too, it's real. The loss of it makes him ache, and at the same time, renews him. Like a used piece of foil, getting washed off, folded up, put back in a drawer.

He flexes his left hand and feels the weakness in it. He thinks of the optical tests they did at the hospital, the MRI. He thinks of the doctor and how he ruled out so many things. Which, he'd said, narrowed it down to one probable conclusion.

"Nice to meet you, Heather. Heather, you know, the flower, it looks soft, and you're soft, so I think your parents did right by your name." Wade jams his hand in his pocket and removes an envelope. "I want you to have this."

"You already paid—"

"This is different."

"I can't—" she shakes her head as she sits up.

"Yeah," Wade stands and places the envelope gently on the dresser, "but you can. You did so much for me, it's…well, it's the least I can do, is all I'm sayin'. It ain't much, but there it is. It's how it's supposed to be."

His feet heavy, he moves out of her room, and he only hears his name softly, like a plea with no real intention. A token protest at best; that, and a distant goodbye.

⁓

Wade sits with the glass of whiskey in his living room, twirling the amber liquid until it almost spills out of the rim. He has to be careful, now. His hand, he knows now, goes through periods of strength, then weakness, then strength. Soon it will always be weak.

He'd called Milt and his son's worry had healed something of the hurt inside of him. Milt offered to pay—pay for everything, including a full-time nurse. Wade just asked him to help him with the Social Security Disability claim that needed to be filed, since his pension won't cover what he needs. Milt promised he would visit soon—with the girls. Wade actually believes him this time.

The dog barks as the doorbell rings. He knows who it is, and he's in no mood to talk to her. But he has to. She's bringing him dinner.

"Hey," Tammy says in her shy voice. "You got a beer?"

Wade says nothing, he just walks to the refrigerator and hands her a can. She places a casserole on the counter. "It's chicken with broccoli. You talk to Cole?"

"Cole's been avoidin' me. I pissed him off...*again*. I can't seem to open my mouth to that kid without pissin' him off these days."

"Well, they got the fence up 'round the units now an' they're doin' fliers...he's already got four units under contract. Ain't that somethin'?" She dishes up a plate for Wade but he's not hungry, not in the least.

"I'm glad. That's good news, anyhow."

"I got news." She sips her beer and raises her eyebrows. "I mean, if you wanna hear it."

"Sure. What news?"

"I'm gonna get my Associate's degree in nine months, an' then I think I'm gonna try for my B.S. and become an RN." Her smile is brilliant and Wade has never seen her look more lovely. He wants to hug her, but he is too exhausted.

"That's...well I'm real proud of you, if you want to know the truth. You come a long way from Flyin' J. What does that dickhead Stuart think 'bout it?" He doesn't care that he's bitter. Everything is bitter.

Instead of anger, he gets a smile. "I cut that dickhead loose. He was an asshole."

"Good. You deserve better."

"So you said. But I ain't lookin' for a man. You know, Annie, she was lookin' for a man from the time she was sixteen. She didn't have no ambitions, you know. Just wanted to be a wife an' mother."

"Yeah. Well, she was good at bein' a mother. She was. And...she took care a me in a lot of ways, so she did right by us all, I s'pose."

"You sound like you don't feel so good, Wade. What's goin' on?"

"It's nothin'. Nothin' I wanna talk about anyhow."

Tammy looks at his untouched meal. "Want me to stick that in the fridge for later?"

"Sure."

Tammy picks up his plate and the weight of loss travels down from his head to his belly, making him want to fold in half. He fights the urge to collapse his upper body on the table and sleep. She pours herself a whiskey and stands near his chair. "So you hear back from the doctor 'bout those tests?"

"Yeah."

"Let's go into the other room an' talk."

"You wanna talk now, huh? You know, I known you your whole life almost an' you never talked. Now, this past year, all you do is talk. I'm not sayin' it's bad, I'm just sayin.'"

"I know. I feel different and I know I act different. Somethin' about takin' charge of my life…you know? When Annie left me that money, I knew I didn't want to waste it on stupid things, I wanted to make right with myself. I knew I had it in me to do more, an' I'm doin' it. So yeah, I feel different an' act different. Don't mean I'm not still the same person down deep, though."

Wade sits next to her on the couch. "And who are you…you know, down deep." He doesn't ask, he just says it, like he doesn't expect an answer. Or like she will suddenly speak from the Land of Womenspeak and say something he can't possibly understand.

She puts a hand on his leg and leans over. "I'm your family, Wade. I'm always gonna be your family."

He turns his head and looks at her. "I know that. I always knew that."

She presses her lips together and looks away. When her eyes meet his, there's something fierce in them.

"Annie didn't do right by you, Wade."

He stares into her face, and with the mention of his wife's name he almost sees her in the expression on Tammy's face. "She did fine by me."

"No, she didn't. And I know it."

"What are you…what're you talkin' about?"

Tammy huffs out a breath and searches the ceiling, finding the words. "I know why you go to the cathouse."

Wade's insides tear open and he wants to scream. But he's too tired, too sad to do anything but stare at her.

"Wade…I know Annie held out on you. She used to brag…she used to tell me that she didn't…like it was some kinda badge a honor that she didn't *give in*. To you, you know, in the bedroom, I mean. She held out on you. An' I know you never went to that place before she died or while you was married. You did right by her, but she didn't do right by you. Most men…well, they woulda gone straight to that brothel, the moment their wives said 'no.' You never did. I know 'cause she'd make me check sometimes. You wasn't ever there, not once that I could see. An' I always felt a little sick inside 'bout her makin' me go an' do that. Like she was…she liked bein' mean about it. You didn't, didja?"

"No," he whispers. "I never did. But after…well doesn't matter. I ain't goin' back."

"I don't judge you, Wade. It ain't like Stu, who had a warm body waitin' on him when he wanted me. He was selfish and…and greedy and…ungrateful…and an asshole. But you…you went there 'cause Ann, she…she didn't do right by you!"

"I don't like it. I don't like that you know that." Wade says, staring straight ahead. "I wish you didn't know any of that. I think…I think I need to be alone."

"Everyone needs family, Wade. And you didn't tell me what the doctor—"

"Right now, I need to be alone. Please." His voice is hollow as he stares straight ahead, his vision blurring as he feels the daze of confusion from her words.

"All right. You know, you should talk to Cole. He's doin' a good thing with his life. An' I know you don't like her, but he an' Cindy…they're good together."

"Good." Wade nods his head. And it is good. He can get over his dislike of Cindy. If Cole can love her, he can accept her. And Tammy is his family. And all he wants is to collapse in bed and dream of a family he can find comfort in. All he wants to do is sleep, sleep until there's no more breath in him.

⁓

Cole shuffles his feet as Wade stands across from him in the kitchen. "You sure marriage is what you want?" Wade searches his son's face.

"Yeah, Pop. It's what we want. An' I know you don't like her or—"

"I like her just fine, Cole. An' it's your life. I get so busy tryin' to fit you in a mold, but you broke the mold, you found your own way. You're findin' your own way. I'm sorry I haven't been there like I oughta."

"Pop, somethin's been goin' on with you an' you won't talk to me. All these doctor visits an...then Mr. Hanson left, an' you seem so...sad. Pop, what is it?"

"I told your brother, an' now I gotta tell you. They think—well, they pretty much told me...Cole. I got MS."

"MS...that's...Multiple Sss—"

"Multiple Sclerosis. It means my body's gonna be shuttin' down. It could come fast, it could go real slow. I may need to go to a home at some point because I won't be...well, I won't be self-reliant anymore."

"No, that ain't what's gonna happen, Pop. Me an' Cindy, we'll take care a you, just like we took care of Mom. I ain't just gonna let you—"

"Cole, you ain't gonna waste your life here, waitin' on me. I don't want that. I'd hate that. I want you happy and, most of all, secure. An' you're buildin' that."

"What did the doctor say? About what's gonna happen?"

"They did a bunch of tests, mostly to rule everythin' else out. That's why they told me at first it wasn't nothin'. There's no way to test. But now...more symptoms are happenin' so they re-did the tests, ruled out everything else...an' this is what it's come to."

Cole stares at the floor for a long time. "Does Milt know?"

"Yeah. Needed his help on some disability stuff I gotta do. He knows. An' he's been real good, too. Even offered to hire me a live-in nurse, if you can believe that. I don't need nothin' like that yet."

"I'm...I'm sorry, Pop. But I ain't leavin' you, you know, to just wallow in this. There's gotta be somethin' we can do to fight—"

"Oh, they got me startin' treatment. Now I got five pills I take instead of two. An' they got me goin' to physical therapy for my hands. They're talkin' about a shot I might have to do, too. I guess it'll be good Aunt Tammy's gonna be a nurse, 'cause I can't see givin' myself a shot."

"Oh, Jesus, Pop. What else can they do?" Cole's voice is breathy, higher.

"Nothin'." Wade shrugs. "There ain't no cure or nothin', so it's just the way it goes."

"Do they got you on anti-depressants?"

"No, why should they? I mean—"

"Because, Pop, you're depressed, it's as clear as day. Tell your doc you're depressed, Pop. I mean it. I've never seen you like this before."

"I ain't takin' no more pills. And anyway it don't matter, right? We can't choose what gets us, but somethin' always does. Your mom got cancer. I got this. Millie had a stroke. It's always somethin'."

"Does Aunt Tammy know?"

"No, I didn't really get a chance to tell her." Wade knows that isn't true, but admitting it to her would be as humiliating as everything else she knows about him. That he'd been made a fool, all of those years, all because Ann needed to prove something to herself. She needed to fight what her body and mind wanted, and she felt like if she could do that, she'd win. Then her body betrayed her and no matter how many times she denied the need, it still ate her whole.

"No," Wade says again, "but I will. I'll-I'll tell her."

Cole walks over and grabs Wade in a bear hug. Wade returns the embrace and then Cole lays his head on Wade's shoulder, like he used to do when he was a little boy. Wade had always taken care of his son. And that's all he wants to do now—take care of him. But it's no longer up to him.

Tammy didn't show up with dinner. She showed up with two suitcases.

He's pacing in the kitchen, and she's still staring at him in that bold, new, unnerving way that he's not grown used to yet.

"I told Cole *I'd* tell you, in my own way. Jesus, ain't nothin' private, ain't nothin' sacred."

"You coulda told me a week ago. Why the hell would you not tell me?"

"And what! An'..an' you come to the rescue by...what? There ain't nothin' you can do or anyone can do! An' you know there ain't no amount of brothels or women or booze or-or even family that can make this any different or any better! I don't care, if you want to know the truth of it! *I don't care* this is the way I'm goin' out!" Wade is talking too loudly now, shaking. All of the anger, the unfairness, the indifference of the world no longer comforting, but a bitter twist inside him. Tammy hasn't changed her position, she's just sitting, shaking her head at him. "I hope it happens fast, I can tell you that! I hope it eats away so there's nothin' left of my brain, nothin' left of the memories, nothin' left of what I had, an' mostly what I lost! You know what I lost? Thirty-seven years married to a woman who detested me! An' I can't ever get those years back! No wonder I'm gonna be a cripple! No wonder! 'Cause the time with her has been eatin' me from the inside out since the first time she told me 'no'!"

Tammy's face flushes a little and Wade is ashamed.

He clears his throat, "I shouldn't a-said that. I loved your sister. I did. I shouldn't have. But you…you just can't."

"I'm sorry. But this is what we're doin'."

"What if I say 'no,' huh? What if I tell you to get the hell out an' tell Cole—"

"You won't." Tammy stands. "You won't tell me that. It's final. Cole and Cindy are movin' in my trailer, an' I'm movin' in here. You need me. And you know what? I *want* to be needed. I been missin' that my whole life. I want that."

"And so what, you're just my little sister-in-law, goin' to school, takin' care of her crippled brother-in-law, an' that's gonna be your life? No, you're gonna meet some doctor, or some guy, an' you're gonna—"

"Maybe someday I will, Wade! It ain't outta the realm of possibility that I'm gonna meet a man, yeah! But meantime, I'm gonna live here, an' you're gonna have to deal with it. I watched you take care of my sister, after everything, after all she done, and you think I'm gonna let you waste away in here all alone feeling sorry for yourself? I *ain't*!" She says firmly, eyes blazing. She stands and steps toward him.

"Well you should!" He wants his words to be final, but they seem impotent and defeated.

They are standing almost nose to nose, glaring. Wade looks into one of her eyes, then the other, back and forth, back and forth, and he can't see her anymore, he only sees eyes, looking into his; purple eyeshadow, black eyeliner, he smells her perfume and he can't stand it another second. He reaches for her and their mouths collide. She has her arms wrapped so tightly around him, it's as if she's clinging to him to keep from drowning. He breaks away and shakes his head, breathy and chest heaving. "This is wrong."

"No," she whispers, "you had thirty-three years of 'wrong.' *This* is right."

She takes his hand and pulls. He follows her into the bedroom and she turns on the side-table lamp.

"I can't make up for what Annie did, or didn't do. But for one night, I can do somethin'."

"One night?" Wade stares at her.

"You know that's the way it's gotta be."

He does know, but he can't say it. She pulls her shirt off to reveal a white, lacy bra, slightly gray with age. She unbuttons her jeans and pulls them down, her panties white and blue striped. Still in her bra and panties, she undresses him slowly and he closes his eyes and allows the familiarity of her and the foreignness of her to come together in him all at once. He lays her back on the bed and there is no money, there is no condom, there is no inspection, and he knows who she is. She is his family.

July 13, 2015

Instead of six more months here, I am leaving next week. All thanks to Wade. He gave me that envelope of money and I didn't even check it until he was long gone. Did I do that so I wouldn't have to give it back? No. If I'm honest, no. I just felt numb that he had said goodbye. I am going to miss him, and it's okay to admit that to myself, it's okay, I think, to mourn it. I just wish I could have done more for him. I'll miss him, I'll miss Terry, the janitor because he was sweet, and of course Gerry. I still miss Gerry. Always making jokes about his legs, always laughing. So funny, and then so sad. Yes, Wade's money was too generous. I just didn't see how thick the envelope was. I wish I had thanked him better. The money is going to not only pay off my car and two cards, there will still be some left over for fall semester at WSU. I liked him, I felt sorry for him...and I do think he's sick. That part is the saddest. But my feelings for him were also trapping me. I couldn't see things clearly anymore. I'm glad he said goodbye, because I don't know if I could have. I'll never forget him. I haven't seen him for a month. I keep expecting to. But now that I'm leaving, I know it's goodbye forever to Wade.

I'm so glad I will be home for when Jacob starts pre-school this Fall. I am counting the days, now. I really have learned so much here. Now that I'm leaving, I see it in a whole new light—everyone and everything. I am even more committed to sex surrogacy because of what I did here.

I ordered the catalog from WSU and it will be waiting for me at home. I applied for my grants already, so we'll see if those come through. If not, I've got Fall tuition covered and that is such a huge relief. Jessica said I could live with them and work part time, go to school, until I can get out on my own. I can't wait. I guess my biggest fear? One day I'll be forced to come back to this place. I should feel lucky that it's an option, but I don't. It feels like a weight around my neck. I won't go there. I don't need to for now.

Even though I'm convinced I want to do the surrogacy stuff, I'm even more convinced I need my undergrad in social work first. I worry a little that I'm leaving here too soon, like maybe there's more to learn. Sex is more complicated than anything I could have ever imagined when I first started out here. So much rests on it. It seems to take up everything in a person's life, one way or another, even if they don't want it to. If it's their biggest desire, it overtakes them. If they can't have it, it overtakes them. If they can't do it, it overtakes them. It's like a giant blanket called SEX covers everything, everywhere, especially in the media, but then it's taboo and "bad" when it's on CNN or it involves a politician. Everyone wants it in their entertainment, nobody wants it in their churches or politics. Or their neighborhoods, even. I guess we'll see if other states will ever wake up and legalize it. You can't try and extinguish something like this. It's too old, and it's too much a part of us.

My biggest take-away from this place is that everyone seems so confused. IT seems so confused. But I've learned that it's bottomless, like this silent, deep, giant body of water, and you can see it for miles, the waves hit the shores, you can see the rocky parts and then all you see is blue, then black. People floating in it, swimming or more often than not, drowning in it. Or I guess many people just tread water any way they can. Try not to sink. I guess that pretty much explains my entire experience here. And before I could sink, Wade came in and now I get to swim away. At least

I'm hoping I can.

I guess what I'm saying is that I don't know that I have learned anything more than how complex sex is—for everyone. We are all mixed up about it, and in it, all at once. It can be really good, or it can be really terrible. Just depends on how deep you are.

More later. I need to rest. I just need the comfort of my bed and long, nice dreams of home.

17

He went back to see her one more time, in the fall, but she was gone. Sienna/Heather had quit back in mid-summer, a month or so after he'd given her the rest of the money Ann had left him. Belle had told him, but didn't mention anything about the money, so he assumes Sienna kept her reasons to herself.

All he'd wanted was a list of Sienna's books. He tells himself he's a reader now, but the truth is, he wasn't ready to sever all ties, and those books had been a tie to her as much as anything else. He decided that he would just read every book from every author she had introduced him to. It's what he and Tammy do together when she's not studying.

He made Tammy re-read *The Stranger* to him, and all of the others he'd read with Sienna. It made him happy that Tammy seemed to enjoy reading them to him as much as he'd enjoyed reading them the first time.

His health had begun to deteriorate fairly rapidly and they had told him it might since he'd started treatment so late. He wears glasses now, but trying to focus on the words in the books is tiring, so he sits on the couch with his head back while Tammy reads in her soft voice all of the words that had touched him with meaning because of Sienna. He had thought he'd loved her, but he knows better now. He loved what she represented to him, which was open arms, a willingness to share herself with him. Money or no, she had been willing. But even that isn't enough to sustain the wise man. Even open arms can be a trap for something unwanted, unasked for and indecisive. They can be a trap for a man who loses his way.

The cane he walks with in public doesn't embarrass him anymore. The fact that he goes everywhere with Tammy does. Because in town, they're talking. But there is nothing for them to talk about. After that one night, she never shared his bed again, like she'd told him. She never will. And he understands that and accepts it. She had taken the parts of her that she shared with her sister and had given them to him in that one night. It's a night Wade will never forget. He doesn't want to re-capture it or even try. He doesn't want anything to sully the memory. In his bed, for one night, a woman had said *yes* for no other reason than she loved him. A woman had opened everything to him and he had no trouble opening back. He hadn't needed a little blue pill, he hadn't needed lingerie or a red silk cloth over the lamp, or an ATM. He'd just needed a part of his late wife, any part, to let him in. Was it enough to heal the wounds made over thirty-three years? In a way, he thinks so. He thinks yes, because it was just one wound, and that one wound seemed to close, not scab over, that one night. And his feelings for Tammy changed after. Suddenly she wasn't a mystery. She was familiar, like a sister, but nothing more. His infatuation had ended as abruptly as the turning off of a lamp. He's grateful for that kindness. It's as if his body, even though it's turning on him, gave him a small dose of compassion by taking away his need. He doesn't miss it. Some days, when he's feeling down, he wishes it had abandoned him long ago. It would have made things smoother, starting way back when.

Sienna had done her part for him, he knows that. But Tammy, she had done something for him that was as authentic as an unbidden bear hug on a cold night. She had released him.

Tammy gives him two injections a day, just like the doctor had shown her, and she studies hard to make something of herself, to give meaning to her life. It was the biggest and friendliest argument they'd ever had— Tammy didn't buy into "meaninglessness" for one minute. She said "that Camus guy was just depressed and needed to be on medication." But Wade understands it on an even deeper level now that his legs aren't working properly, his hand is paralyzed and his eyesight fails. He realizes that he'd been attached so much to things making sense, he'd forgotten that only in the last two hundred years had a lot of things begun to make sense. Before then, the *meaning* had been "God" or "magic." Then science got ahold of them, and the mystery was wiped clean out of people's minds. And now that "thing," that mystery, just...*is*. Things—a lot of things—still make no sense. But he can live with that, and that's why the idea of something being "meaningless" is so sound, so right. The comfort of not knowing. Not knowing where he will be in another six months. The comfort of not knowing where anyone will be. Letting it go and pronouncing it "good." And he doesn't need to sell any part of himself to believe that.

Milt comes once a month with the girls and Carol to see him, now. Bree still treats him like a jungle gym and Carol still wags her finger, but she must see it: the look in his eyes when that little girl scrambles all over him, the smile that spreads over his fool-face. And as Cole becomes more self-sufficient, Milt seems to grant a little grace Wade's way, as if he had no other reason except to be his brother's keeper. But it goes deeper, Wade knows, and he also knows it has little or nothing to do with him. Milt comes once a month because he didn't have the courage to come and watch his mother die. He can't forgive himself for that. But he can come watch his father, because Wade was not the one who was supposed to be invincible—he was bound to disappoint. If that's the way Milt sees him, he doesn't mind so much. If it heals Milt in any way, he can live with that. Milt is going to be just fine, and somewhere down deep, Milt knows it isn't because of his mother, but because of Wade's faith in him, allowing him to find his own way all those years. Yes, Milt knows why he's going to be fine. They both do, and it's enough.

There are days when Cole and Cindy join Milt and his family, and it's all of them, Tammy, too, in Wade's small house, and Wade remembers that feeling, so long ago, of loneliness. But that feeling has been replaced with a certain calm, a feeling of "rightness." He wonders, had Ann still been alive, if he would feel this content. He knows the answer. At least he thinks he knows. It only took one night with Tammy, and things that were wrong were set right again. At least right for him. He can't explain it and he doesn't need to try. Things are just right. And that's all a man can hope for in this indifferent world.

Acknowledgements

I want to thank the many people who helped me research and write this book. For the vulnerability, trust and courage it took for them to share their stories and experiences. I want to acknowledge the amount of courage it took for them to be so vulnerable in a time when being vulnerable about the subject of male sexuality, sex work, and the social and cultural ramifications of being and feeling positive about either or both.

First, thank you Bella Cummins, for opening your doors and allowing me access into your hallowed, heavy-perfumed halls, your "Tea Party," your candor, your convictions, your wisdom. Thank you for the effortless string of verbal gems effortlessly threaded together by your down-to-bone wisdom. I had no idea how much I'd fall in love with your fictional incarnation, nor the real-life person on whom she's based.

Thank you to all the therapists, warm arms, soothing words, laughter, understanding hearts, compassionate minds and willing bodies of the women who work at Bella's Hacienda. Those of you who were there out of necessity, despite your sharp edges, taught me as much as those who were there by choice. Thank you for the stories. I'll never think of "The Incredible Hulk" TV series the same.

To Ruth Greenstein of Greenline and Turtle Point Press, thank you for being the perfect editorial match for my ambition and drive. For seeing the big picture when the process forces me to wear blinders. Thank you always, Jan Hamer, editor, friend, red-line fundamentalist, green-penned minimalist. The perfect blend to challenge me, yet stoke the good stuff when I really, really earn it.

Thank you, Natalie Mayfield, for being good at almost everything I'm not good at, for bringing this book to life with your considerable skill, talent, and know-how. Mostly, thank you for your friendship and everything throughout these crazy few years.

To beta readers Dave Porter, as always, Debra Carter, and thank you to Lacy for opening to me and showing me your world. For being a safe place to wade into my own deep waters and discover how to plumb the depths of my own darkness and lonely fear.

Finally, to K, my always and forever. You helped with so much more than chapters. Thank you for showing me the many ways a human being can be healed and for healing this human being in so many ways.

Photo by Cat Palmer Photography

J.A. Carter-Winward is an award-winning poet, literary novelist, writer, public speaker, visual and performance artist (music, poetry, spoken word). She's the author of five novels—*Falling Back to Earth* (2010, 2017), *TDTM* (2010), *The Rub* (2013), nominated by the Utah Arts and Humanities Council for the "Utah Book Award," *Grind* (2014), named by IndieReader.com as one of 2015's "Top 5 Literary Novels" by an independent press, and *Wade* (2021). She is the author of two short story collections, *Shorts: A Collection* (2014), and *The Bus Stops Here and Other Stories* (2018).

In her genre-defying, award-winning *"no series"*—*No Apologies, No Secrets, No Regrets*—and coming soon: *Work in Progress: Dialogues & Poems,* Carter-Winward's accessible and multi-faceted voice takes on the sacred, the profane, and all that's in between as she examines the breadth of the human experience with inimitable fierceness, humor, and plenty of gut-punch emotion. She's also the author of a stage play, *The Waiters* (2014) and several short screenplays.

As a visual artist, Ms. Carter-Winward's work has appeared in several Utah galleries. Her performances include an original monologue for the local production of Eve Ensler's *The Vagina Monologues,* and as a keynote speaker, guest lecturer, and performer. Her short film *How Bad Can Good Be,* a spoken-word poem/film written, produced, and performed by J.A., has reached international audiences as she strives to create public awareness about the dangers of prescription drug side effects. Ms. Carter-Winward is also a contributing writer for award-winning journalist and author, Robert Whitaker's site, *Mad in America (Science, Psychiatry and Social Justice.)*

Other publishing credits include her poem, "Grace," appearing in the anthology, *We Will Be Shelter: Poems for Survival* (2014), edited by Andrea Gibson, (Write Bloody Publishing); *HSTQ: Spring 2017, Winter 2017,* and the *Spring 2018* editions; *Desert Wanderings Literary Journal*, and several online publications and magazines.

With her dynamic voice and style, J.A. Carter-Winward has been called "one of today's bravest voices in contemporary literature," and "one of the best working poets in America today." Her writing has the power to comfort, provoke, and engage as she continues to chronicle the spectrum of human emotion with her inimitable, multi-faceted voice.

J.A. Carter-Winward lives and writes in the mountains of Northern Utah.

Follow her on Facebook, Medium, and Goodreads.